Big Nobody

Big Nobody

ALEX KADIS

HUTCHINSON
HEINEMANN

HUTCHINSON HEINEMANN

UK | USA | Canada | Ireland | Australia
India | New Zealand | South Africa

Hutchinson Heinemann is part of the Penguin Random House group of companies whose addresses can be found at global.penguinrandomhouse.com

Penguin Random House UK,
One Embassy Gardens, 8 Viaduct Gardens, London SW11 7BW

penguin.co.uk

First published 2026

001

Copyright © Alex Kadis, 2026

The moral right of the author has been asserted

Penguin Random House values and supports copyright. Copyright fuels creativity, encourages diverse voices, promotes freedom of expression and supports a vibrant culture. Thank you for purchasing an authorised edition of this book and for respecting intellectual property laws by not reproducing, scanning or distributing any part of it by any means without permission. You are supporting authors and enabling Penguin Random House to continue to publish books for everyone. No part of this book may be used or reproduced in any manner for the purpose of training artificial intelligence technologies or systems. In accordance with Article 4(3) of the DSM Directive 2019/790, Penguin Random House expressly reserves this work from the text and data mining exception.

Set in 11.3/15.2pt Sabon Next LT Pro
Typeset by Six Red Marbles UK, Thetford, Norfolk

Printed and bound in Great Britain by Clays Ltd, Elcograf S.p.A.

The authorised representative in the EEA is Penguin Random House Ireland, Morrison Chambers, 32 Nassau Street, Dublin D02 YH68

A CIP catalogue record for this book is available from the British Library

ISBN: 978–1–529–15530–3 (hardback)
ISBN: 978–1–529–15531–0 (trade paperback)

Penguin Random House is committed to a sustainable future for our business, our readers and our planet. This book is made from Forest Stewardship Council® certified paper.

For Sheila Rose Pearl Perowne, Christalla Kadis-Kassalova
and Maria Kadis

Prologue

I think it's safe to say that my father was probably always an abomination of nature. He managed to hide it for long enough to woo my mum, a normally discerning and intelligent woman. If the eventual outcome hadn't been so tragic, and if one of the people involved hadn't been an absolute imbecile, and if there hadn't been a dearth of actual romance, their meeting would have made for good romantic fiction.

The ill-starred chance of their meeting was thus: it was twelve months before I was born. They were introduced in an Italian coffee shop in Soho one evening in 1959, after her dance rehearsal. Though English by birth, she was inexorably drawn to the romantic and was an amateur flamenco dancer. She had danced her way across Spain at a time when few women travelled alone. I have an old black-and-white photo of her in her flamenco dress, castanets hoisted high above her head, looking blonde and epic: a roman-nosed Marilyn Monroe meets Carmen Amaya. He was her dance partner's flatmate and fresh off the kebab boat. He looked like a Greek Cypriot Elvis, all Brylcreemed quiff and tight calf muscles. Over the mist of a frothy coffee, served in a yellow Pyrex cup and saucer, she fell for his exotic good looks and his raven Presley quiff. And our fate was sealed.

It is fair to say I carried some guilt. It was actually my fault they got married. They were on holiday, going to Cyprus – by boat – to see his family. She was spectacularly seasick. By the time they had docked, she knew two things. One: she didn't like The Future Fat Murderer AKA George Costa very much, and two: she was carrying his child.

They married in the one-goat village where he grew up. It was a hasty, sad affair of a wedding. He looked like a second-tier spiv; she wore a borrowed wedding gown and held a plastic bouquet. Somewhere in there was a portent. I still have the letter she wrote to her parents, telling them of her 'good news' from Cyprus, trying in vain to put a positive spin on the fact that she was up the spout and marrying the man of her nightmares. They kept the letter as their only souvenir of a wedding they hadn't attended. My mum found it when she cleared their house after they both died. And then it came to me. Along with a half-used bag of Avon cosmetics sadness and a house full of ghouls.

My dad never once spoke of how they met. He never imparted memories. On balance it was probably because he was too stupid to retain them rather than a zen-like ability to live in the moment. It was my mum who used to tell me the story of their tawdry courtship. I would make her repeat the tale over and over, and quietly, inwardly, would shout, 'Now! Get out now!' at moments when she could have saved herself. All of us. Me.

As if it wasn't enough of a blow that he turned out to be a terrible person, my father failed to hold on to his physical attributes. Just like the King of Rock 'n' Roll, he went dramatically to seed. By the time I was planning on killing him, he was no longer what you'd describe as a looker. He had developed a pot belly and chubby stumpy legs, which he attempted to assuage with ludicrous stack-heeled boots. He was barely holding on to the remnants of the quiff: his crowning glory had diminished to a lavishly lacquered all-round comb-over, which was in a battle to the death against an ever-expanding central bald patch. We both knew the bald patch would win. It was just a matter of time.

The years never took their toll on my mum. My *dad* took his toll on her, like he did on all of us. The virtues that he was drawn to – her sense of adventure, her dancing, her freedom of spirit – were the things that he found to be a threat once they were married. And, slowly but surely, he pressed all the beautiful creases out of her until she was as flat as the women he had never been attracted to. I vowed that would not happen to me. When she died, I had two choices: to die with her or to live because of her.

After almost a year, I was still *almost* certain I had made the right choice.

1975

I

I slammed my bedroom door. Hard.
Two reasons:

1. To interrupt the TV viewing of The Fat Murderer downstairs.
2. To see if I could break some windows, thereby further interrupting the TV viewing of The Fat Murderer downstairs.

My friend Soraya had told me, this very lunchtime, that if you slammed a door hard enough, it would break all the windows in the house. I had believed her. Soraya had also said that if you screamed at the right pitch, *loudly* enough, you could make a light bulb burst. I tried that now a few times, with increasing volume. No joy there either. I experimented with a frenzied combination of the two – scream slam, slam scream. And got absolutely nothing.

On the bus on the way home from school that afternoon, I had started reading *Carrie* by Stephen King and now thought how brilliant it would be if, like his title character, I could just exact supernatural levels of destruction using the telekinetic power of my mind. I focused on the door with a laser-like intensity to see if I could slam it with my brain waves, but it just made me feel dizzy. I'd have to practise.

'I don't know why I listen to bloody Soraya,' I mumbled

resentfully, while kicking my vile school shoes off and booting them under the bed. At school, Soraya had styled herself as a soothsayer for the teen masses. She had once told a rapt morning-break audience that if one were to swallow a tapeworm, it would digest all of your calories and you could eat as much as you wanted and never get fat. When I asked her where I could obtain such a creature, she told me I'd have to either lick a cat's bum or snog Calvin Belding from Norrington Boys' School down the road, because rumour was he had a tapeworm and would happily pass it on for a tongue sandwich and a go on your tits. I said I'd rather go for the cat's bum hole than Calvin Belding's revolting face hole: I'd seen it, and even from a distance I could tell it was no oil painting. Anyway, when I happened to mention this to my music teacher, Mizz Liddle, during lunchtime guitar practice, she said it was best to ignore someone as musically bereft as Soraya and, if I wanted to lose weight, to just stop eating so many sweets. When I conveyed this to Soraya, she had countered that Mizz Liddle was most likely a hermaphrodite and, therefore, not to be trusted on issues pertaining to persons who had made a firm decision on their genitals.

With a renewed sense of fury fuelled by chagrin and hormones, I, Constance Costa, The Half Greek Imprisoned Daughter of The Fat Murderer, gave it one last shot: a simultaneous scream and slam. Much better. And I had succeeded in disturbing the television viewing of The Fat Murderer downstairs.

'Pack it in! I'm going to come up there in a minute and give you a bloody wallop,' The Fat Murderer bellowed from below. That's what he meant to say. How it came out was: 'Pack that one ap. Am go to cam ap there and gif you a blatty wallaps.'

Despite working in London for sixteen years, and marrying

a perfect English Rose, The Fat Murderer, AKA my dad, had neither shed his Greek Cypriot accent nor learned the finer points of the English language. Amongst his many rhetoric transgressions, he randomly put an S on the end of words where they weren't warranted. He had friends who lived in *Totten-hams* and *Hack-neys*. A holiday was a *holi-days*. A coat was a *coats*. It didn't matter how many times I said 'There's only one Walthamstow', as my dad would always nod assuredly and say, 'Yes, the *Waltham-stows*', as if it was I who was the moron. It made my sphincter clench just to think that I shared DNA with him.

The wallop was probably an empty threat anyway; since it had become just the two of us this past year, the walloping had subsided somewhat. Which was weird, because I'd have thought that, with less people to wallop, the full wallop consignment would have landed on me. Still, I'd have taken the wallop over the pidgin English any day. It really got on my nerves.

My dad, AKA The Fat Murderer, was an East End tailor by trade, and an idiot by all other counts. He ran his workshop out of a premises on our local high street. If asked, he told people he was 'Tailor to the stars . . .' He wasn't. He made suits for Leyton Orient football players and waistcoats for the waiters from The Corinthian Barbeque and Grill Greek Cypriot restaurant in Loughton.

I had tried to kill him once. My dad. It involved leaving a roller skate at the top of the stairs. I'd seen it in a *Beano* comic. He should have stepped on it, flown down the stairs, legs cycling comically in mid-air, and broken his neck. Instead, he just kicked the skate to one side and shouted, 'Somebotty pick ap this blatty shits.' I vowed to try harder next time.

My present anger wasn't quite spent, so I glanced around my bedroom, looking for something to destroy, and snatched a cup from my desk; but I didn't really want to break any of my stuff. Everything was special: my desk, my books, my albums, my record player, my single bed, my music mags, my stockpile of sweets and booze, my delicious ciggies and my guitar, which would undoubtedly take me on the road to rock superstardom and boundless freedom. And, most precious of all, my wall-to-wall posters: my gang, the guardians of my citadel, my closest confidants, whom I had created and who resided securely in the cavernous, hungry space between my dreams and my reality. They were my world.

I liked it in here. The outside world wasn't meant for people like me. I was destined not to be a part of it but to grip on to the edge with a rictus grin and white knuckles. In here I lived deep in the bosom of what I had built. In here I could survive.

'Put the cup down, Constance, silly billy . . .' They were coming alive now, the gang, stepping out of their flat paper existence, making their presence known, dusting off their charms, fanning up their vanities, vying for my attention. I could see a flicker of a feather boa being rearranged, the straightening of a white bejewelled jumpsuit, the egotistical smoothing down of over-coiffed hair. I heard the incidental twang of an electric guitar, as if it were being set aside in anticipation of a powwow.

'Hey, Constance, babe, got time for a conflab?' It was Marc speaking. Marc Bolan. The love of my life. Now he had arrived, they'd all be coming – The Osmonds, The Jacksons, The Cassidy Brothers. I could sense the electricity in the room, the crackling air.

I grabbed the chair from in front of my desk and propped

it against the door handle, like I'd seen them do on telly, to secure it, just in case The Fat Murderer did get off his fat arse and come upstairs. I knew he wouldn't. My dad never ventured into my room these days, except in the mornings, as he had habitually done since I was a little kid, and always when I was getting dressed. I'd never hear him coming and would instantly be caught unaware when he'd fling the door open and stand there staring like a maniac, asking me what I was doing, as if it wasn't obvious.

I removed the chair from under the doorknob, opened the door and kicked it shut one last time. With feeling.

2

The room had darkened a shade. I turned my gaze to the window. Dusk was falling over East London and I could see a scattering of lights coming on in the houses at the back of our neglected garden. I liked the dark. The daytime was capricious and unpredictable. Anything could happen. But you could rely on the night. The night always fell like a warm blanket over my loneliness; making me feel that here, in the shadows, with the lines blurred, I could pass for normal.

I sat on the edge of my bed, moving aside a pile of *Jackie* magazines and *Record Mirror*s – my two bibles. I lit a cigarette, took a nice long drag, and cast a plume of smoke across the room. Someone coughed dramatically. Donny Osmond ... of course. Donny was very good-looking, but he was a Mormon and I was starting to wonder about the point of clean-living pop stars. Where was the fun in that? When I was a famous rock star, I was going to dine on drugs, breakfast on champagne, and have multiple affairs with other rock stars.

Everyone was looking at me expectantly, but the one I really wanted to discuss my latest gripe with in *private* – privacy would be a fine thing round here – was Marc Bolan. Gorgeous, defiant Marc Bolan, standing astride his Telecaster, resplendent in tight satin pants, long, curly dark hair and sparkly eyeshadow, bending his gender in all directions. Marc was dangerous; all cock and balls and sexy sneer. Much to my perpetual embarrassment/pleasure, my eyes were drawn to his crotch area far more often than they were to his guitar. One of my favourite posters of Marc was on the wall by my bed, with his trouser bump right at eye level. 'Be careful how you turn over in the night, Con, I might poke your eye out,' he had said on more than one occasion. I had made him hilarious as well as spiritual and sexy.

It was the posters of Marc that really stuck in my dad's craw and, therefore, possessed all the more value for me. We both knew what Marc was about. He was about sex and insurrection and growing up. Marc was my passport to free thinking and, therefore, freedom itself. I was desperate to be free ...

I adjusted my pillows, propped myself up, plugged the cigarette into the corner of my mouth, and opened a *Jackie* magazine.

'Oh, don't pretend you're reading, Con. I know you're bursting a vein to tell me ...'

I closed the magazine. I sat up, folded my arms, and regarded Marc Bolan through curls of cigarette smoke.

I put down the magazine.

'Same old, same old, Marc,' I sighed, rolling my eyes and shrugging. 'I hate him,' I said, talking through the smoke, instantly angry and self-pitying. I let the cigarette dangle from my lips and watched some ash drop onto my bottle-green school skirt. I rubbed it into the fabric.

'The Autumn Term Disco is one week away. I just want to be there, like a normal fifteen-year-old – okay, fourteen-and-ten-and-a-bit-months-old – person and that unreasonable lunatic won't let me.'

'Hm, I'd say being a lunatic and being unreasonable tend to go hand in hand.'

This wasn't Marc. It was bloody David Bowie. David could be snitty and obscure and couldn't resist sticking his beak into everyone else's business. I'd only brought David into our world because Marc had said he needed some intelligent company. That had really upset The Osmonds, and I wasn't sure if I shouldn't have been offended as well.

'I will be stuck here, in this hellhole, with him, until I die an old spinster of the parish.'

Marc giggled. 'I don't see you as a spinster, Con. You're way too far out.'

'I'm probably going to have to kill him.' I was both ashamed of how petulant I sounded and satisfied at how much I meant it. I did want The Fat Murderer out of my life.

Marc sighed and rolled his eyes.

'So, what's the dude's issue, babe?'

Babe. I *did* like him calling me babe.

'He says I should stay at home doing homework and concentrating on my education, so I can become a doctor – like a good little Greek girl – which is not going to happen, because as soon as I leave school, I'm going to join a band and go on the road.'

My voice wobbled with self-pity. I sounded infantile. A whining, wheedling little kid.

'Every year I have to make up an excuse to my school friends, like I've got another party to go to or someone died – well, last year everyone *did* die, but that's not the point – the point is that no one ever believes me, and then I have to go into school the next day and listen to everyone talk about how brilliant it was and how I really should have been there.'

I felt despondent now.

'Complete bummer. So, what doesn't he dig?' said Marc.

'He doesn't *dig* any of it. But mostly he doesn't dig the fact that there will be boys there,' I said.

And there it was. It wasn't about age. It wasn't about homework or my education or anything else. It was all about boys. As far as my dad was concerned, I was to avoid all contact with any male of the species in case, I presumed, our sex parts spontaneously exploded. Any encroachment into my nether regions would render me sullied and unable to get a nice Greek Cypriot man to take me as a wife. I don't know what the idiot imagined would happen at a lame disco on a Thursday night in Leyton, but the fact there would be boys there was enough to get his eyes bulging dementedly and to extend his embargo indefinitely.

I unplugged the cigarette from my miserable lips and flicked some ash into my crappy C-minus ashtray. We had all made ashtrays for our parents in school pottery class earlier this year, but I'd kept mine for myself because I had no one to give it to. It was rubbish and my glaze had cracked, because, said Mr Hatton, the pottery teacher, I had paid more attention to getting globs of clay to stick to the classroom ceiling than I had to my glaze recipe. Mr Hatton had terrible halitosis.

I looked at Marc.

'What do you think I should do?'

'I know what *I* think you should do,' said David Bowie. 'I think you should care less about what other people think. If I had cared about what other people thought, I'd never have made "The Laughing Gnome".'

'. . . Or stolen my sound,' said Marc.

They both chuckled indulgently and gazed at each other with narcissistic admiration. That was the trouble with those two – they were fickle and easily distracted.

'I *am* here,' I reminded them.

'Look,' said Marc, 'you gotta funk or be square. Look, me and Dave, we funk.'

David nodded sagely and added, 'But we just don't care.'

'Don't you wanna be a groover?' said Marc.

'Yes, I want to be a groover,' I said quietly.

Marc smiled. 'Then sneak out and go to the disco. Don't be the school freak, babe.'

'I'm not,' I said.

Marc raised an eyebrow. 'You sure about that?'

Was Marc right? Was it possible that I was the school freak? A blast of hot shame went through me like an electric shock. The feeling of shame was a frequent occurrence in my life. The shame of not being able to join in. The shame of not being the same. The shame of the other stuff that I could never mention. Shame from every direction.

Having considered the evidence, I had a nasty inkling that Marc Bolan might be right. And, so it was, at that very point, with the sun fully dipped behind the rows of terraces, casting the back gardens into shadows and shapes, that the night-time failed to deliver its customary comfort and brought, instead, a new haunting: Constance Costa, School Freak.

I had smoked the B&H almost down to the filter. I opened my bedroom window. All was quiet except for a couple of wood pigeons, who seemed to have taken up permanent residence on the back fence, side by side, snuggling in, feathers ruffling. I envied them their easy intimacy.

The air was still and on the very edge of autumn. It was nearly dark now. I flicked the remains of the cigarette onto the lawn below and watched the sparks fly off into the gloom. I hung my head out of the window and practised long dribbling.

I had to think of lemon sherbet so that my mouth watered, and then I let the drool run out and swing in mid-air without breaking it off. I managed a good ten inches and then swung the spittle back and forth, eyeing my target, before it plopped onto the concrete strip that ran along the edge of the shabby lawn below. Missed.

I was aiming for the raggedy vegetable patch where my dad grew disappointing marrows and turnips. The last few sorry vegetables were struggling to ripen and my dad was anxiously checking on them daily. I had no idea why he was so consumed with them. I made a mental note to trample them the next time I was in the back garden.

First, I'd kill his vegetables. Then I'd kill him.

3

The next night, Friday night, was Greek Night. Or, as I liked to call it: Freak Night. It happened every Friday of every week of every month of every year of every decade of every millennium. There was no escaping it. First-generation Greek Cypriot immigrants worked hard all week, sweating long hours over their sewing machines and cash registers. They delayed their gratification until the week's end, when the women made koftes and dolmas and the men played backgammon and drank Metaxa. And we all had to be there. Religiously. The only upside was that I would get to see the one person in my life who didn't make me want to vomit: Vasos.

My dad drove his excruciating red Audi towards Walthamstow through dwindling post-rush-hour traffic. Soraya had said that it was a scientifically proven fact that men who drove large cars were compensating for small genitals. I didn't really want to think about my dad's genitals, but I did resent the car for its celebratory good looks, considering it had replaced the dowdy green Ford Cortina that my dad had killed my family in. It wasn't a vehicle so much as a weapons upgrade. I refused to sit in the front passenger seat and sank down low in the back, face buried in a book, in case anyone I knew might see me.

The Fat Murderer's driving was stupendously bad. As well as giving me whiplash with his heavy-footed stop/start technique, he bequeathed a furious running commentary on other motorists and their apparent lack of driving skills. Everyone was a 'Blatty Baskit' of some variety; he was truly democratic when it came to his dislike of all other road users. He had belligerent nomenclature for every race, sex and age, including but not limited to: 'Fackin' Women Driver Baskits', 'Fackin' Old Baskits', 'Blatty Paki Baskits', 'Blatty Poofda Baskits', 'Blatty Nignog Baskits'. And just in case he left anyone out, every other nationality came under the general term of 'Blatty Xenos Baskits'. Essentially, he disliked any driver who wasn't actually himself. With one exception: if he encountered a nice white bank-managery-type driver, The Fat Murderer was all magnanimity. He'd graciously give way and bequeath upon them an obsequious, wormy smile. And God forbid that anyone *inside* the car should accidentally say or do something that annoyed him. He'd take his eyes off the road completely to turn to the back seat and deliver multiple wallops to whomever he could reach before swerving onto the kerb or into oncoming traffic. How he had only had one major car crash was a wonder.

Tonight, with just me in the back seat, minding my own business, and the evening's traffic thinning, we arrived with thankfully little tumult.

Freak Night was almost always held at Vas's parents' house. The Petrideses had the biggest house of all the Greek Freak parents, and Mrs Petrides liked to be queen bee. My dad parked his penis extension on their driveway and exited the car while I played for time in the back seat, still reading *Carrie*, and pretending I hadn't noticed that we'd arrived. I knew the infinitesimal wait would drive him round the bend. Besides, I was emotionally connecting with Carrie. She, too, had a despotic parent, but even she had attended the school disco. Okay, so she got covered in pigs' blood and blew up the entire school, but she did slow-dance with a boy first. And though Carrie's telekinetic prowess was far superior to my own, I did feel that mine was on the verge of manifesting. So, we had that in common too. I had never slow-danced with a boy.

I let my dad bang on the car window a few times before I jumped and affected surprise. 'Oh, are we here?' I smirked. He just stared maniacally into the car until I unlocked the door and stepped out. He could stare all he liked. His days were numbered.

The Petrideses had money. And, boy, did they like to let you know it. They lived on a private road that backed on to what Mrs Petrides referred to as 'Epping Forest', but which was, in fact, a neglected scrap of wasteland where everyone took their dogs to crap. Their house was a regular four-bedroomed semi-detached, but it stood out amongst the other houses in the street because of the two large plaster-cast lions either side of the entrance gate and the Doric columns that flanked the front door. Mr Petrides hadn't got round to cementing them in, so the columns were free-standing and wobbled dangerously if you touched them. There was a handwritten note sellotaped to one, saying: 'DON NOT LEEN ON WILL FULL DOWN'.

I dreaded ringing the doorbell. It played the first eight bars of the Cypriot national anthem, which didn't qualify as actual shame material but was still majorly embarrassing. As soon as Mrs Petrides opened the front door, I felt a familiar embrace that was both repugnant and irresistible to me. Once you were on the threshold, there was no going back: you were sucked into a vortex that spun you in a web of Greekness so thick it was binding. The familiar sounds of chatter and laughter, the scents of cigar smoke and whisky, and tomatoes and onions cooking; a blend that was warming, exciting, comforting and oppressive.

Mrs Petrides let my dad in first, stopping him momentarily to pick a piece of lint off his shoulder. She watched him until he disappeared into the sitting room before cupping a cold, bony hand at the back of my head and guiding me inside. 'Come on in, Constantina. I give you nice food, make you nice and fat.' Yeah, wouldn't she just love that. Mrs Petrides was obsessed with her figure and ate like a sparrow with its beak glued shut. She loved nothing more than to note how fat other people had become. I ducked my head forwards, shrinking from her skeletal touch. Mrs Petrides got on my nerves. Also, I was pretty certain she and The Fat Murderer were having it off. And that they hadn't waited until after my dad had murdered my mum to get started either.

Inside, the noise level was high-octane and the air was smoky grey and sweaty. The men were in the middle of a backgammon tournament. They had taken over the Petrideses' overheated through-lounge and were shouting in pairs across the tavli boards, which balanced precariously on spindly occasional tables. Olive pips and nut shells littered every surface. Dishes of pumpkin seeds and salted baked chickpeas were piled into saucers, which jostled for space with bottles of brandy and whisky on a large onyx coffee table.

Mrs Petrides had never shied away from gaucherie. The Petrideses' lounge was a study in big bucks and bad taste, all spectacularly lit by a drop-crystal chandelier containing about fifty 100-watt bulbs. There were two life-sized bone china Dalmatian dogs on either side of the fireplace, and the mantelpiece was cluttered with Capodimonte porcelain figurines, which, as far as I could make out, were all of people in varying stages of misery or degeneration: there was a sad-looking beggar boy with patched-up shoes, a fat drunk man who seemed on the verge of hitting his dog on the head with a lamp post, a shrivelled-up old fella with some dead fish, and a bedraggled fruit seller with hardly any fruit to sell. Each was incongruously mounted on a frilly, flower-bedecked base. Mrs Petrides gloated over them because, she said, it was stupid to buy reproductions, which most people did, because they had no value. Hers were genuine. Yeah, genuinely ugly and genuinely pointless. So who was stupid now? Hung above the Capodimonte display, at the focal centre of the room, was the pride of Mrs Petrides' collection of ornamental horrors: a wall-mounted gold clock, as huge as it was ugly, set in a diorama of fake peacocks and plastic amaryllis.

My dad was already in full smarm mode, his porky hand patting Mrs Petrides's diminutive husband on the back a little too heartily, slightly dislodging the three stripes of jet-black hair that Mr Petrides had carefully Brylcreemed across his shiny pate. The Fat Murderer was smiling unctuously to demonstrate what a super stand-up guy he was. He could smile all he liked. He was dead meat.

Mrs Petrides sidled up to The Fat Murderer and handed him a glass of ouzo: water and no ice, just how he liked it. Right in front of me. The emaciated cow. My dad ogled her minuscule tits momentarily. Mr Petrides smoothed his hair strips down. He knew. He knew I knew. My dad saw that we knew. I nodded, knowingly, turned deliberately, and walked out of the lounge and into the kitchen next door.

Against the backdrop of the permanent click clack of the tavli counters and the loud demands for more food from the lounge, the kitchen was steaming hot and crammed with reassuringly wide-hipped aunties on a salt-and-fat production line, all chopping, slicing, rolling and frying snacks. The heat was running down the walls in rivulets of greasy condensation.

'Are you hungry?' asked Auntie Roulla. I liked Auntie Roulla, and her younger twin sisters, Doulla and Goulla. They were all three of them nice to my mum when she was alive, even though she was an interloper and didn't speak their language. I could tell that the aunties knew my dad was a turd, and they lavished kindness upon me where it was much needed. For this reason, and because I was starving, I decided to set my Greek prejudices to one side for now.

The aunties each shared similar and outstanding qualities: namely man-sized but exquisitely manicured hands and the ability to read minds. Nothing escaped their x-ray vision. But then, Greek Cypriot women's intuition was on a whole other level, evolved from a lifetime of affecting acquiescence to the patriarchy. They were world-class experts at second-guessing their petulant and demanding menfolk. They missed nothing.

Roulla eyed me sceptically. 'Constantina, how are you, *agabi mou?*' she said, squeezing my jaw and looking me over.

'What?' I replied, trying some telekinetic blocking to prevent her from reading my mind and discovering that I was a future dad murderer.

'What? What is what? *How are you?* Are you happy? How is school?'

'All right, I s'pose.'

'Look at me, Consta!' she said, wafting stale Rive Gauche perfume and kitchen sweat over me as she tried to catch my eye. I looked down.

'Yeah . . . I'm groovy.'

'What? What you say you are?'

'I'm a groover, Auntie.'

She sighed gently, let go of my jaw, and took a gold-rimmed plate with a picture of Kolossi Castle on it and reached for a bowl of fried meatballs before pausing, winking at me, and picking up a fork instead. She knew I didn't like to eat food that other people had touched with their hands. She began to pile up the delicious homemade snacks, which – as was typical with Greek food – consisted of smaller objects being stuffed inside larger objects: stuffed vine leaves, stuffed peppers, stuffed olives and, my favourite, stuffed bulgar-wheat torpedoes – koupes, also known to me as knobs.

She made to hand me the plate then pulled it back again.

'Constantina, you promise you are okay? You don't lie to me?'

She wasn't going to give up easily. I decided some humorous digression was my best option.

'Auntie, do you want to hear a good joke?'

'Okay.' Sigh. 'Tell me it.'

'Why is all Greek food shaped like penises?' I asked, holding up a long, plump koupa by way of demonstration.

'I don' know, Constantina, why is all Greek food shape like the penis?' she said, smiling and rolling her eyes.

'Because all Greek men like to eat co—'

'No, Constantina! Don't say this joke!'

'What joke?' asked Doulla, who had been washing plates at the sink.

'She likes to say Greek men like to eat *peos*,' said Roulla, indicating a length of about two inches with her thumb and forefinger. She and her sisters giggled. That was fine by me. As long as they were laughing, they weren't probing. Roulla topped my plate up with fried haloumi and olive bread and passed it over to Doulla.

Doulla was on desserts, and added some baklava and tiropita.

Goulla was on drinks. 'Are you thirsty, *googla?*' she asked.

'Yeah, very,' I said. Telekinetic blocking was thirsty work.

'Greek or you don't get no drink,' she said, smiling.

'*Poli dipsasmenos,*' I answered, tripping slightly over my pronunciation.

'Okay, I give you a big drink, darling,' she said, fluffing my hair violently with one of her gigantic man-hands. She handed me a large glass of rose-water cordial. My favourite flavour.

'The others are up the stairs,' she said, before I could respond, spinning me round and out of the kitchen door. 'Go. Don't spill.'

I trudged up the psychedelic staircase (red flock wallpaper and multicoloured Axminster), balancing the plate and trying not to spill the drink, which was tricky, as I was wearing some unstable cut-price platform shoes my dad had negotiated from his friend with the shoe shop on the high street. The Fat Murderer would never pay for anything if he could help it, and almost every purchase was for a favour in return. It occurred to me that, most of the time, the person providing the goods was actually more than happy just to offload them, because, whatever it was, it was, without fail, only ever a poor facsimile of what you really wanted and generally defective to the point of uselessness. One of this pair was a half size bigger than the other, and I had asked for wedges. Hence the shoes were total crap and not at all what I had wanted.

I could hear the other freaks before I rounded the turn on the stairs; coquettish shrills and pubescent snorts. There were about ten of them crammed into the Petrideses' eldest son, Vasos's, box-room bedroom. The room was stifling hot and smelled of cheap scent and hormones. There were half-finished plates of food on every surface. Mike Oldfield's *Tubular Bells* was playing on the orange mono record player on the floor. The needle jumped every time someone moved, and a chunk of Mike's opus was periodically lost or repeated.

Vasos was just six months older than me and he was easily my favourite Greek Freak. He was bright and sharp-witted. He had a beautiful long Grecian nose, almond eyes and slim hands, and had shown me his penis for the first time when we were seven. He had shown it to me frequently since. I had seen him at least once a week for as long as I could remember. Together, we had withstood Greek Freakery beyond the limits of all human endurance.

Our relationship mostly involved me demanding things and him supplying them, which always seemed a fair exchange to me. When we were kids, I had slowly acquired most of his toys, including his prize Airfix Messerschmitt, which I had needed for the airstrip adjacent to my doll's house. When my dad had failed to get us Easter eggs one year, it was Vas who gave me his own. I'd kept it for months, and every week he would ask me 'Have you eaten it yet?' and I would say, 'No. I'm saving it for a special time.' I never ate it; it was too much kindness to consume. As we got older, I relied on him less for material goods and more for an endless supply of expert knowledge and unwavering support. After the accident that changed my world, I had refused to go home and had stayed at Auntie Roulla's for two weeks. Vas was the only one I would speak to and he was there every day after school. I had been trying to get him to run away from home with me for the past year.

The rest of the boys in Vas's room were completely lame. So why the girls were so heavily made-up was beyond me. Cement-thick makeup and Avon perfume choking the air, their skin glistened with highlighters and lip shine and they jangled their bracelets when they ran their hands through their long shiny black hair.

I sat on the edge of the bed next to Vasos and tucked into my food. Here I was again. Another night of feeling like a square peg in a round hole, counting away the minutes and wishing dearly that Marc Bolan would ride in on his white swan and whisk me away to a rock stars' paradise.

I could hear the click clack clack click of the tavli boards downstairs, click clack clack click over and over, the testosterone-fuelled masculine camaraderie. I could hear the women's admonishments, managing, always managing. And, above all other voices, I could hear my dad ingratiating himself into a position of value in his community. Flattering, cajoling, bullying.

A similar scene was playing out up here. Everyone practising their future roles. I already knew that at least two girls and two boys had been promised to each other by their parents. I was both relieved and insulted that no one had asked for me yet. It didn't matter anyway. I wasn't going to get married to a Greek boy. Or to anyone, ever. Unless it was Marc Bolan, but that would have to wait until I was eighteen, in case people thought he was a paedophile. I'd already had enough of those in my life, thank you very much. I was going to learn to play the guitar and become a famous pop star, then I wouldn't need rescuing. I could rescue myself.

There was one other boy present who, I suspected, was the main cause of the sexual tension in the room. Marios

Papachristodoullou was Auntie Roulla's precious only son. He rarely joined us on Freak Nights, as he was old enough to drive and had 'other friends'. I secretly called him Prince Papachristodoullou, because Roulla doted on him like he was royalty. I'd never known anyone to have so many luxurious things. He was already on his second car, he had a chunky Omega diver's watch (for all the diving he didn't do), he had a full-scale Scalextric Formula 1 track, and a brown leather jacket, and he smelled expensively of Aramis aftershave, which was a joke, as he did about as much shaving as he did diving. He was telling a loud story about how he had nearly died when he had crashed into a width restriction bollard on Wood Street in Walthamstow, while speeding in the MG his parents had bought him for his eighteenth birthday that year: 'Another two inches to the right and my arm would've been sheared right off,' he was boasting. It was in bad taste considering what had happened to my family, but everyone was hanging on his every word. All the girls fancied him and all the boys wanted to be him.

Even the New Greeks were hanging on his every word. The New Greeks were the Demetrious – a boy about my age whose name I didn't bother to hear, and his two older sisters, Dina and Adonia. Their family had recently moved to Leyton from Haringey and their dad worked with Mr Petrides. This was only their second Freak Night. I didn't have much time for them. New Greeks meant more Greeks, and I had enough Greeks to last me a lifetime. Prince Marios Papachristodoullou, incidentally, couldn't take his eyes off the elder sister, Adonia. She had sultry brown eyes and long dark lashes and was describing a bikini she had just bought. My eyes were blue, like my mum's. And I didn't own a bikini.

I took a covert look at myself in Vas's mirrored wardrobe

doors. Ugh. It didn't add up to much. I had no long black hair to flick around, no alluring scent to waft, no jewellery to jangle. My hair was mousy brown and just past my ears. I hadn't bothered with makeup, because the only makeup I had was my dead mum's and I couldn't bear to touch it. I was wearing jeans and a checked shirt. With odd-sized footwear. And a roll of stomach fat bulging over the top of my jeans.

I put my plate and glass down on the spare bit of floor not covered with records or Vas's Marvel and DC comics and edged closer to him. Unlike me, Vas was the full kebab. Yet he had nevertheless made his own bid for freedom and had decided early on that he was not going to follow his dad into the furrier trade but do everything within his power to go to university to study literature. He always had his handsome nose stuck in a book. It drove his tiny dad mental.

Vas seemed oblivious to the hormonal fug in his bedroom. He had been reading a *Spider-Man* comic and had barely acknowledged me when I arrived. He looked up now and smiled at me in a way that made me feel like we were the only two people in the room who weren't mentally afflicted.

I leant in closer to him and whispered in his ear.

'Vas, do I look like a boy?'

'What?' he whispered back, grinning.

'Do I look like a boy?'

He ran his eyes up and down me and looked doubtful for a brief moment that wasn't quite brief enough.

'You hesitated. That means I do.'

'No. I mean, you don't dress like a girl, but I can tell you are one.'

'How?'

'Big tits.' Shrugging and gesturing to my general chest area.

'Anything else?'

'No penis.'

'That's not good.' I shook my head in despair. 'Am I fat?' I whispered, almost silently, dreading the answer.

Vas thought for a second. 'I'd say you're well built.'

'Well built how?'

'It's fine. You're fine.' And then, loudly, 'Hey, Conno, have you heard of Uri Geller?' He was admirably adept at deflection for a fifteen-year-old.

'No. What music is it?' I replied, mirroring his loud voice distractedly – I was ruminating on my manly attributes and my burly chassis.

Dina had started eavesdropping and perked up at this. She swept her long, thick hair around with a flick of her head so violent that everyone blinked.

'Oh my God! I don't believe you don't know who Uri Geller is! Everyone knows who Uri Geller is!' she exclaimed, jangling her charm bracelet at Vas to check he was getting how whip-smart she was. 'He's a *psychic*. He can bend spoons with his mind.'

'Oh, you mean telekinesis,' I said, trying for a quick recovery with a dismissive wave of my hand.

I noticed Vas's mouth twitching at the corners.

'What do you know about tekelinisis?' she sneered. They were all looking at me now; even Marios had managed to drag his gaze from Adonia and sniggered. Vas stared at Spider-Man.

'Well, I can pronounce it for one thing,' I said, trying to remember what I'd recently read in my latest Stephen King about Carrie and her telekinetic powers of destruction. I did *not* like Dina one bit.

'And I can do it!' I suddenly blurted.

'No, you can't.'

'I can make a light bulb shatter with my mind.'

'No, you can't.'

'She can. I've seen her do it.' Everyone turned to look at Vasos: his word was considered more trustworthy than mine. He nodded with authority. 'There was glass everywhere. Don't make her angry, because she won't be able to control herself.'

Flexing his instinct for a quick exit, he turned to me: 'Wanna go in the garden for a smoke, Conno?'

I certainly did. I was worried someone might ask me to actually burst a light bulb right there and then. So, I gratefully accepted the invitation and left the freakshow, emitting a casual laugh that I hoped would pass for nonchalance.

Vas and I went into the bathroom. He opened the window and climbed out first. He knew not to hold his hand out to help me, unless he wanted a lecture on sexual equality, which I had been giving him since I had learned about Emmeline Pankhurst in junior school. I followed him out onto the lean-to roof just below the window ledge and into the encroaching night-time. We'd been doing this since we were kids and we were getting too heavy for the corrugated plastic that creaked under our weight. The roof sloped to a height of six or seven feet above the ground at its far end and we had a technique of sliding down quickly on our bellies and grabbing on to the rain gutter at the end to slow our descent as we came down.

We landed like cats, softly and deftly, in the noiseless dark. Such a relief from the bright fervour inside. We walked in sync, bodies side by side, pressed together almost full-length, to the end of the garden, but never allowing our hands to touch. At the bottom of the garden the Petrideses had a patio with a white, dome-shaped Greek oven. The oven had been used earlier that day and still had residual heat. We settled around the back of it, out of sight, sitting on the ground and resting our backs against its white warmth.

The air was cooler than it had been for months. There was a trace of damp somewhere over the curve of the earth making its way towards us. Low clouds made for a starless and moonless sky. We were cocooned. Two refugees in a hideaway.

'That pie-faced Dina girl is asking for a smack in the mouth,' I said.

'Yeah, she's trying a bit too hard, isn't she?' Vas replied, taking the boring middle ground.

'Do you *like* her?' I asked.

'No.'

'Then why are you being fair?'

'I'm not. I don't care one way or the other about her.'

I let that sit for a bit.

'Do you think Auntie Roulla can read minds?'

'Probably. She's bloody spooky.'

'Got any fags, then?' I asked.

'No,' said Vas.

'Typical.'

'You?'

'Yep! Tons,' I replied.

I fished a pack containing six crumpled cigarettes and a matchbook with three matches from the breast pocket of my shirt.

'Where did you get these from?' Vas asked, impressed.

'Nicked them from my dad.'

'Nice one,' said Vas, reaching for a cigarette. 'I'll light it.'

Truth be known, I could easily have afforded my own cigarettes, because I also granted myself a steady cash flow by liberating money from my dad's pockets. The Fat Murderer dealt in cash and always had a huge wad of notes in his trouser pockets. Most of the money went into my Getaway Fund, just in case fame and fortune eluded me for a few years. But stealing his cigarettes on top of that was a perk I felt I richly deserved.

I handed Vas the matches and the ciggie. He lit it like a pro. He took a deep drag and I could feel his skinny muscles relax next to mine. I took the cigarette back and took a few deep drags of my own. It felt like getting high. The complex feel-good rush of nicotine. The sex I'd never had but was so close to wanting.

'Vas?' I didn't risk looking at him.

'Yeah?'

'Do you think we are groovers?'

Vas paused, the cigarette halfway to his mouth.

'Erm. I don't know what a groover is,' he said. 'Is it important?'

'I don't know. Maybe. My friend Marc says it is.'

'Oh.' He took a long drag and flicked the ash. He looked straight ahead into the bushes that lined the back of his garden.

'You look nice, you know, Conno.'

'Oh, do fuck off, Vas.'

'You *do*.'

'Are we gonna run away or what?' I had asked him this a thousand times.

'Probably. Not yet, though. But we will. One day.'

That was always his answer. It used to mollify me, but lately it just made me feel marooned.

Deep down I knew running away was unrealistic, but the hope of another life, of endless possibilities out there at the edge of my universe, was always calling me closer. I was pensive for a moment. Not sure how much to say. Vas knew about my dad. But not all of it.

'I can't take much more, Vas. I mean it.'

'Why? It's not that bad, is it?'

'I just can't bear to be near him. I hate his smell.'

'Yeah, but everyone hates their dad, don't they? A bit? Sometimes?'

'I hate him *all* of the time. He's angry ... violent. Always just waiting for an excuse.'

'My dad hits us,' said Vas, matter-of-factly, still keeping his gaze fixed ahead.

'Well,' I said, 'that isn't going to hurt much. Your dad's the size of an Oompa Loompa.'

'Ha, yeah ...'

'All our dads hit us, it's practically the law in Cyprus,' I said. 'But you really don't get it.'

'Get what, Conno?'

'He's just a nutjob. That's all. Especially since the ... you know.' It was the best I could offer.

Vas nodded and said nothing. We had a tacit agreement that we wouldn't discuss the murder of my mum and two brothers. Until the time was right. He didn't know the half of it anyway.

'Your dad is just ordinary Greek-level mental,' I continued.

'True,' Vas sighed. 'But he really wants me to work in the fur factory. He says he's worried I'm going to grow up queer.'

'So what if you do? It's none of his business. I might be a lesbian, if I fancy it.'

'Do you? Conno, do you fancy it?' He looked at me quizzically. 'Or do you fancy me?'

'Fuck off,' I said, dead-arming him.

'Fuck off.' Dead arm back.

'You fuck off.'

'You fuck off.'

This could go on for some time until one of us conceded the last 'fuck off' to the other. I usually won. This time I let Vas win.

We sat there in happy silence, enjoying the stolen mischief of the night-time together. We smoked the cigarette until it was almost spent, and then lit another one off it before throwing the butt into the bushes, where we watched it glow and die.

We were the same but we were different, Vas and I. He was grounded and had a plan. He believed in himself and his future. And he believed in me. I was all up in the air. A realistic vision of my own future evaded me and I wondered silently if Vas would still like me when I killed my dad. Because the more I thought about it, the more it seemed like a good idea.

'Vas . . .'

'Yeah?'

'Show me your willy.'

'Okay.' Ever obliging, he unbuckled his belt, unzipped his trousers and popped his penis through the orange Y-front opening in his pants.

'It's definitely getting bigger,' I assured him. Penis size was important to Vas, and I wanted him to feel good. Tonight, he'd earned it.

4

It was Wednesday evening. Six whole days since the announcement of the school disco and I had made zero progress on the patricide front and, despite a covert shopping trip the previous Saturday to purchase a groovy outfit, I had no real plan on how to get myself to the disco tomorrow. On the plus side, I was on verge of becoming telekinetic, so the week hadn't been a total write-off.

I was lying on my bedroom floor trying to move a pencil with my mind. It was just about to wobble when Marc interrupted my concentration.

'What's happening with the disco, Constance? It's tomorrow night, isn't it?'

'Yeah, I've begged my dad, but he won't let me go.'

'Ah, that's a bummer, babe. What's the plan?'

'My form teacher, Miss Green, says tomorrow morning is our last chance to give her our disco money.'

'You know what Dave and I think you should do . . .' He smiled at David Bowie, who winked at me conspiratorially in turn.

'Well, I did buy some really nice clothes just in case I *could* go. Do you want to see them?'

'Yeah, let's see your threads,' said Marc.

'We'll critique,' said David.

I didn't think I'd be taking fashion advice from Bowie.

He had dyed his hair ginger and shaved his eyebrows and he thought this looked *good*. But Marc was hot on style. He was never wrong. I opened my wardrobe and took out the two carrier bags I had stashed at the back.

I had sneaked off to Walthamstow market while my dad was working in his tailor shop on the previous Saturday afternoon. He'd promised to treat me if I came in and cleaned his workshop. But there were at least three reasons why I declined:

1. I would have to be in proximity to my dad, literally within smelling distance, and I couldn't stand to breathe in hairspray all afternoon.
2. The treats were never that great and I'd only end up with another pair of manky shoes or something equally galling.
3. My dad had a kettle in his shop that had lost its lid years ago and he was so tight-fisted that instead of just buying a new kettle, he had found an old saucer that fitted loosely over the hole where the lid should have been. Every time the kettle boiled, the saucer rattled and bobbed up and down erratically. The whole arrangement spoke volumes that I could never really put into actual words. Oh, and ...
4. My dad's snaggle-toothed pervert friend and resident creep, Peter Pervy Roy, was invariably there, sitting on a stool at my dad's cutting table having a coffee that would last all afternoon, which meant the kettle would be rattling all afternoon and I'd have to watch Peter Pervy Roy's snaggle tooth dipping in and out of his cup all afternoon.

So, I pretended I had revision and took a small slice of my cash stash and met Soraya and her new best friend, Janice, and we had spent the day buying our disco outfits. As well as some new clothes, I bought a Bay City Rollers album and a poster of their bass player, Woody. Janice and Soraya were crazy on the band and I thought it might be good to go with the flow for once.

It had been a wonderful time of near freedom and, as the market began to shut down, I sat on the blackened kerb minding the bags while Janice and Soraya went to a phone box across the street to let Janice's mum know she was going to stay at Soraya's house for tea. They had asked me to join them. But I couldn't risk it. I needed to be home before The Fat Murderer got back from work.

And then a peculiar thing happened. I instantly identified it as The Calling. Because that's what it felt like. Being called.

'Free Angel' – my favourite track on *Tanx* by T. Rex – was drifting hazily out of a nearby record shop, and I was lost in its cadence when my eye was caught by a pigeon, which took flight and soared above the stalls and over the Victorian rooftops. I watched the bird glide effortlessly towards freedom. As I gazed into the distance, I was hit with an overwhelming longing to be somewhere, anywhere, but where I was. It was as if the horizon itself was calling me towards it, promising a new life just out of reach. Somewhere wonderful, somewhere better. Beckoning me to a place where I belonged. It was a siren call so strong that I almost felt I could take wing and fly straight there. But I didn't know where or how. So, instead, I remained sitting in the gutter, with a bag of secret clothes to wear at a dance I would never attend.

I was immediately struck by an all-too-familiar and

repugnant sense of defeatism rising up. I located The Well of Shame that I kept securely in my stomach and which was a repository for all my feelings of embarrassment, self-pity and weakness. I prised the lid off and I stuffed the feelings in, replacing the lid firmly before anything could escape. I practised breathing and smiling, so that by the time Janice and Soraya returned I could pass for normal again.

'Go on, then. Show us what you've bought,' said Marc, breaking through my reverie.

'Oh ... yeah ...'

I tipped the contents of the carrier bags onto my bed: a pair of high-waisted maroon-satin baggy trousers, a blue-and-white harlequin-patterned twin set, some rope-soled platform shoes and some red-and-white stripy socks. Part groover, part normal. It was a good outfit.

I was excited and nervous. It was the first time I had chosen clothes as a potential groover.

I checked with Marc. 'Is it groovy?'

'Yeah, that is a very groovy outfit, Con.'

Marc smiled and then winked. He paused for a moment, then cast a quick nod at David Bowie.

'It would be a shame to waste that outfit, wouldn't it, Dave?'

Bowie just smiled a crooked smile.

'Marc, it's no good. I'm Greek.' I shrugged hopelessly. 'Greek girls just aren't allowed out. I just have to accept it.'

'Oh man, be there or be square,' said Marc, sounding a touch exasperated, 'You'll be fifteen soon.'

Fifteen suddenly felt very old. Although I ached to age towards freedom, the past year had been lost and I wasn't ready for growing up. I was relieved that I still had until November 5th to remain fourteen.

'Look,' interjected David, though no one had asked him for his opinion, 'what *we* say doesn't matter. You're not a child any more. No one is coming to save you. You have to make your own decisions.'

'My friend Soraya says that you can ask the universe anything and the universe will provide. So maybe I'll ask the universe to save me.' That told him.

'Heavens save us from faux spirituality,' David spat. 'The universe doesn't care about you. The universe doesn't care about any of us.' I was starting to wish I hadn't invited Bowie to join the gang. 'I think you're worried about who you'll become if you keep capitulating to your father's demands. You could turn out just like your mother: sad, repressed, lonely. And dead.'

God, he was relentless.

'She wasn't lonely. She had me. I'm alive. And I'd be happy to be just like her. I loved her.'

'What's her name?' asked Bowie.

'What?'

'Her name,' said Marc.

'I ... um ...'

That was extremely weird. At that moment, my mum's name evaded me. The more I tried to remember it, the more I forgot it, until it had disappeared altogether and there was no chance of it coming back to me. For now, though. Surely only for now?

But it did make me wonder if I was more like my dad than my mum, because he never used her name. On the very rare occasions he was forced to speak of her, he always called her 'she'. Together we were erasing her. I did look like my dad, and had always worried that, one day, when I was least expecting it,

I would turn out to have his character too. I mean, who knows how genes work?

I stared now, from Marc to David, and back again at Marc, who wasn't being very helpful at all and was just twiddling his bloody hair.

I looked to Woody from The Bay City Rollers, who I'd recently stuck on my wall in place of Donny Osmond. He just gaped at me gormlessly.

Fucking pop stars.

I folded my disco clothes and hid them at the back of my wardrobe again. Frankly, the lot of them had put me off the disco altogether.

I treated myself to a little nip of whisky, which I kept in my desk drawer and which I had recently liberated from my dad's drinks cabinet. I actually couldn't be bothered with alcohol most of the time; it made me fuzzy, and I liked to be clear and alert and ready for action, because you never knew when something would kick off. It was a skill I had learned when my mum and brothers were still here.

In our house, peace had been strung across the air like a live wire. When my dad's car pulled up in the driveway at night, the wire tightened and thrummed. If he had had a good day, we were safe. If he had had a bad day or something suddenly met with his specious disapproval, things would escalate quickly. At that point, anyone in their bedroom would have to stop what they were doing, muscles flooding with adrenalin, sweat itching and chafing, fingers tensed and waiting, just in case an intervention was needed. We knew the signal moment and would all bomb downstairs, snarling and pulling him off the unlucky victim. I was proud of us. He wanted to make us weak and we never were.

I thought about this now and sipped my Johnnie Walker Red Label. It was nice and warming. I let it work its way down my throat and into my chest, unbuttoning me, loosening me, freeing my brain, drawing memories from better times.

I remembered the first time we had the idea of killing my dad. It was the boys' idea really. They were twins and two years younger. We had spoken about how to make our lives better. That meant getting rid of him. We would play out scenarios where he might get electrocuted, harpooned, drowned. But we could never come up with an idea we all agreed upon. Or that was remotely feasible.

I was older now, and I was on my own, and I would make it work. I had to make it work.

I heard the front door open and close, the disgusting jangle of keys on the hall table. He was home. 'Marc and David might think they know everything,' I thought, 'but they don't.' I did have a plan. It involved a little packet secreted in my desk drawer which was about to be put to use.

5

The Fat Murderer was in the lounge sitting in front of the television, his back to the door, one stumpy leg hooked obscenely over the arm of his armchair, his floor-standing onyx ashtray by his side, Rothmans burning away. His cigarette packet, a glass of whisky and a plate of peanuts were on a small occasional table set slightly behind him. The peanuts really got my goat. No one could make peanuts as irritating as he could. He had this way of grabbing a handful and jiggling them around in his fist before slinging them into his open mouth. I hoped he'd choke on them.

He hadn't heard me come into the room because he had the football on and was engrossed in the game. Football gave me a stomach ache. I hated the testosterone noise of the crowd baying for blood. All the men judging, jeering, cheering when they had done nothing but watch. Who the fuck did they think they were?

I stood behind my dad and alternated my gaze between his bald patch and the match on TV; two things occurred to me:

1. I could get that onyx ashtray and crack him over the head until he was good and bloody and be done with it right now.
2. England were beating the crap out of Czechoslovakia. (Poor Czechs. Probably quite weak and feeble from living on just cabbage and fags.)

Oh and

3. His bald patch was definitely getting bigger. Hurrah.

I felt for the small packet I had concealed in the left-hand back pocket of my jeans for reassurance. My freedom in an envelope. Then I checked he was fully engrossed in the game and, very slowly and very carefully, just out of his line of sight, I extracted two cigarettes from the pack on the table and put them in the right-hand back pocket of my jeans.

'Come on, England, you blatty baskits,' he said to the telly, rolling nuts around in his fat fist.

'I want Czechoslovakia to win,' I said loudly, standing right by him. (There was always the hope that I might shock him into a heart attack. After all, he was fat, old and stressed. How much could it take to push him over the edge?)

I was about to go into a very carefully constructed five-phased plan of action and needed to start on a good foot. If we reached Phase Five ... Well, there would be no going back. This was my last chance before tomorrow's disco and, if it didn't work, I'd be the school freak for real.

'I'm hungry,' I said. 'Shall I make dinner?'

'Yeah, go on. I bring some steaks from the butcher's,' he said, eyes on the match.

'Okay, I'll do that and some salad.' I hovered for a bit. No sense in going to Phase Five without trying phases one to four first. 'I'll just watch a bit of football first ...' I said, attempting a camaraderie that almost made me puke. Football, though. God.

'Yes. It's a good match. Come and sit down, Conniecon.' Conniecon, for Christ's sake. 'Come, on, don't be a stranger,' he said, between peanuts. I don't know where he'd got the 'don't be a stranger' phrase from, but he was using it all the time recently.

It was annoying. He moved his leg from the arm of his chair and patted it, saying, 'Come on, sit down.'

Urgh. Vomit job. I spent most of my time trying to avoid being in the same room as him. I certainly wasn't about to perch on the arm of his chair where he could *reach* me. I sat on the opposite side of the room on the green Draylon chesterfield and felt the two cigarettes crunch in my back pocket.

'Dad,' I started. I really detested using that word to address him. It implied a closeness I reviled. It sounded pleading. Okay. Phase One about to commence: The Reasonable Request.

'Can I please go to the school disco tomorrow night?'

'I have says NO.' He was still looking at the TV.

Right, Phase One done, then. Phase Two: Sensible Bargaining.

'But Dad, you don't have to do anything. It ends really early; I won't be home late. Soraya's dad will drop me home after—'

'I says NO.' Still watching the Czechs getting slaughtered. Wow, we were whizzing through the phases. Phase Three: Logical Argument.

'Everyone else is going. The entire school. All the teachers will be there. Nothing bad will happen. It's probably even safer than any normal day at school, as there will be so many extra adults there.'

'You're too young to go to the disco. Next year, maybe.' Eyes still on the television.

'You said that last year. It's next year *now*.'

I was on the edge of the sofa now. Still logical but not for long. Phase Four: Losing My Shit was looming.

'You can go when you're old enough.' Eyes still on the box.

'Like, when?!!! I'm nearly fifteen. I'm old enough now. I'll be the only one left out. It's just one night. *One* night.'

'You've got homework,' he said, eyes still fixed on the bloody TV screen, as if to infer that football was more important than me.

'I *haven't*. It's a Thursday. We don't have to hand it in until Monday. I can do it at the weekend.'

'Let's see how you do in your school report this year and then we'll see if you can go next year.' He flicked his hand in my direction, as if swatting off a persistent fly. Smug fuck.

'All my friends are going.'

Silence.

Pleading wasn't a phase, but I couldn't help myself...

'Pleeeeeaase. I won't talk to any boys and you can come and pick me up early. I could just go for an hour. Just an hour. Pleeeeeaaaasse. I'll be the only one. I just want to be like everyone else!' Silence.

And...

Phase Four initiated: 'IT'S NOT FUCKING FAIR, YOU FUCKING BASTARD,' I screamed.

Oh, he was looking at me now, all right. I thought he might blow a gasket, but he remained immovable. A small, weak man wielding power over the powerless, like a cruel child kicking a sick puppy. I swallowed it all: the pain, the fury, the ignominy and the loathing, and shoved it into The Well of Shame. Then he dangled a bone tied to a piece of string. He turned to look at me.

'Where is the disco?' Urgh, peanut stink right up my nose.

'The school hall. And the teachers will all be there and some of the parents.'

He thought about it for a long minute, then looked back at the Czechs getting slaughtered.

'Go and do the dinner.' Hint of a smile.

'So? Can I go then?' Good little doggy, ignore the peanut stink.

'No.'

String tugged sharply and the bone out of reach. I bet he was really enjoying this.

He jiggled his peanuts and threw them merrily into his gaping hole and went back to watching the telly, and the other underdogs getting their hopes and dreams beaten out of them. Like the Czech footballers, I could feel my old friend, despondency, rising, but this time it had company: defiance. And I still had Phase Five ...

'Okay.' This was it. He'd have to go. If I accepted The Fat Murderer's rules, then they were my rules too. And I didn't think I could stand a future that contained just the two of us slowly dying in this mausoleum of a house, self-medicating with fags and whisky.

Time for Phase Five: The Poisoning of The Fat Murderer.

6

I could never look at the bright yellow kitchen cabinets without thinking of my mum. She had wanted them for ages. She had asked my dad a thousand times and he always said the same thing: 'We'll see.' Five years he made her wait, always saying he'd think about it, he'd see ... Then she had inherited money from her parents and was finally able to afford to buy nice things instead of putting up with the cheapskate facsimiles that my dad would insist were 'just as good'. She chose yellow because it would make our dark kitchen feel sunny even when it was cold and rainy.

My mum had put a large mirror on the kitchen wall opposite the window so that it reflected the flowers on the windowsill outside. She wanted it to be a happy place. Some days, it was: during the hours between us coming home from school and him coming home from work, when it was just the four of us making dinner, drinking coffee, doing homework, chatting, laughing; then it was a happy place.

I guess my mum knew, as I did now, that you can have all the yellow cabinets and flowers you can lay your hands on. It doesn't make a room happy if the people in it aren't happy. As soon as he stepped into the room it was as if the yellow had turned sour and both the flowers and our spirits had wilted. Now there weren't any people at all. Just me and him. And there was no laughter. And there were only weeds in the window box.

I stared blankly at the cabinet doors. I was actually going to do this. I bent down and opened the cupboard next to the stove. I took the frying pan out. I placed it on the gas burner. I opened the fridge and took out the steaks, a cheerless package wrapped in bloodied white butcher's paper. While the steaks fried, I assembled the ingredients for a Greek salad – red onions, cucumber, tomatoes, feta, olive oil and, just for my dad, nature's poison: three little laburnum seeds, which I had foraged from next door's tree, which overhung our back garden. I added capers for camouflage.

We ate on our laps. Him staring at the telly. Me staring at him. My blood ran hot then cold as I watched The Fat Murderer shovel the deadly seeds into his cruel mouth.

By tomorrow he'd be gone.

7

Next morning, Disco Day, I sat at the kitchen table, toast in hand, watching my dad appreciating himself in my mum's mirror. He was cheerfully blow-drying and lacquering the circumference of his head. He didn't look very dead. He didn't even look peaky. Maybe laburnum seeds took a while to get working... I'd check with Soraya today, as she had given me a cast-iron guarantee that laburnum poisoning was instant and almost undetectable.

The Currently Undead Fat Murderer had added a new cerise V-neck velour pullover to his wardrobe, which he wore now over his shirt and tie. It stretched obscenely across his fat belly.

'Nice top,' I said, with a heavy hint of sarcasm.

He gave his circlet of hair a lengthy spritz and disappeared in a cloud of spray. I coughed and engaged in some dramatic waving of both hands.

'Jesus, you're choking me. Can't you do that in your bedroom? I can taste it on my toast.'

'Shaddap. Don be so blatty rudes.' Another big squirt wafted over me.

I'd be burping that up for hours.

'How do you feel today?' I asked, tasting the bitter chemicals on my tongue and surreptitiously examining his face for signs of imminent expiry.

'Okay, why?'

'Just wondered. Why are you so dressed up?' I asked, curious now.

'I'm going to be home late tonight.'

'Why?'

'I am going to the casinos.'

'What, all of them?'

'What? Don't try to be blatty funny.'

'Who with?'

'Uncle Peter.'

'Urgh. He's not my uncle. He's a pervert. Peter Pervy Roy,' I said, pushing my luck a bit, still assuming that, at any moment now, my dad would begin clutching at his throat and die.

'Don't be blatty rude,' he said, without so much as a cough or a rasp.

Peter Pervy Roy – he of the endless snaggle-toothed dipping into coffee, was, in no uncertain terms, a disgusting perversion of humankind. He could make your skin crawl just by looking at you. He was mid-thirties, tall and skinny, with sand-coloured hair. He had a sharp, oversized Adam's apple that bobbed up and down when he spoke and he wore trousers so eye-wateringly tight that they squashed his knob and bollocks into a weird flat patty. And then there were his dipping teeth. The two front ones crossed over and made his lip protrude lasciviously. He made no bones about staring at my bum and even made sure I saw him do it. He'd twist his neck round to follow me with his roving eyes. Sometimes he'd pull me onto his lap and talk about how I was 'getting a figure' while he stared at my chest. His bony hands were swift and slippery, sliding over places that weren't theirs to cover.

I bit into my Sunsilk Firm Hold on toast.

The Fat Murderer patted his glazed bonce once more all round, took a last loving look at himself in the mirror, and grabbed his blazer and car keys. He stood in the doorway and gave me a smile. For one foolishly self-indulgent second, I thought he was going to give me a last-minute reprieve.

'Do your homeworks tonight, okay?'

My head started to thump, an intense syncopation at the base of my skull. I imagined doing a Carrie and summoning some knives from the knife drawer with my telekinetic powers, flinging them into my dad's hands, pinning him to the door frame, showing him who had the real power. Instead, I screamed inside, a huge open-mouthed window-smashing light-bulb-exploding scream.

'Be good, Conniecon.'

And he was gone.

'Stop calling me fucking Conniecon,' I mumbled uselessly.

I still had ten minutes before I needed to leave for school. I went into the back garden to kick a few vegetables, but there was a light drizzle and I didn't want my hair to go flat. It was already pretty lifeless, even after a vigorous blow-dry with a pint of setting lotion. The wood pigeon couple were bustling through the English ivy that clambered up the back fence, scoffing the last of the blackish berries with alacrity. Their simple goal of eating and cooing, eating and cooing, eating and cooing was hypnotic. The beat in my nervous system gently eased and slowed, coo oooo coo, coo cooo coo . . . I swayed and cooed along. And I felt a little better.

Theirs seemed like a good relationship. Uncomplicated. All they cared about was the fence and the berries and there was plenty of both to go round. I wished they'd come closer.

I would have loved to stroke their smooth soft feathery hot bodies, to rub my face on their tiny heads.

'What are your names?' I asked, softly.

No reply. Just doubling down on the scoffing.

'I think you are called Betty and Ron.' I tried it out a few times. 'Betty and Ron, Ron and Betty.'

They continued to ignore me. Berries disappearing down their gullets as fast as bullets.

'Hm, maybe you're too regal for Betty and Ron. How about Elizabeth and Ronald?' They both looked up then, and I swear they sort of nodded. Maybe my telekinetic powers were animal biased? I shut the back door, grabbed my shitty school bag, and went to face my destiny.

That day, disco Thursday, school felt like a holiday, everyone free and silly. Dr Doron, all-round killjoy and headmistress at Leyton Manor Girls' School, reminded us in morning assembly that this was still a study day and, should any girl be caught exhibiting undue frivolity – which included giggling flirtatiously, rolling our skirt waistbands over to make our skirts shorter or wearing the wrong tie knot – she would put the entire school in detention.

Several of us immediately pulled down our skirts and tightened our ties. According to Dr Doron, loose ties were consistent with loose morals. It was one of her many bizarre and arbitrary school rules, including:

1. No dropping of apple cores in the playground. This was because her beady-eyed sausage dog, Molly, had once nearly choked on one, much to the delight of staff and students alike, who all suspected that Molly was no ordinary dog but an avatar of Dr Doron, sent

forth into the playground to sniff out illegal activities, such as smoking, chewing gum and girl-on-girl snogging practice.
2. No brushing of hair in public, as this was precisely – *precisely, girls* – as indecorous as cutting one's toenails in public.
3. No fraternising with the boys from Norrington High, especially Calvin Belding – he of the tapeworm – who had breached all protocol between the two schools and had taken to circling our school gates at home time like a ravenous dead-eyed shark.
4. There were many more school rules, but no one listened because rumour had it that Dr Doron was a bitter spinster whose vagina had sealed up through lack of use.

Everyone called Dr Doron Dr Moron, even some of the teachers. In particular Mizz Liddle and Mrs Fullerlove, the PE teacher, who didn't give a toss if we dropped apple cores. They dropped them too. And they did smoke and did practise girl-on-girl snogging in the playground. With each other. One of the Deborahs saw them when she went to collect the balls on the netball court after practice one afternoon before last summer term ended. 'They were properly going at it,' Deborah said. Soraya said this was proof that at least one of them had man parts and it was probably Mizz Liddle, as Mrs Fullerlove had big bosoms and a husband.

I forgot myself in the rampant disco fever and started to pretend I was a part of it. It felt good to get carried away with the general air of excitement. By lunchtime I had half convinced myself it was a reality and had even paid the 15p entrance fee so my name was on the list. I watched Miss Green, our form teacher, write my name down and saw it looking all normal and just a part of a list of other normal people. One 10p, two 2ps and one 1p jangled into the collection box – a pretty Pears soap tin that was so Miss Green it made me want to cry.

We sat for lunch with The Three Deborahs: Blatchford, Brownlow and McNichols. They all ate school canteen food, which I never did. It looked disgusting and, also, the dinner ladies didn't seem particularly fastidious when it came to food hygiene practices. Sometimes the plates had bits of old dried food on them. I had a Curly Wurly and a packet of crisps I'd brought in from home.

Once we had sorted out our outfits for the evening, the talk turned to the Norrington boys and, more specifically, who would get off with Calvin Belding. I didn't understand the fascination with Calvin Belding, other than that he was a convenient source of weight loss thanks to his resident tapeworm. I'd seen him from a distance, hanging around outside our school at home time, prowling around the railings, all slack-eyed and drooling, with colourless bum fluff on his face and Art Garfunkel-style bonkers frizzy hair. He was older than us, sixteen, but his larynx was still waiting for its big moment to descend, so his voice came out as an amusing squeak. I bet he was even worse close up.

Much more to my liking was his intriguing new friend, Paul Johnson. While Calvin was practically licking the school railings, Paul Johnson hung back across the street. He possessed quintessential English attributes: a slight build, a pretty face, straight blond hair and, best of all, he had recently moved to London from Yorkshire and spoke with a charming exotic accent. Why Paul was friends with Calvin I had no idea. I hoped he'd be there this evening.

Despite my dad's refusal to die in a prompt and seemly fashion, and despite him reminding me that I wasn't allowed to go out this evening, I had become inextricably caught up in my own ruse. At that moment, I firmly believed that I, Constance Costa, would be going to the Leyton Manor Autumn Term School Disco. I really did. I thought the laburnum seeds would surely be kicking in by now and that, with any luck, I'd come home this evening to find my dad stone-cold dead, one hand grasping his stilled heart, his limbs as stiff as his lacquered hair. The very thought lifted my spirits immensely.

8

When I got home that afternoon, two odd things happened.

The first odd thing was that the phone rang. Our phone never rang. It was The Fat Murderer calling to check that I had come straight home from school, to remind me that I was to stay at home this evening, and to demonstrate, unwittingly, that he was still very much alive.

I stomped up the stairs and into my room. 'Fucking Soraya,' I said to Marc.

'Hm,' he said, shaking his curls out of his eyes. 'The laburnum seed poisoning didn't go to plan I'm guessing, babe?' Marc said.

'Soraya said that laburnum seeds were – *without fail* – fatal to anyone who ingested them,' I said, almost hysterically.

Bowie smirked. 'She still hasn't learned to question the sagacity of the ramblings of a self-anointed teenage soothsayer, has she?' he said, addressing Marc and not me.

I gave him a withering look.

'I don't understand what went wrong. He ate it all. I saw him,' I said.

I lit a ciggie and stood in front of my bookcase. I found my *20th Century Encyclopaedia*, which my dad had bought me without ever knowing it, as I had cut out the middle man and taken the money straight from his pocket. I flicked through the Ls.

Heaving a prolonged and agonised sigh, I lugged the hefty book over to my bed and began to read aloud.

'Okay, "All parts of the laburnum are poisonous, especially the seed pods, which contain the alkaloid cytisine. If eaten can cause headaches, nausea, vomiting, frothing at the mouth, convulsions and even death in humans." See? He should be dead by now.'

I read on: 'Oh . . . "You would have to eat many of these seeds to come to harm, however, and mortality is extremely rare . . ." Shit. Soraya had told me that a man her dad knew had died after consuming just one single seed. She said it dropped off a tree and into his barbecue when he wasn't looking.'

I looked up at Marc and David in utter dismay.

'My dad didn't even froth at the mouth . . . I should have checked before I . . .'

'I think that's a pattern with you, isn't it?' said The Orange-Haired One. 'One could be forgiven for thinking you were scared to actually do it.'

He really knew how to twist the knife.

Then the second odd thing happened. I was just about to change out of my school uniform when there was a knock on the door. No one ever knocked on our door. Except the nosy old bag next door who stuck her neb in on the night of the murders and had made it her mission to do so ever since.

I opened the front door just a crack and – you could have genuinely knocked me down with an actual feather! – there was Vas. This was only the second time that one of the Greek Freaks had visited unannounced. The first time was last year, when it all happened. And that was Auntie Roulla and didn't really count. And now here was Vas. My Vas. I couldn't believe my eyes.

Neither of us said anything for a long moment. I stared at him. He had his school uniform on and a hint of a moustache on his top lip – classic Greek-boy geek chic. He looked down at his feet and shuffled them a bit. And with a covert glance at me, said, 'Is your dad in?'

I wondered what the hell he was doing here.

'What the hell are you doing here?' I asked.

'Can I come in?'

'Huh?'

'Is your dad in? Can I come in or what?'

'What?'

'Is your dad in? Can I come in?'

'Stop saying the same two things. Yes, you can come in,' I said, opening the door and making way for him to push past me.

'Is your dad in?'

'Fucking hell. No. He's out with his pervert friend.'

'Oh. Good.'

He was acting very weird. Which was weird because Vas was never weird.

'Why are you being weird?' I asked him now.

'I'm not,' he said, which was a lie, because he definitely was.

'What are you doing here? Has someone died?' Your mum, with any luck, I thought, then felt bad for thinking that and then thought I shouldn't feel bad for thinking it because she was an ossified old moo who was shagging my dad. So I re-wished she was dead and felt fine about it.

'No. No one's died.'

'So what's happened?'

'Nothing has happened. I just popped round. Why are you making it a thing?'

'You *popped round*. Right. 'Cause you're always just popping round. Here comes Vas, popping round as usual.'

'Yeah, all right, all right, Conno.' He dumped his school bag. He seemed bigger. Solid. Tangible. Kind of ... exciting.

'Do you want a whisky and a ciggie?' I asked him, riding an unexpected surge of ebullience.

'Yeah, go on!' he said, relaxing a little. He followed me into the back room where the drinks cabinet was and stood beside me. God, we looked like such a pair of Greek geeks in our school uniforms. But I also liked the way we matched. I poured two medium-sized whiskies. He was hovering a bit too close and I could hear him breathing.

'Can you not breathe on me, please,' I said, looking at him.

He ignored that and carried on respiring over me loudly.

'I've never seen you in your school uniform before,' he breathed, taking a glass from me. 'Do you always look this messy?'

'Yes. I do,' I said, looking down at my loose tie and untucked shirt.

'Some of your buttons are undone,' he said.

'I was in the middle of getting changed when you knocked. Deal with it,' I said.

'I can see your bra.'

'So? Stop gawping. It's not like I'm nude. What's the matter with you?'

'Nothing. Where's your cigs, Conno?'

'In my blazer pocket,' I said, nodding down at my breast pocket. Vas slipped his hand in and withdrew the pack of B&H. Normally I wouldn't give it a second's thought on a Freak Night, but this, here, where I lived, in the real world ...

it felt ... close ... intimate. Now I was feeling weird. He sipped his whisky. He looked around the room.

'What you been doing?' he asked now.

'Oh, you know, endless partying with rock stars ... flying to San Francisco tomorrow on a private jet. You?'

'Yeah, same. What you reading?'

'Why are you asking?'

'Just, you know, making conversation.'

'I've almost finished *Carrie*.' I shrugged. 'You still reading *Spider-Man*?'

'No.' He sounded a bit defensive. 'We started doing the metaphysical poets at school. You know, Donne, Herbert, Marvell.'

I made a loud snoring noise.

'I actually really like them,' said Vas, a bit tetchily.

'You actually do, do you?' I said, with an exaggerated eye roll. Bloody hell, this was turning into a right old bore-off.

He lit a cigarette and took a desultory drag. He looked a bit lost. I usually saved most of my pity for myself, but I found myself sparing a little for him and regretted my sarcasm.

'Vas, is everything *really* okay?'

He nodded. 'Yeah, I just wanted to see you, check you're okay.'

I shrugged.

'Have you had your tea?' I asked him. Food always worked for me. Maybe some calories would pep him up a bit. He was ridiculously thin. His bony old crone of a mum probably had them all on the grapefruit diet.

'No, I'm starving.'

'I could make us eggs 'n' chips. Yeah? Can you stay?'

'Yes, I can stay,' he said, smiling. 'Can you do your buttons up, though? You look like a right slob.'

Jesus.

We walked into the kitchen, Vas trailing behind me, still breathing but not quite as erratically, thankfully. I still couldn't quite believe he was here. In my kitchen. Tonight was a horrible night: it had been an entire week since deciding to kill my dad and I had failed, David Bowie and Marc Bolan had been useless, and while everyone else would be at the Autumn Term Disco, I would officially be designated School Freak by my absence. And here was Vas.

'Thank you for being here,' I said. I meant it too.

'Thank you for being here so I could be here,' he said, and clinked glasses. We knocked back the whisky.

'Okay, you peel the potatoes and I'll cut them into chips,' I said, turning to hand Vas a bag of spuds at the exact moment that he shouted 'Hey Conno, catch!' and threw a tomato at my face.

'Ouch, that hurt,' I said, rubbing my face. 'Why did you do that?'

'You were supposed to catch it in your mouth!' he said. 'Go on, try me!'

'No, I don't want to throw vegetables at you.'

'Not *at* me. *To* me. Go on, I've got skills.' Skills. He'd never said 'skills' before.

I sighed and picked up the tomato. This was the problem with people doing nice things for you – you were obliged to reciprocate and indulge them in their idiocy. I tossed the tomato towards Vas. He bobbed his head and caught it in his mouth. I had to admit, it was quite funny. I mean, who knew getting someone to catch things in their mouth could be entertaining?! I got a bit carried away after that and threw several grapes, a radish, and a chunk of haloumi. Each time Vas caught a new thing, it was funnier than the last. And every time he threw something at me, I missed it. Which was funnier still. Why it was funny I had no idea, but we were laughing until we doubled over. Vas had come alive and his eyes were sparkling and, I had a feeling, were I to look in the mirror, mine would be sparkling too.

Vas had a way of slotting into a space as if he had always been there. Now we sat at the kitchen table eating our English dinner together as if we had always done so. I watched as Vas dipped a chip into his fried egg and then placed it in his mouth, chewed and swallowed. I found it suddenly fascinating. I had momentarily lost my appetite – which was a first for me. Even straight after the murders I'd managed a couple of shish kebabs. Now it felt like I was chewing cement and all the saliva in my mouth had pooled somewhere lower in my body. I felt very hot.

'You not finishing yours?' Vas said, digging his fork into my chips and transferring most of them to his plate. I shook my head mutely and continued to stare at his mouth.

'Why are you staring at my mouth?' he asked, wiping his lips and checking his hand.

'I was looking at your ridiculous bum fluff moustache,' I said, for quick recovery.

He did a half shrug. 'You're just intimidated by my burgeoning masculinity,' he said, scraping the remaining scraps onto his fork. I snorted derisively. He ignored that.

'Nice,' he announced, leaning back in his chair. He pulled his shirt out from his waistband and undid the top button of his school trousers. He wore his trousers low on his hips and I could see a faint line of black hair disappearing into his pants. I hadn't noticed that before.

'God, I'm bursting,' he said, patting his stomach.

Weirdly I felt like bursting myself, but in a very new and unusual way.

We sat, not speaking for a while. Then ...

'I'd better get home, Conno.'

I didn't want him to leave. While he was here, the kitchen was a sunny place again.

He got up, slipped his school blazer on, and hefted his rucksack onto his shoulder.

We stood on the doorstep for a while, both of us reluctant to end our interlude of normality.

'Well, see you at Freak Night tomorrow, then,' I said, finally breaking the spell.

Vas shifted his rucksack from one shoulder to the other, then, with an air of decisiveness, put it down on the step. He flicked his hair out of his almond eyes, which, I couldn't decide, looked either dreamy or like he needed to go to the toilet. He had also gone a very deep shade of red – almost purple, in fact.

'Have you ever wondered what it would be like if we kissed?' he blurted out, looking at everything except me.

'Erm, that's a bit out of the blue,' I said, glancing down at his line of belly hair for about the tenth time and gulping quite loudly. I wished I could stop staring at it, but it was like my eyeballs had a will of their own.

'Well, I mean,' said Vas with a pretend carefree shrug that looked more like a spasm, 'we're gonna have to kiss people at some point, so maybe we could practise on each other so that, when we have to do it for real, we'll be good at it.' He said it so cheerfully and with such an air of practicality that it took less than a nanosecond to piss me right off.

'Oh, what, so you can go off somewhere and snog someone and show off more of your tragic "skills"?'

'What? No ...'

'I'm not having you practise on me so you can be good at it when you want to have a *real* kiss,' I said, with intense irritation. 'The first time I kiss someone it's going to be with someone who wants to kiss me for *me*, not because I'm just the closest thing handy for a trial run.'

'Well, what about if I did want to kiss you for you?'

'But you don't.'

'I do, I do, Conno. I was just talking bollocks before,' he sighed. 'Why do you think I'm here?'

'To show me your *skills*.'

'Christ, Conno, I just really want to kiss you.'

'Well, I don't know why you didn't just say that in the first place instead of wasting all this time.'

'So ... can I? Please?'

I could think of worse things to do, and he had returned to a more normal colour now.

'Okay,' I said.

He leant forwards, keeping a big space between us, and pressed his lips to mine. Which would have been nice, except that he was breathing quite heavily again and he had one of those bogies up his nose that makes a whistling sound, which I found very distracting.

'Was that all right?' Vas asked, gently. 'Did you like it?'

'Your nose is whistling,' I said.

I instantly felt bad.

'But it was a nice kiss. I've got no others to compare it with, but I could tell it was a good one.'

'Okay, well, see you tomorrow.' He stepped off the doorstep and walked a few paces before turning around. He looked very serious. 'Thanks for the chips.'

Not the best romantic parting gambit, I thought – 'Thanks for the chips' – but I expected it was the most Vas could manage if his feelings were as complex and confused as mine were right now.

9

I went back upstairs, lit a cigarette and wandered over to the window. The cool of the dying day against the glass was soothing and I rolled my forehead from side to side. It felt good. It helped me think. I wished Vas was still here. If he kissed me again, I'd be ready for it this time. I would stop and take in the moment, let it linger. I would kiss him back. I wouldn't tell him that his nose was whistling.

I opened the window and flicked the still-burning cigarette into the garden, where it hit a pathetic ailing winter squash. There were no shadows or shapes this evening, just a flat twilight drizzle. I looked for Elizabeth and Ronald but they weren't there. Some crows were starting their end-of-day cacophony, trying to get everyone into the same tree for the night. I bet there wasn't a teenage crow out there going 'Sorry I can't come. I'm not allowed. I'm a freak.' I closed the window, shutting out the noise, but I kept the curtains open so that I could still see out. I never drew the curtains. I couldn't bear to separate the outside from the inside completely.

And that's when it happened again. That same sensation I had experienced when I was sitting on the pavement in Walthamstow market the previous Saturday. That siren; drawing me towards something big. Something good. The promise of a dream fulfilled. The Calling, making its way through the ether, slipping over my shoulders and chest and down into my legs. I knew how this would end without even knowing where it was going to start.

I opened my desk drawer and took out my mum's makeup bag – one of her few things I had rescued before my dad had eliminated her presence entirely. I unzipped the little bag and ran my fingers over the few pieces inside; there wasn't much: a lipstick, an eye pencil and a few blocks of eyeshadow. I didn't feel sad, like I thought I might, though I couldn't think about not being able to remember her name at this moment. I sort of felt she'd understand and tell me it was okay, because a name was just words. It was memories that really counted. And as I took out her half-used relics one by one, I did have memories. I smiled when I recalled her doing my makeup when I was small and drawing huge lips on me with bright red lipstick and huge blue half-moons for eyes. She would have told me to stop canonising her makeup. Were she still alive, she would have said, 'Oh, for God's sake, Constance, you twit – it's not doing anyone any good sitting in a bag, is it? Use it and enjoy it.' So that's what I did.

I played *Ziggy Stardust* but I could barely hear him, because the crows were still massing and cawing and calling and calling and filling my head with their opinions and noise, and colours came like a glass-shattering sunburst and it was electric and I was freaking out to Bowie in a moon-age daydream and Ziggy was squawking like a pink monkey bird. I danced around my room feeling the sting of guitar strings on my flesh, making me tingle, and all my senses rearing up on end, and then I got the disco clothes from the back of the wardrobe and put them on, blooming into them as they touched my skin, those maroon slithery trousers sliding up my legs like hands, the twin set, tight-fitting and new, the rope-soled shoes making me feel tall and significant. I dried my hair into little flicks and wisps. I applied my mum's pale lipstick and black eye pencil. I will remember your name, I promised. I saw my reflection in monochrome in the darkened window, not daring to confirm it in colour in the mirror, liking the curve of my breasts, the way the satin fabric fell over my hips. I liked how the lipstick felt gliding over my lips; everything feeling smooth and sensuous and slippery.

I couldn't even recall the bus ride; the next half hour was a blank. But, as I stood at the school hall door, on the threshold of so much, feeling the heat of the room, with Barry White growling 'you're my first, my last, my everything', beating in time with my heart, I knew who I could be.

Soraya and Janice were there along with The Three Deborahs. All dancing in a circle and sideways eyeing up Calvin and his friends, who weren't acting quite as cocky as usual and looked like seasick pirates now they were finally on the island they had circumnavigated for so long. The girls waved crazily when they saw me and I joined the circle and became wonderfully and completely normal. I melted into my group of friends on the dance floor and we were one, losing ourselves in the sheer pleasure of being teenagers, alive and together. Mizz Liddle was in charge of music, so we were a bit concerned that she might make us dance to Tchaikovsky, but she was a hot potato that night and played the soundtrack to our young lives.

'Aaaarrggggh, Rubettes!!' screamed Janice, and we all swayed and waved our hands above our heads singing 'sugar baby love, sugar baby love'. Things went up a gear with 'Rock the Boat' by The Hues Corporation. We had no idea who Hue or his Corporation were, but we all stood in a conga line rowing our boats and singing: 'Rock the bo ooooh ooh oooooat!' After we rocked the boat, we Rocked Our Baby for George McCrae. We all then chucked our babies in the air to get down with Benny and The Jets. The Deborahs went crazy, jumping up and down and screaming when David Essex came on.

Miss Green, our pretty, petite form teacher, joined in. She was the best; apart from Mizz Liddle, who was fierce but my first favourite. You knew where you were with Mizz Liddle. She was currently giggling with Mrs Fullerlove, who was helping Mizz Liddle with the records and smiling at her in a way that reminded me of Elizabeth and Ronald on their garden fence. Only with records instead of berries.

Mizz Liddle put on some Gilbert O' Sullivan, which none of us liked much. 'Still,' I yelled, 'at least it's not Gilbert *and* Sullivan!' We all laughed, but Deborah Brownlow was laughing much louder than all of us, far louder, in fact, than a normal human being. She flicked her long curly red hair all over the place and Calvin and co looked over and The Deborahs looked back. One of Calvin's zit-faced cronies came over and started to dance with her, and then they were snogging just like that! To Gilbert O'Sullivan. A penny dropped. It was a bit like Greek Night and the Freak Girls. If you wanted to get a boy to notice you, you had to flap your head around and shriek. That didn't seem to be very attractive to me. If I was a boy, that would put me right off. And anyway, Vas had kissed me and I had never flicked my hair. Although, I was thinking of trying now, because there was Paul Johnson, standing slightly to one side of Calvin Belding, looking bloody gorgeous, and then I stopped thinking about anything because – oh my God! We all went totally mental singing along to The Rollers, arms aloft, the disco ball spinning colours across our faces, our lungs bursting with song and dance. I sent a telepathic message to Marc, telling him how amazing this was and wishing he were here to dance with me and to hold me down before I burst into a million particles. Bowie must have been earwigging, because the next song was 'Rebel Rebel', which is the worst song he's ever written and off the worst album too – *Diamond Dogs*, more like a Dog's Dinner – but then I felt a sudden fondness for the old weirdo and we continued to fly around the school hall on wings that couldn't fail us.

And then came the slow dances and I looked to Paul Johnson, which made me feel guilty about Vas, but then Calvin Belding and his tapeworm were creeping across the dance floor and 'Wanna dance with me?' he asked, in his scratchy little mouse voice, and everything went super slowed-down. I really, really didn't want to. It felt like I was cheating on Vas, which was stupid because Vas wasn't my boyfriend and we'd only had one nose-whistly practice kiss, plus it was only Vas. But if I was going to cheat on Vas, I'd rather make it worth the effort and cheat with Paul Johnson. And Calvin was pretty spotty close up, and had a face like a soggy pancake, but 'The Air That I Breathe' by The Hollies had started and Calvin moved in and I thought I'd better say yes, to be normal, and then we were close and he spent three minutes pressing his crotch into mine, which was quite disgusting actually. I felt weirdly hot but not in the same bursting way I had when I was with Vas, and was grateful when Dr Doron the Moron opened the hall doors to let some air in.

At the end of the song, Calvin's pancakey face came towards mine with his tongue practically flopping out onto his chin. There was no way I was going to have that in my mouth, not even for a coveted tapeworm. Even in the disco demi-light I could tell Calvin wasn't massively judicious when it came to dental hygiene. As he zoomed in for the big ending, tapeworm wiggling, all closed eyes and sluggy tongue and furry teeth, I clamped my lips together like a vice and he sort of ended up just sucking round my mouth while I held my breath, trying not to inhale any germs. And that's when I saw, over his shoulder, a flash of pink velour in the open doorway.

Everything contracted and the sound of the room echoed somewhere in the distance. Most of my internal organs had relocated to my throat. The Fat Murderer was standing there, manic eyeballs rolling and sweeping like bloodshot searchlights, trying to find me in the crowd. His furious face was surrounded by a perimeter of wild hair, which stuck out at right angles to his head. Before I had time to process, he was in the room, grabbing my arm and pulling me out of the school hall and away from who I had become.

Miss Green, our lovely form teacher, had been lost in her own reverie and now lowered her comely arms. Her face changed and her eyes looked as if they had never seen such ugliness. She made to move and then, instead, rooted to the spot. I wanted to hold a hand out to her and scream 'help me', but then the shame kicked me into action and I looked away. The last thing I saw was the confusion on Calvin's stupid face and the look of concern and shock in Janice and Soraya's eyes as I allowed myself to be commandeered out of the hall, through the school gates. The red Audi was parked by the kerb directly outside, engine ticking over menacingly. The Fat Murderer booted me onto the back seat.

To put a shit-flavoured cherry on top of a shit-flavoured Bakewell tart, Peter Pervy Roy was sitting in the front passenger seat, snaggle tooth slithering out from under his top lip, all saliva and slippery grin. What a horrific double whammy.

My dad jumped into the driver's seat and manoeuvred his pink velour belly behind the steering wheel. He twisted around to look at me in the back seat. His head looked like it was going to detonate. It was twice its normal size. I wished he would just drive away, but he had other priorities. He reached between the two front seats towards where I sat in the back and struck me several times across the head and face with full force. I almost laughed because he looked ludicrously funny with his face all swollen up and piggy-eyed like that.

'You think its blatty funny, do you?' he screamed, little yellow rat's teeth bared. I didn't care. I was used to worse and I had taught myself to absorb the shockwaves, store them in The Well of Shame and shut the lid. Too many times, when I was younger and less defensive, I had squirmed across floors in dark rooms, screaming, pleading and wondering when it would stop. No more. Tonight, I had taken one small step towards The Calling and there was no going back. I wouldn't be cowed. I was already calculating how far I could push this. And, on some level, I could sense that he knew it. I felt dangerous.

'I blatty told you to stay inside the house tonight,' he yelled, voice getting louder towards the end of the sentence. He was on a mad, psychotic roll now and it would move in slow motion until he was spent. He threw a few more open handers. 'Why do you wearing blatty makeup on you face? Where did you get it?'

I didn't flinch, I pushed it down. I glanced towards the school gates. I saw Miss Green run out and then turn and run back in again.

'Whyyoudonfackinanswerme?' he bellowed, nostrils flaring, eyeballs bugging out like lollipops. 'Eh?' Slap. 'Eh?' Slap.

I went with the blows. I wouldn't give him the triumph of intimidation. My jaw clenched, then I exhaled and said evenly and with control, 'It was my mum's makeup. MY MUM. I'm entitled to it.'

That threw the murdering bastard for a moment. He didn't want to get onto the subject of my mum. If I could have just said her name right then, that would have stopped him in his heartless tracks, I was sure. But it just wouldn't come to me. Nevertheless, even the thought of her hung in the air perilously. I let it hang. I looked him square in the eyes, flashing soundless violence and eye daggers. Peter Pervy Roy shifted in his seat. He was starting to look uncomfortable.

Semi-recovered, my dad started anew. 'Have you been dancing with the boys?'

There it was. The danger zone. Boys. Sex.

I felt a deep daring and the thrill of risk gave me a control I hadn't felt before. 'Yes, I did dance with a boy. And I'll do it again if I want,' I said, with measured hatred. I was sick of living this half life and my calm wavered dangerously as I spat, 'And what are you going to do about it? Nothing. You can hit me all you want on the outside, but you can't touch me inside. You can't reach *me*.'

I was expecting him to leap out of his seat and into the back of the car with me to unleash his full madness, when Peter Pervy Roy stepped up, catching my dad's arm in mid-swing.

'Ah, come on, mate, she's a teenager, she's only out having a little dance.'

I never thought I would be grateful for Peter Pervy Roy's presence, but my dad seemed to snap into some semblance of sanity, as if he had just been reminded that we had an audience. This was the first time his charm offensive had slipped in front of an outsider. He mumbled an ill-formed threat, faced forwards and revved the engine. I glanced sideways and saw Miss Green coming back out of the school gates with reinforcements: Doron the Moron and Mr Hatton, the pottery teacher, followed by Janice, Soraya and The Three Deborahs. Bringing up the rear were Mrs Fullerlove and a furiously determined Mizz Liddle, who charged through them all. Just as her hand touched the car door, The Fat Murderer put his fat foot down and we left them by the kerbside, along with any hope of my rescue.

The ten-minute journey home was conducted in threatening silence.

When we arrived at the house, The Maniacal Fat Murderer didn't put the car in the drive but instead parked out front by the kerb and kept the engine running. I got out of the car and he drove off at high speed.

10

It had started to rain; a spiny, sharp rain, pricking my face and hands. There was an overload of electricity in the air, the smell of burning wires.

I attempted to pull my house keys out of my trouser pocket, but the mortice key got hooked around the lining. I tugged sharply and the lining tore, freeing the key. I stopped, breathed. I aimed the key at the door and, with absolute, unswerving precision, unlocked the deadlock. Then the Yale. Stepped inside. Slammed the door. Good. Okay. All pieces of me present and correct.

I flew up the stairs in the darkness, straight into my room. I was pleased none of the gang were awake, as I had started to shake and needed some time to gather my strength. Only I couldn't. I couldn't make my body work the way I wanted it to. I was juddering all over, spasmodically. I watched my hands disappear and reappear. My face was numb and I couldn't feel my nose or lips. I checked the mirror to see if they were still there and I was embarrassed to note that I was making a weird gibbering noise, saliva dripping from my mouth and snot from my nose. I tried to hold it all in, thinking about how this would look if Vas were here to see it. But I was so fed up of holding on, I let it go. Time moved of its own volition.

I must have been like that for some hours, because when I finally heard a small noise and looked up at my alarm clock, it was dead on midnight and the rain had picked up a steady pulse.

'The weather is just about right for the occasion, isn't it?' said a voice by the window. Marc.

'Yeah,' I half laughed, half snorted.

'Clean yourself up, Con. This is his mess, not yours, and you don't have to wear it.'

I went and got a pink toilet roll from the bathroom and came back, sat on the floor cross-legged and wadded some up. I spat on the wad and rubbed it around my face. My face was sore and my jaw felt stiff and useless. I had a cut on my forehead where my dad had caught me with his wedding ring. How dare he still wear it. I blew my nose and threw the paper in the wastepaper basket. I felt better. Much better. My head was clearer than it had been in a long while. It was only now that I saw I had lost a shoe. I looked down at my maroon satin baggies. There was a huge tear fraying at the knee and my knee was scabbing up. I had no idea how that had happened.

I did a few things:

1. I took down the big poster of Woody from The Bay City Rollers, folded it carefully and put it in the bin. It had been a swift love affair but I was too old for him after tonight. I felt the sediment of years past and those yet to come settle on my chest.
2. I changed into jeans and a sweatshirt and socks, folded what was left of my disco clothes carefully and put them back in their carrier bag at the back of the wardrobe.
3. I went into the garden, in the rain, and, in my stockinged feet, trampled every vegetable until they

were mush and my socks were wet through and caked in mud and winter squashes up to my ankles.
4. I went into my dad's bedroom and rifled through his wardrobe, feeling the pockets of his trousers. I found two pairs with small wads of cash in them and relieved them of their burden. I took off my filthy socks and stuffed one in each of the trouser pockets. On my way out of his room I took a packet of cigarettes and a lighter from his bedside cabinet.

I returned to my room, sat and faced Marc.

'Marc, I remember things. And some things I don't want to remember.'

'Con, you must speak your fears to know they are true, otherwise they will always haunt you. To see the stars, you must first look into the darkness.' Ever the poet.

'I'll talk for three cigarettes then stop.' I took a cigarette out of the pack and lit it. I inhaled the nicotine deeply into my lungs, feeling that rush and release.

'It started when we were small. I remember the cellar. He would lock us in. It was dark down there. The boys were terrified, they were so tiny and confused. They didn't know what was happening or why. They hadn't done anything *wrong*. I used to hear my mum reasoning with him, waiting until he calmed down. It happened so many times. At first, we used to scream and cry and bang on the door to be let out. In the end I made it into a game. We had some toys down there and a torch and we would play and I would make up stories for the boys. When he unlocked the door one time and said we could come back up, I said, "We're staying down here, we like it." And we used to spend our time playing down in the cellar even when he didn't lock us in. He soon stopped doing it after that, of course.'

I lit the second cigarette from the first, even though it hadn't fully burned down.

'That doesn't mean that things got better. One evening the boys had just come out of the bath. I expect they were playing up but, you know, they were babies ... *Batman* was on the TV and I had a terrible headache ... It was snowing outside and he made them stand on the doorstep, naked. They were three years old. I waited, pretending to watch *Batman*, my head screaming, hoping someone would walk past the house and see them, knock on the door and demand to know what the hell was going on, to rescue us. But people never do. I let the boys in after a couple of minutes. They were red with the cold. He didn't say a thing to me, which was odd now I think about it.'

'Why do you think that was, Con?' asked Marc. 'You know, looking back as an older person.'

'I don't know. How do you know why bad people aren't bad when you expect them to be bad? Maybe he knew he was crossing a line and that I might tell about the other stuff.'

'What stuff?'

'No, not worth raking it all up. It's all in the past ... mostly ... I think.'

I knew David Bowie wouldn't be able to keep out of it.

'Constance, it doesn't matter when it happened. Our past is always in our present.'

'What?' I knew exactly what he meant, but I was playing for some time.

David sighed. 'All of time is present all of the time.'

'Maybe it's just best to leave certain things behind,' I countered.

'You can't leave things behind. Understand that and you'll know how to move on,' said David.

'Oh, I know how I'm going to fucking well move on. I'm going to kill The Fat Murderer. It's my only way out.'

The rain had stopped and the air had grown dead and cold. My feet were frozen and dirty. My breathing was shallow and quiet. I was still. Everything preternaturally calm.

I said, very slowly and deliberately, 'Okay. I'll try. I don't really know how to say it. It's obscure and I don't know what it means.'

I twirled the cigarette slowly in the rubbish ashtray, knocking off lifeless white embers until it was just a red-hot bevelled point.

'And what if I'm remembering it wrong? What if I was getting the wrong end of the stick? What if it was normal?'

'Did it feel normal?' asked Marc.

'No. It did not.'

I twirled the cigarette some more. It had burned halfway.

There was a long silence after that.

'I can't talk about this any more,' I said, and took a drag on what was left of the cigarette and stubbed it out. 'Enough.'

I sat.

The colour of the sky had changed so subtly that it was only the smell of chill daybreak that told me it was morning, cold vapours snaking through my open window, the scent of brown leaves and drizzle on dirt, the sour mash of rotting vegetables and the gorgeous, plaintive cooing of Elizabeth and Ronald, reassuring each other, reconfirming their love, taking in the coming day without a care in the world.

I thought of Vas. I thought of my mum. I thought of her death at the hands of The Fat Murderer and I thought of my own hidden guilt; a culpability I had never spoken of. And I thought of murder.

11

It was Friday evening, 7pm, and I was sitting in the kitchen fully dressed and with my coat on for two reasons.

1. Maybe my dad would return home and we would go to the Petrideses' for Freaky Friday as usual. I was stupidly nervous about seeing Vas for reasons a) The Whistling Nose Embarrassment and b) my face was a mess and I didn't want him to see me wearing my shame.
2. Maybe my dad would return home, go apeshit and I'd have to do a runner.

I hadn't seen my dad since last night, which was fortunate, as it meant he wouldn't know I'd bunked off school. I had written myself a letter of absenteeism: 'Dear Miss Green, Constance was unable to come to school on Friday as she had period pains. Yours sincerely, Fat Ignoramus.'

I would obviously rewrite it (using my left hand, so it looked like it had been written by a patriarchal imbecile), and put his real name at the end, but I enjoyed writing Fat Ignoramus.

I had struggled about bunking off. I liked school. But there was no way I was going to face everyone after what would be forever known as The School Disco Disaster of 1975. I could have ridden the shame. I was an expert at that.

But I felt frail, like an outline of myself with nothing filled in any more.

Instead, I had decided to spend the day reading the *Bhagavad Gita*, practising some chord sequences out of my Bert Weedon's *Play in A Day* guitar book and eating Curly Wurlys. It wasn't particularly edifying as a day of leisure, though. For three reasons:

1. I realised that my guitar was really shit.
2. The *Bhagavad Gita* was very boring. I didn't see why Krishna had to be so opaque about everything. His entire message seemed to be 'one can kill only the body; the soul is immortal'. I'd pretty much said the same to The Fat Murderer in the car last night after The School Disco Disaster of 1975. Krishna had nothing to teach me. I decided being a killer was far more useful than being transcendent, so made a list of ways to murder my dad instead. So, in some way, I had had a spiritual awakening after all.
3. The Curly Wurlys had shrunk since I last bought some. What on earth was happening to chocolate bars???

I heard the key scrape in the lock and the front door squeal and click. I heard his keys clinking and clanking on the hall table. I knew he was checking himself in the hall mirror. Making sure every hair he had left was in its place for Mrs Petrides, no doubt.

I put the note to Miss Green in my monstrosity of a school bag. I say 'bag', but it was more like the sort of thing that a backstreet abortionist would have carried with him in Victorian times. I had asked for a brown leather satchel with a strap that went across my body. My dad had, of course, presented me instead with a Gladstone bag. Who, in the twentieth century, has *a Gladstone bag*? I was agog when I first saw it. If a battered suitcase and a very mouldy briefcase had produced a bastard child, this would be their progeny. I presumed the old Scrooge had found it at the bottom of a skip, judging from the stink. I clipped the mortifying item shut and made a mental reminder to buy myself a new bag from an actual shop.

Our journey to the Petrideses' was strange. The atmosphere in the penis extension was stultifying. I was expecting to endure some more mad ranting and raving, but my dad was bizarrely serene, which felt more unhinged, more sinister. He just asked me questions. What did I do at school? 'School stuff.' How did I feel? 'Fine.' Was I hungry? 'No.' Did I want to give Greek Night a miss and go to the cinema? 'No.' What did I want to do for my birthday? 'Nothing.'

He shook his head as if I were being unreasonable.

Just before we got out of the car, he took my hand (cue vomit in mouth) and prized open my fingers (vomit threatening to spurt out) and dropped a small trinket in my palm. It was a gold bauble encrusted with semi-precious stones attached to a short thin gold chain. Ah, the old atonement-jewellery trope. Cheap and insincere. My dad made suits for a bloke who owned an H. Samuel Jewellers, and whenever anything went tits up and he couldn't think of any other way round it, he'd get you a piece of wonky jewellery: always something bizarre that you'd never pick for yourself, and no doubt the bloke from H. Samuel's was desperate to get rid of.

'This for you, Conniecon.' Jesus. I looked from the bauble, which I noticed had a stone missing from one of its mounts, to his greasy face, which was pulling an expression of disingenuous contrition, and then put it in my pocket, saying nothing.

'You don't want to wear it?'

'No.'

'If you don't like it, I buy you something else. We can go to the H. Samuel's and you can choose something yourself.'

I didn't respond.

'Come on, cheer up, Conniecon. We just had a little row. Comb your hairs over your eyes, and if Roulla says about your face, tell her you did this in school.'

Still silence from me. I was starting to learn that silence could be powerful. I looked at him. My gaze unwavering. He shifted in his seat.

'Okay? Come on. Don't be sillies.' More of a threat than a cajole.

I got out of the car and walked to the Petrideses' front door. I knocked with force. Mrs Petrides opened the door and, before she could yap her flap, I pushed past her. The last thing I wanted was to hear her inane prattle.

I started up the stairs to Vas's room but, as luck would have it, Auntie Roulla was coming down from the toilet. I put my head down and mumbled '*Yassou thea*', and tried to pass her on the turn. She was like a hawk after a rabbit. Her gigantic hand darted out and she clasped my chin in her red-painted talons and turned my face up to hers. She looked at me for about twelve hours, with her lips pressed into a thin, grim line before saying anything. When she did speak, all she said was, 'Go upstairs, Constantina *mou*.'

Vas's bedroom window was open, because Marios was having a fag. It was just past dusk and the air was already biting. It felt good against my hair and skin, made me comfortably numb. As soon as I appeared at his bedroom door, Vas took one look at my face, jumped up, tucked a bunch of books under his arm, grabbed a bowl of pastries and steered me to the bathroom and out of the window. He had brought poetry books for himself and a new bestseller for me that he knew I wanted to read. He had always bought me books with his pocket money. Anything printed on paper was worth the outlay as far as he was concerned.

We assumed our usual position at the bottom of the garden. I tucked into *Jaws* by Peter Benchley and he into the poetry of John Donne. We kept a small distance between our bodies, but I could still feel his warmth. We kept sneaking looks at each other, but said nothing for some time. Eventually, Vas sighed, and turned his book down onto his lap. I thought he was going to talk about our kiss or my face. But, instead, he looked directly at me and said that the metaphysical poets really understood the inextricable connection between spirituality and physical love. I replied, in reference to my own book, that I thought the woman was stupid to go swimming at night-time when she was due to have a period and probably deserved to get eaten by a shark.

Vas nodded in agreement and picked up his book again, crossed his legs, and placed the bowl of pastries in his lap. They were loukoumades, tiny sweet fried dumplings drenched with honey. They were delicious. I watched him surreptitiously as he distractedly picked one up, let it linger at his lips, then chewed and swallowed, the muscles in his neck working, never taking his eyes off his book.

'You all right, Jack?' I said, after a while. 'Enjoying those, are you?'

'Have one,' he replied, absently tilting the bowl towards me and, for a scorching nanosecond, a thought passed through me as quick as lightning: I imagined what it would be like if he placed the loukoumade in my mouth. Why? Why on earth would I think that? First of all, his hands were probably full of germs; I'd seen him rearranging his balls about ten times already this evening and I can guarantee he did not wash his hands after going to the loo because, whenever he went, there was never a gap between the flush and the door opening. Secondly, whatever had happened between us after school yesterday was, clearly, inconsequential. We were back to being Vas and Conno.

We sat in companionable silence for half an hour or so. Although my eyes were on the pages of *Jaws*, they just skated over Peter Benchley's words. Now I was safe in our hallowed cloister behind the Greek Oven, with the sky open and infinite above us, I began to sift through the events of the past week, fanning them out, working from the edges to the centre of it all.

In just seven days I had demoted The Osmonds, I had instated and swiftly banished Woody out of The Bay City Rollers, got rid of everyone else except David Bowie and Marc Bolan, semi-kissed two boys on the same night – one lovely and one chuck-up material – slow-danced with the chuck-up one at the school disco, been subsequently shamed in front of the entire said school disco, and had tried, but failed, to kill my dad. And Vas had gone from reading comics to reading poetry (from Marvel to Marvell, I had said to him, and he laughed a proper ha ha ha!). It had been a long week by anyone's standards.

I couldn't get to the centre of it, though. It was as if my concept of time had shifted. Usually, I could work through events and, after some sorting and filing the crap down in The Well of Shame, I could find equilibrium. At first, I thought that too much had happened in one week to make sense of it all, to normalise it. But then it struck me, as sharply as if one of the stars above us had sent down sparks to ignite my senses: I didn't want to normalise it, because I didn't want to be normal. Somewhere in this cataclysmic farrago of a week, I had changed. I wanted to be me. I didn't want to be Janice, or Soraya, or even Miss Green, because I was going to take my own life into my own hands. And to be me I had to be without my dad.

'What?' said Vas, suddenly looking up from his musty old book.

'What?'

'What did you just say?'

'I didn't.'

'Yeah, you did, something about being without your dad.' He looked at me, scrutinising me in that intense way he had.

I shrugged.

He let it go.

'Share,' I said, nodding to his book. He looked down, heavy dark lashes mingling with the vanishing light. His hair was curling over his ears and touching the back of his sweater. He looked like a picture of Lord Byron he had shown me once, but too young yet for the danger to radiate. He read in his steady voice, no treble, no bass, just his reassuring mid-frequency and truth.

'I wonder, by my troth, what thou and I did, till we loved.'

'God, you utter wet.' I couldn't help myself.

'Share,' Vas responded, nodding towards my paperback.

'The fish had moved away. It swallowed the woman's limb without chewing.'

Vas looked at me dead-eyed for a second and I gave him a 'What?' look. Then we both laughed and I gave him a good dead arm. He didn't reciprocate but moved away, imperceptibly, creating a bigger space between us. I had come to rely on the warmth of his proximity. I shouldn't have made that comment about his nose whistling. I had really blown it. He looked at me unequivocally now, staring for longer than he should have.

Eventually, 'God, Conno . . .' He extended a hand towards my face and traced the deepest bruise with his index finger. He had never touched me this way before. It was thrilling.

'I want to help,' he said.

'The only person who can do anything is me, Vas.'

The reality of my situation was descending upon me like the night coming down on our heads, heavy and compact. I would bide my time. I would kill my dad. Properly this time. And then I would run.

I was on the verge of sidestepping this whole issue and asking Vas to get his willy out, but suddenly I didn't really want to see his willy, and something told me he probably wouldn't want to show it to me. I didn't want to go back to being just Vas and Conno. I wanted to be *us*.

'Calvin Belding tried to kiss me.' I blurted it out.

'Who's Calvin Belding?' Vas withdrew his hand from my face, as if he'd received an electric shock.

'Creepy kid from Norrington.'

'Where?' He sounded annoyed now.

'On the lips.'

'No, where did it happen?'

'School disco.'

'Oh. Was it good?'

'Okay as disco's go, I suppose.'

'No, the kiss.'

'Oh. No, it was dreadful. I didn't want it. He came at me all of a sudden. He's got a tapeworm too. I kept my mouth closed.'

I don't really know why I told Vas about Calvin. It wasn't to make him jealous, though if he could be jealous, that would be a bonus, but I wanted to be honest with him, I think. And then the real reason . . .

'Ours was nicer . . .' I said it quietly. I felt shy. But I wanted Vas to know. 'Much nicer. I don't think I did it very well, but if there is a next time I'll do better.'

'Prove it.' Vas smiled.

Keeping the small space between our bodies, Vas brought his face towards me and kissed me, on the lips, briefly but wholly. He pulled away for a second, then kissed me again. I tasted his lips, they tasted of the loukoumades, honey sweet, and I wanted to make them open with my tongue. He would have gone for it too, I reckon, had there not been a multitude of fake screams and crashes as the Freak Brigade came sliding down the lean-to roof, girls falling deliberately so the boys would help them up. I despised their ersatz vulnerability.

'Oi, oi!' shouted Marios. 'What you two geeks doing back there? Trying to bend spoons or what?' He really was an absolute legend in his own lunchtime, that one. The girls were giggling and hee-hawing like a bunch of donkeys.

'No, we're snogging,' I said, just as he came round the curve of the oven.

'Yeah, right,' said Marios, sitting down and making a huge farting sound as he hit the ground. He pulled a whoopie cushion out of his trousers and waved it at his entourage. Cue more gurgling.

'No, we were,' said Vas.

Marios looked at us for a long second and shook his head.

'You two need to see psychiatrists.'

He grabbed Vas's book and read aloud. '"It sucked me first and now sucks thee, and in this flea our two bloods mingled be." Urgh, disgusting, why don't you just look at nudey pictures like normal people?'

He moved closer to me and looked at my face.

'Holy shit, Constance. I hate to think what the other fella looks like.'

Vas was very quiet. Marios checked the others were far enough away not to overhear.

'It's all kicked off big time in there,' he said, with a nod to the house. 'My mum's gone totally apeshit at your dad, Con. I'm not surprised. Did he really do that?' Dear Auntie Roulla, I thought.

I felt Vas close the small gap between us, my flesh gratefully softening around his hot bony shoulders.

'What happened?' Marios asked.

'I went to the school disco, without permission.'

'That's all?'

'Yeah.'

'Fffffuck . . . life shouldn't be this hard.'

'It's easy for you, Marios. You've got everything you could ever want. You're Auntie Roulla's prince. She thinks the sun shines out of your arse.'

'It does,' he said, smiling.

'How do you get away with being such a privileged imbecile?'

'Only child, innit.'

'Yes, but Auntie Roulla is no fool.'

'Ah, but I was born with an atrial septal abnormality.'

'A what?'

I looked at Vas, who replied. 'A hole in the heart, Conno. Marios was born with a hole in his heart.'

And one in his brain, I thought, but instead said, 'Oh . . . sorry about that. Does it hurt?'

'It's not even there any more, but I was pretty unwell for my first year before it healed.'

'Oh, sorry again,' I said, for want of anything to add.

'Don't be. I don't remember anything about it. But my mum does. And that's the important thing.' He laughed and tapped me on the nose affectionately.

'So, you are just a sneaky privileged imbecile after all.'

'Thank you for the compliment, Constance.'

'You're welcome, Marios.'

'Right, I'll leave you two weirdos to do whatever weird stuff you like to do.' He might have been an imbecile, but he knew when to call it a day. 'I hope you pull through this, Constance.'

'I've not got fucking cancer, Marios,' I said, to his retreating back.

'Right,' said Vas. 'Where were we?'

I was just about to say, 'Tongues, I think', but Vas opened his book and carried on reading boring old John Donne.

He was great at kissing, Vas, but terrible at romance.

12

As it turned out, school wasn't as bad as I thought it would be when I went back the following Monday. Luckily for me, there were two other incidents that had occurred which, thankfully, overshadowed The School Disco Disaster of 1975.

1. I had got off with Calvin Belding. If going stiff as a rock and having a pancake-faced Spotty Muldoon suck on you like a limpet while cramming his knobbly crotch into your knicker area is getting off, then, I suppose I did. The Deborahs, in particular, wanted to know what it felt like. Did he do tongues? Did he come up for air and go back in again? Did he smell nice? Was his hair soft? Was he wearing Old Spice or Brut? Did he touch my bum? Could I feel his entire penis? Am I going out with him now? My kiss with Vas had been infinitely more exciting than having Calvin's slobbery chops all over me, but I didn't bring it up. Greek Night and school were two separate worlds and, anyway, it was none of their business.
2. And thank you God for small mercies: Mr Wellesley, our maths teacher, had been suspended!!! Everyone knew that Janet Morgan, the head girl, had been carrying on with him for about a year. It was obvious because they went red every time they passed

one another in the corridor and, sometimes, they would just stare at each other in maths class for ages. It wasn't as weird as it sounds. Mr Wellesley was really young and trendy, with long Jesus hair, and looked about eighteen, and Janet looked about eighteen because she was tall and had big hair like Farrah Fawcett-Majors. Anyway, Janet had told her best friend, Tracey Evans, not to tell anyone, but she thought she was pregnant and it could only be Mr Wellesley. Tracey Evans had immediately told her mum, who told Janet Morgan's mum, who asked Janet if it was true and it was. Mrs Morgan told Mr Morgan, who went ballistic, and they both came to the school to see Doron the Moron and insisted she call in Mr Wellesley. He had to leave his class there and then and put Janet (ha ha, irony or what?) in charge of the class and go to the head's office. They called Janet in. Janet told her mum and dad and Doron the Moron that she loved Rick – *Rick* Wellesley!! He said he loved Janet, and Mr Morgan said he was going to crucify him, which was very apt what with the whole Jesus look, but instead Mr Morgan tried to strangle Mr Wellesley. The mad choking sounds made Dr Doron's sausage dog, Molly, get stressed and she puked in the corner, and Dr Doron's assistant had to wipe it up with Kleenex while Dr Doron and Mrs Morgan tried to prise Mr Morgan's hands off Mr Wellesley's scrawny throat. We heard it all first-hand from Doron the Moron's assistant, who went to flower arranging class with Soraya's mum. Janet certainly embraced disgrace with dignity. She stayed at school and played the Queen of Tragedy, everyone fussing round her and asking her if she needed to sit down all the time. She loved the attention. She wouldn't love it in six months' time when she was pushing a pram containing a tiny baby Jesus lookalike and changing its shitty nappies every five minutes. Her bloody tiara would slip then, I bet.

Apart from a visit to the school nurse, who asked me if everything was okay at home (Yeah) and Miss Green asking me if I needed extra time for homework (No), I'd got off lightly.

13

At home, The School Disco Disaster of 1975 was never mentioned again. I thought my dad might try to make amends and get me something nice for my fifteenth birthday, but November 5th came and went with a remarkable lack of flourish. The morning started with a cheap birthday card left on the kitchen table with twenty pounds inside and the touching line 'To Connie from George'. I would not endure another birthday like this. I had to set myself a deadline. Not a stupid one that I couldn't meet, but a workable one, one that would give me murdering incentive. I threw a gauntlet down to myself and swore an oath, out loud, on the latest *Jackie* magazine, so that it mattered: 'I, Constance Costa, the imprisoned daughter of The Fat Murderer, do swear on this holy *Jackie* magazine, that I will kill The Fat Murderer before I reach my sixteenth birthday.' I added 'Amen', just in case there was a God and just in case she was listening. And then I chucked the *Jackie* in the bin. I was done with magazines. They were crap.

It was time for Project Pork Chop.

I had listed every form of 'accidental' death that I could think of during my spiritual-awakening day off school after The School Disco Disaster of 1975, but none seemed feasible. A shove from a great height wouldn't work, as I'd almost certainly never be on top of a building high enough at the same time as my dad. I had no idea how to cut brake cables on a car.

A drug overdose would have been okay, except I tried making a cup of coffee with twenty ground-up paracetamol and it tasted terrible. He'd never swallow that. Any other method – stabbing, suffocating, etc – would have been tricky to execute, and would have landed me in prison, which would negate the whole bid-for-freedom thing I was trying to achieve. Sadly, poisoning was still my only viable option.

Soraya had said that she knew someone who knew someone who had died from eating a refrozen pork chop, but I was treating Soraya's intelligences with some circumspection these days. I needed to make sure I had as much information as possible so that it wasn't a repeat of the laburnum seeds debacle.

I went to the library, but that was a waste of time. I asked the school librarian, who was known as 'Old Coffee Breath', for a book on food poisoning, but instead she asked if I wouldn't prefer to take out an Enid Blyton or something with a 'roaring good storyline' while exhaling caffeinated bacteria all over me. I had a flick through the *20th Century Encyclopaedia* but there wasn't much in there about death by pork, and I dared not ask the gang in my room because I'd only get judgemental stares and told I was 'reverting to childish behaviours to solve an adult problem' or bla bla bla *whatever*.

Then I had a brainwave: Mrs Pollard or, as we liked to call her, Pollard the Bollard. Which had twofold merriment because:

1. It rhymed.
   and
2. She was straight up and down with no curves, like a bollard.

Pollard the Bollard was our slightly sad-looking science teacher. She always looked like she might be on the verge of a nervous breakdown and I wasn't surprised. Firstly, she had to teach O-level biology to fifteen-year-old girls who had zero interest in the subject. Secondly, she had, as far as I could make out, a husband who could do with a large helping of poisonous pork chop himself.

Pollard the Bollard hadn't always wanted to be a teacher. She had told us once she'd wanted to be a toxicologist and solve murders for the police. Then she had met her husband, who said he thought teaching would be a more suitable profession, as the hours would be better when they had a family, and she'd get a pension. But then it turned out her husband was a Jaffa – seedless. So, she had neither the job she'd wanted nor the family she'd hoped for. Her husband was a dead loss, if you asked me. She was clearly a pushover. A character trait of which I had every intention of taking full advantage.

After the last period on Thursday, I took ages to pack up my bag. Soraya and Janice had to go to netball practice, so they couldn't wait for me, which was useful. Pollard the Bollard was sitting at her desk grading papers. I coughed loudly to get her attention. She looked up distractedly.

'Everything okay there, Constance?'

I could tell by the way she asked me that she knew. All the teachers knew what had happened, even if they weren't personally present at The School Disco Disaster of 1975.

I nodded. 'Yes, thank you Poll—*Mrs* Pollard.'

'Is there something I can help you with, Constance?'

It was now or never. I walked up to her desk with what I hoped was a quizzical but relaxed air.

'Miss Pollard, you know when we were doing microorganisms last month …'

She set her pen down.

'Yes, I believe you were particularly interested in them, Constance. But, again, I must remind you not to worry – not all microorganisms are bad.'

'Well, this is about that,' I said, segueing expertly. 'You know you were saying that some of them can be deadly to humans? Like you had studied in toxicology?'

'Yes.' I had her attention now.

'Well, I was thinking, Miss, if there are microorganisms in our food?'

'But, again, Constance, as I explained last time, the dinner ladies do wash their hands and the school canteen doesn't serve food riddled, as you suggested, with bacteria.'

They don't. And it does, I thought. But, instead, I acquiesced.

'Oh yes, but there are bacteria in food, aren't there?'

'Yes, certainly there are, good and bad. When we grew bacteria on agar jelly, that can easily happen on food too. The bacterium needs something to feed on and food is a good source of nutrition.'

'Miss, can you get food poisoning off meat?' I asked. I realised I was clutching my Gladstone in front of me at chest height. I wished I had put it down at the start. Now I felt like I had to keep holding it.

'I should think so, yes,' she said. 'If it's not cooked properly.'

'Could you get it off, say, pork?'

'Certainly, pork and chicken are both quite unstable if treated unhygienically.'

'How much pork would you need to eat?'

'Well, it would depend on the bacterial load and the type of bacteria. *Trichinella spiralis* can be very dangerous.'

My eyes lit up at that.

'How dangerous exactly? Please?'

'Well,' she said, enjoying this as much as I was, 'pork infected with trichinella can lead to trichinosis, and that's very horrible.'

'Is it? How so, Miss?'

'Well, the symptoms are terrible. You could get diarrhoea and bad stomach pains. That's if you're one of the lucky ones.'

'What if you're one of the unlucky ones?' I said, feigning concern but feeling a pleasant fervour building inside me. My fingers were tingling. I wasn't sure whether this was because of my excitement or because I was iron-gripping my abortionist's bag. Mrs Pollard tried to look grave but she was as excited as I was. We were talking toxins now and, for different reasons, we both had a vested interest.

'Well, there's muscle pain, fever, feeling sick . . .' Oh, good.

'What if there isn't any trichinella in the pork? How do you get it in there?' I asked, trying to sound insouciant. I put my bag on the floor.

'Ah, well, you can't *put* it in the pork. It's got to originate from a worm that the animal ingests from eating, say, unhygienic food scraps.'

'Oh.'

Sensing my disappointment, she said, 'But there are plenty of other bacteria that can occur in pork, Constance.'

'Like salmonella and things?' I said, trying to match her rally.

'Yes, salmonella, but also campylobacter, listeria and many others. There are also roundworms and tapeworms in pork too, so you should always cook it very well.'

'How much would you have to ingest to, say, die?' I asked, affecting my best casual air.

'Oh, I don't know. It really depends again on the bacterial load in the pork and how much of it you eat.'

'Would a pork chop do it?'

'Why, yes, I suppose so, if it was very infected and the person eating it was weak.' Hm. That might put a fly in the ointment. The Fat Murderer was as strong as a rhinoceros.

'Constance, may I ask, are you enquiring from a scientific perspective or a culinary one?'

'Oh both, Miss. I was just fascinated when you told us about toxicology and I'm just trying to think about my future.'

'We should look at your A-level choices and see whether, in addition to Biology, you might want to think about Chemistry.'

Yeah, over my dead body. I hated science and was only going to do Biology A-level because it would have knobs and bollocks in it, which I was currently finding to be an increasing fascination.

'Yes, I think that would be a very good idea,' I said. I would be long gone by then, anyway, so it wasn't really an issue.

'I should go, Miss,' I said, stepping back and tripping on the bloody bag. 'Thank you for your time.'

'Any time, Constance. It's good to know you're applying what we do in class to your life outside school.'

Oh, I would certainly be doing that.

14

December was bizarrely mild this year and there wasn't so much as a snowflake in sight. The council had erected the usual underwhelming Christmas tree in Coronation Gardens and it had disappeared the following day. Soraya said that there had been several mysterious disappearances in the area, and it was because Leyton was on a powerful ley line – hence the 'ley' in 'Leyton' – which went all the way to Stonehenge. That was priceless even by Soraya's standards. I asked her where she'd heard this nugget of info and she couldn't 'remember'. She was all mouth and no trousers that one. And, anyway, the man from H. Samuel's the jewellers had seen some boys cart the tree off in a Sainsbury's trolley.

December 13th was the anniversary of The Multiple Murders of 1974, a whole year since The Fat Murderer had murdered my mum and brothers, and the murdering cretin said nothing – no commemoration, no recognition. To be honest, I didn't want to linger on it too long myself.

I had one family snapshot that I kept inside a book on my bookshelf. I contemplated it now. It had been taken by one of the Greeks during a Freaknic – a Greek Picnic – when I was about nine. My mum and dad were at each end and I was in the middle with a twin either side of me. The photo always made me laugh, because a nine-year-old Vas was in the background swinging from the limb of a tree. He spent the entire day up that tree. He had the nickname *Maimou* – Monkey – for weeks after. I carefully folded back the bit with my dad on it and tore it off. I lit a match and burned him; a fitting memorial. It helped with the sadness. I couldn't afford to be sad. I had to focus on avengement and escape. In that order.

I was on the trail of the lonesome pine these days. Janice, Soraya and The Deborahs had all started chewing gum loudly and had joined a youth club in Walthamstow, where they played pool with boys. It sounded brilliant. They didn't bother to ask me to come because it was pretty obvious, by now, that I was a dead loss and not allowed to do anything at any time with anyone. Ever. Amen.

Freak Nights had gone up the spout a bit too. They were less frequent and more craptastic than usual, for reasons too numerous to count:

1. I think my dad was avoiding Auntie Roulla after The School Disco Disaster of 1975, because when they did see each other, she looked at him like he was something the cat had dragged in. Hence we rarely attended.
2. We weren't allowed in the garden because the lawn was soggy and Mrs Petrides didn't want us treading mud into her precious tasteless carpets.
3. We weren't allowed to go upstairs to Vas's room, because they 'wanted our company in the lounge', which was just a lie because we all knew that Mr Demetriou was a draconian old buffoon who had clocked that Prince Marios and his daughter, Adonia the Beautiful, had the raging hots for one another.

4. Sometimes Vas wasn't even there, because, his witch's broom of a mum had said, he had started going to a chess club with some friends. Well, that was a double revelation: I didn't know he played chess. And I didn't know he had friends.

Anyway, all this meant that I got to see less of Vas than was humanly endurable. Just as we had started the kissing phase of our relationship, there was now no chance, at all, of dedicating more time to it. The recollection of Vas's mouth on my mouth set off a fluttering in my body, which travelled all the way from my throat to my gusset region. I had replayed our last kiss so many times that the memory was wearing thin. I had even begun to add extra bits to the scene in my imagination to make it last longer.

Even though I ached to see him, I had told Vas not to come over after school again because it was just too risky and I couldn't deal with the consequences. The Fat Murderer was growing madder by the day. The freedom I had acquired for a merciful period post-The School Disco Disaster of 1975 was becoming increasingly brittle. When we were together, things felt volatile, edgy. I didn't fully understand it, but it had me on permanent red alert nevertheless. If I thought about it too much, I began to feel fuzzy, like I was disappearing.

We were playing a malevolent game of hide 'n' seek, he and I: I tried to be nowhere and The Fat Murderer was everywhere. I stopped playing records at night so that I could hear him craftily coming up the stairs. He would burst into my room demanding to know what I was doing or who I was talking to, filling the door frame, all malignant fumes of sweat and hairspray and rancid breath, his eyes rolling around the room looking for some imagined transgression. I'd wait until he closed the door and then resume talking to Marc and David, at which point The Fat Murderer would throw the door open again and demand 'Who do you talking to?' I could have kept that up all night; it was really very tragic but also very amusing, and there was always a chance that I could nudge the fat idiot towards a nervous breakdown.

Luckily for me, he spent some evenings with Peter Pervy Roy, and went hunting on the weekends with his cronies from the Rotary Club. As if he hadn't done enough murdering in his lifetime, he now spent his Sundays trampling the countryside shooting at poor unsuspecting birds and watching them falling helplessly out of the sky, making their babies orphans. My dad's speciality. Our dilapidated garden shed became festooned with hanging pheasants and dead wood pigeons. He was always gutting something in there. He was like a fat Greek Charles Manson, only not as good-looking and twice as mental. And he had guns locked up in metal boxes in the upstairs landing cupboard. I made a note to myself to check them out.

I was hanging all my hopes on Project Pork Chop. And this time I wasn't taking any chances. I had been thawing and refreezing the piece of meat for about three weeks in the garage, where we kept a large chest freezer. When I was sure it was good and dripping with bacteria, I planned to undercook the chop and serve it to my dad for his dinner. I was worried about his strong constitution, so I was also going to serve him some garden peas from a blown tin that had been in the cupboard since before my mum died. I had read that blown cans were an indication of botulinum, which was incredibly deadly. Fingers crossed!

It was during this period that my dad, in his steady ascent to the very top of Mental Mountain, decided to cultivate his own escargot. One day, while loitering around, waiting to make sure he was occupied so that I could go through his pockets in his bedroom, I noticed the idiot going into the shed with a large Tupperware tub and a bag of flour. I was curious to see what he was up to.

I wandered down to the shed, and peered inside. I knew what he did in there, but even I wasn't expecting … Armageddon. Dead-eyed birds hanging on hooks from the ceiling, a freshly eviscerated wood pigeon on the workbench, soft bloodstained feathers adrift, its limp neck dangling; discarded, bloody guts cast aside as if they were of no consequence. The Fat Murderer looked up and pulled his greasy chops into a horrific grin, which he probably hoped passed for a smile. He was plonking garden snails onto a bed of flour in the Tupperware dish. I fought to overcome my desire to kill him there and then with the shovel that was propped against the door. I imagined bashing that hideous grin off his face and then, when he was down, driving it into his fat neck to finish him off.

Instead, I said, 'What the hell are you doing?'

'I'm making snails,' he said, matter-of-factly, bullying a doomed mollusc into the flour.

'You can't *make* snails.' I didn't need to add 'you idiot', because it went without saying.

'Escargots, Conniecon. I feed them with flour and they shit and it cleans them inside.'

'How very appetising,' I snarked. 'I don't think that's how the French do them.'

'Of course, is exactly the same. One dozens escargots is cost one pound. These ones are free.'

'You're on your own, mate. I'm not eating garden snails that have shat out flour in a Tupperware box.'

'Don't say mate and this shat.' He blew quickly these days, and although I was wary of it, I couldn't resist giving him a prod. He was volatile, but I knew Auntie Roulla had him in her sights and I was banking on a layer of protection I hadn't had since my mum died.

I looked philosophical for a moment, then: 'Okay. You can eat your own shitty snails. I hope they choke you.'

He was promptly incandescent, hair standing outwards, oily nose getting too close to my face. I could smell his cheesy breath, coating my face with a sweet-sour gust. His eyes were too close, too mad, the whites bloodshot and yellowed. The closeness was stifling. Sickening. A catalyst for something unformed, almost remembered by us both, stopped us in our tracks for an endless micro-moment.

I didn't want to be in the Armageddon shed with him any longer. I had to get out. Now. And though, on the outside, I was nonchalant and smirky as I sauntered away, inside I was scrambling to get out quickly under the corpus of a half memory from an unlit corner of my mind. Eleven-year-old me in the bathroom, door locked, screaming outside and, inside, being slung around the bathroom like a rag doll, the boys and my mum banging on the door, him looming over me, face engorged, smack after smack after smack, too hard, covering my head and face and body. Fear and primordial survival chemicals had struck me blind back then, and I had only seen the darkness and not the opaque. But now I saw it.

When he was in one of his frenzies, he had a way of pretending he had stopped, letting you think it was over, and would briefly walk away, before coming back for more. You never knew when it would really stop. And this one time, this time in the bathroom, he pushed me to the floor, and it was so undignified as I was wedged between the pink bath and the pink toilet, he walked away, made to slide the bolt open, changed his mind and came back for more good measure, and I saw now what I had failed to see in the blackness of that moment. He hadn't just been angry. He had been aroused. It hadn't been a reprimand. It was something else. He was coming back because he hadn't had quite enough. He needed to be sated. I remembered this now and relived the sensation.

I was retching as I reached the top of the stairs. I felt a rising panic and it took all my might to cram it into The Well of Shame, which was getting full to overflowing these days. I went into the bathroom now to calm myself, my mind pitching and banking in tumultuous recall, pink reeling on pink, too much pink. I didn't know why I decided on the bathroom, but I think I needed to revisit the scene. Replay the events in my head. Place bodies. Map out movements. To travel back into my brain to a time it had happened and to view it through older eyes. Just to make sure I was right. What was I right about? It was a feeling, something I had seen . . . the physical evidence of that excitement, acrid odours and sickening eyes.

I couldn't feel my feet or my hands. I was afraid that, if I looked at them, they wouldn't be there.

Memories were coming back. It wouldn't be long now.

I green-lit Project Pork Chop.

It couldn't happen soon enough.

15

'Iiiiiiitttttt's Chrrrriiiisssstttmmmaaaaassss' was all I could hear. On every radio in every shop, blaring out of every car. Slade heralding the most depressing time of year. And to make matters worse, we were to spend Christmas with The Greeks, *at our house*.

On Christmas Eve my dad brought home a manky-looking silver tree with the baubles already attached to it, which, I swear, though he denied it vociferously, was the one that had been in the window of the In and Out shop on the high street since last Christmas. It was faded and dusty and half the baubles had come off. We couldn't find the fairy lights, and then remembered they'd got thrown away two years ago when they'd almost set the tree alight. Neither of us cared that much about the fairy lights.

I had been watching festive crap on TV for weeks and experienced not a single Christmassy twinge. All the TV ads for toys and games just made me feel angry and detached. What did I care about Lego and Barbie dolls? I did want an Etch A Sketch, though. I was probably too old for one, but I didn't care. I had been dropping some heavy hints to The Fat Murderer, but I was managing my expectations at a very low level.

And while I had been looking forward to the *Top of the Pops Christmas Special*, I saw in the *Radio Times* that it was being hosted by Radio 1 DJs Tony Blackburn and Noel Edmonds.

I supposed it was better than last year, when it was Tony Blackburn and Jimmy Savile. Tony Blackburn AKA The Mayor of Cheesetown. And cigar-chomping maniac Jimmy Savile AKA Pervington Pervy. I mean, what the hell were the BBC thinking? Blackburn was bad enough, but Savile was something else entirely. He was The Pervmeister General. You could tell. All that eye wiggling and his puke-making catchphrase: "Ow's about that then?' I bet he had terrible cigar breath too. And what was going on with their hairdos? Literally no one in the real world had hair like any of them. And they were all smug as fuck. I'd rather miss *Top of the Pops* entirely if watching it meant looking at those self-absorbed fops. Even the thought of the wonderfully slapstick comedy of *The Morecambe and Wise Christmas Special* failed to elevate my mood.

The forlorn Christmas tree just about topped it all off perfectly. My dad, finding a rare path through the landscape of his self-obsessed psychosis, must have sensed my disappointment with our efforts.

'Get some candles, Conniecon. From the garage. We light them tomorrow when people coming and it will look like Christmas.'

Yeah, Christmas in hell. Although, all those naked flames around his lacquered hair might be interesting ... most humans were 60 per cent water, but he was mostly grease and hairspray. He'd go up like a bonfire.

I rooted around in the garage and found the candles. They weren't very nice ones, but I made candle holders out of satsumas, which I had seen on TV, only on TV they'd used apples, but we didn't have any, so the candles wobbled a bit and got covered in juice, but generally they looked good scattered around the living room. We didn't have an angel for the top of the tree, so my dad drew a face on a satsuma and stuck that on, which he thought was just hilarious. I couldn't help but get carried away with the upturn in festivities (plus I'd been at the drinks cabinet), and a laugh slipped out. He put his hand on my shoulder as we looked at the satsuma angel and then I got hold of myself and went into an elaborate contortion and moved out of his reach.

On Christmas morning I woke early and, before Marc and David were awake, I crept downstairs to see if there was an Etch A Sketch under the pitiful tree for me. Nope.

I thought I was the first one up, so was startled when I heard a strange gasping noise coming from the kitchen. I walked quietly out of the lounge and down the hall and peered into the kitchen. My dad was standing at the open back door, in his repulsive brown underpants, gazing out at the dead garden. He was bracing himself against the architrave with one hand and had a glass of whisky in the other. Somehow it was a miserably complex tableau. I had no idea what it meant and wasn't about to dwell on it. I just knew there was so much there, in that doorway, that I didn't want to see. I crept away again and went back up the stairs, stepping wide on the treads that creaked.

I dressed with extra attention and washed and dried my hair. It had been three weeks since I had last seen Vas and twice as long since we had touched. I craved the sweet communion of a kiss so badly it hurt.

By the time everyone arrived, I was pretty tipsy on snowballs. The Fat Murderer had said I could make myself one, and I was rather heavy on the advocaat and light on the 7UP, and he seemed either not to notice or not to care that the one snowball had lasted for hours and the advocaat bottle was half empty. He also gave me twenty quid from the pocket of his jacket, which was hanging at the bottom of the stairs on the newel post, and didn't notice when I picked out another twenty later. *Kala Kristouyena*, Con!

The Demetrious, who were still relatively new to the freakshow, were the first to arrive with their two daughters, Dina the Mealy-Mouthed and Adonia the Beautiful. I had not forgotten Dina's attempt to embarrass me that Freak Night back in September, when I'd thought Uri Geller was a singer instead of a spoon bender. Nor had I forgiven her for backing me into a corner so that I was forced to claim I could do telekinesis. Though I did pity her – if schadenfreude can be classed as pity – because she had a face like an undercooked Fray Bentos meat pie, while Adonia, who was two years her senior, was more radiant than ever. It was as if all the good genes had been used up by the time Dina was made. Adonia's face fit together so nicely, and I was perturbed to admit that she was kind and clever as well as beautiful. She was going to be a solicitor. The Demetrious brought along their fifteen-year-old son, but I still couldn't be arsed to talk to him or remember his name. It began with a D. Or a T.

The Papachristodoullous – Auntie Roulla and Uncle Mikis – arrived next, along with Prince Marios, who muttered a distracted 'Hi Con', and made his way straight over to Adonia. Uncle Mikis handed over the Greek essentials for survival: two bottles of Metaxa and two of Commandaria, a bottle of Johnnie Walker Red Label and a 200 carton of Rothman Internationals.

Auntie Roulla grabbed me by the cheek and wiggled it up and down a few times until it hurt, and then wished me a tearful *Kala Kristouyena*, and handed over a ginormous poinsettia plant. 'This is for you, my darling, because I know your mummy always liked the Alexandrinos plant, and it break my heart last year when you didn't have one.' As if death wasn't on my mind enough already, now I had to watch a poinsettia die. They always did. I'd throw this one in the bin later to save myself the agony of watching its inevitable demise.

Auntie Roulla had made a huge saucepan of stuffed vine leaves. She'd made koupes (knobs) and keftedes (balls) as well. Doulla and Goulla were close behind, and came armed with husbands, children, and baklava, kristopsomo bread, taramasalata, tahini, olives and karidopita, the best spiced walnut cake on Planet Earth.

The Petrideses came late, as they had to wait for the lamb to cook 'just right'. They'd baked it in their Greek oven in the garden. It had been in there since the night before, so I don't really understand why they had to be late, but I suspected that Mrs Petrides wanted to make a big entrance. She came in, all empty padded bra and wiggling her arse, wielding a huge roasting tray covered in tinfoil. She got her wish, as everyone gathered around her, shouting '*banayia mou!*' and 'bravo!' as her tiny husband peeled back the foil to reveal huge chunks of lamb and potatoes. I was about to ask her why she hadn't done a turkey like normal people, but saw her glancing at my dad, who gave her a weird suggestive look over Mr Petrides's head, and a bit of sick came up in my mouth.

Vas was the last to come into the house, and it was just the two of us in the hall while everyone else was getting on with the business of pinching cheeks, kissing, back slapping and shouting their heads off. I felt a bit overeager when I saw him, which made me annoyed with myself. With everyone Greeking it up big time in the lounge, I thought he might have seized the opportunity for some special sign of affection. Instead, he hovered at the front door, his head down. He had been growing his hair for the past three months and his fringe hung low over his face. He wouldn't look me in the eye.

'Hi Conno,' he muttered, to the floor.

Well, this wasn't how it was supposed to go.

'All right, Merry Christmas and all that.' My voice sounded odd. I was all sixes and sevens: excited, disappointed, hungry for him, and embarrassed by my own neediness. It was hard not to let all of that show.

He didn't look up or reply.

'You coming in then, or what?' It came out shrill and shrewish. Why couldn't I control my voice?

Vas stared at his shoes and shuffled forwards.

'Oh, come on, soppy bollocks!' I said, losing my patience.

He looked up defiantly and OH MY GOD!!!

'Woah!! What the – what the *hell!* Vas, what's on your face!' I bellowed.

'Fuck off, Conno.' He was wearing black-rimmed National Health specs with a big pink plaster over one lens.

'Oh, my giddy aunt! You can't wear those,' I said, with utter contempt.

'I have to.'

'But you look like a complete spastic.'

'It's bad to say spastic.'

I leant against the wall, snorting and laughing in derision.

'Oh yeah, very funny. I've got a lazy eye, okay? It's medical.'

I was being horrible. I knew it. It was just that, although the glasses were hilarious, they also made Vas look older, and I had a pang of anxious realisation that soon he'd be grown up and off to university, and where would that leave me? Horrible was all I could manage.

'Oh God, Vas, you are gonna get killed at school!'

'My mum chose the glasses.'

His mum, in true Greek fashion, had gone for the cheapest option. She probably took advice on how to be a tight-arse from my dad after they'd had a puke-inducing bonk.

'She has done you up like a kipper!' I scoffed.

He came in and shut the door behind him and looked at me long and hard.

'What's different about you?'

'Nothing.'

'Why is your voice suddenly all high and girly and piercing?'

'It's not.'

'It is. You're all jumpy and weird. Are you drunk?'

Great start. I took his coat and threw it on the hall floor.

'Come on in, then. The freaks are all here.' I walked ahead of him and heard him sigh behind me.

By the time lunch was served, Greek chaos was in full swing. Everyone had caught up with me booze-wise. Cigarette smoke filled the air. Kids were running amok, dripping grease and crumbs everywhere, and adults were eating, shouting, smoking, drinking and belching simultaneously. Vas and I were put on the kids' table, which was highly unacceptable. I started to kick off about it: 'I'm not sitting with the kids. I'm an adult. Adonia and Dina are with the adults. Me and Vas are fifteen, we don't want to eat with the kids we—'

I was just gathering momentum when Vas – the Judas – interjected quietly and clearly in this new superior manner he had acquired since I last saw him, 'I don't mind', just as my dad raised his voice and shouted, 'NOT TODAY, CONSTANTINA!' They were both starting to really piss me off. I sat, like a big self-conscious giantess, towering over the kids. Vas sat at the other end of the table and chatted with his little brother.

He always managed to look comfortable wherever he was. That also pissed me off. He was supposed to be on my side. We hardly spoke. Other than for me to yell along the table, 'So, Vas, have you admitted to your dad that you're a homosexual yet?' Vas looked at me with mournful eyes. I knew it troubled Vas that his father doubted his son's sexuality just because he was a gentle soul. I didn't feel at all bad. He was being a wanker.

Early evening everything came to a halt to watch *Spartacus* on television. The Greeks loved *Spartacus*. I didn't mind it. Especially the bit where they all shout 'I'm Spartacus'. Tony Curtis starts it off and his mini dress only just covers his meat and two veg, which is quite exciting, as he's good-looking for an old person. Only I couldn't hear any of the dialogue, even that bit, because the kids were going hyper, the women were screeching over the kiddie noise, and the men had started to play tavli and were shouting over the screeching. That click clack was intolerable.

Later on, at the time when all decent folk would be winding it up and getting ready to go home, things started to get lively: the ouzo and the Greek records came out and the dancing began.

'Come and have a dance, Connie,' said my dad, holding out a moist, pudgy hand. His face was bloated with booze and sweat. I looked to Vas for support, but the prick had his nose stuck in a book and was deliberately not making contact with his one available eye. I managed to keep my Christmas dinner down and shook my head, and my dad turned away and started slapping his feet and hopping around with the other maniacs, shouting 'Oooopah!', making my mum's crystal chandeliers jangle like an echo in the empty space she'd left behind. He was practically dancing on her grave. A few of the kids had discovered the satsuma candles. One kid was eating a satsuma, peel and all, and another was trying to eat a candle. Vas glanced up at me. I stuck two fingers up at him and slipped away up to my room.

16

Once inside my room, my mood plummeted. I couldn't fathom why. I had been feeling quite pleased with myself. After all, I hadn't joined in. I had refused to eat any of Mrs Petrides's show-stopping lamb roast. In fact, I had taken a mouthful and spat it into a napkin when she was looking. That had put a stopper in her ceaseless cock-a-doodle-dooing. And best of all, I had outdone Vasos and left him downstairs with the other freaks while I had retreated to my private quarters, where, I had made it patently clear, he wasn't welcome. So why did I feel so loathsome? I looked to the gang. Their silence was deafening.

'Oh, what now?' I said, defiant.

David, of course, was the first to speak up.

'Oh, Constance, Constance, Constance.'

I found my packet of B&H. I lit one, sat on the bed, and sighed.

'I was a cow to Vas, wasn't I?'

Silence.

'Wasn't I?'

'Sorry, we assumed that was a rhetorical question,' said Bowie, raising one non-existent eyebrow.

'Yeah. I was,' I said, 'I just couldn't stop myself.' I felt terrible now. My proclivity for the destruction of anything good was exemplary. I had proved that the night my mum and brothers had died.

'So why would you do that?' said Marc. 'Why would you be so cruel?'

I answered without guile. 'Because nothing about me is real. Because he's growing up and I'm not allowed to grow up. Because he's going to go to university and he'll get a job and get married and have children, and I'm going to end up in prison or begging for soup under Blackfriars Bridge, along with all the other people that don't fit in. Because . . .'

'Weirdly specific,' mumbled Bowie.

'Because,' urged Marc very, very gently, 'you have no idea of how you will ever have a future.'

'And,' said Bowie, kinder now, 'you have no idea of how you'll ever find a place where you fit in.'

'And,' I said, very simply, 'I like Vasos, a lot, and I'm just a big nobody.'

'And now,' said David, 'he's sitting down there feeling alone and awkward. Your mum would be so disappointed.'

I was ashamed of myself. It was a different kind of shame to the shame in The Well of Shame. This was more painful. This shame stabbed and said you are not a nice person. *Just like your dad.* I felt truly awful. I felt like nothing. I was nothing. I had no one else to blame this time.

I went to take a draw on my B&H but my mouth had disappeared. This was happening more frequently: parts of me evaporating. I could never anticipate when it would happen or how long it would last. What if, one day, I disappeared altogether and ceased to exist? That might be nice . . . I stubbed out my cigarette and went over to my desk. I put the Bensons and the matches on the surface and took a piece of fresh paper from the drawer. I found a pen, sat back on the bed, and started a list:

THE MANY THINGS I HATE ABOUT MYSELF

1. I am nothing.

I looked at it for a long time, trying to think of what else to add, but after some contemplation, I thought that just about said it all. I tried it out for sound: 'I am nothing, I am nothing.' I thought, if I said it enough times, I'd get used to it and then it wouldn't hurt so much when I finally vanished completely.

The door creaked open and I screwed up the sheet of paper and sat on it quickly. It was Vas. He came straight in and sat down next to me on the bed. I opened my mouth to speak. To say sorry. But the way he looked at me made me shut up for once in my life. He hesitated for a small moment and then, as if he'd made a big decision, held the back of my head with his hand and spoke: 'I'm not gay.' He pulled me towards him, a bit too fast for comfort. I wasn't sure if he was going to kiss me or headbutt me. I waited, part in horror and part in fascination. And part in desperate need. I let him kiss me, part my lips with his tongue, press his body against mine, lay me down on the bed and kiss me again, and again and again. Somewhere along the way, Vas had learned how to touch. I thought three things:

1. Vas had been learning more than how to play chess this past month.
2. Well, that's the friendship gone to buggery.
And

3. Friendship is an elastic concept anyway.
   Oh, and
4. If teeny Mr Petrides saw this, he would be pleased that his son was kissing a female.
   Oh, yeah, and
5. If my dad saw us now, he'd probably kill Vas. And then me.

After what felt like a long while but not nearly long enough, he lay by my side across the bed. I leant on one elbow and looked at his body. His T-shirt had ridden up and I traced the fine line of belly hair down from his navel with my finger. It fascinated me. He caught my hand.

'Stop, Conno,' he laughed. 'I won't be able to control myself.'

'What do you mean?' I asked.

'Just . . . stop touching me – there. Just lie with me.'

I lay down again and we held hands, which was lovely, though the fact that I wasn't allowed to touch Vas's precious belly hair when he had had his hands all over me felt a bit one-sided. I looked towards Vas and saw the lamplight glinting against the one lens of his spectacles and I started to giggle.

'Fucking hell, Conno . . . I already feel like a right tosser.'

'It is funny, though, isn't it?' I laughed.

'Yeah, I suppose it is. I suppose I could take them off for a bit if you want to have another go?'

'Nah, keep 'em on. It gives you character. I believe John Donne once wrote, "If it t'were only that you and I could raise our spirits through National Health spectacles. I, in terrible sulk and you with lazy eye . . ."'

'So, you have been looking at the Metaphysicals, then?' Vas smiled.

'A bit.' I smiled. 'Wanna cig?' I asked him, letting go of his hand and sitting up.

'Yeah, go on.'

I got up to fetch the packet and the matches from my desk.

'Conno? Conno?' He sounded odd. Hollow.

'What?' I replied, turning, fag in mouth, match about to strike.

'What's this?' He was holding up my list. He had smoothed out the crumples and was looking from the page and back to me again. I rushed forwards to take it from him but he was quicker and snatched it backwards out of my reach. He looked scared and pale. To be fair, he always looked a bit scared and pale, but he looked more scared and more pale than usual.

'You don't *mean* this?' he said, confused. I felt ashamed. Childish. Found out.

'It's not important, Vas. I was just, you know, feeling sorry for myself.' I could feel the gang cringing on my behalf.

'Conno, you're not nothing,' he said quietly.

'Vas, it doesn't mean anything.'

'Conno, you *wrote it down. It's got a fucking title*. Why do you hate yourself?'

'I don't. I really don't. Can't we do some more kissing and forget about it.'

'No. Not yet.' God, he was like a dog with a bone. 'Why do you feel like you're nothing?' he said deliberately and stubbornly.

I surrendered and sat down on the edge of the bed next to him, fags and matches in hand, the cigarette bobbing up and down in my lips as I spoke.

'Sometimes I just do,' I said.

'Is it your dad?' said Vas, removing the cigarette from my mouth and tucking it behind his ear.

Shrug. Long silence.

'Great, well, I'm glad we cleared that up,' he said.

'Vas.'

'Yeah?'

'Do you ever feel like you're disappearing?'

'No.'

'Sometimes I feel like I am disappearing. I don't matter to anyone.' As soon as I said it, I wished I hadn't. But sometimes you just blurt things out. And if I couldn't trust Vas with my deepest fears, then who could I trust?

He held both my hands in his and looked suddenly so much older than his years.

'You matter to me.' He said it so easily. I almost believed him.

I thought he might be going in for a kiss again, but there was a knock on the door.

'Fuck, is that your dad?' Vas whispered urgently, letting go of my hands and looking less earnest and more terrified.

'Nah, he never knocks; he'd be in here by now if it was him.' I called to whoever it was to come in.

It was just Marios. He said he wanted to be alone with Adonia, but her parents were keeping a close eye on her, so could we come out to the garden with them and then turn our backs so they could snog. God, I was bored of this repressive shit. Adonia was, like, twenty-two or something and should be able to kiss whoever she wanted to kiss.

I said I didn't mind and, anyway, me and Vas could have a smoke.

Marios looked grateful. 'Thanks, Con.'

He was about to leave the room and then stopped and looked back.

'What have you two been doing?' he asked.

'Snogging,' I said.

'No, really?'

'Yes. We were kissing and I touched her boobs. A lot. And a bit of bum,' said Vas. 'And then we discussed existentialism.'

Marios shook his head and said, not unkindly, 'You two really do deserve one another.'

He left the room and we sat on the bed side by side, both thinking our own thoughts. Vas sighed, screwed up the piece of paper and aimed it at the bin. He had a way of not lingering on the negative. He looked at me, smiled, and ran his fingers through my hair. What we had, what we were when we were together, felt fresh and uncomplicated again.

'You're a mess, Conno, you know that.' Just a statement of fact, not a judgement.

I wasn't sure I entirely agreed with him. Thank God he didn't know about Project Pork Chop.

It was Boxing Day morning by the time everyone had drunk-driven home. I had to hand it to the aunties, they had left the place looking better than when they had arrived. The fridge was packed with leftovers that would see us through to New Year, though, so there was no chance of feasibly proposing a pork chop dinner.

I continued the freeze/thaw process. Although the sooner the better, I was in no immediate rush; I had more than ten months before my deadline of my sixteenth birthday. I was pretty sure I'd have The Fat Murderer tucked up safely in his extra-large coffin way before then.

1976

17

January 3rd, 1976, was fixing to be an auspicious day. Two good things happened:

1. It was a Saturday night and, usually, on Saturday, my dad went to the casino with Peter Pervy Roy, but Peter Pervy Roy's wife (who would be stupid enough to marry that snaggle-toothed slime bucket?!) was having a baby, and so I had my first proper chance to finally execute Project Pork Chop.
2. I was in the bathroom squeezing blackheads when I heard The Fat Murderer rummaging around in his gun boxes in the airing cupboard on the landing. I slipped the bolt on the bathroom door and slowly opened it just a crack. I had his back in my direct sight and, beyond that, an open gun box, which was, I was extremely intrigued to note, stuffed full of cash. My cash, thank you very much.
Oh and . . .
3. He put the key to the gun box . . . wait for it . . . *under* the gun box! Wow, Brain of Britain strikes again.

This was a good day: I knew where he kept his stash, and Project Pork Chop was about to be accomplished with skill and precision.

I had defrosted the chop and dutifully undercooked it. I'd

even, in a final flourish of commitment to the cause, given it a cursory wipe on the sole of one of my outdoor shoes, in the hope that some dog shit bacteria might be transferred onto it for extra measure. I served it with the peas from the blown can heated to a botulinum-building lukewarm temperature. I watched in horror and hope as The Fat Murderer sliced a piece of pork off the bone and shoved it in his face. He took one bite and said the meat tasted funny and he was going to 'give the blatty butcher a bollocking', and then suggested we went out for fish and chips instead.

Months of time and devotion dashed to smithereens.

When we got back from the chippy, my dad suggested we watch telly together. Although I had enjoyed my meal, I was still pissed off that he wasn't going to die, so I left him on his own watching *Kojak* and smoking fags. I snatched a few ciggies on my way out of the room and stomped upstairs, where it was ice-cold and bleak. I had left my window open, but the weather was warm and wet for the time of year. The real chill was coming from the gang.

I sat on the bed, looking out of the window at the flat, grey sky. I listened out for Elizabeth and Ronald, but I think they had moved on for fear of ending up in the shed along with the other dead wood pigeons. I didn't blame them. I'd have flown off too if I could have.

I lit a cigarette, though it didn't taste nice. 'Lucky escape or another monumental failure, Constance?' David, of course.

I had pinned all my hopes on Project Pork Chop. That it had been such a non-starter after all that effort was pretty demoralising.

'Monumental flop,' I said.

Perhaps it was the dismal feeling of failure weighing me down, or the burden of my murder mission. Whatever it was, quite unexpectedly, the time had come to unload.

I took a deep breath. I spoke softly and plainly, without embellishment.

'When I was seven years old, my Cypriot grandfather came to England for the first time. He stayed with us for six weeks. Every opportunity. If I passed him on the stairs, he would make me stop and put his hands in my pants. When we went anywhere in the car, he would sit in the back with me and touch me. He would put his finger to his lips in this ghastly secretive way and tell me to shush, while all the time he would probe and touch and his stink filled my nose and my mouth and went down my throat; sweat and old age and perversion, rolling off him, depravation, desperation. On the days when both my parents were at work, he would collect me from school and I would have two sickening hours with him until my mum came home. It was a nightmare. I would hide away but he would always find me. I told my mum. She told my dad. My dad told her I was lying and to ignore me. He got very angry. So, she did the best she could: told me to try to avoid my grandfather. To tell him to stop. To shout for her and she would come straight away. She kept an eye on him, but she couldn't always be around. How must that have made her feel? That she couldn't protect me. That the one person who could have helped was my dad. And he chose not to. Now, let me tell you something else. Two years ago, my grandfather was evicted from the village in Cyprus. My dad's brother's wife – Irini – had caught my grandfather encouraging her three-year-old daughter to touch his penis. She told my dad's brother, Christakis. He believed his wife. He protected his daughter. He moved my grandfather into an old people's home in Nicosia and never saw him again. Did my dad ever say sorry to me, or my mum? No. Who was my dad angry with? His dad? No. His brother's wife. For lying. The day I found that out was the day he killed my family.'

18

My mum always used to say February was a 'low month'. If you were considering topping yourself, February would push you over the edge, and March too, if you missed the February time slot. I got through both months without resorting to suicide, thanks to music and Vas.

I had also invented a strategy of release and control, like a pressure valve. Within the four walls of my bedroom, with Marc and David, I could be myself, raw and real. At school, I was the master of disguise. I understood that there was safety in being part of the herd. At least on the outside. I had normal conversations: I laughed with my friends. I did my homework. I was a normal amount of good and a normal amount of bad. But affecting normality was profoundly tiring. I kept getting that sensation of evaporation. Of losing parts of myself. I was replacing the parts of me that were disappearing with new, even less stable parts.

The one good thing about the isolation is that it gave me time I wouldn't otherwise have had. And I had plenty of time. I had time to find new music. I grew into Pink Floyd, The Stones, The Moody Blues. I wore them like new clothes, and with such panache. I drank Bob Dylan until I was inebriated. The first nanosecond that I heard 'Visions of Johanna', the words draped themselves over me like fragile filaments of empathy. 'Ain't it just like the night to play tricks...' The Night was always mine, and I knew that Dylan had left the song for me to find through the tangle of time. And it was time that turned me to the old poets – the romantic fools, Byron and Wordsworth, and Keats with his lovely 'Ode to a Nightingale' (I suppose it wouldn't have had the same romantic imagery if it were 'Ode to a Wood Pigeon', but I thought of Ronald and dear Elizabeth when I read it, because I'd never heard a nightingale sing). I fell in love with those last two lines:

> *Was it a vision, or a waking dream?*
> *Fled is that music: – Do I wake or sleep?*

I read them over and over and always thought of Vas.

And I had time to find what would become my first love: classical guitar. I had learned to read music now, not just chords. And my playing had become so much better since I had got a new guitar. Yes, I had a *new guitar*!

The purchase of a new guitar had been a collaboration between me and my music teacher, Mizz Liddle. And my dad. Though he wasn't actually aware that he was involved. Mizz Liddle had the appearance of a small, bespectacled twelve-year-old boy. Some of the girls said she was a lesbian, as if that was supposed to be something to worry about, and as if Mizz Liddle would touch any of them with a bargepole. She was my first favourite teacher and she didn't suffer fools gladly.

Mizz Liddle thought I would play better if I wasn't playing a child's starter guitar. She said my playing was coming on surprisingly quickly. I don't think she had any idea that I literally had nothing else to do with my life other than practise. I expect she thought my swift advancement in playing was solely down to her amazing tuition.

One day she had said that she would be delighted – *yes, delighted was her actual word* – to accompany me to some guitar shops in Denmark Street in the West End of London to purchase a new instrument, if my father was willing to spend the money. And he certainly was. I had the money already and could easily top up again with some more out of the gun box or any number of pockets. As long as I lifted the cash slowly and steadily, my dad was never any the wiser.

I pretended to Mizz Liddle that I had gone home and discussed getting a new guitar with my dad, who had asked me to convey the message that he was grateful for her patronage and would gladly pay for a new instrument. I don't know if she fell for it. But she'd seen what The Fat Murderer was like at The School Disco Disaster of 1975 and she was probably glad to have a reason to avoid him. She went along with it anyway. Nothing got in the way of music for Mizz Liddle.

Denmark Street was full of musical instrument shops. And my day there with Mizz Liddle was completely and utterly and mind-blowingly *amazing*. Diamond-encrusted freedom. The sun was shining and we went to a cafe for sandwiches and coffee where Mizz Liddle explained that the official form of lesbian address was actually Ms and not Mizz. Who knew?! *Ms* Liddle said the title wasn't only specific to lesbians but not to trouble my brain with details and to just call her Liz. It was the most grown-up thing I had ever done and it made me feel like an equal instead of a freakqual. I said 'Liz' a lot that day.

We strolled from shop to shop looking at guitars. God, it was heaven. They were in every shop, on every wall. They were on stands, hanging on racks, in cases, out of cases, Spanish, Japanese, American, British ... and all hues – blues and reds and sunburst oranges. It was guitar nirvana. I wanted a Gibson Hummingbird so badly. It was the best one and I loved its title. But it was too expensive. I could have afforded it; I just didn't want to spend all The Getaway Fund, in case I had to get away. I looked at Gibsons and Martins because that's what Dylan used, but Liz said that I should wait until I had decided how dedicated I was before I put my father to such an expense.

The man in the shop had long brown hair and was about as thin as Liz. He had suede-brown eyes and said he had overheard us. He said, leaning in close to me (microbes spraying all over me, no doubt, but they were probably okay, as he seemed clean and was very good-looking, a bit like Jackson Browne), he was willing to share a little-known secret. I was about to tell him that a secret should be not known at all by pure dint of its being an actual secret, but then imagined Marc saying, 'For once in your life shut your big fat gob, Con', and thought better of it.

The Jackson Browne look-a-like's warm eyes were alight as he brought a beautiful, richly varnished acoustic out of its snug, orange fur-lined case: a Japanese-made Kay classical. Everything about it was gorgeous, and the man in the shop said he thought it was better made than most American guitars. He said a lot of people thought Kay guitars were made of wood laminate, but this one was solid wood with rosewood trims and a perfectly balanced bowl back. He said not to be swayed by fancy brands, as they weren't always better. For a moment I did hesitate, because it sounded like a logic very similar to my dad's, and I didn't want to end up getting the thing that resembled the thing but was a cheaper version of the thing and, therefore, not the thing at all. But it wasn't. I could tell.

And I trusted Liz, who picked it up, sat on a stall, and played Carulli's Andantino in G. It sounded beautiful.

Liz handed the guitar to me.

'Try it for yourself,' she said.

I held it on the balance and watched it sway back and forth perfectly. I sat down and placed it over my thigh. I tried the piece she had just played. It didn't sound quite as good, but it felt good. The guitar might not have been a Hummingbird, but it was a nightingale, and it sang to me.

19

Above all else, I had, during this period, fallen for Vas. Freak Nights were mostly back on, but Vas was sometimes at chess club. I hated those times. He said he did too. He told me he didn't really care about chess, but his mum and dad insisted he went because they were worried that sitting around reading all the time was unhealthy. Nevertheless, we worked around it and made our oasis of calm amidst the Greek chaos. We sometimes met after school just to kiss at the bus stop until my bus came along. They were heavenly minutes.

Although I had known Vas since the beginning of time, it was only now that I finally *saw* him. I *felt* him. I loved him from the depths of his soul to the surface of his skin. I didn't know how to say it, or even how to think it, but, when I tried, what I came to was that I was *thankful* for him.

On the weekends, when the weather was dry, we would meet in the park. I loved sitting and reading poetry over his shoulder, though I didn't always get it as easily as he did. I didn't see why the metaphysical poets couldn't just say what they meant. I had a strong inkling it was really just all about sex. Maybe this was Vas's pornography. Poetry porn! Sometimes I got bored and just stared at his hair or the backs of his hands until he caught me and would laugh lightly, and say, 'Conno, for fuck's sake, stop freaking me out.' Then he'd kiss me. Whether we were kissing or reading or just being silent, it was all the same. It just felt . . . right. All the time.

Vas had been reading the Mower poems by Andrew Marvell and he had written some lines on a piece of paper for me:

The Mower Against Gardens
No plant now knew the stock from which it came;
He grafts upon the wild the tame

'That's you,' he had said, with what I thought was, and hoped wasn't, sadness. 'The wild grafted to the tame . . .'

I blu-tacked it onto my wall next to my bed, just far enough from Marc Bolan's trouser department that I could view them separately.

20

I couldn't believe it was already April. *Where had the time gone????!* I had just seven months before I was sixteen, which was the absolute last date by which I had promised to murder The Fat Murderer. I had taken my eye off the ball somewhat on account of spending most of my time thinking about Vas and being a famous guitarist. I really did have to get a move on, otherwise, instead of being a super-liberated rock goddess, I'd end up being married off to a hairy Greek Cro-Magnon man who expected me to clean his house and bang out hirsute babies nineteen to the dozen.

April had always been my favourite month when my mum was alive. She *was* April; an early burst of sunshine, bright and petal soft. When she got home from work, we'd sit in the garden, she and I drinking coffee and eating Walnut Whips, the boys playing in the dirt somewhere. I loved the sweet smell of first-cut grass, the colour burst of tulips, the generosity of lengthening days.

Sometimes, when the cold crept in, April could feel pernicious and lonesome. It felt like that this year. The warmth was there but only skin-deep. The sun was there but never shining on the place where I was standing. The days were longer but they were hollow and toothachey and gave me time I couldn't use because I was too busy *wasting* time. So, when it was decided that Greek Night would venture into the normal world during the second Friday of the month, it felt ominous.

The Curzon Cinema had announced that it was going to screen *Hello, Dolly!* and it had been decided by Auntie Roulla, and the rest of the Papachristodoullous, that we were going to have a full-on Greek Freak Night Out at the cinema to watch it. This would mean a major military operation the size of the D-Day landings. It would involve several cars. Buckets of food and added comforts would take up most of the car space, so someone would have to sit on someone else's lap and the kids would have to squat in the footwell and someone would have to go back for a second carload, because someone's *yaiya* and *bapou* were over from Cyprus and they'd have to come too. I knew the drill and it would be an utter shambles.

Marc had been excited on my behalf when I mentioned the proposed cinema trip.

'Oh, I love the cinema. I haven't been to the pictures for ages. I get recognised, you know, and everyone bothers me. Will Vas be going to the cinema?'

'Depends if they make him go to chess club,' I said. I begged the God I didn't believe in to let him be there, as I played warm visions of us secretly holding hands in the dark, cigar-scented velvet theatre.

Hello, Dolly! had been playing at The Curzon on and off since 1969. It was a big favourite with the aunties. It was basically the all-singing all-dancing story of a very annoying bunch of people trying to make other people fall in love with them, though there was literally no one good-looking enough to cause even the tiniest commotion in your knicker area. Moreover, the songs were torture, especially when Auntie Roulla sang along in impeccable Greeklish, much to the irritation of the other cinema patrons. We'd already seen it about a hundred times. The Greeks only watched three films: *Spartacus* at Christmas, *Ben-Hur* at Easter and *Hello, Dolly!* the rest of the time. I had suggested we break with tradition and see *Tommy*, which was playing on the larger of the two screens, but that suggestion went down like a lead balloon with my dad: 'Whadoyouwantoseethatblattyrabbishfor?' he had spat, as if the very notion of me having an alternative idea was anathema, '*Hello Dollys* is with the Barbara Streisand.'

The Greek Meet was planned for 7pm outside The Curzon. A pink-streaked sky had faded to a purple dusk, casting a flattering shade over the grubby grey street. It had been a warmish day, but as soon as the sun dipped, it was coat weather. Before my mum died, she had bought me a new coat with some of her wages that she had set aside. It was just between us, she had said, and not to tell my dad. It was a fashionable powder-blue belted rain mac, which, she had stated, was 'so with it, it was almost past it'. I hadn't worn it since the so-called accident, but thought it was time to do so, as April was her month and maybe it would help me to remember her name and what her voice sounded like, because that had gone from my memory too. It was as if there was a wall in front of my brain and everything I needed to remember about her was behind the wall. I couldn't see over it and I couldn't knock it down. It didn't help that there was no trace of her in our house. The Fat Murderer had really done a thorough clean-up job after the crimes. As far as he was concerned, she was done and dusted and out of the way, so he could boink Mrs Petrides, who'd wear a dead woman's shoes before they were cold, the grave-robbing old baggage. Also, I noticed, quite soon after my mum was killed, that when someone dies no one ever says their name. It's always 'your mum' or 'your wife', as if the name died with the person. I sometimes thought I could ask someone – maybe Vas or Auntie Roulla – what my mum's name was, but I couldn't bring myself to do this for two reasons:

1. I was really ashamed to admit I couldn't remember.
2. I had this very deep-seated feeling that it was important to work out how to break down that wall and find those memories for myself.

Anyway, that's why I wore that blue mac. I also wore jeans I'd bought with my Christmas money and some red Kickers shoes, which I had splashed out on with money from my stash. I felt good.

My dad and I waited outside the cinema, by the kerb. The two of us in proximity was stifling even in the open air, so I started to mentally categorise the dog shits on the pavement, just for something to do. I ordered them chronologically, whitest first and brownest last. I had almost run out of shits when I heard the low throb of a car being driven in the wrong gear. I looked up in time to watch in awe, along with random pedestrians who had stopped in their tracks, Auntie Roulla gliding up at glacial speed in her huge silver Mercedes-Benz. We only knew it was Roulla by the car numberplate, GR33K LDY, because she sat so low in her seat that she was practically invisible. It was a wonder she could see anything over the steering wheel.

She scraped the hubcaps along the kerb for a good six or seven feet before mounting the pavement with one wheel and stalling to a halt. 'Blatty Nora,' my dad said, elbowing me subtly and chuckling. I really had to double down on killing him.

Suffice to say that Auntie Roulla was not a natural when

it came to driving. She was better than her husband, Mikis, though, who had failed his test three times and finally ended his lessons with a crash that had projected the driving instructor out of the windscreen and all the way to Whipps Cross Casualty department. No wonder Marios had already had his first car crash at seventeen. Bad driving was in his genes.

Roulla got out of the car with more dignity than she had a right to, waved to the arriving Petrides, ignored my dad, and started to pull a few children out of the footwell. She then opened the boot and proceeded to unload Tupperware while a succession of more silver Mercedes arrived and disgorged children, grandparents, and copious amounts of food.

The males of the species pooled at the entrance to the cinema and stood around avoiding dog shit, smoking, shouting, slapping each other on the back and generally not helping. The little kids were running riot in and out of the revolving doors. And there was Vas (thank you, dear God I don't believe in, for not making him go to chess club – carry on like this and I may have a change of heart), looking abruptly taller and like he needed a good meal. He was all sudden growth spurts and hollow cheeks these days. He had turned sixteen on April 1st and looked more like a man than a boy, with some newly acquired shadow around his jaw. He had new spectacles, which didn't have a plaster on one lens, and he looked bookish and gaunt. Just the way he would want to look.

He had his hands in his denim jacket pockets and his head ducked down in a way that he thought made him look tortured, like James Dean. He smiled a thin smile and nodded. 'All right, Conno?'

I nodded back and said, *'Hello, Dolly!'*, again. Glad to see we are keeping up with modern culture and integrating.' He rolled his eyes and gave me a feeble dead arm. I could sense he was a bit off tonight.

'What's up?' I asked him.

'Conno, do you ever feel like you wanna kill your dad?'

Do I! I thought, but instead said, 'What's he done?'

'I'm choosing A-level subjects and he is driving me fucking crazy.' He went into a very good impersonation of teeny Mr Petrides. 'Don't choose Literature – it's just reading; don't choose Art – is just drawing; don't choose History – is just the bloody past, who cares about these things. Vasos, if you don't want to come to the fur factory, then get a skill, be a tiler, is good money, people always need tiles, no one needs someone who can draw . . . endless.' He took a breath. '*And* he got my mum to have a serious word with me about my sexuality. She said they were worried because I refused to show an interest in girls.'

I laughed. 'Well, last time I checked, I had several body parts which would testify to the contrary!'

'Yeah, sod it. I'll have to have a feel later to remind myself, though . . .' He grinned impishly, then said, 'Clock the barnets, Conno', looking sideways in the direction of the aunties.

'What?' I asked, but before he could answer, Auntie Roulla was yelling at me. 'Constantina, come and help!' she shrilled, from under the strain of a pile of food tubs. I hesitated for a microsecond and The Fat Murderer was already on my back. 'Go and help your aunties,' he said, giving me a shove in Roulla's direction. 'She *just asked* me,' I replied, through gritted teeth. 'Give me a chance.'

'I'll help too,' said Vasos, but my dad clapped his hand on Vasos's shoulder and steered him away, chatting to him with his best and most obsequious insincere smile. That was the first thing that threw me this evening. My dad never bothered speaking to Vas.

I walked over to where Roulla was parked and stopped dead. I had been too busy looking at Vas to notice before, but now I *did* clock the barnets! Auntie Roulla had been to the *kommotirio*, the Greek hair salon. Her thick black hair had been died a deep maroon and was shaped and lacquered into what could only be described as a large crash helmet. She primped her coiffure and smiled ecstatically. 'You like my 'do, Constantina?' She hooked a carrier bag of cut-up fruit over my arm. It had a small hole in the bottom and fruit juice drizzled slowly down the front of my mac.

I swallowed and said, 'Yes, Auntie, it's very . . . big. And nice.'

She took this as the ultimate compliment and piled some tubs in my arms.

'We all go together,' she said, nodding towards her sisters, Doulla and Goulla, as they were manoeuvring their equally huge hair out of Goulla's silver Mercedes-Benz. Doulla's rock-hard dome was purple and Goulla had gone ginger, though she was calling it strawberry blonde. I wondered how all that hair had fit into one car.

Auntie Roulla took a critical look at my hair. 'You know, Constantina, your hair is getting darker, is nice colour now, *kastano* instead of like the mouse, we can give you Toni home perm, make your hair nice and big too. Look thicker.'

'I don't want a Toni home perm,' I said.

'I do it for you. I like your makeup,' she continued. 'Not too like a *poutana*. You looking like a real lady these days.' She leant in and whispered, 'Your mummy would be proud.'

That was the second thing that threw me. No one had

mentioned my mum since Christmas, and I'd been thinking about her all day today. I felt both touched and guilty because I'd sort of forgotten to think about her as much lately.

The third thing that threw me was the group of four boys going into the cinema foyer. It was only bloody Calvin bloody Belding with his goons and one non-goon, the gorgeous Paul Johnson, who was still as slight and as pretty as ever. I doubted they were at The Curzon this evening to sing along with the cast of *Hello, Dolly!*. They were probably going to see *Tommy*, the splendid rock opera about a deaf, dumb and blind kid – that's really bad luck – who is good at pinball. How he managed that was something I'd pay to see. Like all normal people.

I prayed the boys would be gone from the foyer by the time we all marched in. The thought of the real world colliding with my Greek world was excruciating. I was suddenly cripplingly aware of what we must look like, this circus of screaming, shouting, crash-helmet-haired, olive-skinned, food-bearing nomads. Why couldn't we just get a packet of Poppets and see *Tommy* quietly and inconspicuously like everyone else? Why did everything always have to be such a spectacle?

It took ages to move our swarthy entourage and their belongings into the cinema foyer and, as my luck would have it, Paul Johnson and co were still standing around smoking while waiting for the theatre to open.

And then the fourth thing happened. It came out of nowhere, lightning-flash fast and incomprehensible.

The Greek Freaks and I were standing in a straggly circle around our supply cache. The Demetrious, whatshisfaces junior and senior, were arguing at the ticket kiosk over which seats to sit in. The aunties were shouting at the kids. Calvin and his goons were play-fighting. Except Paul Johnson, who was trying to catch my eye. I tried to look everywhere other than at him. I saw Vas look at them. And then look at me. I saw my dad look at Vas, and then glance over at them, and then at me and back at Vas again. I wished everyone would stop looking at everyone else. I could feel the air split, the atmosphere crackle and spark.

I followed my dad's eyes across the foyer, then to Vas, and then back to the boys.

At the same moment Paul Johnson smiled and waved.

My dad slapped me hard on the cheek. With his palm.

And then again, twice. With the back of his hand. His wedding ring crunching my cheek into my teeth. 'Stop looking at these fackin' bastards!'

Right there.

In front of everyone.

IN. FRONT. OF. EVERYONE.

I could feel my face begin to disintegrate with red hot shame, burning me away, my fingers almost translucent ... and then. So slowly it came to me, but all mixed up. His face, bitter and spiteful, childish and twisted, his violence and his grabbing, his fury as he drove away the night of the crash. That wasn't just fury. It was deeper. And then a sluggish revelation; something I should have identified long ago coming together. He knew what his father had done to me and he didn't care. He could have stopped it but he didn't. *He let him do it to me.* It was his sickness too. I wanted to vomit. My breath was gone and my mind moved in slow motion. He shouted something but I only heard a ringing silence.

All the Greeks looked shocked and stood frozen to the spot,

even Auntie Roulla, whose maroon hair against her colour-drained face made her look suddenly ill and old. She held on to Marios, who was struggling to come forward.

The Fat Murderer struck me again, this time hard enough to knock me down. Paul Johnson shouted, 'No, stop!' He made as if to come over, but Calvin put out a slow arm to prevent him.

A scorching adrenalin jab of humiliation shot through me as I scrambled to get up off the dirty floor and my mind sharpened as quickly as it had dulled. I went into conservation mode and did what I always did: opened up The Well of Shame and started to stuff the feelings inside. I would discuss this with Marc Bolan and David Bowie when I got back to my room. They would know how to make it okay. Then, quite suddenly, a seismic jolt moved the focus away from me.

Vas, ever the peacemaker, nodded a kind acknowledgement to Paul Johnson, at which point seasoned kid-basher Mr Petrides looked at Vas, then at Paul Johnson and then back at Vas, and it was as though his last penny had dropped into place as he turned to his scrag-end of a cow of a wife and said, 'See, I told you. He's a bloody bender.'

Vasos hit himself on the head with frustration and let out a high, piercing and frankly womanly scream. He turned and swiftly exited the foyer, leaving the revolving doors spinning in his wake. Mr Petrides followed Vas outside. Through the glass doors, I could see Vas lighting a cigarette with shaking hands. He drew on it furiously. His entire body quaking, thighs and calves thickening with blood-suffused muscle, sinews in his neck alive and taut. He looked like a man.

My dissipating particles came back together at lightning

speed. I wanted to go out to help Vas, but one of the little kids had tried to follow Mr Petrides outside and had got the hood of his anorak stuck in the revolving door, jamming it half open. Doulla tried to extricate him but he was stuck fast. We could hear every word that was said on the street outside. As could everyone else.

'You think you are clever, smoking!' Mr Petrides smacked the cigarette out of Vas's hand. It spun onto the pavement, where the hot ashes sparked and skittered across the street. 'You want to be like these bloody useless English boys?'

I saw Calvin and his goons shrug and light up fresh fags.

'Or do you like them because you want to be with the men?'

Mr Petrides gestured back to the boys inside, and it was clear he meant Paul Johnson when he said, 'Is this the one you like – the one who looks like a woman? Another bloody poof?'

God, poor Paul Johnson . . . he was really getting it this evening.

There was a fleeting moment where it looked as if Vas was going to cry. And then he blew like Krakatoa.

'FUCK OFF!' It was a guttural eruption, full of venom and command. Very un-Vas-like.

My jaw hung open. This was my cool-as-a-cucumber Vas. Losing his shit. And losing it big! In public!!!!

Mr Petrides went to shout back but his face froze – I think all our faces froze – as Vas moved in towards him, one fist raised as if to strike. His breath was coming fast. His eyes were black.

'No, you cunt! You fucking cunt! You touch me again and I will kill you, I swear to it.' I looked at Mrs Petrides, who was – the utter opportunistic old bint – holding on to my dad's arm with both hands. My dad was shouting at Doulla to hurry up and get the kid out of the revolving doors. Roulla was shouting at my dad for shouting at her sister. Uncle Mikis was shouting at Auntie Roulla, telling her she was making it worse. And through it all I could still hear Vas. It was as if he had swallowed a foghorn. A litany of pent-up bile was spewing out of him now.

'I am sick to death of your fucking shitting pissing cunting crap. I will smoke if I want to, I will eat what I want, I will read what I want to read, I will fuck whoever I want to. I'm not going to marry fucking Dina – sorry, Dina – and I'm not going to be a bloody furrier or a tiler and I'm going to university as far away from here as possible, so you might as well get that into your thick fucking bastarding shitting cunting skull once and for all.'

All I got from that was 'marry Dina', like another slap in the face. Vas and Dina? *Dina?* Even *Dina* chosen over me? Dina with her undercooked Fray-Bentos-pie face and the personality of a blobfish?

With a suddenness that made everyone jump, the kid was disengaged from the revolving doors, which then swivelled round, hitting Auntie Doulla in the face. She clutched her nose, which had started to bleed profusely, and followed the rest of the Greeks out onto the street, just in time to see Vas smash his fist into his dad's stomach. I laughed. I couldn't help it. I clapped my hand over my mouth, but it escaped round the edges. His dad staggered back and straight into a nice big brown dog turd.

Vas and his dad had a momentary stalemate while Mr Petrides wiped the crap off his shoe onto the edge of the kerb, swearing in Greek. He stamped his titchy feet and then, trying to recover some of his power, he moved towards Vas.

Vas was still fired up, rampant. 'You are killing me. I don't want your bloody life. I WANT MY LIFE.' He screamed it so loud that his voice was ragged and torn.

The little kids started to cry. Vas's mum started screaming and begging my dad to do something before she had a heart attack (that would have been a silver lining, but no such luck), and Vas's dad hopped around like a wiry little chicken and started kicking Vas in the shins, first with one foot then the other, while Vas stepped aside, avoiding each punt. I think he could have floored his dad, but even in an incandescent rage, Vas still had a scrap of regard left for his father's dignity. A bolt of respect for him brought with it a bolt of respect for myself.

I looked around at us, The Greeks, at the outsiders gawping, at poor beleaguered Paul Johnson and the goons back in the foyer, everyone looking and rubbernecking and no one doing anything to help. I thought of the times when my brothers and I had all wished for someone, anyone, to come along and help us, rescue us. To show they cared about the suffering of other human beings. Of children. Of women. Of people who were not as physically strong and were unable to defend themselves. When other drivers looked into our car while he was laying into us and just drove on; when neighbours heard him smashing things in the kitchen, my mum screaming, her head hitting the wall with a sickening thud, and no one knocked; when people passed two little boys, pink, naked and frozen on the doorstep in the snow, and continued on their way home; ate their dinner and pushed the uncomfortable image from their minds because it was *none of their business*. Well, it was.

It *was* their business. It was happening in their world, so if it wasn't their business, if it wasn't their responsibility, then whose was it?

And I think that's what made me hook my arm around Mr Petrides's throat and get him in a stranglehold. Mrs Petrides screamed at my dad again – for fuck's sake, she just couldn't shut the fuck up. She clawed at his chest then pretended to faint for a second. My dad shoved her away and tried to pull me off Mr Petrides, but I gripped on tighter and Mr Petrides started making weird choking sounds as his tiny feet, still slippery with shit, came off the ground and started kicking in mid-air.

The fingers that prized my arm off him were Vas's. He was wheezing and snot was coming in and out of his lovely nose in fast spurts, his teeth were set in a snarl and he looked ugly and dangerous. My dad pulled me away from Vas and dragged me along the floor, scraping my red shoes and hollering and yelling over and over that this was my fault, that everything had been my fault, and that I was 'a fucking fat cow'.

I felt the sting of the slap on my face, the sting of the staring eyes, the sting of the loss of face – as if I had any face left – and the sting of the insult. I felt the shame and ignominy and destruction and loss and sadness and hate and dashed hopes and dreams boiling inside me. The Well of Shame was full. I couldn't push anything else in there. It started to simmer, the lid wobbling perilously like a pressure cooker.

And then. The lid. Just. Came off. It came off with such a force that I staggered backwards and had to catch myself before I fell. I felt drumming in the base of my skull and the bottom of my spine, faster and faster, the pain blinding and numbing all at once. And that's when all the words I wanted to say got backed up and a frothing, churning, wrath burst forth, which I caught hold of and channelled into one sentence, loud and weirdly sonorous: 'You knew what he did to me' – over and over. My body started to become lighter, losing its solidness and form. I couldn't control it; I couldn't bring it back together again.

Everything stopped.

21

I woke up at Auntie Roulla's. I was on her bed, lying on a pink candlewick bedspread. My head was aching and my mouth was dry. The room was typically bonkers and classic Auntie Roulla, which made me feel better. Mad flock wallpaper in bright green and gold, heavy red velvet curtains that had every curtain accoutrement known to mankind: swags, tails, scoops, tie-backs, pelmets. The lamps on each side of the bed were glass, flaming Olympic torches held aloft by a duo of naked Aphrodites.

Auntie Roulla had a lot of stuff. The room had two gold-framed prints: a picture of a fat little boy grizzling and another of a ginormous swan and a naked man and woman. The Petrideses had the same two pictures. My dad had wanted them too, but my mum had drawn a line. The crying kid and the swan gave her the creeps. Me too.

A shelving unit covered a large part of the wall opposite the bed. It was crammed with nick-nacks, most of them a tribute to Cyprus. My favourites were a clock shaped like the island and a miniature replica of Kyrenia Castle, and a plastic drinking bird with a green tail feather that dipped its head in and out of a glass of water over and over. On the dresser Auntie Roulla's Rive Gauche perfume sat alongside creams and compacts and rings and bracelets galore.

Somehow, the Papachristodoullous' excesses didn't offend

me as deeply as the Petrideses' gaucherie. Auntie Roulla's clutter felt silly and sentimental and gave the room warmth. I picked at the candlewick bedspread while avoiding Roulla's searching gaze.

She was sitting on the edge of the bed with a glass of *sideritis* herbal tea and a bowl of egg and lemon soup. Food: the Greek cure for everything. It was a celebration, a commiseration, a comfort, a cure.

I sat up and took the bowl of soup from her and sipped the lemony rice in silence. It was delicious. When the bowl was empty, she took it from me and handed me the tea. I sniffed it experimentally and shook my head and handed it back to Roulla, whom I regarded carefully. She looked exhausted. There was a dent in her hair. Her voice sounded thin and tired.

'Darling, is very good for you,' she said, coaxing. 'This is very special herb tea from the mountains of Kakopetria in Cyprus.'

'It's not from the mountains, it's from the Greek shop in Leyton. It smells like sick.' I shook my head again. 'Where's Vasos?'

Roulla shrugged and turned her mouth downwards, Greek for something and nothing. 'He's at home. Everything is okay.'

She rubbed her eyes with her fingertips, smudging her black eyeliner so it made dark half-moons under her already darkened eyes.

Roulla's jewellery twinkled in the bedside lamplight. I reached towards her chest and played with the strands of gold that fell from her neck onto her breast. We were both holding our cards close, working out which way we would gamble with the conversation we were bound to have. I relented, for something to do, and picked up the mug of tea/sick and sipped it, making faces.

'Constantina...'

'What?'

'I have one question, darling.' She pasted a warm smile over serious intent, but it didn't fool me. I knew where this was going.

'What it means you knew what he done to me? What did someone done to you? Did a man do a bad thing to you? Did your father know it? Why didn't he help you? What should he have stopped?'

That was more than one question, but I didn't feel it was the right time to point that out. I buried my face in the mug and inhaled the sickly aroma of herbs from the motherland.

'What?'

'Did your father let something bad happen to you?'

I realised how hard this must be for her, to break ranks. Mikis, her husband, would disapprove of her interfering. It was unfathomable how the Greeks could be so intrusive and yet so against intervention.

'What?' I said, blinking into the mug.

'Don't say what to everything, Constantina.'

'Sorry.'

'Is something happening at home?'

'No.'

'Constantina, I worry for you. What is happening at home? Who is doing things to you?'

'No one. It's nothing.'

'Not nothing, my darling. When you came to us with the bruises on your face last year, I asked your father what happened. He says you had a fight in the school disco and came home with bruises. This is true, yes?'

I shrugged.

'Tell me, *ayabi mou*, what is happening? Who does things to you? I can help.' She wasn't going to let this go. How could I possibly explain? The shame of letting that vile old man touch me. The desolate feebleness of asking for help and getting none. Of being branded a liar. And was any of it still relevant? Did these things have a sell-by date? And how could I explain that what was happening now felt so similar? The method was different, but the impetus and the result were the same. The grabbing, the staring, the sour odour of sexual jealousy, the blunt-instrument control of my development, the unremitting check on my womanhood. How could I explain to her a concept for which I had not yet formed words?

'You are always angry.' I had forgotten Roulla was there for a second.

'What?'

She sighed. 'What? What? What?'

'I'm not angry, Auntie.'

'Why do you hate your father so much? He tells your uncle Miki that you just sit in your room? Talking to yourself every night.'

'I don't talk to *myself*.'

Her dark eyes flitted from my eyes to my mouth and back again, looking for clues.

'You miss your mummy, yes?' That was a conversation-closer if ever there was one.

'Where is he?' I asked.

'Your dad? He is downstairs.' Her lips went into the straight line I knew so well when she expressed disapproval.

I had no idea what to say. I just wanted it all gone.

Roulla knew she was running out of time and options. She was weighing up something, a tactical change, which, her good sense told her, before she had begun, would get her nowhere. But she was desperate.

'He misses them also,' she ventured. And my eyes shut down instantly. She kept going valiantly, kindly but uselessly. 'Is very hard for him, Constantina. He has lost them too. Now he thinks he is losing you.'

I couldn't listen to any more of this crap. I could just about take the revolting tea and cringeworthy sympathy, but there was no way I was going to let her chisel away at my hard heart to create a soft spot, to feel *pity* for him. I was disappointed in her. I knew she knew better. I swung my legs over the bed, noting that my jeans were ripped on both knees. Every time I bought some new trousers, that bastard ruined them. I put the mug on the bedside table with spiteful deliberation.

'Where are my shoes, please, Auntie?' I asked, through gritted teeth.

'Constantina, listen to me. You think you got no one, but you got us, your Greek family.'

'Where are my *shoes*, Auntie?' I said, starting to panic. I didn't want to hear what was coming.

'Your father, he is just doing his best . . .' she finished lamely.

'Auntie Roulla, where are my *fucking shoes*, please?'

She waved a limp hand to the shoes by the overstuffed gold-velvet nursing chair in the corner. They sat there on the vivid Axminster, sad and red, like end-of-the-pier clown's shoes, their toes scuffed, a fitting testament to the evening. My coat was on a hanger hooked over the wardrobe door. The dribble of fruit juice dried and sticky.

The car journey back from Auntie Roulla's was quietly satisfying. A paradigm shift had occurred between me and my dad. It was intangible but darkly present. We both felt it. And it was due to the unexpected presence of our newly born guest, The Monster, who was sitting between us.

We had been a reluctant duo, my dad and me. We were both desperate to either tear away from each other or tear each other apart. But, now, the dynamic had changed. We had become a threesome. We had been joined by The Monster we had awakened through our public display of dysfunction. It had been there all the time, nascent, waiting for its moment. I didn't know whose side it was on. We would find out.

We all three of us knew that talk was redundant, so we travelled in silence. As he pulled into the drive, my dad looked at me strangely, with an expression I hadn't seen before: a mixture of fury, disbelief, fear, regret, and yet disingenuous for all that. He simply said, as if all transgressions would be mitigated by this statement, 'When you are married, you can choose to do what you like. Is your husband's problem. But, for now, you are young and I don't want you looking for boys. I will find you someone nice and Greek to marry. And this is the end of that discussion.' I was about to point out that there hadn't actually been a discussion. But then I remembered he was a raving lunatic, so I ignored him.

As much as I was sure I was never going to let him arrange a marriage for me, I was equally sure of a few other things: I was never going to be rescued. Marc Bolan was never going to whisk me away to a purple paradise where we would play guitar together and hang out with Bob Dylan. And Vas would never run away with me. He was going to university. I had heard him say it, loud and clear. Everything was changing again. At least, before The Great Cinema Showdown of 1976, all the pieces were in their rightful place. I knew where everything was. Now the picture had fragmented and the pieces were scattered. I wasn't sure if that was good or bad. There was a buzzing building in my head.

I got out of the car; I opened the front door and went straight upstairs. The Monster didn't know whether to follow me or stay with my dad. If it knew what was good for it, it had better come with me. Otherwise, it was *sayonara* for the pair of them.

22

It was Friday night, two weeks after The Great Cinema Showdown of 1976, and I was abject with boredom. I had re-read a few *Record Mirror*s – Gary Glitter, Showaddywaddy, Alice Cooper . . . I mean, seriously, how did these dodgy-looking codgers end up as pop stars? Frankly, if it went on like this, The Fat Murderer could have a hit record. The thought of that made me do a small sick-up in my mouth. So I consumed a coffee Walnut Whip and a Curly Wurly, purely for medicinal reasons.

The Fat Murderer hadn't come home, so I presumed there was no Freak Night this evening and that he'd gone to the Greek Kafenion with the other Friday night knobs to play tavli and eat baklava. Everyone was avoiding everyone now, because no one knew what to say after our spectacular Greek showdown at The Curzon (The Greek Showdown, starring Constance Costa and Vasos Petrides, coming to a cinema near you!). Mr and Mrs Petrides had absconded altogether and taken Vas and his brother to unglamorous Clacton-on-Sea for the Easter break, which was unprecedented, as Greeks never went on holiday unless it was to Cyprus. Vas had tried to call me from a phone box, but the pips kept going, so we only managed: 'Hello?' 'Can you hear me?' 'Yes, I can . . .' 'Oh fuck, Conno, I've dropped my money . . . I'll try to call you back, pip pip pip', etc.

I opened the window to consider a bit of long dribbling, but as a concept it had kind of flagged, plus it was bloody freezing. I had a look for The Calling, but I couldn't get the feel for it. I had two options left.

1. Do homework.
2. Start up a conversation with Marc and David.

Neither appealed, so, as a final act of desperation, I called Soraya. Her mum answered the phone and shouted, 'Soraya! Phone. For you. Again. It's Constance.' *Again?* How come Soraya was getting phone calls? She was a pain in the hole. No one phoned me. Was there a secret phoning club that I wasn't a part of? Probably, actually. She took ages coming to the phone, which made me anxious, because The Fat Murderer AKA The Cypriot Ebenezer Scrooge – Ebezaki Scroogiopoullos – would go nuclear if the quarterly phone bill exceeded 20p. When Soraya finally made her glacially slow passage to the phone, she was full of news.

'Are you calling to talk about Mizz Liz Liddle?' she said.

'Ms,' I corrected. 'What about her?'

'She's only gone and shacked up with Ms *Jayne* Fullerlove.'

'How do you know?' I asked, frostily. Ms Liz Liddle was mine, not hers, and I didn't like not being in the know.

'My mum knows someone who knows Ms Fullerlove's husband, and he told her at their yoga class.'

Soraya, not bothering to pause for breath nor for me to get a word in edgewise, concluded that this was not just concrete but *incontrovertible* proof that Ms Liz Liddle had finally undergone a full sex change and had a penis sewn on, which would have been taken from a male corpse. I said

I didn't think that was a thing. Soraya insisted it was, because her uncle had registered as an organ donor in the event of his death and she'd seen the small print. You had to promise to donate all your organs, of which a penis was one. It would have to be worked with a pump, though. I tried to visualise that but failed.

She then started banging on about Janice's new boyfriend, Martin, who was 'very ginger', and how Martin was going to fix Soraya up with his friend, Carl, who was also ginger, 'but not as much as Martin'. And how Deborah McNichols was dating Calvin Belding, who had tried to finger her through a hole in her tights.

I had to get off the phone for two reasons:

1. Soraya's voice was starting to grate. She was managing to both get on my nerves and depress me.
2. I did not want to hear another word about Deborah McNichol's 'hole', nor anyone else's genitalia come to that.
   Oh, and
3. She'd been yammering on for eons and Ebezaki Scroogiopoullos would burst a vein when he saw the phone bill.
4. And, most importantly, I had started to think that Soraya might be one sandwich short of a picnic.
   And
5. She made me feel like everything around me was moving on and I was the only thing left standing still.

I said goodbye while she was halfway through telling me why Deborah McNichols was a slag.

I went back to my room, picked up my lovely new Kay guitar, opened my practice book and, with a prolonged sigh, started on a piece by Ferdinando Carulli. About the only thing that wasn't changing around me was music. Thank the good Lord I still had that.

23

The following week I had an unfortunate *interlude* with The King of the Pervs.

It was a warmish mid-week evening and almost dark. I had spent a happy hour researching potential methods of patricide. Electrocution could work. Our bathroom was always freezing cold. We had a wall-mounted two-bar electric heater over the bath. You had to stand in the bath to turn it on, so the rule was that you turned it on before you ran a bath. To be safe. Just in case. All I needed to do was loosen the brackets and kindly run The Fat Murderer a nice bath. He'd have to stand in the water to pull the cord, the heater would fall off the wall, and his clogs would be instantly popped!

The Fat Murderer was at the Kafenion. He said he'd be home by ten, as he was meeting Peter Pervy Roy and they were going out for a steak at The Corinthian Barbeque and Grill Greek Cypriot restaurant in Loughton.

I was in my room playing *The Dark Side of the Moon* by Pink Floyd in my knickers and a T-shirt, fag plugged in the corner of my mouth. I was counting my Getaway Fund, to see if I had enough to feel safe in case I had to run off once I'd fried my dad in the bath. I was lost in smoke and music and the wash of melodies and concepts, the way The Floyd made the beautiful and the grandiose sit side by side with the commonplace. David Gilmour's guitar-playing ... consciousness exploding. After discovering The Floyd, I couldn't really listen to The Osmonds any more. I felt bad for them, but what are you going to do?

I had added a poster of Dave Gilmour to my collection. He was on the back of the bedroom door so as not to upset anyone. He was the most beautiful man I had ever seen. Had it not been for Vas getting in the way, I'd have fallen for Dave big time. He hadn't said anything yet, but I knew he was listening to my guitar-playing and would let me know when he was ready to help.

I counted nine hundred and twenty pounds. Not bad. I was just about to pop into my dad's room to fleece another eighty quid to make it up to a neat thousand when I heard a knock on the front door. I looked at my alarm clock. It was 9pm. I hadn't been playing my music loudly, so it couldn't possibly be the old bag next door. And no one else ever knocked on the door because they were either dead or had their own key.

I knew I shouldn't have answered. But curiosity and hope got the better of me. I crept quietly down the stairs, keeping my body pressed against the wall. I could see a tall shadow through the frosted glass panel. The knock came again. It was a sly knock.

I sat at the foot of the stairs, staring at the door, trying to work out the shadowy figure. It pressed its head against the glass panel trying to look in. 'Connie, is that you I can see sitting on the stairs there?' Fuck. Peter Pervy Roy. Why was he here? I thought about not answering, but then he said, 'I'm a bit early for meeting your dad. He'll be back soon. Can you let me in, love? It's getting nippy out here.' It wasn't nippy. I'd had my bedroom window open and it wasn't even remotely nippy. I thought about just going back upstairs and shutting myself in my room, but then I remembered how Peter Pervy Roy had saved me from a proper walloping after The School Disco Disaster of 1975 and had a moment of weakness. The idiot that I am.

I opened the front door and let him in, pulling my T-shirt down over my thighs, suddenly aware of my state of semi-undress. He walked past me in his abominably tight trousers and into the kitchen, as if he owned the place, sat himself at the kitchen table and said cheerily, 'Go on, then, if you insist.'

'What?' I said, while rummaging in the hall cupboard for my mac. It still had the sticky fruit stains down it from The Great Cinema Showdown of 1976. I put it on and buttoned it up all the way.

'Cup of tea?' said Peter Pervy Roy. 'Two sugars. I bet you don't take sugar, eh, sweet enough already, yeah?'

God, I was already regretting letting him in. He was such a moron. If there was an Olympics for Morons, Peter Pervy Roy would get a gold medal in every category.

I walked into the kitchen and filled the kettle, setting it on the gas stove. I took a mug out of the cupboard and, with my back to him, spat in it and added a teabag and two sugars.

I brought the mug of tea over to Peter Pervy Roy and extended it towards him. He let my proffered hand just hang there in mid-air without taking the cup from me. He lifted the corner of my mac.

'What you got this on for? Expecting to get wet?' His lips slipped apart over his snaggle tooth.

I should have poured the tea in his lap and scalded his disgusting squashed genitalia, but instead I put it on the table and ignored the question. He ran his creepy finger down the fruit dribble. 'Who's put that sticky mess there, then?' He made a suggestive face, eyebrows all wiggly and mouth half-cocked. I had no idea what he was talking about. 'Fruit,' I said.

'So, what have you been doing, flitting around the house in your knickers, then?' he asked, dipping his teeth into the mug and not taking his eyes off mine. I already knew where this was going. He was so tedious. He was The World Champion of Tedium.

'I've been in my room,' I said evasively, now looking at the kitchen clock. 9.15pm. 'My dad will be back soon,' I said, taking a small step backwards, trying to put some space between us.

'Your dad's meeting me here at ten. Plenty of time yet,' said Peter Pervy Roy. He took a big slurp of tea and put the mug down. He got up from his chair and walked round to the front of the table. He perched his scrawny backside on the edge of the table, arms folded.

'So, what have you been getting up to in that bedroom of yours, then?' I could smell beer on his breath. Yuck. He must have come straight from the pub. Peter Pervy Roy was a predictable piece of goods: pathetic pub Monday to Friday, cruddy casino Saturday, roast dinner and a bath on Sunday. Lucky Mrs Pervy Roy. She had really bagged a prize one.

'Homework,' I said.

He spent a moment considering that. He picked up his mug of tea, took a smarmy slurp, went to take another, and instead said: 'So, how's your love life?'

'I haven't got a love life.'

'Ah, don't worry, your secret's safe with me. I bet you're a right little sex maniac on the quiet, aren't you?' he said, having another smarmy swig.

God, I wished I had taken the whole telekinesis thing more

seriously. What I wouldn't have given now for the power to make him choke on his tea.

'I've got loads to do, so I'm going back up. You can stay here and wait for my dad. I think he said to me he would come home a bit earlier than ten, as he wants to have a bath so he'll probably be here really soon.' I was peddling and he knew it.

'Shall I come up and help you with your homework? I'm good at conjugating verbs?' Jesus fucking Christ almighty.

'No thanks. I'm doing maths. I'm going up now. Bye.' Then, just to make it clear: 'You stay here.'

Peter Pervy Roy stood up, a greasy grin breaking over his teeth.

'What are you hiding up there? I'm coming up there with you, have a look at your little secret.'

That's the last thing I wanted. I'd left the wad of cash on the bed and a fag in the crappy ashtray. Plus, every single cell in my brain was approximately 100 per cent certain that it would not be a good idea to let this lascivious imbecile into my bedroom.

I leant against the kitchen worktop and folded my arms across my chest. Then I unfolded them, because it felt protective and I didn't want Peter Pervy Roy to think he scared me. The thing is, I wasn't sure where to put my hands, because they felt useless hanging by my sides and aggressive on my hips. So, in the end, I put them in my coat pockets.

'You getting chilly?' said Peter Pervy Roy. 'I'll warm you up.' God, he was relentless.

He put his tea down and closed the small space between us. He put his hands on my arms and started rubbing them briskly, as if to make them warm.

'I'm not cold,' I said. It came out louder than I had expected. I was starting to feel repulsed. And, also, quite pissed off. And maybe a bit scared. But not as much as I thought I might be. Also, since I had emptied The Well of Shame, I had felt less out of control. That was odd – the minute I stopped trying to control everything, I started to control everything. And I had The Monster.

I put everything on pause for a moment while I flitted back in time to when I was twelve and confused, and Peter Pervy Roy was ogling me and talking about my figure and making me feel odd and like I was doing something wrong. And here he was again, obfuscating with cheery talk and feigned innocence. But I was older now and knew what his game was. The fifteen-year-old me felt a great protection for the younger me. I didn't have to put up with this shit. The Monster made his presence known and growled.

'Take your hands off me,' I said, with venom. Then: 'GO AWAY', as loud as I could manage and possibly a bit hysterically. Peter Pervy Roy stepped way back, holding his hands up in supplication.

'Whoah, Constance, what's this? I'm just trying to be nice here.' He added an unconvincing 'hah hah hah'. He was pretending to be cool, but I could tell he was shitting himself. 'Constance, I think you're confused. Your uncle Pete's just being friendly.'

Uncle Pete, my arse. I was outraged that someone as moronic as Peter Pervy Roy had the sheer temerity to think he could make me question my perception. The Monster growled louder and showed its teeth.

'I'm not confused,' I said, levelly. 'I'm telling my dad about this.' I had no intention of telling my dad and, even if I did, he'd do precisely nothing. History had been testament to that. But it was the first threat that came to me.

'Tell him what? Nothing's happened,' said Peter Pervy Roy, with his palms up in supplication. 'I think your dad knows you're a saucy little mare, doesn't he? You need a firm hand, you do.' And there it was. My dad had treated me worse than this in front of Peter Pervy Roy, so I supposed Peter Pervy Roy thought I was fair game. Maybe that was my value stamp. In their eyes. Not in mine. Not any more. The Monster started to salivate.

'My dad is still my dad and I will tell him,' I said, my voice growing louder again. 'And I'll tell all his friends and everyone that knows you, and I'll tell my teachers and they'll get the social worker round your house and talk to your wife. I'll go to the pub and tell everyone there as well.'

'Connie, this is ludicrous. No one will believe *you*.'

'I don't care if they believe me. They don't *need* to believe me. They will have heard me say it and then everyone will always think it every time they see you. That's Peter Pervy Roy. He touches kids.'

'What did you just call me?' He had the cheek to look taken aback.

'I will make a shit bucket of trouble for you. I will, watch me.' I was suffused with bravado! I worshipped The Monster. It was on my side. Feeding me with its reckless bile. I felt rash and careless of the consequences.

Peter Pervy Roy clamped his lips over his greasy choppers, turned towards the table, and oh so casually picked up his mug of tea and drained it, as if he had all the time in the world and wasn't cacking his scraggy pants. He put the cup back on the table and turned and attempted an indifferent smile.

'You've got the wrong end of the stick here and I could do without this aggravation, I've got enough of my own. You're lucky I won't be telling your father about this.'

He walked towards the front door and I followed close behind him, which made him tuck his backside in and walk faster, as if I was going to – hahaha, big irony – assault him. He looked back over his shoulder. 'You're damaged goods, anyway,' he sneered. 'No one's gonna want you.' I had a moment where I thought I might chase after him and drop-kick him in the spine. But then I also thought I just couldn't be arsed.

24

Because the Greeks had to do everything back to front and arse upwards, Greek Easter wasn't at the same time as normal people's Easter. It arrived a week after everyone else's but, this year, celebrations were postponed because the weather was gloomy. Good weather was imperative. With Greek Easter, there were no easter egg hunts and roast lamb dinners, no pastel-coloured fluffy bunny toys and bunches of tulips. In Greek World, Easter meant only one thing: the start of Barbecue Season, so good weather was imperative. Greeks across the land would rush to get bags of charcoal and rusty old grills out of their garages and sheds. They'd load up the silver Mercs with the entire contents of their kitchens and drive to a remote field somewhere in Essex. There was a one-in-three chance they'd find the field, because no one possessed either a map or a sense of direction. When the good weather arrived two weeks later, festivities were back on, with a Greek Freak Fervour saved especially for the consumption of shedloads of incinerated meat.

I thought back to when we were all kids – even Marios – and we would spend our days building dams, climbing trees, constructing wigwams and pretending to smoke twigs that we'd set on fire in the embers of the coals. The time was boundless and charmed and would stretch out into the early evening, when the dusk would pacify, the chatter would quieten and the adults would snooze while we played somewhere just out of hearing. As I got older, I became bored with these trips, feeling increasingly out of place. Now I couldn't wait to be there because I would see Vas.

This would be the first chance we had had to speak properly since The Great Cinema Showdown of 1976, because of the Petrideses' suspiciously timely family holiday and insufficient Freak Nights. I was looking forward to seeing him and finding out just what the whole deal was with his uncharacteristic and, frankly, deranged behaviour at the cinema. And also dreading it: it felt like things had changed. I'd never seen Vas lose control and it seemed like the boy I knew had evolved, secretly, into a different person. We had always had a rhythm, Vas and I, and I was worried that we wouldn't get back into it.

I was going to make sure I looked the very best I could. I had cut up the jeans that my dad had scuffed when dragging me off Mr Petrides and I wore them turned up extra short with a pale-blue sleeveless shirt. I had pestered The Fat Murderer for some Grecian sandals and he had got me some from Tony, the co-conspirator of The Two Differently Sized Shoes Fiasco of 1975, who managed the shoe shop. I wanted brown Grecian sandals and he got me bright red, most likely because they were cheaper, but both shoes were the same size, so I counted it as a rare footwear triumph.

As we left the house, my dad, ever the harbinger of positive reinforcement, said he thought I was too fat to wear shorts and that I should cover up my legs. I told him not to worry about it because I'd be taking them off when we got there.

'What you mean you taking it off when we get there?' he asked, looking confused as to whether he should shout or worry. I patted The Monster on the head affectionately. Good

Monster. Since The Great Cinema Showdown of 1976, and The Peter Pervy Roy Victory of 1976, I had felt empowered in ways I was unable to articulate. I had The Monster to thank for that.

'All the other girls will be wearing bikinis, so I've got one in my bag. I might just go topless, though.' That shut him up. Too fat. Bloody cheek. I admit, I had put on a few pounds and my shorts were incredibly tight. I had been keeping a fully stocked larder in a carrier bag in the back of my wardrobe: Texan Bars, Curly Wurlys, Rolos, Mintoes, Freddo the Frogs, Walnut Whips. An ideal evening would be to do my homework, count my money, and then munch my way through a couple of albums and maybe a good book. It made me feel loved and special. It made me feel solid when I started to fragment. I made a mental note to pull back on the self-love and limit the chocolate to two bars a night. Nevertheless, coming from that fat bastard it was beyond irony.

It was a warmish morning; a dull sun baking the dirt on the dual carriageway. Although we had only been travelling for fifteen minutes, the convoy of silver Mercs pulled up on the grass verge that ran along the edge of the A12 heading into Essex, so that the men could stretch their legs and confer over the route. I watched as they waved their arms about, pointing up the dual carriageway towards Romford, making suggestions for going left, then right, etc. This would happen several times on the journey and sometimes they'd incorporate some snacking and then all have a manly wee behind the bushes. It was all very tasteful.

By the time we had covered most of Essex, and our caravan had found its convoluted way to the lane by the field, the sun had made its mind up. It was shining brightly on a waterfall of white blossom trees, which cascaded down a grassy slope so newly green it hurt to gaze upon it; fecund with cow parsley and sedge and dog's tail grasses, all nodding towards a trickling brook at its foot. A song thrush flew over my head and I turned to follow its flight up the hill, where it disappeared into a stand of aspens on the horizon. For the first time in months, I got a delicious sense of The Calling. Was it the horizon or was it the birds that did it to me? I think it was both. The birds were so free. They were born to be free; parent birds taught their babies to fly, to soar over their own horizons, unencumbered and blessed. I wanted that so badly, to leave all this sorrow and anger on the ground and fly far away, to a renaissance that I knew could be wonderful if I could only reach it.

Meanwhile, the Greeks were setting up camp in Greek time, which is basically lightning speed. They can throw themselves down on any spot of land and have it looking like they've been there for years in record time. Blankets were laid, edge to edge. Tubs of fragrant cucumbers and tomatoes, onions, lemons, bunches of summer-pungent coriander, minty haloumi floating in milky brine, a greasy five-pint can of peppery olive oil, and huge flanks of meat wrapped in pink-stained white butcher's paper were all placed on the grass. Knives and forks and mismatched plates were put in the centre of the blanketed ground, along with paper napkins and Greek breads. Doulla had made flaouna, the cheesy minty Greek Easter cakes that I loved so much. I asked if I could have one and my dad told me to stop thinking about what I was going to stuff in my face and start thinking about how I was going to help with the cooking. Roulla gave him a look and nodded to Doulla, who smiled and handed me a pastry, saying, 'Enjoy, my darling.'

Everyone got busy. Men doing the men stuff and women

doing the women stuff. Which irked me somewhat. The men got to carving the pork and lamb into huge chunks. Spearing them onto the long metal skewers was Vas's job. I guess his man parts were finally big enough to handle meat. The women chopped the salad in the Greek way: holding the tomatoes and cucumbers in one hand while carving off irregular lumps straight into the salad bowl with a sharp knife.

The Fat Murderer told me to help with the salad, but I said wasn't about to get roped into sexist role play, and then just shirked off and read 'The Lady of Shalott' by Tennyson, which I was trying to learn by heart. Soraya had said that, if you memorised things, you wouldn't get dementia when you were old. My mum's mum had died of a dementia so bad that the last time I saw her, on a geriatric ward, she was happily counting old Christmas cards with her foot in a bowl of custard. I thought I might try to avoid that if I could.

Adonia and Marios, who were now – huge announcement that no one cared about – engaged, were allowed to giggle side by side down at the brook, keeping an eye on the kids. I'd give it ten minutes before at least one of the kids would run back crying with a bee sting, a bloody lip or a wet bottom.

Whatshisface junior came over to try to talk to me, but I was monosyllabic enough for the dullard to give me up as a bad job and pitch in with the skewering instead. I now hated him on principle, as not only was he a dullard but he was also the brother of undercooked Fray-Bentos-pie-faced Dina, who thought herself good enough to marry Vas. And now her sister, Adonia the Beautiful, was going out with Prince Marios. What a bloody family. Who the hell did they think they were?

It wasn't until after the food had been consumed and the drink drunk that the adults, sated and sleepy, had a fag and a lie-down in the warm afternoon glow. Before long, mouths dropped open and emitted snores, which meant the younger ones could slope off. Vas and I were sitting at opposite sides of the same blanket. He caught my eye and raised his eyebrows. I checked The Fat Murderer and he was sleeping like a baby – a hideously deformed one. Vas and I both stood simultaneously and crept away.

We walked in careful silence up and away from the itinerant spread, The Monster trailing way behind us, towards a row of aspens at the crest of the slope; bright leaves gleaming and brushing up against each other like new lovers. Their spindly offspring growing up around them, fresh and unblemished.

It was hard work keeping up with Vas, now that his legs had got longer. I was getting a proper Greek sweat on; hair pasted to my forehead, armpits squeaking with perspiration, and tight short shorts working their way up my backside a little further with each step. It wasn't quite how I'd envisaged presenting myself to Vas after our hiatus.

We found a spot in the swaying grass at the base of a tree. The sun had dipped in the sky and the rays slanted low over our heads. Vas sat with his back resting against the slim white trunk and I sat opposite him, legs crossed, wriggling from side to side to release the tight short shorts that had inserted themselves firmly between my buttocks. Vas was first to erupt.

'Fucking hell, Conno!'

'Fucking hell, Vas!'

We clutched at each other.

I said, grinning, 'The Great Cinema Showdown of 1976!'

'Good title.'

He shook his head and his fringe flopped from side to side. His hair had grown longer and was wet at the ends from the sweat of our climb. I liked the way it looked on him, glistening in the sultry glimmer of the waning afternoon. He took his T-shirt off and pretended to clean his glasses, but really, I could tell, he wanted to showcase the four chest hairs he had grown since we were last together. He settled back against the tree again, rolling his T-shirt into a support for his neck.

'You went ballistic at your dad!' I said, laughing loudly now.

'You tried to *strangle* my dad!' he replied, laughing as loudly. 'It was really hard to drag you off him. You're really strong for a girl, Conno. I'm surprised you didn't get arrested for GBH.'

'I'm an outlaw, running from the feds.'

'We're the Bonnie and Clyde of Walthamstow!' Vas said, punching me in the arm.

I returned the punch, a bit too enthusiastically.

'Ouch! You're like that *Beano* character, Pansy Potter the Strong Man's Daughter! That's my nickname for you from now on. Pansy.'

I was relieved. We were back. We were quiet again for a while.

Then: 'So,' I said, feeling foolish and brave. 'There's a "from now on" for me and you, then?'

Vas looked at me kindly, his head to one side. 'There will always be a from now on for me and you, Conno. Who knows where we will end up? But we will always have had this.'

Have had. HAVE. HAD. Sounded like an ending rather a continuation to me. That wasn't really the reassurance I had been after. I decided to let that go for a minute.

'Vas, why did you go so crazy? I mean, it was me who was getting it that night. Not you.'

Vas had been looking down at his hands in his lap; he now snapped his head up to look at me. 'You know, Conno, sometimes I think you are so wrapped up in your own misery that you choose to forget other people have things going on.'

'Wha'?' I gawped.

'Wha', wha'?' he said, mimicking me but not meanly. 'That's all you ever say, is "wha'?"!'

'No, I don't,' I said, annoyed.

He sighed. 'I don't blame you. I think it's fair to say you've had the shittiest of all times the past couple of years. I do. Honest. But even if someone else's time isn't as bad as yours, it still might be bad for them.'

'Fucking hell, Vas, it's not a competition.'

'But that's the point, sometimes I feel it is. I can never tell you how I feel or what's happening to me because you'll always say, "Well, it's not as bad as I have it, Vas, you don't know how shit my life is, Vas, let's run away, Vas." I have to think about *my* life, Conno. I can't just be an addendum to your existence.'

The Monster bared its teeth.

'Frankly, I don't know what an addendum is, *Vas*, but all you have to do is tell me. I can't read your mind, can I? You're always so Secret Squirrel about everything. Fucking chess club and unreadable books and unfathomable expressions and fucking Marvell and chest hair – pathetic, by the way – and marrying fucking shitting undercooked Fray-Bentos-pie-faced fucking dopey Dina – and don't tell me I'm being cruel. She's a bloody waste of DNA.'

Well, this wasn't going to plan at all. I was just considering delivering a hard kick to his knob and bollocks and walking away, but then I remembered Marc and David's words from last Christmas, when I had scoffed at Vas's nerdy spectacles and Band-Aid arrangement: 'Why would you be so cruel, Con, why?'

'Are they really making you marry Dina?' I asked, with as much sympathy as I could muster.

Vas barked a laugh. 'Don't try to sound concerned. I know you think it's hilarious.'

'Well, it's Dina.'

'Yes . . .'

'Dopey Dina.'

'Yes.'

'Dumpy Dina.'

'Yes, Conno, I know how alliteration works. You can be cruel sometimes, you know.'

'So, are you going to marry her or what?' I asked, ignoring another slight to my character.

'*Of course I'm not going to marry her*. I don't want to have marriage *arranged* for me. I want to go to university and find someone of my own.'

That stung a bit, I have to say.

'Right. Thanks, Vas,' I said quietly.

Tut. 'No, don't take it that way, Conno.'

'No, I get it, that's fine.' I had waited weeks for this reconciliation with Vas. I had hoped he would thank me for jumping to his defence that day at The Curzon. In my head I had been the heroine of the piece. I had come to his defence and strangled his dad. I was expecting a fanfare. How was this degenerating so fast and how was I emerging as the villain here? And why was I feeling less like his someone special and more like a spare-part stop-gap?

'You've got the Vas Plan. I get it. You're going to get your exams, go to university, meet someone who's not damaged goods and live happily ever after. I'm pleased for you. Really.'

'Damaged goods? Who's damaged goods?'

'No one.'

'When did you start saying that?'

'Someone called me it.'

'Who?'

'What do you care?'

'Fuck's sake, Conno. I care. *I care*.' Vas reached to sweep my hair off my forehead. I swatted his hand away. 'Who said it?'

'Peter Pervy Roy.'

'Who the fuck is Peter Pervy Roy. Do I know him?'

'Yeah, the one with the tooth.'

Vas racked his brains for a second or two. 'Ah, yeah, I know him. Skinny, creepy-looking. Goes to the casino with your dad?'

'Yeah.'

'Why did he call you that?'

I shrugged. 'Because he's a cunt.'

Vas nodded. With caution, he moved my sticky fringe away from my forehead. This time I let him.

'Conno, do you know why I walked out when your dad hit you in the cinema foyer?' he asked suddenly, very serious.

'Because you were in a mood with your dad, who wants you to be a tiler and thinks you're a homosexual and saw you eyeing up Paul Johnson. I saw it too,' I said petulantly, still sore about the marriage thing. Although I had vowed never to marry, it was unthinkable that Vas – clearly – didn't want to marry me.

'No, well, yes. No. I wasn't *eyeing up* Paul Johnson. I was trying to acknowledge him caring enough to want to come over to help you.'

I could only manage a grumpy 'Hurgh.'

'But it was complicated. Yeah, I was pissed off with my dad. I was on the edge already. But I couldn't stand to see your dad do that to you. To humiliate you like that. To try to make you look so small. In front of the boys. To ... I don't know how to say it ... stunt your growth ... steal your femininity ... oh, I dunno what I'm trying to say ... *own* you ...' He trailed off. 'I'm talking crap.'

He wasn't. He was right. It was all those things.

'So you threw a humungous epileptic fit.' For me. ME.

'Yeah. Gargantuan.' Vas nodded, just once but with sincerity.

I let that sink in. Really sink in until that softly candid confession had taken root into a deep and bottomless understanding. Vas had fallen on his own sword, thrown up a smoke screen. He had thrown a wobbly to draw the attention away from me. So that I could salvage some scrap of self-respect. In front of The Greeks. In front of Paul Johnson. How could I have doubted his intentions? I didn't have the words to know how to acknowledge something that profound.

'Thank you,' I said, quietly. It was all I had.

Vas shrugged. 'Well, my dad had it coming anyway. And you still managed to make it all about you, didn't you?' It was a statement, but a nice one, sympathetic. 'And ...' He took a deep breath and looked back down at his hands in his lap.

'What?'

'And I saw the way that blond kid looked at you.' He cast his eyes downwards.

'What? Paul Johnson? He fancies Janice.'

'No, he fancies you.'

Was it possible? Could someone actually fancy me? *Me?* AND. BIG AND. Could Vas be jealous? I somehow found an uncharacteristic iota of decorum and managed not to ask him. Instead, I said, 'Do you think that's what my dad saw, then?'

'Yeah, I do,' said Vas. 'I could see it in his face. It was ... nasty. And weird, you know?'

I could have expounded on this. But I couldn't go there today. Not with the sun mellowing and the grass between us softening, drawing us closer together.

'I don't fancy Paul Johnson. He looks like a girl.'

'No, he doesn't. He's blond and good-looking and English.'

'So?'

'So, I'm Greek. The full kebab with extra tahini sauce. You hate everything that's Greek.'

'That's not entirely true. Loukoumades are all right.' I poked him in the ribs.

He *was* jealous. *He was only actually jealous!* I couldn't have been more overjoyed at another person's sadness and insecurity if I'd tried.

'So,' I said, 'you feel sorry for me and then you feel insecure about me, so you react by punching your dad?'

'Yeah,' he laughed, weakly. 'That's about the size of it. It's been brewing for ages between me and my dad, though, ever since I chose the arts for A-levels—'

I didn't really care about that right now.

'I like you,' I said, 'not Paul Johnson.'

'I know,' he said, sounding as old and wise as the trees around us. 'Fuck it.' He shrugged and my Vas was back.

'Kiss?' I asked nicely.

He nodded mutely and I leant in. We kissed for a while, not touching. His tongue explored my mouth and a flutter of butterflies in my stomach took blissful flight.

He pulled away after some minutes. I wished he hadn't. While it was happening, it was all that was happening.

'Conno, you know you can tell me stuff,' he said, 'I won't think you're damaged goods.'

'Okay,' I said, 'I will. But not today.'

The afternoon was too pretty to soil with my dirty stories. I wanted to bathe in this warmth, soak up every ray of ripened sunshine, inhale every scent, feel the tingle of his touch, like lemonade bubbles bursting on my skin.

'What do we do now?' I asked.

'I think we should have sex,' said Vasos.

'Yeah. That's not going to happen.'

'I'll show you my willy. It's got bigger.'

Ironically, after all the years of inspecting the contents of Vas's Y-fronts with a judicious detachment, it seemed a bit more ... involved now. I did think it might be nice to have that closeness with Vas, to own his body, to let him own my body. A fresh start. Cleansed with love and friendship and four magnificent and actually very alluring chest hairs.

I turned away from him, looking down the hill. I could just see the Greeks below. No movement. I took off my shirt and leant back against his skinny, four-haired bare chest. I wanted to feel his skin on my skin. I wanted his skin to be my skin. New skin, new life, new person. I felt The Monster purr.

'Conno?' Vas was twirling a strand of my hair.

'Yeah?'

He tugged the strand of hair.

'What do you reckon?'

'What if someone comes?'

'They won't. They'll be asleep for ages yet. We'll see them before they see us if anyone comes.'

It was inevitable that Vas and I were going to have sex at some point, but the thought of it made me nervous in case I got it wrong. I wasn't sure I was ready for it. Plus, the way the girls talked about sex at school it seemed like hard work. And a bit hit and miss. Oh well ...

'Yeah, go on then,' I said briskly, surprising myself. 'What's the best way to go about it?'

'It's not supposed to be an act of efficiency, Conno,' said Vas, laughing.

'Stop laughing at me! I've never done this before,' I said.

'Neither have I.'

'Yes, but boys think about this stuff all the time, don't they? And anyway, you're good at everything, aren't you?'

'Bloody hell, Conno, pressure or what!'

'Oh, come on, Vas, let's just get on with it before I change my mind.'

'Okay. Well, we're supposed to have foreplay first.'

'What's foreplay?' I asked.

'You know, a build-up to it.'

'A build-up to what?!'

'To our climax.' Vas sounded less sure of himself now.

Our climax? Our climax. I was starting to worry. I mean, I knew what a climax was, of course I did, but I had never really thought about the actual mechanics of sex, let alone some highly coordinated grand finale that was expected at the end. What if I didn't have a climax?

'Stop looking so worried, Conno. We can go slowly.'

I would have rathered we go fast and get it over and done with really, but I nodded and let Vas kiss me on the neck a few times. That felt nice, so I turned to face him and we lay down together. It felt good to have him press his body against mine and I was lost in his smell, the taste of his mouth, the sensation of his hands in my hair, the tiny drops of perspiration that drip, drip, dripped from Vas's fringe onto my face, like the softest rain. My mind had ceased its endless searching and stilled, totally enveloped in this blissful and beautiful moment. I didn't know what was supposed to come next but I knew I wanted it. I wanted him. I had missed him so much.

Vas unzipped my shorts and started to pull them down, but they were really incredibly tight and had ridden quite far up my bum crack. He tugged harder.

'Can you lift up a bit, Conno, please?' said Vas.

I lifted my buttocks off the ground. Vas tugged some more with no luck. He knelt up now and used both hands.

'Fuck, Conno, I can't get your shorts down, have you glued them to your arse?' Vas said, sounding a little exasperated.

I stood up and, with a lot of wriggling, helped him pull my shorts free. I felt silly now and kind of didn't want to get back to the sex. But I'd started so I'd finish.

I knelt in front of Vas and he undid his trousers and it was at this point that I realised something that had never occurred to me before. And why would it?

'Vas, do all penises only have one . . . outlet. Is that normal?'

'Yes, it's bloody normal,' he said.

That seemed like an obvious design fault to me and not entirely hygienic.

'So how do you know what's coming out and when?' I was genuinely flummoxed.

'I don't know. The body just knows, Conno. I mean, what do you want me to do about it?'

I really hadn't thought this through at all. I'd totally gone off the idea of having sex and I think, by the looks of things, Vas had too.

He did his trousers up and I stepped into my shorts.

We sat side by side, his arm around my shoulders, my head tucked into his neck.

'Can we try again soon?' I asked him, after some time.

'Yes, of course. As long as you can just shut up for two minutes and let me do my thing.'

'I will. I promise.'

'And wear something that doesn't require heavy machinery to remove.'

'Okay. I'll try.'

I smelled his neck. It was sweaty and sweet.

'Stop smelling my neck.'

'I like it.'

'Oh God . . . it's a good job I like you so much, Conno,' Vas sighed.

For me, there could have been no better climax.

25

Christ, it was all anyone was going on about. The Wedding. Turns out, Marios and Perfect Adonia had been shagging like rabbits and Adonia was up the duff! That was going to put a stick in her 'I'm going to be a lawyer' spokes. She'd be making oven macaroni and breastfeeding Marios's brats for a living from now on.

Don't get me wrong, I didn't judge them for shagging. Me and Vas were doing it quite regularly. Finally. It was tricky, at first, but we eventually got into the swing of it and it promised to be a good summer for two reasons:

1. We were having sex.
2. Our parents had no idea.
   Oh, and
3. Vas appeared to be very good at it.

Being good at sex was important to Vas and, I had to admit, it was extremely addictive. But I didn't want Vas to get too big-headed, so I told him I didn't think it was all it was cracked up to be and, given a choice between intercourse with him and, say, Curly Wurlys, I'd go for miles of chewy toffee covered in creamy Cadbury's milk chocolate any day of the week. He said that was the horniest thing he'd ever heard. He was incorrigible.

Arranging the time to have the secret sex was almost more

exciting than the actual secret sex. We both joined a number of after-school clubs that we had no intention of attending, and this gave us our early evenings to wander through the plains of Hollow Ponds in Leyton, snatching romance and privacy where we could.

The best thing about the sex was that it made me feel like I was one half of something. That was nice. Because it wasn't exactly a picnic being a complete amount of me. The worst thing was having to use a condom, which Vas insisted on. Condoms were, frankly, disgusting items; they were filmy and viscous and felt sleazy. But neither Vas nor I wanted to end up in Marios and Adonia's situation, so I put up with them 99 per cent of the time, as long as I didn't have to touch them or look at them.

The school summer holidays were idyllic. We'd both passed our O-levels with good grades – Vas more so, because he was a swot – and with nothing else to do, we felt free. Sometimes, during these golden times, Vas and I didn't even have sex. Sometimes we spent entire days just lying together, smoking, reading, talking about what we would do with our lives once we were eighteen and independent. I think I liked these times best. I said I had decided to become something called a session musician, which meant playing guitar for bands in the recording studio and on stage, when the bands were too untalented to play themselves. Vas was still unwavering in his desire to go to university and study English Literature. I tried to be supportive.

We had a little institution we had set up, Vas and I, called The Mind Gift. This involved giving each other a parting gift of a quote or a thought that explained what we were thinking about, or how we felt that week. He would often quote one of his beloved metaphysical poets. I'd quote Dylan, or Pink Floyd, or sometimes just something silly, like 'Do the hustle, do it!' Just to make him laugh. Most of the time we were pretentious, though.

And thank you, dear Lord God who may or may not be real, Greek Nights were back on schedule. On those occasions Vas and I were blasé, determined not to give the game away. We spent those evenings reading, eating, passing the odd comment, almost ignoring each other. It was quite erotic. The Monster sat idly by, casting a protective shadow. I felt that in allowing The Monster inside, I had less room there for my dad. I had secured myself a new world with a guardian at the gates.

But I had allowed happiness to confound me and had forgotten that this new world was not a forever world. August was almost done and, as our summer of ecstatic sunshine and blue skies began to wane, I became aware of two things, both of which settled over me like a pall of black smoke:

1. That The Summer of Vas and Conno would soon be coming to an end and, with it, our freedom. We would be back at school, at the mercy of Freak Nights and confined to bus-stop snogging. It wasn't enough. And one day it would all come to an end, and that time was creeping nearer with every new day. Vas was already talking about his A-levels and university and it depressed me. I wanted time to stand still.
2. That I had completely and utterly forgotten to kill my dad. It was ten weeks until my sixteenth birthday, the day I'd vowed to have killed him by. He should have been dead by now and I was not one inch closer to being free of The Fat Murderer. Where had the time

gone?! Soon the nights would be drawing in and I'd be trapped once again.

Perhaps it was the black smoke, perhaps it was that Vas had steadily unlocked me with his poetry and his caresses, perhaps it was neither of those things, perhaps it was simply that the time had come. I had carried with me an urn of emotional ashes since the day my mother died. It was my secret burden and contained a part of the story I had admitted to no one, not even Vas. Recently, its contents had threatened to spill over. I was taking great care not to let that happen. And then The Fat Murderer cracked the vessel open with four one-syllable blows.

26

The nagging had started when I met Vas in Coronation Gardens, our local park, that afternoon. It was a particularly hot and sticky late August day, when the freshness of summer was past its prime and the fug of London heat sat grimy on our skin. It had been the hottest, driest summer on record. The park was parched and the flowers were dead.

We bought bland ice-cream cones. The gormless pigeons that lived for scraps on the hot concrete ground were cumbrous and slower than usual. A small group plodded over, shuffling back and forth, eyeing my cone. I snapped off the end and sprinkled a few featherweight crumbs on the ground for them. As they shambled closer, all the other pigeons got wind and flapped over tiresomely, kicking up feathers and dust into the clammy air. Thwarted by their own clumsiness and confusion, the pigeons missed their opportunity, and some chippy sparrows nipped in and out, stealing the crumbs from right under their beaks. The pigeons never got angry, though. They just waddled around in dopey circles, hoping for a chance crumb to land at their feet. There was one pigeon who was so dozy that he failed to grasp a single crumb, no matter how hard I tried on his behalf. A crumb would land within a quarter of an inch of his beak and his first reaction would be to turn and dodder away from the morsel, as if he was dubious of it, as if he was unsure the crumb could really be for him.

It occurred to me that bird life was no different to people life. It left me feeling aggrieved.

By the time I got home, I was irked and intensely out of sorts: hot, sticky, grubby and headachy. The Fat Murderer was already home from work. As soon as he heard the front door slam, he shouted, 'Where do you been?' It was on the tip of my tongue to say, 'Having sex with Vasos.' Instead, I just said, 'Library.'

I went into the lounge. He was watching *Charlie's Angels* on the telly. He had his shirt buttons undone (cue heaving and retching) and his neck tie hung over the back of the chair. I stood behind him and thought about taking his tie, wrapping it around his throat and strangling him, watching him jerk and writhe until he stopped. I would get back on track. I would kill him, but I just didn't want to get caught and end up in prison. I'd last about five minutes in a female prison, with everyone putting razorblades in everyone else's dinner and getting shivved in the showers. I'd have to make sure I was the biggest lesbian's girlfriend so that she'd protect me. Essentially, I was a coward.

I lingered for a bit. I did this occasionally as a sort of contractual fulfilment: he would see me; I would see him. Job done. He looked me up and down, spitefully, then looked at glamorous raven-haired Angel Kelly Garrett, who was doing a crap acting job of looking tough, and said, 'Now, that's what you calling a good-looking woman.'

He was just trying to find new ways to cut me down. He couldn't get up to his old tricks because we were two against one now. Me and The Monster against The Fat Murderer. Besides, since The Great Cinema Showdown of 1976, Auntie Roulla had been keeping a very shrewd eye on my dad. Several times she had asked me if everything was okay at home. She had even said that I could live with her and Uncle Mikis if things got bad. She said I could have their third-best bedroom, as Marios and Adonia would be shacking up in their second-best bedroom for a few months before they got their starter home.

I took another look at the back of The Fat Murderer's head. 'Oh, for *Christ's sake, fuck off you moron*,' I spat.

'What did you say?' he snapped, threateningly, half getting up out of his chair.

'What are you going to do? Kill me too?' I started to walk away and continued to do so as he said, quite clearly, '*It was your fault.*'

I went to my room.

The air there was heavy and darkly clammy with the guilt I had barely kept at bay since the day my family died.

Foolishly, I had left my bedroom window open and about a zillion midges had wafted in. They made a beeline for me and were zinging around my head. I closed the window and went on a killing spree, whacking them with a T-shirt until I had squashed them all. There were satisfying black and red smudges on the ceiling and walls.

A bluebottle had been surreptitiously working its way towards a half-eaten Curly Wurly bar I had left in my crap ashtray on my desk. It crawled across Dave Gilmour clumsily, as if it didn't give two hoots about the fact that he was the greatest guitarist in the known universe. It wafted over to Bowie, who waved his hands around theatrically while Marc Bolan rolled his eyes and said, 'Drama queen or what?'

When the bluebottle thought no one was looking, it landed craftily on the ashtray, sidled onto the chocolate bar, and started rubbing its revolting germy bluebottle legs together.

I hated bluebottles. This one had probably been sitting on a dog turd somewhere and now it was in my room depositing faecal microbes on my stuff.

I reached under my bed. The first thing that came to hand was the smaller of the differently sized platform shoes from so long ago. I smashed it down on the bluebottle, sending the ashtray and the chocolate spinning across the desk and onto the floor. 'And you can fuck off too,' I said.

I poured a teeny Drambuie. It tasted like medicine, but my dad's drinks cabinet seemed to be winding down, so it was a like-it-or-lump-it situation. I retrieved the crappy ashtray, which had broken in half, from the floor and lit a cigarette. I walked over to the bedroom door. I unpinned the top left-hand and right-hand corners of Dave Gilmour from Pink Floyd so that he dropped, face downwards, against the door. I didn't want him to hear this. I pulled the chair out from under the desk and turned it around so that, when I sat, I was facing David and Marc. I knew what I was about to do and the thought of it gave me instant serenity.

'Got something you want to get off your chest, Constance?' asked Bowie.

'I think it's finally time,' said Marc.

They were very intuitive, for a pair of egocentric pop stars who mostly cared about themselves.

I nodded slowly. I took a drag on the cigarette. Placed it in one half of the crappy ashtray and folded my hands in my lap. I sat up very straight. Things I had buried for so many thousands of moments had found their time. I just opened my mouth and words and memories spilled out like lubricant, oily and slick.

'I want to talk about the night my dad murdered my mum

and my brothers. Everyone, even Vas, just thinks it was an accident. But it wasn't. It was stone-cold classic murder. Accidents happen randomly, that's why they are called accidents. If you behave in a way that makes an accident inevitable, then it's not an accident. It's done on purpose.

'It was a Friday evening, a few weeks before Christmas, and we were all supposed to be going to The Greeks. My mum had cooked koftes to take. She made the best koftes. Even Auntie Roulla said so. She was so tired that night, my mum. She had been at work all day. The boys were playing up.'

I watched the smoke from my untouched cigarette curl upwards and disperse, curl upwards and disperse. I tried to say their names. But I felt, if I said their names, it would somehow seal their deaths. But that just seemed stupid now. They were gone. Everyone was gone in one way or another. Janice and Soraya, The Deborahs, Ronald and Elizabeth, my wood pigeon lovers, my family ... Nicos and Loukas, my baby brothers. I could even sense Vas slowly vanishing, ebbing away from here and flowing towards his own existence. It was what it was.

'He was always chipping away at their happiness. As they got older, I saw them growing stressed. I saw their little eyes reflecting a worldliness that shouldn't be seen in children's eyes.'

I paused and wondered whether I should be letting sleeping dogs lie for fear of inflaming the savagery that had threatened to tear me apart for so long.

'The night they died, Constance?' David prompted.

'It was Greek Night. My mum had made the koftes. I was in my room doing homework and the boys had been sent up to their room because they had been naughty. But they were play-fighting and laughing and jumping on and off the bed. I went to their room and shushed them. We all crept to the top of the stairs and held our breath, listening to the raised voices downstairs.

'My dad had received a letter from his brother in Cyprus that morning. His brother had told him that their father, my grandfather, had been banished from the village because he had been caught diddling my three-year-old cousin. My dad accused his brother and his brother's wife of lying. That was the day I decided I wanted nothing to do with my dad. He had been told what my grandfather had done to me. Here was indisputable proof that it had to be true. That I had been telling the truth. And he was still denying it. Because if he didn't, he would have to admit that he had allowed it to happen. I get that now.

'That's what they were arguing about: about my grandfather and what he had done to me and how my dad hadn't believed me. I became aware, immediately, of the familiar noises. The code red sounds. The "run to the rescue now before it gets too out of hand" indicators.

'It all got so huge so fast. We all ran downstairs. My mum was on the floor by the kitchen bin. Like she was refuse. By. The. Bin. My dad picked her up by her arm and twisted it hard behind her back. I thought he was going to break it. I couldn't believe what I was seeing. I was so mad. So terribly mad and impotent. We all pulled him off her and he was turning on each of us one by one, so it was a mess, because everyone was pulling and dodging and screaming.

'The koftes were all over the floor and we kept treading on them. It was quite funny but also very sad. My mum had been too tired to make them but she had made the effort and she had made them so beautifully and now they were nothing. It was all for nothing.'

I put out my cigarette. I wasn't going to smoke it. I picked up the Drambuie then decided against it. It smelled horrible.

'He insisted that we still went to Greek Night. We all got in the car. My mum sat in the back seat, trying to calm the boys. I was in the front seat. Everyone was shaken up and we were all trying to be normal again. My mum looked shattered, the boys were crying but trying to do it silently, everyone looked hollow and empty and he looked … it's hard to say in a few words, because it was complex. Replete? Like he'd just got a load off his mind. Like he'd just eaten the best dinner of his life. Like a big weight had been lifted off his shoulders. Like he'd just won a raffle. He was thriving. And we were all dying. And then I got out of the car and I refused to go, and he flared up again – he was incandescent with rage. I hated him so much. I just couldn't be in the car with him. Or any of them. I didn't want that to be my life. I thought, if I got in the car, I would somehow be signing a deal, agreeing to it, becoming a part of it. At that moment I hated them all. I think my mum could see that. I wish I had been able to give her a different message. I was selfish.

'He drove off and left me there, outside the house. I didn't have a coat or door keys. I could see my mum looking back at me as they drove away, she looked like all she was thinking about right then was me. And there was nothing she could do.'

I paused for a moment. No reason. I just fancied stopping for a sec. Marc and David said nothing. Just waited.

I could hear a faint intermittent buzzing somewhere in the room. I listened carefully, holding my breath. I stood and followed the grating noise. It was coming from somewhere behind my desk. I pulled the desk away from the wall. The bluebottle was on the floor, spinning on its back. Going round and round in senseless circles. It was fatigued and would stop between every few rotations for a couple of seconds and then start again, spinning and fizzing and going nowhere. Just getting more worn out. What a terrible way to end a life, I thought. Only half dead and no hope of ever flying again. I put it out of its misery.

'When the police came, do you know what the first thing I thought was?' I said, sitting down again. 'I thought, they don't come out for domestics. So, what are they doing here? I had been sitting on the doorstep. I remember Mrs Seagal from next door asking me if I was locked out. I said I'd forgotten my key but that my mum would be back soon. When the police car arrived, she came out again and told them I was a latchkey kid.

'I didn't know what it meant, but I remember the policeman asking if she was a friend of the family. She said no, and he told her to go back in her house.

'Auntie Roulla got out of the police car. Marios was there. He was crying. That's when I got confused. She kept telling me to come with them, but I wanted to know what was going on. Maybe one of the neighbours had heard the fight and reported it. Or maybe Auntie Roulla felt sorry for me and had come to get me when I failed to turn up for Greek Night. I knew, though. I knew he had killed them. I knew that night, in the kitchen, before we got in the car, that he was going to kill us all.'

I lit another cigarette and had a few puffs for want of something to do with my hands. I thought I might be going off smoking. It was starting to not taste nice and, now that my hair was longer, I could smell the smoke on it. I picked up a few strands of hair and brought them to my nose. Nasty.

I picked up a *Jackie* magazine and tried to read a poll they had done about whether people preferred showers or baths. Half the people said they felt a bath was more relaxing and deeper cleansing. The other half felt that it was like sitting in your own filth, so a shower was a fresher experience. I really did have to stop buying *Jackie* magazine if they were going to waste my time with a load of meaningless shit like that. I rolled the magazine up and threw it in the wastepaper basket.

'I asked Auntie Roulla to tell me what had happened. But she wasn't much help, to be honest. She'd gone completely off her rocker and was crying and saying things in Greek that I couldn't understand. She kept trying to kiss me, but she had spit in the corners of her mouth and I thought of how Mrs Pollard had told us that human saliva was more germy than a dog's, so I wouldn't let her.

'"There's been an accident," the policeman said. It wasn't an accident. I knew it then and I know it now. He's a lunatic behind the wheel at the best of times. It's like he likes to get you in an enclosed space so he can shut you in with all his madness, keep it all contained so it can bounce around and charge at you again and again. He loves the power. The control. Your lack of control. I saw how angry he was when he drove away that evening. I remember my mum looking at me through the back window as if she knew she would never see me again.

'When my dad came back from the hospital, he said the crash had been my fault. He said if I hadn't made up the lie about my grandfather, they wouldn't have rowed. He said if I hadn't got out of the car, they wouldn't have continued to argue and he would have seen the oncoming vehicle sooner and not had to swerve and hit the wall. He made me feel guilty, as if I was the reason for *everything*. I kept thinking, maybe he was right, you know? If I hadn't got out of the car, maybe I could have calmed things down. Maybe if I had helped with the boys and not gone to my room. Maybe if I had stayed in the kitchen to help with the koftes instead of being selfish. Maybe I could have changed the way things turned out. And until he said it again tonight, part of me had believed it. But the way he said it just now ... he doesn't believe it either. I was just a kid. He should have been protecting me. And them. Instead, he killed them. It wasn't the car crash. The car was just the artillery. It was him. His jealousy and psychotic need for control. I may have survived that night, but he's been killing me every day since. It's all him.'

I sighed. It was a casual sigh. More a deflation, really. What was done was done. There was an intense ringing in the room, as if there was a sound beyond silence, so still and stifling was the air. I could hear the ten o'clock news on the TV downstairs, tinny and far away. I could tell it was the news by the bongs. Bong: the world is about to end. Bong: the government are rubbish. Bong: someone murdered someone. Bong: the Queen's hat blew off. Bong: someone exploded a bomb somewhere. Bong: an old lady's cat got stuck up a tree. Bong: my family are dead and they're never coming back.

27

November, God help us all, heralded two things:

1. Friday, November 5th: my sixteenth birthday. No card from The Fat Murderer. Who was still ominously alive, because I was too obsessed with Vas and too busy studying for my Grade 8 classical guitar test to get my act together. Plus, A-levels were really hard work, much worse than O-levels.
2. Sunday, November 21st: the arrival of the wedding of Prince Marios Papachristodoullou to Adonia the Beautiful Demetriou.

As well as being rather busy with music and shagging, I had, frankly, run out of feasible ideas for (preferably painful but undetectable) patricide. Then, I had an unexpected breakthrough while watching an early Sunday morning American cop show: a tyre blew on a speeding car. The car hit a central reservation and turned over, bursting into flames, incinerating its driver. A beleaguered American detective surveyed the scene and picked up an object. 'What ya got there, chief?' said his congenial but hapless sidekick. 'This, here, Dan, is our murder weapon. A passivated drywall nail, 1 7/8s of an inch, if I'm not mistaken.' The jaded chief stared into the middle distance and continued, 'Caused a slow puncture. When driven at high speeds, an underinflated tyre is a blowout waiting to happen.' The chief took a brief drag on his smoke. 'Dan, we're looking for someone who knows their drywall.' Well, that was low-budget TV music to my ears! I had no idea what drywall was, but I knew how to stick a nail in a tyre. It was a lot easier than undetectable poisoning or elaborate electrocution; certainly a lot less messy than bashing my dad's head in with the onyx ashtray and less effort than strangling him with his tie. It really perked me up so much that I also crept into The Fat Murderer's room while he was still snoring his head off and took another twenty pounds to add to my Getaway Fund. I was up to one thousand two hundred and eighty pounds now. I was minted.

On the day of the wedding, I got up early and took a hammer and some tacks from the shed while trying not to see all the dead birds hanging there. I tapped two tacks into the nearside front tyre of the ghastly red Audi. The Fat Murderer would be going on the North Circular Road this morning, as he was picking up the buttonhole flowers for the wedding from the florist in Tottenham(s). He was bound to speed on that road. I was quite excited. By the time the wedding was over, I'd be free.

Greek weddings were huge and chaotic. They were an enormous, indulgent, mad, free-for-all bonanza where everyone ate, drank and danced to excess. If there wasn't at least one knife fight between waiters from rival restaurants, and at least one kid taken to hospital because he'd gone blind with alcohol poisoning, your wedding was a washout.

Adonia's mum and dad, the Demetrious, didn't have much money, but Uncle Mikis and Auntie Roulla owned a dress factory that made dresses for Debenhams. They were rich but they didn't flash it around in the same way as the

Petrideses. Except for now. They were going to make sure that their son's wedding superseded every other Greek bash this side of Cyprus, even if it was a shotgun wedding – or perhaps because it was.

It was The Big Day and Auntie Roulla was in her element. She had all the bridesmaids in the Petrideses' lounge: me (yes, I was a bridesmaid – much to Vas's unending amusement), Dopey Dina and a few other freaks I hadn't met before, who were relatives of either the Demetrious or the Papachristodoullous. She had her newly marooned hair in rollers under a hairnet and had adorned herself with every piece of jewellery she owned. She was jingling and jangling as she leant over me, all overbearing amounts of Rive Gauche perfume and light perspiration.

I was dressed like a giant fairy in a peach-coloured, floor-length satin creation. I had peach-coloured high-heeled satin shoes on and shiny flesh-coloured tights, which, I'm sure, were children's sized and were so tight that my legs looked like sausages about to burst. The dress was too snug around the waist and had made pillows out of my bosoms and belly. I looked like I'd been upholstered rather than clothed. And, of course, the shoes were too small. Auntie Roulla had got a job lot from a friend's factory and it was first come, first served. I hadn't been quick enough; I took a size six but all that was left was a size five. Dopey Dina took a five and had snagged a size six pair, but she wouldn't swap with me, because, she said, they came up small. Shoes would be the death of me.

'Constantina, why your headdress in your hand and not on your head, *agabi mou?*' said Auntie Roulla, poking my hair.

She had insisted I went to bed in hair curlers the previous

night and, at first light, had embarked on Project Big Hair. She had back-combed my existing hair and then pinned it over a false hairpiece that looked like a large hairy doughnut, which she balanced on the top of my head. The doughnut was much lighter than my own hair colour and there wasn't enough of my real hair to cover it sufficiently. Though Auntie Roulla sprayed the construction into a rock-hard shell, you could still see bits of the blonde hairpiece showing through.

She had delivered on her promise, though; my hair was certainly big. Like a voluminous empty bird's nest. She had topped it off with a rigid plastic peach-coloured tiara festooned with plastic peach blossoms, which I had taken off almost as soon as she had pinned it into place.

'Auntie, do I have to have this fake hair on?' I asked.

'Yes, Constantina, *mou*. Because you got no real hair,' she said irritably.

'But it's a different colour to my real hair. It's going to look stupid,' I moaned, hoping that, if we focused on the doughnut, she'd forget about the tiara. No such luck.

'It don't look stupid because it is covered up with your real hair and we put the headdress back on the top. Don't worry. You look gorgeous! Trust me.'

Auntie Roulla grabbed the tiara irritably out of my hand and started to pin it back onto what was supposed to pass for my hair, stabbing me in the scalp with hair grips. She spat on her fingers and used the spit to smooth down some of the displaced hair and then secured it all with another cloud of hairspray. My hand automatically went to my head. She slapped it back down.

'Constantina, you take this thing off one more time and I get very angry, okay?'

'Okay, Auntie,' I said, and stared despondently at my pinching satin shoes. 'Don't take them shoes off, Constantina, because your feets gonna blow up and you won't get them back on.'

'But Auntie, please, everything is so small ...' There was already a tiny hole in a side seam of my dress where the satin had begun to fray.

'Darling,' Roulla said, looking at me with an expression of candour, 'these not small. You just got fat,' she said, pinching my midriff with her newly varnished claws. 'Just don't breathe out till after the wedding, okay?'

She nodded over at the other freaks in peach.

'Talk to the other girls, Constantina. Don't be like you.'

I didn't give a toss about them, so didn't bother talking to them. It's not like we were going to be friends after the event, so it wasn't worth the investment.

Fortunately, it wasn't an issue, as, at that moment, Goulla and Doulla arrived with hefty makeup bags and grouted and plastered us with an orange foundation that worked for none of our skin tones. We had lurid blue half-moons for eyelids and crimson cheeks and lips. I looked like my dad. In drag.

We were all given a small plastic peach-coloured shoulder bag to wear, and each of us was supplied with a lipstick for touch-ups, a comb and a small bottle of hairspray. We were allowed a few personal items. I couldn't fit a book in there, so I just had my door keys and the piece of poetry that Vas had given me so long ago. I read it now for ballast: 'No plant now knew the stock from which it came; He grafts upon the wild the tame'. He must have had a premonition about me and my hairpiece.

The groom and his groomsmen were at Auntie Roulla's

house with Mr Papachristodoullou and my dad. The Fat Murderer had made the wedding suits for the men – double-breasted two-tone mohair with big lapels – and was supposed to be doing last-minute fittings and alterations, but was, no doubt, liberally ingratiating himself like a big fat murdering worm.

Adonia was at home with her mum. She was having a professional makeup woman coming in to do her hair and makeup. I hoped, for her sake, whoever it was had a lighter touch than the aunties.

At 2pm the bride arrived at the Petrideses', and she and her maids were bundled into a white Rolls-Royce adorned with fat white ribbons and balloons. There was a huge fuss made over loading Adonia's long dress train onto the laps of the bridesmaids, and we were given stern instructions not to allow it to become soiled.

The church part of the wedding was insane. Every Greek Cypriot in the entire universe was in attendance. We did the whole walk-up-the-aisle bit in a very haphazard formation, holding Adonia's dress, which, I noted bitterly, was not fucking peach-coloured but a very tasteful off-white. She couldn't have actual white, said Dumb Dina, on account of the fact that Marios had knocked her up. 'Those are the rules,' she had said. 'Only virgins can wear white.' 'Whose rules are they?' I had asked. 'God's,' said Dina. I honestly don't think she could tell her shoes from her feet, that one. She was that stupid.

It wasn't until we were halfway down the aisle that it became apparent we should have practised this bit. There's no 'Here Comes the Bride' music at Greek weddings. Had there been, we might have been able to have kept some sort of rhythm. As it was, everyone was shouting their heads off in

Greek and we were knocked sideways by the pandemonium. We were all moving at different speeds and we had to keep stopping, as Mr Demetriou, who was on Adonia's arm, kept pausing to chat to people he knew along the way. Then Dina accidentally stepped on the dress and Adonia was jerked backwards and we all stepped on each other's feet. Feet that were already in agony.

When we finally reached Marios at the front of the church, I was shocked. I had always thought of him as the eldest of us freaks, fully formed and adult. But now I saw he was just a kid, like us. He looked like a little boy in grown-ups' clothes, two sizes too big. Adonia was only two years his senior, but looked much bigger and older than him. She looked like she could be his mum. I had a hard time imagining them snogging, let alone having sex and making a (undoubtedly hairy) baby.

I was deflated to observe that The Fat Murderer was not, as I had hoped, lying mangled and dead on the North Circular Road, but was alive and standing next to Mr Papachristodoullou, trying to look significant and failing miserably. He was sporting a white carnation and a fiercely smug expression. Maybe English tyres were better quality than American ones. Maybe it was just a very slow puncture and he'd get the lethal blowout later, on his way home.

The ceremony was infinite and beyond tedious. The priest rambled on in Greek for literally years. I mean, what is there to say? Do you, large older-looking lady, take this small schoolboy to be your lawfully wedded husband? Yes? Good. And do you want her? Yes. You're married and it serves you both right. Amen. Job done.

Instead, there was a lot of swapping around of headdresses

between the bride and groom, dabbing of stinky stuff on heads, wafting of incense and general claptrap for eons. The priest smelled of whisky and bergamot. I wished I had a nip of whisky.

Even though it was November, it was boiling in the church. I had started to sweat. I was top of a very sweaty sweat league. I bet it could be proved scientifically that Greeks have more sweat glands than other nationalities. If there was a Sweating World Cup, the Greeks would play the Turks in the final, and win.

Sweat had started to trickle from under my bosoms, making my bra feel tight and scratchy. My head itched and the tiara dug in at the sides, making my temples ache. My too-small tights had gone renegade on me. The waistband had begun to roll down and had created a kind of extra tyre around my hips. The crotch had fallen and had created what my mum used to call a 'parcel' between my legs. I tried pulling them up surreptitiously through my dress but the dress was too tight and slippery for me to get any real purchase.

My feet were killing me in my stupid satin child-sized shoes. I had been hopping from foot to foot for about an hour to try to give each foot a period of respite. But it was no good. They had to come off. I prized one off and my foot popped out of it like a cork. The relief of the cold church floor on my burning sole was divine deliverance. Auntie Roulla was right. I couldn't get it back on again. I took off the other shoe and kicked them both towards Vas, who was sitting in one of the front pews and hadn't stopped staring incredulously at me throughout the entire ceremony. He was really enjoying this. It was payback for The Plaster Over the National Health Spectacles Debacle of Christmas 1975. My dad, eagle eyes all over me, shot me a warning look. How dare he? I felt The Monster inside me rear up slightly.

At the back of the church, it was bedlam. So large was the crowd that most of the people who had come to the wedding ceremony had to wait outside. As large herds drifted out for a smoke and a snack, larger ones drifted in for a look, while the kids climbed over the pews and dropped food everywhere. Everyone was talking at the tops of their voices, trying to be heard above the rising clamour. The priest was shouting louder and louder to be heard above the cacophony. Then he started singing in his holy voice, saying Kyrie Eleisons, swinging incense into people's faces. No one took much notice of either the singing or the incense. They just carried on eating and yelling. Once in a while, someone would cross themselves just to keep the holy theme going, but it was cursory at best.

Finally, the hellish shebang was over and we turned to walk back up the aisle. Adonia and her mum faffed about with her dress and made us all get back into formation. As I started to walk, on tiptoes so that no one would notice I didn't have my high heels on, my tights decided to complete their downwards journey and rolled to my ankles. Thus shackled, I could only take tiny steps, which meant I had to totter along at double speed to keep up with the other bridesmaids. I looked back at Vas, whose shoulders were shaking helplessly. I started to laugh too. I caught my dad's eye as our procession passed by him and my Monster flipped him the finger.

28

The reception took place at Walthamstow(s) Town Hall, where I was in the ladies' toilets, wriggling out of those recalcitrant tights. I had tried pulling them up countless times, I had even tried putting my knickers on over them, but whichever way I tried it, gravity always won.

I was in the first cubicle, because I had read an article that had said this was likely to be the least used and, therefore, the least bacterially infested. The article said to never use cubicle two, as you might as well eat faeces. I left the door open to allow any microbes free egress as an extra precaution. I was trying not to let my bare feet touch the floor and had placed squares of toilet paper on the chipped green tiles. Thankfully the town-hall people had seen sense and equipped the loos with Izal Medicated toilet paper. It had no absorbent properties whatsoever, but it was hygienic.

Just as I was stepping out of my tights with the knickers attached, Auntie Roulla burst through the entrance to the toilets, door banging in her wake, echoing around the cold hard surfaces. She looked deranged.

'Constantina, *agabi mou*, what you doing?'

I thought it was pretty evident that I was taking off my tights and knickers, but nevertheless . . .

'Taking off my tights and knickers. They keep falling down.'

'Don't be silly, Constantina. They stretch. One size fit all. Put them back on.'

'No! Auntie, they don't fit me. *They're too small.*'

Auntie Roulla waved her hand as if weighing up something.

'*Mila kai portokali.* Is apples the tights is too small, is oranges you too big.'

'I'm not bloody wearing them. And this dress is too small as well. And the shoes. Can't I just change into my normal clothes?'

Auntie Roulla's nostrils flared to twice their usual size and her eyes bugged out at me as she leant into the cubicle.

'*Gaouli mavro . . .*'

She snatched the tights with my knickers attached and shoved them in her handbag.

'You don't take that dress off tonight. I mean it, Constantina. You are my lovely girl. I like you better than Adonia, *O Theos* forgive me, is shame you not Greek enough to marry my Marios, but you are very hard work.'

I knew what she meant. I let that one go.

'Constantina, put fresh lipstick on, please.'

'I've lost it.' I'd thrown it away.

She fished around in her handbag and produced a bright red lipstick, which she ran around my lips.

'Where is your hairspray?'

'I've lost it.' I'd thrown it away.

She closed her eyes for a small minute, trying to regain what was left of her ragged composure, spat on her fingers and smoothed my escaped hair upwards, poking it into the hole in the doughnut, then repositioned the tiara.

'Are you sad Marios is married, then, Auntie?' I said, artfully, as I began to roll my dress back down over my thighs.

I hadn't really given much thought to how this whole pregnancy shotgun marriage might have affected Auntie Roulla. She'd done such a good job of putting on an ecstatic face. I could see now that she was tired of the façade.

'They so young,' she said defeatedly, slumping against the toilet door. 'Life is so short and so precious. My Marios was hole-in-the-heart miracle child. He was so small and weak. I did a deal with God. I said, "God, if you let my boy live, I will make sure his life is perfect." I tried so hard for him to have this good life. Not for him to make a girl pregnant and get married while he is still a teenager. His life is not free now. He has responsibilities. It's too soon.'

'But why did they have to get married, Auntie?' I asked.

'To hide the shame,' she said.

Auntie Roulla looked devastated. I felt incredibly sad for Marios, and also a bit remorseful for contemptuously calling him Prince Marios. All that pressure to be the perfect son and now he was being forced into a marriage he wasn't ready for, just to save face.

'Adonia is nice, though, Auntie,' I offered. 'And she's really pretty.'

Auntie Roulla nodded sadly.

'At least Marios didn't shag Dopey Dina, eh?' I said, eyebrows raised suggestively.

'*Alithkia*. Very true. If I cut her head open, I would find a cauliflower in there.'

'Auntie! I'm telling!' I teased.

'Don't you tell, you cheeky. Or I tell everything on you! And

I got more on you. I see you and Vasoulakis!' She raised her eyebrows back at me, as if to say 'got you there'.

She started rooting around in her handbag for her perfume.

'What? Does everyone know?' I gasped.

'No, just me. Everyone is thinking that Vasos will turn out to be a nancy boy. Because he's soft and reading the poems.' She found her Rive Gauche and gave us both a generous spritz. I coughed. She pinched my nose, gave me a kiss on both cheeks, and gripped me in a vice-like hug. She smelled of the Rive Gauche and fried onions, which I found strangely comforting. 'Make Vasos wear the rubber johnnies if you making sex, yes? Don't have a baby.'

'Er...'

'Come on, let's feed you and make you happy. You looking too thin.'

'Auntie, can I just have my knickers back, please?'

'Is okay, no one going to see your froufrou. Nice to get some air. Keep your legs together, though.'

It's too late for that, I thought hilariously to myself.

I followed Roulla through the double doors into the reception hall. The heat and noise hit like a tsunami. The stink of perfumes and armpits, spirits and food rolled across the room. Shouting and laughter and music came crashing down, dragging me under, drawing the breath from my lungs, turning me upside down.

The bad-tempered, heavily perspiring waiters wore tight black trousers and white shirts and smelled of cigarettes and new sweat on top of old sweat. They moved like dancers through the tables, delivering plates of nuts and chickpeas, hummus and tahini, souvlaki, seftalia, dolmas, pastries, koftes and mountains and mountains of hard, sour Greek bread.

And everyone was in their best finery and in full showing-off mode. The ladies wore faces thick with makeup, waving varnished fingernails, clattering their 24-carat Cyprus gold, bustling across the room from table to table to catch up on or to instigate fresh gossip, stopping occasionally to spit-wipe a child or two.

The men were grouped at the tables, ties off and shirt buttons undone, jackets on the backs of chairs. They leant in closely, plotting and eating and knocking back the whisky, with a hand slap on the tabletop every so often. Business was done here, alliances made, marriages brokered.

The dance floor at the far end of the hall was full, although I don't know how they could hear what they were dancing to. Right now, a DJ was playing Nana Mouskouri, who was fighting to be heard over about a thousand excitable Greek Cypriots all communicating at top volume.

I had lost sight of Auntie Roulla. I couldn't see anyone I knew. I was knickerless and marooned. And I was hungry and thirsty. I hadn't eaten since breakfast and had sweated out pretty much all my bodily fluids. I looked around for Vas but couldn't see him. I looked, instead, for somewhere to sit and refuel. There were six or seven rows of tables, which ran lengthways along the hall. Each row held monumental displays of alcohol and cans upon cans of anapsyktika. The Greeks love their anapsyktika. If there was a fizzy drinks Wimbledon, it would be game, set and match to Cyprus.

I took a seat halfway down one of the less populated tables. I took a glass from the centre and poured myself a large whisky. A waiter pranced over, deftly removed the whisky from my grasp and placed a bottle of warm, flat Pomagne in front of me. 'This is a nice drink for the ladies,' he said, with a greasy smile and a boob graze. 'Fuck off,' I replied, and grabbed the whisky back and knocked it down in one gulp. Sexist prick.

I took a lump of bread and drew a plate of tahini nearer to me. I started to swallow bread and tahini in huge mouthfuls, barely chewing. I poured another whisky.

The whisky and the food made me start to perspire again. I parted my knees as much as my dress would allow to let some air up into my 'froufrou'. It was bliss. I sat back and looked over the cavernous room. Still no Vas. I could see guests moving to the edge of the dance floor. Making space in the middle. The DJ went off and a live band kicked in with 'Siko Horepse Sirtaki'. It was time for the bride and groom to perform their money dance. I got up and wandered over to observe with the other onlookers. Marios and Adonia each had hold of the corner of a handkerchief, which they twisted and curled as they circled one another in slow deliberation to the bouzouki music. When the handkerchief became too twisted, Marios would snap it away from Adonia, flap it and untwist it and then she would take up her corner again and the whole process would start all over. I thought this had to be an analogy for married life, but I was a little too tipsy to work it out. Plus, I didn't care much. As long as it wasn't me getting married. It was a mug's game.

The Fat Murderer was the first to pin some money on the bride. The obsequious cretin. Five twenty-pound notes, one after the other so that there was no doubt about how much he was giving. He then held the pin box so that other people could collect one and pin their money on the couple. The richer they were, the more money they would pin on. Uncle Mikis was standing by, checking who had been generous and who hadn't, which I thought was in bad taste, as not everyone had as much money as he did. I felt sorry for the poorer people, because they were being shown up. It wasn't their fault they were poor. I hoped that I wouldn't end up poor, though – it was a shit life.

Before long the hapless couple were covered in cash, it was wafting and trailing and fluttering as they twirled and whirled. My dad spotted me, pressed a pin and a fiver into my hand, making sure that Mr Papachristodoullou saw, and gestured for me to go up and pin it on the bride. I stuck the pin in her dress and tucked the fiver down my bra. I think my dad saw it, but what was he going to do? I had two very large whiskies and a Monster inside me. I was indestructible.

29

I stood back at the perimeter again, watching and feeling a bit like a spare part, when I felt a poke from behind me that landed right in my bum crack. I turned to remonstrate, but it was Vas.

'Oi oi!' he said cheerily. He was even taller now and lankier. He smelled of whisky and cigarettes. He was a bit tipsy too. I felt a reckless flutter in my stomach. I had the urge to kiss him right there and then in front of everyone. I turned my back to him and continued to watch the money machine march on.

Vas did a loud burp down my ear from behind me and then said, over my shoulder: 'Where you been, Conno? I've been all over looking for you.'

'No, you haven't.'

'I bloody have. Here's your shoes. I brought them from the church.' He dropped them on the floor by my feet, which were filthy but cooler now and less swollen. I managed to squeeze the shoes back on.

Vas slipped his arms around my waist and leant into me. 'I *have* been looking for you. I'm feeling quite randy.'

'Randy? Who says randy?'

'I do. I am randy.' He kissed my neck.

'Vas, everyone's going to see!' I whispered, and shirked away from him, giving a sideways glance at my dad who was, of course, clocking everything.

'Fuck 'em.'

'Fuck 'em?'

'Yeah, fuck 'em. I'm sixteen, you're sixteen. It's legal. It's natural.'

I turned my head to look at him over my shoulder.

'We don't come from a natural world.'

'For God's sake, hold your tongue, and let me love.'

I rolled my eyes.

'I don't think my dad would consider quoting John Donne a good enough reason to allow a public display of affection. He'll think we're fucking.'

'We *are* fucking,' said Vas, with a hoarseness to his voice which meant he really was feeling 'randy'.

The wedding dance onlookers had dispersed and a few people had started to float onto the dance floor to the band's vocalist not quite pulling off Demis Roussos' epicene falsetto. 'Ever and ever and forever and ever you'll beeeee the one . . .' I hated that song.

'God, do you think that will be either of us one day?' said Vas, looking over at Adonia and Marios. *Either* of us. Not *us*. This was not the first time Vas had intimated that he had no intention of ending up with me. I had always proclaimed I'd never get married, not even to Marc Bolan or Dave Gilmour out of Pink Floyd, but that was just kids' stuff and I knew they weren't really real. But Vas was really real, and the thought of either of us being with someone else was unconscionable.

'What do you reckon, Conno?' he said, tightening his embrace and resting his chin on my shoulder. He had a bit of a stiffy, I noticed. I could feel it in my back. It made me nervous. I had worked hard to keep Vas and I a secret, and now stupid, drunk Vas was blowing it for both of us.

I turned to face him.

'That's very specific wording, Vasos Petrides.'

'Huh?'

'What do you mean, *either of us*? What? Are we just doing it until you find someone better? Am I not Greek enough for you either? Why don't you go and stick your feeble knob in Dina's back and marry her? I bet she can't wait to become a part of the archaic institution of Greek female slavery. She'll be right up your street. You can be king of the patriarchy and she can be your nice Greek serving lady.'

'What the fuck, Conno? It was just a turn of phrase. I meant *nothing* by it.' Vas held both hands up in supplication. He looked hurt and confused. I noticed his semi had miraculously abated. That made me feel sorry for him. Vas had been all perky and now I had flattened him – in spirit and in body. I felt bad. Though, on the bright side, it was very metaphysical. He'd probably look back and appreciate this moment.

The fierce wind went out of my sails and was instantly replaced with a gentler breeze. I looked at Vas.

'I'm sorry,' I said. 'My dress is too tight and this thing round my head is killing me. And I fucking hate this wedding.' And that Fat Murderer is still alive and bogging at me continuously, I wanted to say, but refrained.

Vas, being Vas, was always ready to move away from the bad towards the good.

'Let's slow-dance,' he said, one eyebrow cocked. He moved in till our bodies were touching. Daring me.

'Vas, you wouldn't be suggesting this if you weren't all whiskied up.'

He moved in closer still, pressed against me.

'Yeah, maybe you're right, Conno. But maybe we need to get whiskied up now and then. Walk a wobbly walk.'

'What do you mean, walk a wobbly walk?'

He looked down at me, his jaw tight. He took his glasses off and put them in his trouser pocket. He had little red marks either side of his nose. He sounded serious now.

'I can't walk in these straight lines for the rest of my life.' He gestured around the room as if to demonstrate. 'Neither can you. You know you can't. We weren't made to fit. I feel like I'm constantly waiting for Armageddon to arrive and I'm always trying to prevent it. I feel like messing it up a bit.' He pulled me close, pressing his cheek against mine and whispered throatily, 'Fuck. Them.'

This wasn't the first time Vas had wanted to tear it all down in public. I recalled The Great Cinema Showdown of 1976 and I understood it better now. That wasn't just about not wanting to marry Dina, or not wanting to be a furrier. It was about Vas daring to be who he wanted to be. We weren't so different.

He pulled back and stared at me for a moment. He traced my bottom lip with his fingertip.

'Why does everything have to be a major secret? Why are we forced to lie and hide? Why do we have to feel bad for who we are and what we want?' he said, sadly. He wasn't just talking about us. He had had The Calling too. I was sure of it.

I kissed his fingertip, which was resting on my lips now.

'All I want to do is have a dance with my girl. Is that so wrong?' His gaze was steady. 'Conno, will you please fucking slow-dance with me?'

'Yes,' I said, putting my arms around his neck. 'Let's slow-dance . . . to this terrible, terrible music.'

I think, for the first time ever, I felt like I was becoming a real adult, even more so than when I was allowed to call Ms Liz Liddle 'Liz'. This felt . . . like a tipping point. This was a decision I was making for me. For us. I checked with my Monster, and it had settled. I wasn't scared. I didn't look around to see who was watching. I just leant into my friend's warm, slightly odorous body and let him move me to the music. As the fake Demis finished warbling his bonkers symphony of love, Vas held me there, on the dance floor, breathing gently, his chest rising and falling against my own. The band segued into a hellishly Hellenic version of 'I'm Not in Love' by 10cc. We began to move slowly, melding into one another.

'I forgot to say earlier, you look absolutely awful by the way, Conno,' he said into my ear.

'I know,' I answered.

'I mean, really, truly hideous.'

'Yes. I know.'

'I mean, worse than all the other bridesmaids.'

'What? Worse than Dina?'

'Much worse.'

'Thank you. Auntie Roulla thinks you're a nancy boy.'

'Everyone thinks I'm a nancy boy.'

He let his hands slide down to the base of my spine.

'Where are your knickers?' he said feeling around the space where they should have been.

'In Auntie Roulla's handbag.'

'Of course they are.'

I would have liked that dance to have gone on for much longer, but it was aborted about halfway through. The Greeks didn't have much patience for slow-dancing. And they certainly didn't have much patience for 10cc. Uncle Mikis signalled the band to stop playing and had a quick word with the band leader, who nodded. The musicians started tuning up their bouzoukis and lyras.

A buzz went round the room and more people moved onto the dance floor. Everyone knew what was coming. 'The Kalamatianos,' said Vas. 'The what?' I asked. 'The bloody circle dance,' he replied with an eye roll. I'd taken part in this ritual dance before and it was utterly unfathomable to me: it involved several circles of people all going in different directions. I never knew which way I was supposed to be going and always ended up treading on everyone's feet. I could see Auntie Roulla making a beeline for me. And my dad wasn't far behind her.

'Shall we get out of here?' said Vas, seeing what was coming.

'Yes!' I said, feeling bold and elated and rebellious all at once.

Vas took my hand and pulled me through the crowd, grabbing an open bottle of wine from a table.

We ran, laughing, through the main doors and out onto the expansive forecourt of the town hall. It felt good to be away from the heat and the noise. The air was cool and soothing. We sat on the broad edge of the huge water fountain at the centre of the town hall's expansive frontage. Now that it was dark, the fountain was lit up and glittered like an immense, infinite crystal chandelier. Every droplet glistened as it was tossed into the air and then, meeting its crystalline acquaintances, cascaded down like showers of ecstatic diamonds; as if their sole purpose was to shine for our pleasure. We were high. We laughed at everything. Until we were silent.

It was quiet out here. Just us, and a lone waiter across the terrace, smoking a cigarette, and the sound of distant traffic.

The air was cold now.

Vas passed me the bottle of wine and I took a deep drink.

I was very thirsty. He guzzled down a good slug as well. I felt instantly woozy and warm. It was exquisite.

'God, Conno, we did it, didn't we? We went public,' said Vas, shaking his head slowly from side to side.

'Yep. Cat's out of the bag now.'

'Do you think you'll get it when you get home?'

I thought about it. I thought about my Monster, shielding me. And I thought about Auntie Roulla and her protective evil eye, which was all over my dad. And I thought about how I wasn't scared any more. How I was impermeable. I thought that, whatever my dad did to me, he couldn't affect me unless I allowed it. He could hit me, but the pain would always stop. He could touch me, but I could rewrite the memories and replace them with better ones now that I had them. Whatever he did to me, I could make myself untouchable.

'No.' I drank some more wine and passed it back to Vas.

We sat and said nothing for some time, passing the wine back and forth until it was gone and we were both good and drunk. Vas nudged me.

'Conno, I'm feeling horny again. Is there anything you can think of to help me out?'

'Wobbly walk or not, I'm not being caught *in flagrante* outside the town hall!'

'Fair enough,' said Vas. Then . . . 'Not even a han—'

'No.'

We were quiet again for some time. Vas was first to speak.

'You know—'

'I said *no* . . .'

'No, not that. I don't feel like it now. I've just realised, you smell like Auntie Roulla. It's put me off a bit.'

'She sprayed me with Rive Gauche. It's horrible, isn't it?'

'That misunderstanding we had back there . . .'

'I said I'm sorry and I really meant it.' I did too.

'No, I mean, yeah, but what I mean is, that wasn't really our argument, you know?'

'Well, it was mostly my argument, wasn't it?' I admitted shamefully.

'It's *their* argument. Their stupid old ways from the old country. We wouldn't be arguing if we weren't tiptoeing around them and each other all the time. Let's promise not to let their hang-ups be our hang-ups. It will tear us to pieces if we don't protect what we have.'

'Okay.'

'Promise?'

'I promise.'

I was shivering a little now. I thought how gallant it might be if Vas had a jacket to put around my shoulders. Like in the films. But, typically, Vas wasn't wearing one.

'I'm cold,' I said, stating the obvious.

'Me too.' Vas put his arm round my shoulders.

'Your skinny little chicken arms aren't going to warm me up, are they?' I said, derisively.

'Well, I was rather hoping you could warm me up with your enormous rolls of fat,' he said in return, snuggling up.

We both smiled, then. That was undeniably our most precious confession of love for one another. We would never top this moment. This was our time. We were young, we were brave, we were in love, we were both ready to face the worlds we would create for ourselves. We knew our worlds wouldn't collide. We were going in different directions already. But for now, we both knew that we had this. And we were going to look after it. Each other. That was enough.

'Thank you for bringing my shoes,' I said.

Usually, I didn't think about Marc Bolan and David Bowie when I was with Vas, but I thought of them now, waiting at home for me, my dear friends, there in the realms of my waking dreams. I would have a less sorry story to tell them this evening.

30

I knew that something wasn't right the moment I got to the front door. I could feel it in the ether, like red dust rising before an earthquake. It was 2am and the red Audi was parked in the drive. The night around the house was cold and still, vacuous. There was no birdsong. There was one light on in the house. Mine.

I fished around for my door keys in my plastic peach-coloured shoulder bag. I clutched the keys with numb fingers. I didn't see the poem from Vas, which I had stashed in the bag earlier today, flutter to the floor. I pressed the key into the keyhole, but the door swung open at my touch. I stepped inside.

I had left the wedding around midnight. My dad was involved in some backgammon tournament when I told him I wanted to go home because my feet hurt. He looked irritated that I had disturbed him. I was also smirking quite cockily and breathing out booze fumes, so they might also have been contributory factors to his goat being got. He said I had to stay because it was my duty as a bridesmaid to be there until Marios and Adonia had left. I pointed out that they were going to be there until the bitter end and the end was nowhere in sight. I reckoned they were probably lasting it out, trying to delay the start of their lives together for as long as possible; I didn't blame them. The prospect of going from exciting illicit nookie to married mediocrity and a screaming kid in the Papachristodoullous' second-best bedroom wouldn't be my preferred lifestyle choice either.

Auntie Roulla had bustled over. She gave him her look. Her look was a bit mad now, as she was tired and was on her second wind, which was never a good thing.

'She's tired,' she had said to my dad in clipped tones. 'I make sure she get home safe. I put her in one of the cars now. Come on, Constance, get your shoulder bag and say goodbye to Marios and Adonia.'

My dad turned back to his game. He said nothing more.

As she ushered me away, I heard Auntie Roulla mumble under her breath, '*Pezevengi*.' She really hated my dad. It was good to have a kindred hate-spirit. That made three of us: me, The Monster and Roulla. The Triumvirate of Triumph!

I was saying my goodbyes to Marios and Adonia when Auntie Roulla was called away. Typically, a kid had gone from table to table draining all the remnants of undrunk drinks and was now in a state of collapse.

'*Banayiamou!*' said Roulla, in annoyance, 'Constantina, *agabi mou*, wait here and I come back and walk you to the Mercedes driver. I get Kyriakos to drive you home.'

'Don't worry, Mum,' said Marios. 'I'll walk her to a taxi. We haven't spoken all night, have we, Con?'

'I'll go too,' said Vas, slurring slightly.

The Papachristodoullous had hired cars for the night from the Apostolos Andreas Taxi office in Leytonstone. Five Mercedes-Benz cars were parked outside the town hall, on standby to ferry people home if they were too drunk to manage it themselves. Most people were quite happy to drink and drive, so the taxis had remained mostly empty. Vas, Marios and I walked across the bright, chilly concourse, past the untiring crystal fountain and out of the main gates to the line of waiting cars.

'So, you two have a good evening?' asked Marios. He took off his jacket and put it around my shoulders.

'It's been brilliant,' I said. I meant it too. I glanced at Vas.

'Yeah, really good, thanks,' said Vas, looking first at Marios then at me and then back at Marios and blushing slightly.

'So, for once I don't need to ask what you two have been up to,' Marios said, with a stern smile, folding his arms across his shirt front, 'because I think we all know the answer.'

Vas and I both shrugged, uselessly.

'Look,' said Marios, 'it's none of my business. And you know what, it's none of anyone's damn business. But don't do what we did. *Me and Adonia*,' he said, to make sure we understood when he got no response from either of us.

'Look, you do what you want to do, okay? But I suppose, what I'm saying is, I wish me and Adonia had done all our dancing in public. Look where doing it in private took us . . .'

Vas and I nodded in unison.

'Everything will be fine,' I said to Marios. 'You're Auntie Roulla's Miracle Hole-in-the-Heart Prince. You've got a charmed life.'

'Yeah, maybe . . .' he replied.

He gave me a kiss on the cheek.

'I'll leave you two lovebirds to it, then.' He turned and walked off without a glance. He had a slump in his stride that made me want to call him back and tell him that we could all run away together and escape right now if we just jumped in a car and told the driver to go somewhere, anywhere, towards that indefinable someplace else that The Calling had tried to lure me towards. But, of course, I didn't.

We waited until he had gone back inside and then Vas and I faced each other.

'Good night, Conno.'

'Good night, Vasso.'

We kissed, lightly brushing lips, once, twice, three times.

'You know,' he said.

'I know,' I said.

'And I know too, yeah?' he said.

'Yeah,' I said.

I got into the back of the car and watched him begin to walk away. He suddenly turned and ran back and motioned for me to unwind the window.

'What?' I asked.

'Just checking that you know what I meant when I said that you know and I know?'

'Yeah. It means you love me. And you know that I love you too. Doesn't it?'

'Yeah. Oh, good. We're clear, then.'

'I don't know why you just didn't say that instead of wasting all this time.' I smiled.

He reached inside the car and gave me a proper kiss with tongues and then did something he had never done before: he drew my bottom lip between his teeth and gave a small proprietorial bite. It was incredibly sexy. 'I do love you, Conno. I do.'

I asked the driver to stop a mile or so away from my house. I had warmed up in the car and wanted to get out and walk, to prolong the evening, to wrap myself in these new dreams and hopes, to relive every sensation, every moment, to replay that same moment, that same dance, that same kiss, that same sentence. That bite.

I waited for the car to disappear and then took my shoes off and rashly dropped them into a bin in the front garden of the house I was standing by. I put my arms through Marios's jacket. It was quite tight. Either I *was* getting fat or Marios was really small. I didn't care. I felt beautiful. I had danced with a boy. Not a pancake-faced, tapeworm-harbouring creep like Calvin Belding of The School Disco Disaster of 1975, but a boy with whom I was intimate. A boy with a beautiful long Grecian nose and thick dark lashes, black curls drifting down his neck. A boy who made me aware of my body, the way it moved. A boy who elevated my mind. Someone who made me proud to be me. I was validated because someone as good as Vasos loved me. No one else. Me. Beautiful me.

A blackbird was singing its heart out somewhere nearby, sweet and unbridled, its lover singing back from high across the treetops, a flurry of notes cutting though the darkness. The air was biting. I took several deep mouthfuls. I walked slowly away from home and towards the main road, in my bare feet, checking the pavement for dog shit and sharp objects.

I was no longer tired and decided to sit on a bench on the high street, feet tucked up under my dress for warmth. I opened my bag and pulled out the piece of paper with the quotation from Marvell's 'The Mower Against Gardens', written in Vas's neat, slanted hand.

> *No plant now knew the stock from which it came;*
> *He grafts upon the wild the tame*

It took on a new meaning now. I was the wild. He was the tame. We were one.

I watched a melancholy fox scouting for scraps. He stood still and stared back, not unkindly. It was some while before I realised that time had passed. I walked the rest of the way home barely feeling the cold ground under my feet.

Now I stood at the foot of the stairs. I wasn't breathing. I could hear noises I hadn't heard before. I was confused. Maybe it was Peter Pervy Roy finding out just what I had up in my bedroom. Maybe it was a burglar. Or a poltergeist. Soraya had once said that if I kept practising telekinesis, I might summon a spirit accidentally. I knew it was none of those things.

I walked slowly up, step by silent step. I got to the top of the stairs and looked around the corner and along the hallway. My bedroom door was open, the light was on and someone was there.

In a trance-like state, I walked into the room. My dad was in there in just these brown Y-front underpants, his huge belly sticking out over the waistband and the Y part slightly falling open. He looked crazed. His face was engorged with blood, swollen and incensed. His remnant hair was like a malicious clown's wig, sticking out in all directions. His short, thick limbs were demonic, bestial. He was sweating and breathing heavily. He was breaking my records one by one by slapping them down sharply on my desk

'Stop,' I said, lamely. 'Stop.' I searched for The Monster to find he had swapped sides and was standing diabolically beside my dad, eyes glinting, and with a grin that said, 'You fool, Constance, you didn't really think I'd be on your side, did you? We monsters have strength in numbers. We stick together.'

My dad saw me now. He grinned with malevolence like an old cuckold who had found his ultimate revenge. He looked happier than I had ever seen him. Like he was delighted I could join them both.

'Is this the fackin' shit you listening to?' he said, pausing just for a moment before slapping down *The Dark Side of the Moon*.

'W'as this fackin' shit?' he said, smashing down Dylan and Santana.

I rushed into the room and pushed him away from the record pile.

'STOP! Stop!' I screamed.

He stamped spitefully on the remaining pile at his feet.

'You fucking bastard!' I screamed, pushing him away from the records and scrambling to pick up the ones that weren't yet in pieces.

'You calling your father a fackin' bastard?!' he screamed back. 'I'll show you who is the fackin' bastard.' He pulled me by my ear and dragged me across the floor, shoving me into the wall, where I slumped.

He turned to David Bowie. 'Who is this fackin' bastard?' he said, ripping him off the wall and tearing him into pieces.

'NO!!!!' I shouted. 'No, please, please ...' I got up and ran to cover Marc Bolan with my body. The Fat Murderer shoved me aside and ripped him down too.

'No ... no ... not him, please, no ...' I was whimpering. I fell to the floor, legs no longer able to keep me upright.

He ripped them all down, tearing them into two, three pieces, screwing them up and throwing them at me. He scooped up my books from the shelves in armfuls – 'Is this the shit where you getting your ideas from?' – took them out of the room and threw them down the stairs. 'I put them in the rubbish.'

'I hate you,' I sobbed. 'I hate you so much, you murdering fucking bastard.'

'I show you who is the bastard,' he said. He loomed above

me, his open hand suspended, as if he were mustering extra force to deliver his blow.

'Go on, do it, then,' I screamed, while, inside, I knew I would be okay no matter what happened next. 'You can't touch me.' I sort of snorted a laugh. 'You can do anything you want to me, but it won't go inside. You have no power. You only see my shell. You don't know who I am. You can't DO ANYTHING TO ME.' A hysterical noise came out of me.

For some reason The Fat Murderer stepped backwards and lowered his hand. He grasped a pile of *Jackie* magazines and threw them at my head and returned to his task: complete annihilation. I had no idea how long it went on and what happened, because time had slowed and my consciousness was suspended.

Once he had finished destroying everything and everyone, he hovered over me and spat in my face. 'Look at you. You fackin' joke. You fat lump, you fackin' fat lump. Nobody will ever want you.' Then, just as he was leaving, he took a step back, saw David Gilmour on the back of the door, and ripped him down as well. In a way I was glad. I couldn't have looked David in the eye ever again after what he'd just witnessed.

I waited. I wanted to be certain he wasn't coming back. I heard him dressing, whomping down the stairs, then clattering in the kitchen; the jangle of keys and, finally, the front door slammed. It opened again and then shut quietly: The Monster, loyal and in tow.

What I really wanted now was to talk to David and Marc, but he had killed them. Oh, I knew they were just fucking posters, I always *knew*. So what? I needed to believe they were real because I was alone and young and they were all I had and they were safe; we were all safe in my imagination because it was the only place The Fat Murderer couldn't reach.

I walked over to my dressing table and looked in the mirror. What a mess. What a hideous, awful, laughable, hateful mess. How did I ever think I was beautiful? I had been so deluded.

My stupid thin English hair had come undone on one side and hung down in a lacquered clump; the plastic peach blossoms on the tiara had fallen off and got stuck in there somehow. The fake-hair doughnut had slipped forward and dangled tragically over my eyebrows. My dress was filthy and the seams had started to pull apart and fray in several places. Marios's horrible wedding-suit jacket was stretched tight across the tops of my arms, making them look distorted.

My old friend, bile-bitter shame, flooded through me like venom. Oh my God. Was this what Vasos had been looking at when he said he loved me? It had to have been pity.

'What are you looking at?' I spat at my reflection, through gritted teeth. 'You are useless. You are worthless. You are a nothing.'

A familiar numbing tingle had begun to work through my body. My face was becoming blurred around the edges, fragmenting, pieces breaking away and drifting. I watched with grim fascination as, piece by piece, my muscle and bone floated upwards and dissolved. Becoming the nothing I was always meant to be. So dark and woozy and nice to be nobody at all. God, it felt good just to let go, going, going . . .

. . . but not gone. No. Not gone. Not yet. From somewhere deep inside the darkest part of my brain there was a small light flickering. I wanted so badly to just go. But I wanted to be the one who survived. I didn't want to be nothing. 'You're not nothing.' Vas's words from that blessed Christmas evening when we had first put our bodies together and touched. And tonight . . . 'I love you, Conno, I do . . .' It had to be real. *It had to be.* I had felt it. I had known it. Galvanised, I grasped, with trembling fingertips, the infinitesimal scrap of hope that still existed in the depths of my consciousness.

'No. NO.' I stared hard in the mirror, trying to make my face reappear. I couldn't control it; I couldn't fight it fast enough, there was no centre of gravity, nothing to hold on to. I hit myself on the head with the heel of my hand. I felt that.

'I am here.'

I said it aloud.

I hit myself again. Harder.

'I AM HERE,' I said, louder this time.

I hit myself again. Harder still.

'I. AM. HERE. I AM HERE.' I was shouting now. 'I AM HERE I AM HERE.' Each time hitting myself harder and harder on the head until I was back.

I was exhausted. I lay down on the bed.

I wanted to talk to Vas, to thank him for bringing me back, but I knew that my dad would rip him away from me the same as he had everyone else.

31

I didn't exactly know how I felt immediately after The Great Bedroom Apocalypse of 1976; I didn't feel anything big. Apart from a thumping great headache, I didn't even feel bad. I just felt painfully new and raw. Almost purified.

I had lain for a while trying to sleep, but I kept thinking about my mum. And how awful it was not knowing her name. I mean, this was ridiculous. I thought that if I could just remember even the first letter of her name, it might jog my memory. I went through the alphabet but nothing registered. The more I reached for it, the further away it got, until, eventually, I slept. When I awoke, it was dinner time. I had slept all day. I took a bath. Dressed in jeans and a T-shirt. I put my hair up in an elastic band. I swallowed four Anadin for the headache, then I cleared my room of every remaining vestige of music except for my new guitar and sheet music. I packed up all my clothes except for jeans and baggy T-shirts. I raked the crappy shoes from under the bed and just kept a pair of sneakers. I threw away my toiletries and my mum's Avon.

The Fat Murderer was in the kitchen when I went downstairs. I had paper carrier bags stuffed with magazines (mostly torn), records (mostly broken), posters (mostly screwed up) and clothes (mostly too small). He was pushing a meal of lamb chops, salad and chips into his face. As usual, I hoped he'd choke on it, but no such luck.

I was really hungry.

'Do you want some dinner?' he asked, mid-mastication and looking steadfastly at his plate.

'No, thanks. I'm not hungry.'

He looked up from his plate now and stared at me.

'What?' I said.

He held up two small tacks. Oh. Brilliant. Another one bites the dust, I thought. Though, seeing them now, they didn't look like the 1⅞ passivated drywall nail that the world-weary American detective had found in the TV cop show. They looked a lot smaller.

'I picked these from my tyre,' my dad said.

I shrugged. 'Bully for you.'

'They the exact same tacks from the shed,' he said, loading some meat into his face hole.

'Wow. You should be a detective,' I said dryly.

'Do you know how they get in the tyre?' he said, while masticating a lump of squelching gristle.

'Why don't you tell me?' I stared him out.

He stared me out. Squelchily.

'Anything else?' I asked breezily. 'No? Good. I'm busy. I'm having a clear-out. I'm going minimalist. I'm fed up with all this stuff.'

I waved the bags containing the ruins of my shattered sanctuary and waltzed off. I knew it was a bitter form of refuge. But I wasn't going to be beaten.

And I had a three-part plan:

1. Keep myself to myself. As mad-haired Garfunkel and equally mad-haired but in a different way Simon of Simon and Garfunkel once sang in their epic song

'I Am a Rock', I was now an island. That was the new totally self-sufficient and emotionally detached me. The one exception to this rule was, of course, Vas.
2. Continue to steal as much money as I could without getting caught.
3. Soraya had told me about this new thing called sleep apnoea. Basically, fat people choked in their sleep, stopped breathing and croaked. That was a gift and a half. I would suffocate The Fat Murderer with a pillow when he was asleep and it would be declared an accidental death.
Oh, and then
4. I'd leave school and start looking for jobs to do with music.

As it turned out, there were three-toed sloths moving faster than my brain and the first thing that happened, before I could see it coming, was Vas being sent to boarding school in Dulwich, which I looked up in the *London A–Z* and it might as well have been on the other side of the universe.

That adulterous old carcass, Mrs Petrides, proclaimed it to us all on the first Freak Night after The Great Bedroom Apocalypse of 1976. It had been three weeks since the wedding and Marios and Adonia were just back from their honeymoon, and before they had even had a chance to tell us about it, the old boot blurted it out. She just couldn't wait. She was literally crazy with vicarious hubris. She announced, looking at my dad and then at me, and then at my dad again, while Vas looked down resolutely at his shoes, that Vas was so good at his A-levels that he had been fast-tracked for Oxford University to study Literature and Philosophy; moreover, he had received a partial grant to a private boarding school for bespectacled boffins to get him through his A-levels a year earlier. He was to start the following Monday. Presumably the Petrides had relented now the cat was out of the bag about Vas's heterosexuality, and they considered him man enough to be allowed to forgo tiling for a living without fear of bringing disrepute upon the family. I knew The Fat Murderer was at the bottom of this. And Vas and The Fat Murderer and Mrs Petrides and Auntie Roulla and everyone else in the room knew it too, and we all knew we all knew. The spiral of knowing was infinite.

My dad didn't take his eyes off us for a single nanosecond, so Vas and I had no opportunity to discuss this latest hellish revelation. Auntie Roulla tried to get us both into the kitchen to help her with food, but Uncle Mikis shot her a look. Eventually she stopped trying.

The next day Vas phoned me while The Fat Murderer was still at work.

'It'll be good for you,' I said, in a strangulated attempt to be supportive.

'I'm gonna miss you, Con,' he replied.

'We'll see each other over the Christmas holidays.'

'The thing is, we won't. That's kind of the point ... I'm staying at Dulwich to do extra tuition over the holidays because we've got mocks in January. Same over Easter as well – got to be ready for the A-levels.'

I began to deflate but managed, 'Well, we will have the whole summer.'

There was an ominous distance over the line. I could feel Vas slipping from me by the second, exiting this trifling world of ours and entering a superior life. One he had always wanted.

A life that didn't include me. A life that was bigger than a mutual exchange of teenage love between two repressed Greek teenagers one ecstatic, drunken night in Walthamstow. He was heading towards a life he deserved. It had always been on the cards. It had just come sooner than I had expected.

'What?' I said, prompting Vas from his silence.

'Hasn't your dad told you?' said Vas.

'Told me what?'

Big gap.

'What, Vas? Just *say* it, for fuck's sake.' I mean, surely there was nothing my dad could have dreamed up that was any worse than anything else he'd done...

'He's booked flights for you both to spend the summer in Cyprus.'

I had no air left. He had done it. The Fat Murderer had surpassed himself.

'And then, you know, I'll be at uni by the time you get back... my course is four years...' Vas continued.

It was all going ... going ... gone.

'So, what are you saying?' I asked Vas. I knew exactly what he was saying but I needed to have it spelled out to me, because right now I was having difficulty believing it.

'It's just ... there's no way, Conno. I can't see how we get round any of it. There's just no time ...'

'We can make time,' I said feebly.

'Conno, we've been fighting time all the time and we're still losing time.'

'You said the word "time" a lot of times there, Vasso,' I said, with weak laughter, trying to grip, with broken and bloodied fingernails, on to the very edge of what we still might have. 'Come on, Vas, we've managed against all the odds so far.

We just need a bit of luck on our side and that's bound to come along.'

'Conno, I think we were born into bad luck, you, me, Marios – our entire generation.'

'That's a bit bleak, Vas, even for you.'

'I've tried to figure out why everything feels wrong. I think it's because we're the first ones, you know, and no one knows what to do. We're the kids of immigrants and our parents are trying to be a part of a new world but they're still stuck in the ways of the old world. And we're caught in the crossfire. My children, your children will hopefully be the lucky ones because we won't want them to suffer in the same way we have.'

There it was again: mine, yours. Not *ours*. As if that wasn't a big enough kick up the chuff, he carried on.

'The children of the future will be born into a world where they are allowed to belong.'

I wanted to say 'Oooh, la di da, get you' in response, but felt it was inappropriate so kept my trap shut. And I had to admit he'd hit the nail on the head. But I didn't give a squirrel's nuts about the children of the future. I cared about me, now.

'Yeah, but we could just see each other when we can, or we could wait.' God, I was feeble.

'Look at us,' continued Vas, as if I hadn't spoken. 'We can't just date like normal people. I feel guilty every time I see you. Like we're doing something wrong, which is *insanity*. If Marios and Adonia had just been allowed to date, they might have got it out of their system and not ever married, and now look at them: they're stuck with a kid on the way.'

'Well, I'm not going to make you marry me and have kids ...' My mouth was just making noises. I already knew this was a done deal. Might as well give Vas a helping hand. 'Do you want me out of your system, then?'

'No, Conno, but while you're in my system, I'll never get away from this place. I have to grab this moment. I'm scared that if I don't get to Oxford, I'll end up skinning rabbits for a living like my dad. I'm scared. I'm really scared. Aren't you?'

'No. I'm not scared, Vas.'

I was. I was absolutely terrified. And angry. I'd save sad for later.

'. . . So, that's it then?' I said.

'Con, I'm under so much pressure. Your dad is getting to my mum and dad and it's just so much pressure. Please understand.'

'*You're* under pressure? All the pressure I've been under and I have never folded once where you were concerned, Vas. Either you're incredibly weak or those fucking Greeks did a bloody good number on you.'

'I'm sorry,' he said, and put down the receiver.

It was safe to say 1976 had ended badly. On Monday, December 13th, the second anniversary of the murders, I commemorated the loss of my family and added Vas to my private ritual of mourning.

1977

32

Tuesday, June 7th, 1977, was going to be a first-class, toe-curling embarrassment of the Greek variety. It was the Queen's Silver Jubilee. There were street parties all over England to celebrate Queenie's twenty-five years on the throne and the Greeks were joining in. Which meant, once again, we would be exposed to the normal world for the freaks we were. The Petrideses had ordained that we would all attend the party in their street, because it was a private road and there would be less chance of riff-raff turning up. Or as Mr Petrides put it, raffriffs.

Everyone was supposed to bring some food for the community. The Fat Murderer and I had stopped at the Greek grocer's on the way and I was carrying a tray of sticky kataifi pastries, which were attracting insects like flypaper. I was just about to announce that we were embarrassing ourselves by bringing non-English food to a quintessentially English occasion when I saw that most of the trestle tables had been laden with boring paste sandwiches, which were already curling up at the edges, and cheap packet biscuits. Bugger that for a game of soldiers. I was going to make sure I put aside a few of the kataifi for myself.

I had wondered how the Greek Freaks would fit into such a patriotic affair with English people. I now saw they had no intention of fitting in whatsoever. The Petrideses weren't bothering with wobbly old trestle tables and paper plates. They had their best crockery out and had – oh Lord help us – moved their sofa and armchairs onto the front lawn and, instead of a picture of the Queen, had hung a poster of Prince Philip in their front window. 'Is Phil the Greek!' said my dad, as if the Queen's husband was a personal friend of his.

'All right, Con?' said Marios, in a flat voice. He was kneeling over a rusty old barbecue on the Petrideses' front lawn, flapping a bit of cardboard to get the flames going. Ashes were wafting all over the place. He didn't look so much like Auntie Roulla's golden boy these days; it was as if a bit of his shine had worn off.

'Christ, are we having an actual barbecue, out here on the front lawn?' I said, choking on some ashes.

'Oh yeah,' said Marios. 'This is just for the loukaniko sausages. She's cooked an entire sheep in her bloody garden oven,' he added, nodding towards The Scarlet Woman, Mrs Petrides, who was busy directing The Fat Murderer and her comedy husband, who were bringing out two huge stereo speakers from the house.

'Please, God, no . . .' I said to Marios.

'Oh, yes,' he said, wafting a little more aggressively. We watched as Mr Petrides wheeled his record player out on Mrs Petrides's hostess trolley. It was connected to the electricity via a long extension lead, which ran across the path where everyone could trip over it.

The aunties were carrying out vast platters of roast potatoes and chopped salad, while Mr Petrides stood by the extension lead, saying, 'Be careful of the wire.' Every two seconds.

'I thought Vas might come,' I said.

'I bet you miss him, don't you, Con?'

That was the understatement of the century. It had been six months since my phone call with Vas and I had only just started to wake up in the mornings without a cloud of doom hanging over me.

Mr Petrides had put on a Greek record and the shockingly loud bouzouki music made the entire street look our way just at the very moment Mrs Petrides and Auntie Roulla appeared, each holding one end of the onyx coffee table on which sat a very large, smoking-hot baking dish heaped with Greek lamb.

'Everybody is welcome!' Auntie Roulla said to the crowd of onlookers. I wanted to die and was about to say, 'Oh, Auntie, no, they won't like our food . . .' when one of the neighbours, a bald man in a beige cardigan, whizzed over with his paper plate in his hand and said, 'Oooh, don't mind if I do.' A woman in a floral dress came next, saying, 'Is there enough to go round?' Silly question! Of course there was enough to go round. We were Greeks. We knew how to eat. No curly sandwiches and stale custard creams for us. I felt a rare spike of pride for my countrypeople, then remembered I was supposed to hate us and squashed it back down. By the time The Fat Murderer had put a Nana Mouskouri LP on, there was quite a crowd. Uncle Mikis was handing out glasses of Commandaria and Doulla and Goulla were teaching the little kiddies how to do a Greek circle dance. Bloody hell! We were only popular! I was pleased we were integrating, but the English had enormous appetites. They were going through the lamb like locusts. I pushed through the greedy gathering to make sure I got my plateful before they cleaned us out.

I sat at one of the trestle tables with my plate. Dina had spotted me and came over. 'Fuck off,' I said, with my mouth full of lamb. Oh, she knew she was gonna get it. At the previous Freak Night, Dina had told me that Vas had a new girlfriend who went to a private girls' school in Dulwich. She said the girl was a year older than Vas and thin. And English. I decided there and then that, were I to meet Dina in the outside world, I would punch her in the face so hard that her teeth would shoot out of her arsehole. Anyway, she got the message and sodded off.

As the evening wore on and dusk fell, I wandered inside the house to go to the loo and check on the kataifi. Marios followed me into the hallway and said, urgently, 'Come upstairs with me. Me and my mum want to have a word.'

Auntie Roulla was in Vas's old bedroom. It made me feel odd to be in there with all his stuff. She had Marios and Adonia's puke machine of a baby on her shoulder. Fate could be cruel, I thought. The new kid had two very good-looking parents but DNA had intervened and it had come out looking like a tiny undercooked Fray Bentos meat pie.

Marios closed the bedroom door. The room smelled of Vas. 'Con,' he started, 'have you thought about what you're going to do about Cyprus?'

I had moaned to Roulla about going to Cyprus pretty much every week since I had found out about my dad secretly booking flights there for the summer. At first, I was horrified at the prospect of a holiday with The Fat Murderer. I had panicked, and attempted and aborted the sleep apnoea plan, which involved me standing over my snoring dad with a pillow and then chickening out in case he woke up before he died. I hadn't done much on the killing front since.

Then I had had a change of heart. The summer landscape looked bleak if I stayed in England. It would be hell without Vas. Janice and Soraya were going interrailing with The Deborahs and I would be a Noddy No Mates. Suddenly an all-expenses-paid holiday in the sun didn't look so bad.

'Con?'

'What?'

'Have you thought about it?'

'Yeah, I mean, I suppose I've got to go, haven't I?'

'You don't have to go. You're sixteen, Constance, and that means, legally, you can make your own decisions. You are allowed to leave home if you want to.'

He was right. I had been so focused on killing my dad by the time I was sixteen that I'd sort of forgotten that, once I was sixteen, I was no longer under his legal lock and key. My catalogue of failures had continued for so long that, eventually, it had rendered the killing of The Fat Murderer not entirely necessary. I was as disappointed as I was relieved.

'So, you could stay here. We'd support that decision, wouldn't we, Mum?'

'Well, it's no biggie, is it?' I said, a bit puzzled. 'It's just for a few weeks.'

'Yeah, but you can't guarantee that, can you, Con?' said Marios, sounding a bit serious.

Roulla looked like she was about to burst and jiggled tiny Fray Bentos a bit too enthusiastically. It burped up a sicky on her shoulder.

'Give the baby to me, Mum,' said Marios. 'I'll take her to Adonia.' He paused at the door. 'Mum, just tell Constance. Okay?'

Auntie Roulla looked ashen.

'What's going on?' I asked, starting to worry a bit. 'Tell me what?'

'Constantina, I need to say something to you which my husband forbid me to say,' Roulla blabbed urgently, casting a quick glance at the door as Marios closed it behind him.

'What? What is it, Auntie?' Fucking hell. So dramatic, I thought.

'Listen to us. You don't have to go to Cyprus, *agabi mou*,' she said, with a hard emphasis on each syllable. 'You can stay with me.'

'Auntie, I think it will be all right. I was thinking I would go on holiday. When I come back I can—'

'No, is not holiday. Darling, you know your father . . . he is not to be trusted.'

'Well, he kind of leaves me alone now that Vas isn't here.' The Vas ache came back. I pushed it away.

'If you go to Cyprus, maybe something will happen and you—'

The bedroom door burst open and I could hear the revellers in the street below singing 'God Save The Queen' and someone adding, 'And Phil the Greek toooo!'

'*Se proeidopoió*, Roulla!' It was Uncle Mikis. He had come up the stairs unheard, like a stealth bomber. It got mental immediately. He fired off rapid Greek at Roulla, most of which I couldn't understand, but caught the words: 'leave it alone, none of our business, I have told you.' Roulla held her own, but Uncle Mikis shouted louder and longer and she backed down. I had never seen her show weakness before and it was a shocking eye-opener: for all her man-management and kitchen savvy and hole-in-the-heart child pampering, she was still just a woman in a man's world and a man had put his foot down. About what, I wasn't sure. I really did have to get away. These Greeks were driving me insane.

'Go down the stairs, Consta,' said Roulla, as Uncle Mikis shooed me out of the room. I could hear ferocious whispers as their argument continued.

As I walked past the kitchen, I saw The Fat Murderer in there scoffing the two kataifi I'd put aside for myself. I hoped one went down the wrong hole and asphyxiated The Fat Murdering Life-Ruining Bastard.

'How many of those have you shoved down?' I said to his back. He turned to look at me, his face full of my pastries, and said, 'What did Roulla say to you in the bedroom?'

'Nothing,' I replied. Then, 'I'm not coming to Greek things any more. They're shit.'

I was quite surprised, and a little disappointed not to get at least a small argument, when my dad just shrugged and said, 'Okay, you don't have to come if you don't want to.'

When we left that evening, Roulla kissed me goodnight and squeezed me a bit too hard, transferring the odours of Rive Gauche and baby sick onto my hair. She whispered urgently, 'Constantina *mou*, my lovely girl, please remember I tried for you.'

33

Having made the decision to go to Cyprus, I needed to make sure I had a firm plan in place for when I got back. I needed to sever all ties to the past when I left home, otherwise the trail would lead my dad straight back to me. I wasn't returning to school. Some of my biggest heroes hadn't got so much as an O-level between them; even David Gilmour out of Pink Floyd hadn't completed his A-levels, and look where he was now. Gilmour would have been impressed with my progress on guitar. I was playing well.

Before I said farewell to academia once and for all, I wanted to play a special piece for my guitar teacher and saviour, Ms Liz Liddle; she of the boyish chest and 'flatmate', Ms Fullerlove. She had given me a lifeline. The months since The Great Bedroom Apocalypse of November 1976 would have been a lot worse without guitar lessons. And I wanted to pay her back.

After our final lunchtime guitar practice, before we broke up for summer, I held back while Ms Liz Liddle packed away her guitar. I wanted to say something. To acknowledge how special to me she was. And to explain why I wasn't coming back next term. I had fallen in love with her blunt kindness and it was the least I owed her.

'Constance, you don't want to be late for first afternoon period. Get a move on.'

'Erm ... Liz?'
'It's Ms Liddle in school, Constance.'
'Oh, yeah.'
'Oh, sod it, call me Liz! Who cares! What's your next period, Constance?'
'Oh, sod it, who cares!' I said, chancing my arm.

She clicked the locks on her guitar case and stood it against the wall. She sat on the edge of her desk and folded her skinny arms across her flat chest.

'I think we both know we're not coming back next year. Don't we?' she said.

'Oh, I didn't know you weren't coming back. Is it because you're going to run away with Ms Fullerlove?'

She cracked a little smile at that.

'I've been offered a job to teach at Guildhall School of Music and Drama.'

'That's humungous, Liz. Congratulations.'

'Thank you, Constance.'

'Is Ms Fullerlove leaving too, Liz?'

'Yes, she's going to stay at home to look after our dogs, and she'll tutor children after school. We are thinking of having a baby too.'

'Oh.' I didn't know what to say to that. 'How's that going to happen?' I asked eventually.

'We have a male friend who will be a part of the arrangement.'

I wasn't sure who would do what in that situation, but I thought, if I were them, I'd just keep it simple and stick to the dogs.

'And where will you go?' she asked me now.

'I think I'm going to run away for a bit, Liz.'

She nodded. A lot. 'I thought as much.'

'How? How did you think that, Liz?'

'Because you're a runner. You never want to be where you are. I can tell by the way you play. You are never quite here. When you play a note, your mind has already rushed on to the next note and the next. You can fool yourself, Constance, but you can never fool your audience. You *have to* be in the moment. You *have to* be real. You need to take a stance when you play. You'll only be able to do that when you know who you are. You might say, less con, more stance.'

She grinned and let that hang for a few seconds.

I thought about it. Then thought I didn't want to get off course, so ignored it.

'Liz, I think, sometimes, I haven't shown you how much I have appreciated you. When you took me to get my guitar, the coffee and the whole day out, and the whole calling you Liz thing. I don't think you could know how special it was to me.'

'I think I do.'

'I think, Liz—'

'Yep, you can stop saying Liz for two seconds, Constance. I won't hold it against you.'

I laughed. 'Yeah, sorry, Liz. It's just that,' I took a deep breath, 'I think you knew that I hadn't really got my father's permission.'

'I suspected as much. You did a very good job of keeping me from talking to him.'

'Well, my dad doesn't really value my love for music. To say the least,' I said, recalling him trashing my beloved vinyl during The Great Bedroom Apocalypse of 1976.

'No.' She nodded. I wasn't telling her anything she didn't know. I could see that.

'I thought it was very kind of you because you might have lost your job.'

Liz took a beat and then smiled. A huge, warm, generous smile.

'Well, I simply can't see a fellow music lover go hungry, Constance. And I simply could not see you playing that ridiculous child's guitar any longer.'

There was nothing else to say after that. I thought that we were about square with one another.

'So, I've been practising something and I wanted to play it for you to say a proper thank you and to show you that I haven't taken you for granted. That you didn't take your risk in vain.'

'Okay. Are you about to do a bit of showing off, Constance?'

'Yes. I am.'

'Go on, then, blow my socks off.'

I picked up my guitar, positioned it on the inside of my left thigh the classical way, the way she had taught me, placed the fingers of my left hand on the fretboard and rested the fingers of my right hand on the strings. I realised I was trembling a little and the first few notes were shaky. I had never been nervous playing before, even when I was rubbish, not even in front of David Gilmour out of Pink Floyd. But this, this had to mean something. And sincerity was not my forte.

I played her the adagio from the *Concierto de Aranjuez*, the notes mellifluous and uplifting, tragic and epic. It was one of my mum's favourite pieces of music. Ms Liz Liddle listened to it all without flinching or smiling. Afterwards she said, 'Once you've learned to play that piece with honesty as well as technical perfection, come to see me at Guildhall.'

'I will,' I said. And I meant it.

Although I hadn't quite received the unbridled praise I was expecting from Ms Liz Liddle, she had handed me the foundations of my new life. She had offered me a place at Guildhall and, eventually, I would go. Not only did I have a new existence to look forward to, but I now had one with meaning.

34

The journey to Cyprus was unexpectedly enjoyable. At the Cyprus Airways check-in desk, we checked in our suitcases and my guitar. My dad asked for seats in smoking. I'd have been happy to sit there, but the thought of four hours with our arms touching – neither of us was made for airline seats – was repugnant. Plus, the thought of him having to get up and go to the back of the plane to smoke was edifying.

'Oh no, that will set off my asthma,' I wheezed, for the sake of the check-in lady.

The Fat Murderer looked at me quizzically. 'You don't got asthma,' he said, doubtfully. He really knew nothing about me.

'Can you seat me in non-smoking, please?' I said, rolling my eyes at the check-in lady.

'Okay, no problem,' the desk lady said. 'I can put you, Mr Costa, in a smoking seat and your daughter in a non-smoking seat, if you'd prefer.'

Clearly, he didn't prefer. 'Both non-smoking.'

She returned our passports, which The Fat Murderer went to put in his jacket pocket. I snatched mine out of his hand and stuffed it into my new money belt, which I had bought from a camping shop in Walthamstow market and which contained my Getaway Fund. The Fat Murderer kept eyeing it up.

As it was, his insistence that we sit together turned out to be futile, as I spent most of the flight chatting with the stewardesses behind their curtain. They were a riot! I'd started a conversation with them when I went to the toilet. Turns out one of them had a husband who was in a semi-famous band. When I said I wanted to be a session musician, she was delighted. I mentioned I'd lost my mum and boyfriend and they kind of adopted me for the duration of the journey. They gave me free drinks and cigarettes and, when I admired their made-up faces, they gave me a makeover and asked if I'd like to sit with the captain in the cockpit for landing. It was a phenomenal flight. When I re-joined my dad, smelling of fags and whisky and with a face painted like a middle-aged prostitute, he looked like he'd eaten shit. Which, figuratively, he had.

We were met at Larnaca airport by my dad's brother, Christakis, his beetle-eyed, sharp-tongued wife, Irini, and their two children, Maria, twelve, and Xenia, who was six. Irini initiated a hugathon that threatened to be interminable. I noticed she avoided hugging my dad and gave him a curt nod instead. I sensed a kindred spirit.

Christakis was much nicer than my dad. He was better-looking too, which was amazing, considering his innumerate self-inflicted deformities. He was a carpenter who made beautiful furniture, but at the expense of his limbs. Having previously sawn off four of his fingers and broken his nose with his own hammer, he had attained local hero status by having fallen on his bandsaw, almost cutting himself in half, and surviving! He had been put back together a bit twisted and he was lucky to be alive. His local nickname was Cut-In-Half Christakis. Irini worked full-time raising the family and taking care of the house and gardens. I liked them both.

The Fat Murderer and I were staying in the house Irini and Christakis had built with their own hands: a 1970s single-storey villa with a shady front veranda. Their house was on the same plot as the empty two-roomed stone house my dad and his brother had grown up in. My grandfather had still lived there until three years ago, when my aunt had him banished from the village. They kept it locked.

They also possessed one of the few televisions in the village. There was never anything on it, except the news and one Greek film, which seemed to be on every evening and involved a lot of screeching women being shaken to their senses by moustachioed men, but it was a symbol of their well-earned status nevertheless. Cut-In-Half Christakis and Beetle-Eyed Irini had done okay.

The Fat Murderer couldn't resist letting them know how much more he had: flashing his wad of cash (somewhat lighter, thanks to me) and endlessly boasting about his big house and fancy German car. Uncle Christakis listened patiently, every now and then twisting counterclockwise to straighten out his cut-in-half body, but Irini looked like she wanted to stab my dad in his piggy eyes. I liked her more each day.

35

I was unexpectedly and almost instantly drawn to the cadence of village life, dusty and resonant with the chirping of cicadas and the odours of backyard husbandry. Time had a different stamp here. No one consulted a watch. The movement of the day was all: it started at dawn, so that pressing tasks could be completed before the sun began its daily scorching of the earth. Well-diggers, ironmongers and goat herds all industriously trying to beat the rising heat. Women stayed inside during the brightest hours, protecting their skin from the unrelenting sear of the rays.

When the sun was at its highest, everything ceased. The shops and cafés closed their doors. Houses shut their shutters. Bed sheets were pulled back and hot, weary bodies laid down. Donkeys collapsed gratefully under the shade of olive trees. The chickens stopped their clucking. Even the cockerel, who crowed pretty much all hours. A profound stillness and silence, a deep peace. This was the time when I liked to walk alone, wandering through the village and inevitably making my way down to the oldest part of town.

As the sun passed its zenith, with the air barely cooling, and the hibiscus flowers readying to close for the night, Dhali became industrious once more. The swallows strafed the skies for insects and the cicadas tuned up for their evening chorus. Now the ladies emerged from their afternoon rest to water their arid gardens and prepare the evening meal.

This was my time with Irini. We'd sit together sipping ice-cold rose-water cordial while stripping string beans for dinner, her knees spread wide to make a hammock of her dress. Beans went into the pot, the husks into her skirt, which she picked up and carried to the chicken coop out back. It made the chickens go bananas, especially the cocky cockerel, who bustled and pecked his way to the front so he could get the best bits. He was an absolute arsehole, that chicken. And he was tough when we ate him. He had the last laugh.

Irini would always use this time, when it was just the two of us, to teach me Greek and to quiz me on life in London. I was surprisingly good at learning the language, but not so forthcoming on the Q&A side of things. It was fine when she wanted to know how much things cost or what sort of shops we had in England, but the exchange was always a prelude to her angling for information I didn't want to give.

'What is life like with your dad, Consta?'

'Okay.'

'What was it like when your *bapou* came to England?'

'Not great.'

'Were you ever left alone with him?'

'Um ...'

'What did your dad tell you about why the old man had been exiled from the village and sent to a retirement residence in Nicosia?'

I was ducking and diving. I knew why she was asking. Her six-year-old, Xenia, had been one of the other victims of my Greek grandfather's abhorrent behaviour. I had done all my hurting and healing and avoided any response that would open that can of pervy old worms. As much as I understood her need to talk about it, it was just too complicated to get into.

To be honest, it was quite easy to fob her off; as an inquisitor, she was good, but she was no Auntie Roulla.

Dinner was always wonderful, mostly because my dad was hardly ever there (he was 'doing business', he said. More likely he'd found some new women to 'do' now that he couldn't get his pudgy mitts on Mrs Petrides's fossilised old carcass), but also because the food was simple and homegrown and fresh and made with as much love as Irini could pour into it: piles of macaroni with boiled chicken (from the coop in the garden, but hey-ho, that's life, if you're unfortunate enough to be a chicken), grated haloumi, string beans and cool mint sponge cake. We ate at the Formica kitchen table, together, doors open, happy to catch the twilight sliver of peacetime between the resting flies and the waking mosquitos.

When darkness came down, it came softly and completely; the heady scent of jasmine soaking the night, filling every pocket of air, curling around railings and verandas, through the trees, finding its way into your pores until you were infused, floating, drunk on the scent. I would stand and inhale for minutes at a time, so insatiable was I for this nightly opiate.

Now the men put on their clean shirts, the women fresh dresses, and they would take their *peripatos*, a slow amble around town, stopping to gossip with neighbours or to pause to watch the screechy women being shaken to their senses by the moustachioed men on one of the rare boxy black-and-white televisions that had been rolled out onto verandas for everyone to share; the tinny noise dissolving into the evening air. Here, the night was evocative and space was infinite. God, I couldn't stop myself from falling in love with this country.

Who'd have thought it, I thought, then felt hypocritical for thinking it and then thought I was allowed to change my mind so rethought it and felt justified.

More often than not, my dad's childhood friend, Leonidis, and his family would come and join us for a walk. Leonidis had a confident ease about him that comes with self-made wealth: he had made his fortune by opening the first disco in Nicosia, the island's capital. He was good-looking, successful, pleasant and respected. Everything my dad wanted to be and wasn't. He also had a full head of hair. My dad's hair was more hair lacquer than actual hair these days and, I was bedside myself with glee to observe, faring badly in the humidity.

Sometimes, we would end the evening drinking coffee on Leonidis's veranda, which was beyond mind-numbing, as Leonidis and The Fat Murderer would talk about money and property developing and I'd be stuck trying to make conversation with Leonidis's intellectually challenged eldest son, Stavros. I'd always stay for the minimum time and then slope off. On this particular evening, getting away proved more difficult than usual. The Fat Murderer had been discussing a property he intended to build on the plot next to Leonidis's admittedly impressive villa. He looked more mental than ever. His Elvis quiff had gone flat and sat on his bonce like a hairy pitta bread, his eyes were all squirmy and he had a smile that would have been at home on the face of a maniac. Which, of course, he was.

'Constantina,' said The Fat Murderer. He never called me that. 'Did you see Leonidis's television?' He pointed to the unmissable TV on the veranda. 'Leonidis is making a lot of money. This is the best TV you can buy in Cyprus.'

'Jolly good for Leonidis,' I snarked.

'Look at it!' he said now, reverting to English.

'All right. Hold on to your pitta bread. I'm looking,' I said, actually looking, 'and it's playing the same crappy film as all the other tellies. So what?'

The Fat Murderer plastered a slick smile on his face, greasy with self-adoration, and ruffled my hair. He looked around the veranda and nodded as if we had just had an agreeable exchange.

'Tell Leonidis about your guitar-playing,' he said now, back to Greek. 'She's very good,' he said to the rest of the company. 'Go fetch your guitar and play for us, Connie.'

'What? You've never shown any interest before. I'm not doing that. I'm not a performing monkey,' I said, smiling nicely, still in English.

'Connie, I says to get your blatty guitar and play for us. Or talk to them. Show you are interested.' English.

I wasn't going to do that. I thought two things:

1. He'd bought a first-class ticket to Loonyville, that one, and it was a one-way trip.
2. I sensed a weakness in him that I was going to enjoy.

'No,' I replied, sticking to English. 'I'm not playing just so you can be popular in front of your boring mates.'

His eyes went cold but his revolting smile remained locked in place. 'Don't worry, you can leave soon. Just talk to your Uncle Leonidis and show him how nice you are.'

'Fucking freak,' I said, under my breath.

'What did you say?'

'I said, I'm off, mate,' I replied, and headed to the old town.

Fortunately, Stavros didn't follow me this evening. He was always hanging around, asking where I was going and who I was meeting, which was none of his business, but Stavros was quite dishy in a caveman sort of way, so it wasn't a hardship, as long as he didn't talk much, and it took my mind off Vasos slightly. Every time I thought of him and his new girlfriend, my heart bled.

My dad didn't seem to mind my spending time with Stavros either. In fact, he encouraged it. If he spotted me slipping away, he'd say, 'Don't be rude, Conniecons. Take Stavros with you.' I supposed he thought we were probably cousins and so there would be no chance of any hanky-panky. It was almost worth having a bonk just to prove him wrong, but if Stavros was as boring in bed as he was in conversation, I'd probably fall asleep before the good part.

Who I really wanted to spend my evenings with was Hambis, Kyriacou and Panayiotis. The Greek Philosophers.

36

I first met The Greek Philosophers in Old Town Dhali. I had discovered the place within a few days of our arrival. It's draw for me was magnetic and mystical. The newer houses in the village sprawl were roomy and echoey with straight lines. The old town was small and its houses dilapidated and wonky, noiseless with earth and dust. Its pace was set by the octogenarians who peopled it. I was enchanted by the utter otherworldliness of it. It had been untouched by time; it was in the past and the past was before all the bad stuff had happened. In England, everything reminded me of all the dead people. Here there was none of that.

The old town was set around a small square of well-trodden dirt with a row of old cafés, which were set high up on a crumbling stone veranda underneath ancient Phoenician-style arches. The cafés smelled of bergamot and mastic, aromas folded into the air by the heavy wings of moth-like ceiling fans. They were frequented by old men who drank small cups of aromatic sweet coffee until midday and moved on to something stronger as the day wore on. I thought this might be a nice way to live out your days. Maybe I'd do that when I was old.

The houses had blue-painted doors that, like the people, were faded and venerable to me. I was curious to see who would come out of them. If I got a brief glimpse inside as a door opened, a thrill of nostalgia would course through me, a kind of old belonging I couldn't quite catch. Almost The Calling – but calling me back instead of on.

I had been sitting on the high veranda outside one of the cafés, legs dangling over the edge, heels kicking against the low wall. The café owner had sold me an ice cream and then shut up shop. I was the only one there, in the silence and heat. As it was siesta time, I thought everyone else would be asleep, so I was more than a little surprised when one of the blue doors I had watched so often and so hopefully, opened.

I stopped breathing. I waited for a moment or two then slid off the veranda. I edged closer to get a proper look. An elderly man with clean, fluffy white hair stepped from the shadows into the sunlit doorway. His shirt was threadbare but freshly laundered and his trousers hung off him like they had once been fitted to a plumper man. Had it not been for his belt, they'd have fallen down. He gave off a smell of coal tar soap and Orthodox church incense. I recognised him as one of the old café men I had been observing.

'Come inside, if you wish,' he said. His voice was gravelly. As if it hadn't been used yet today. 'I have seen you looking before. You are welcome to see. Come in.' He kept a straight face but his eyes smiled.

'Erm . . . I don't know who you are, though,' I said, stupidly, taking a step back.

'You have seen me before, many times at the café. I am the same person here.' He gestured, taking in his house.

I hadn't considered that, when I was watching, the watched would be watching back. It was always a shock to me that life wasn't a one-way window. I licked my melting ice cream, which plopped off the cone and into the dirt.

I took another stupid step backwards, the remaining cone still in my hand.

'I know who you are,' he said lightly. He ignored the fallen ice cream. '*E gori tou rafti.*' The tailor's daughter. 'Your mother is dead.'

Well, that was short and to the point. I liked him instantly for his bluntness. It was clean, somehow.

'But your father, the tailor, he is not dead.'

'Not for want of trying,' I mumbled in Greek, not meaning to be heard but quite hoping I was.

'Ah, well, it's true, when we have experienced great and tragic loss, we can spend the rest of our lives blaming the living as if it will resurrect the dead.'

I didn't know quite what to say to that. Then I stepped through the open doorway and lingered momentarily in the shaft of pale golden light that draped across the threshold, bearing dust motes into the unknown, enveloping me, drawing me inwards.

Inside, the tranquillity was so transcendent that even the empty streets seemed restive. The house was dark and cool; just one room with a flagstone floor. There was, in one corner, a metal-framed four-poster bed with spotless, embroidered ivory bed linen, a narrow wardrobe next to it. Against the wall there stood a wooden table with two rickety wooden chairs that had once been blue, the paint worn so thin by the rub of time that the dark wood beneath was now barely covered. On the table stood an oil lamp, a pile of old books and an open newspaper. A small stove in an adjacent corner. That was all.

'I am Kyriacou. This is my house. I live here with my wife. She is dead too. But every day we still live here together.' He tapped the side of his head.

I looked around the room to make sure he didn't have a rotting corpse in a chair somewhere.

'*In my memory*. People never die if we love them,' he said, nodding as if he knew I agreed with him.

I didn't.

'I can't even remember my mum's name.' I wasn't expecting to say that. It just came out.

'Trauma,' he nodded, knowledgeably. 'The mind hides things to protect us until emotional wounds have healed. But the heart never forgets the name of love. You'll remember soon enough.'

'What if I don't?'

'You are Greek. You are strong. You will heal.'

'Hm.'

'Do you know what your name means? Constantina means steadfastness, dedication and perseverance no matter the obstacle.'

If you say so, I thought, then, at his invitation, I sat in his dead wife's rickety chair and we drank Greek chai, taken black and laced with cinnamon and star anise, and he showed me photographs of all the people he'd once known and who were now deceased. It was a surprisingly cheery way to spend an afternoon.

That was my first audience with a philosopher. Whenever I took a walk alone, I inevitably wound up in the old town. Kyriacou introduced me to his best friends. I instantly liked everything about them: their freshly laundered shirts, faded and well-worn but clean and carefully ironed; their white whiskers and sparse Brilliantined white hair. And their wise faces as old as the ruins of Dhali.

Hambis, who was the oldest of all of them, became my

favourite. He was so old he practically had one foot in the afterlife: he had pink, watery hamster eyes and a madly shaking whisper of a voice. He had an orchard just beyond the old town, which he still kept, and was unerringly kind.

Panayiotis was younger than Hambis and Kyriacou. He and his twin brother had both gone into the priesthood and had taken vows of celibacy. While his brother stayed on and became the bishop of the impressive cathedral of Panayia Evangelistria in Dhali, Panayiotis had turned atheist when he met the woman he wanted to marry and, presumably, bonk. This happened forty years ago, but he was still referred to as the Fallen Priest in the village: *O Pesmenos Papas*. As luck would have it, his wife died a few years after they'd got married.

To the uninitiated, they may have appeared as three decrepit old geezers who drank and played cards all day. But I had the benefit of hearing their wisdom and experiencing their virtuosity and, to me, they were The Greek Philosophers: a dying breed, the last bastion of a Cyprus that would soon be gone. They weren't for moving forwards, they were for standing still, marking time until there was none left for them.

We sat night after balmy night under the crumbling arches drinking ouzo and muddy Greek coffee. They gave me cigarettes and taught me to play tavli and diloti. I was terrible at both but didn't care. I just wanted to hear their memories and their opinions. They were well read and I loved their stories of ancient Idalion, the site on which 'modern' (that was a joke) Dhali was built. I almost believed they'd seen it all first-hand. They talked of the Trojan War . . .

'Happened right here!' warbled Hambis.

The siege of the Phoenicians . . .

'Happened right here!' said Kyriacou.

And the one we philosophised over most of all, The Great Lovers Tiff of 200 AD, when Adonis, Aphrodite's bit on the side, was killed by her partner, Ares, the God of War . . .

'Yes!! This happened right here!' insisted all of them.

'But was justice done?' asked Kyriacou.

'Justice is never done if people are not allowed to love who they want to love,' said Panayiotis, getting a bit heated.

'Ah, you would say that,' said Kyriacou. 'Because of love you fell twice: you fell for a woman and fell from the church. *O thio forés pesménos papas*. The twice-fallen priest!'

'I'm not talking about me,' said Panayiotis, raising his voice a touch. 'And you know this. I am talking about our young people who are arranged into marriages where there is no love. How many of those women would seek a lover if they could throw off the shackles of obligation and be free to love?' He knocked back his ouzo in one and slammed the glass on the table.

It always got interesting when there was slamming.

'We don't know if it's even true,' said Kyriacou.

'My brother is the bishop here in Dhali. He was consulted. He told me. We know it's true,' replied Panayiotis, angrier still.

'What's true?' I asked, trying to follow the rapid Greek.

'What do you think, Constantina?' asked Hambis, now in his wobbly whisper. 'Would you allow a husband to be chosen for you? Could you be happy with this?'

'*Na proséchaaeis*' (be careful), said Kyriacou, quietly.

'Careful of what?' I asked, but was ignored again.

'Of course, she won't be happy!' boomed Panayiotis. 'She is a modern woman from another world. A world we don't understand.'

I'd had enough shouting Greeks for a lifetime, so I nipped

it in the bud by announcing that it really didn't matter what I thought, as no one had ever wanted me for an arranged marriage because I wasn't Greek enough. And, moreover, I said, to close the subject once and for all, where Adonis was concerned, the idiot had it coming to him because you don't cheat with someone whose current boyfriend is the *actual God of War* and then act all surprised when he kills you. Hambis nodded sagely at this, which pleased me, until I realised he wasn't nodding, he had *nodded off*.

Stavros would wander into the old town occasionally to join us and buy drinks. He would always get a warm welcome from Kyriacou, though Hambis and Panayiotis were a little more reserved. 'Big pockets filled with his father's money, that one,' grumbled Panayiotis to me, confidentially. I kept quiet. After all, my own pockets were full to bursting with my father's money too.

Panayiotis had a point, though. Stavros was imbued with a confidence to which he might not have been entitled, had he been reliant on his own chattels rather than those of his wealthy family. He kept reminding me that, one day, he would have enough collateral to start up his own night club in Nicosia, and then he'd be rich like his dad. 'Good for you,' I'd say with distaste. I couldn't help but think about Vas's earnest struggle to be independent, his decision not to earn his wealth from his father's lucrative furrier business but to make a life of his own filled with poetry and art. Sexier by far, no matter how many times Stavros flexed his bronzed muscles or wiggled his one continuous caveman eyebrow suggestively.

All in all, these were halcyon days: these strange elderly men, who were in the final whispers of their lifetimes, taught me to like Greek Cypriot people, Greek Cypriot things, to like the *Greek in myself*. They helped me see that it was not the entire cultural landscape that I reviled, but just two men, my grandfather and my father, who had painted my vista black.

And Stavros added a bit of harmless scenery. He was stupid, but easy on the eye. And on one occasion he presented me with a delicate gold filigree bracelet, which I quite liked. Considering I ignored him most of the time, I thought that was rather big-hearted of him. I also thought: beware of Greeks bearing gifts. Then I thought, don't be cynical, Constance. Turns out I was right first time.

37

The time flew by in Cyprus. It was hard to believe it had been a full seven weeks since we had left England. Now every moment was precious. It was Friday afternoon and our penultimate weekend.

The weekends were usually spent at the beach. My cut-in-half uncle closed his workshop at lunchtime, swept up the sawdust and any recently severed limbs, and loaded up his pick-up truck with watermelons and meat. He and my dad would sit in the front cabin and smoke, and myself, Stavros and various cousins and aunties would pile into the rusty flatbed and hang on for dear life while we were bumped and swung over rocky roads and tracks towards the east of the island. One hair-raising hour later, burning hot and covered in rust scrapes, we would fetch up at the remote little Fig Tree Bay in the province of Protaras: hot white sands that sloped gently into the turquoise sea, brilliant and blinding, sunlight glimmering greens and blues on the crystal, pond-still Mediterranean.

My uncle had set up a barbecue and was skewering meat onto metal spikes with a recklessness that didn't bode well, considering his proclivity for self-harm. My aunt was cutting up salad and my dad, taking the easiest path to gratification, was slicing up the watermelon and soaking up gratitude as he handed out slices and insincere smiles to his thirsty devotees.

'Conniecons, give this watermelon to Stavros,' he said in Greek, waving a large dripping slice in my direction.

'Let him get his own,' I replied in English. 'And stop calling me that. It's bloody creepy.'

'I says to take it to him now,' he said, reverting to English, and quietly so no one else heard. Except Irini. She heard all right. Nothing escaped her beetley eyeballs where my dad was concerned.

'Isaystotakeittohimnow! Dowhatyoublattytoldforonceinyoublattylife,' he spat, forgetting he had an audience.

'Oh, please piss off and leave me alone,' I said, and headed to the water. It was quite liberating being able to swear at him without repercussions. He was so set on being liked that he wouldn't dare show his real self. I had to admit it was a very agreeable way of spending my last days with him before we returned to England and I started my new life without him.

And then I was in the sea and it was bliss; the silky water smoothing away the irritation. I floated, chiffon ripples around my body; the exotic scent of watermelon carried across the surface. I took this moment to embellish my dream of a near future with guitars and musical friends and Ms Liz Liddle at Guildhall. It was going to be so good!

I was wearing a new swimsuit, which I now realised was quite low-cut – a mistake for someone with a physique made of moving parts. My knockers kept floating up and out of the top and I had to keep tucking them back in, which was annoying, but, still, I was fairly at peace until Stavros came splashing in, flicking water at me as if we were on frolicking terms. He indicated the small island about a hundred metres off shore, which we had swum to every time we came here. '*Koursa se,*' he suggested. It was wanky to ask me to race him, because he was a much faster swimmer. He was all testosterone and no sense, Stavros.

We climbed onto the island, carefully avoiding the clusters of black spiny sea urchins. The rocks were jagged and hot, but it was worth the pain to be able to stand adrift in the firmament, the blue of the water merging with the faultless blue of the sky. We wandered about picking up trifles and sea treasures. It would have been perfect if the monobrowed twerp hadn't kept trying to hold my hand.

'Get off me. I'm perfectly capable of climbing a rock without your help,' I said, as he wound his wet fingers through mine.

'It's dangerous,' he replied, in his sleepy way. 'I am strong,' he said, sort of pumping up his, admittedly, rock-hard bronzed pecs. 'I can protect you.' I thought about Vas's puny chest and his four fragile chest hairs and pushed the desire away.

'Right. Well, I don't need protecting, thank you very much.'

Stavros continued to look at me – or more precisely at my chest. I followed his gaze downwards and realised one of my boobs had plopped out of my swimsuit again. I tucked it back in hastily and pretended it hadn't happened. 'Let's just swim back to the shore – I can smell the meat cooking. I'm hungry,' I said, and turned away from him.

I started to hobble over the rocks towards the edge. Stavros followed, managing the crippling surface much better than I could. I stumbled and he was there, putting his hand on my elbow to steady me. I mumbled a begrudging 'thank you', at which point, one hand still on my elbow, he slipped the other round my waist and pulled me into him, smoothly. I didn't like the feel of our wet swimwear touching, his hard hairy thighs rubbing against mine. He bent his head to kiss me. He had some sunburn on his nose and the skin was flaky. Up close it made me feel queasy. I ducked under his arms. 'No, no, no, no, no! Don't do that,' I said, half amused and half repulsed. What the hell did he think he was doing? I had never given him a signal that intimacy was on the cards. Had I? I knew I shouldn't have accepted that bracelet from him. Maybe it was some sort of contractual agreement I wasn't aware of and this was its fulfilment. He moved towards me. 'Stop right there,' I said, hand raised, palm towards him. 'Stavros, I do not engage in physical relations with someone unless we are having a relationship. So, touch me again and there will be trouble.'

He shrugged. Then smiled a proprietary smile that really pissed me off. I made a note to give him back his shitty bracelet.

38

It was during our last week in Cyprus that the inevitable happened. I had been with The Greek Philosophers all morning, trying to understand the whole EOKA situation. Kyriacou had been with Grivas – he said an armed rebel uprising was the only way to national freedom, Hambis was with Archbishop Makarios, and Panayiotis had said that Cyprus was safer under British rule after all, because now the Turks had moved in and Cyprus was divided; so better the devil you know. They kept asking me for my thoughts, but I wasn't really that invested. Once I left Cyprus, I would never come back and, now that my time here was ending, I had started to think about my future and how I was going to make it all work.

That was what was on my mind when I returned to my aunt and uncle's house, thinking to play some guitar and count up how much money I had left in my money belt. I got two surprises instead:

1. It was siesta time, so I peeked into my aunt and uncle's bedroom to find my uncle alone, snoring loudly with his manhood tenting the sheet he was sleeping under. Urgh, but, also, I couldn't help wondering how he'd managed that in his sleep!? Still, at least that was one appendage he hadn't managed to saw off.

2. I went looking for my aunt and that was my second surprise. Unless she was sleeping, Irini was busy. Now she was still as a statue, sitting in her sparse, clinically clean kitchen, lips pursed, beady eyes unfocused.

The back door was open onto the dusty yard, wearied flies wafted in on the air. It took a few seconds before she noticed me. She got up, went to her refrigerator, and pulled out a large bundt cake. She cut two slices without talking and placed two plates on the table. I sat opposite her, resting my sticky hot arms gratefully on the cool grey tabletop.

'*Adi*,' she said. Let's do this.

We had arrived, as we were always destined to do so: my *bapou*, the kiddie-fiddling Greek grandfather.

'Eat your cake, Consta,' she said, stuffing a large lump in her own mouth, her furtive eyeballs darting from left to right as if she were looking for spies hidden in the corners.

'You say you know what happened. Here. Before your mother died. Yes?'

'Yes,' I said. I had already told her this during one of our many food-prepping sessions on the veranda.

'But do you know how it happened. She stuffed another piece of cake into her mouth, for comfort, I thought, or to stop herself from screaming. I knew all about that. She led me to the open kitchen door and pointed across the dusty yard to where the empty, ancient house belonging to my grandparents still stood.

'It was when your cousin Xenia was just three years old,' she said, leading me over to the windowless, crumbling shack. She took a large key from her apron pocket, inserted it into the rusty old lock, turned and pushed open the creaky, aged wooden door. We stepped inside. Cold flagstone floors. Two rooms, cool and still. She pointed to a shadowy corner.

'I came looking for Xenia,' she said, in slow Greek, so that I could catch everything she was saying. 'I hadn't seen her for fifteen minutes. I sensed that something was wrong. I walked through here,' she walked through the doorway, I trailed behind, 'and I saw him in the corner, right there, his trousers down, his penis in his hand, trying to persuade her to take it.'

She mimed what she had said, to make sure I understood it. It was obscene to watch. I felt ill. I guessed the hurting and the healing I thought I had gone through hadn't worked quite as thoroughly as I had thought. Some intensely nasty images came to mind now.

'Your uncle had him removed from the village. He's in a retirement home in Nicosia now.'

'I know,' I said. 'I was hoping he'd be dead by now.' I unzipped my money belt and felt inside it for my passport and money. Just checking they were still there. I had become more obsessed with checking as our departure date loomed.

'No. Unfortunately he is alive. Your father wants to take you to see him before he goes back to England. Did you know that? Did he tell you?'

'No.'

I looked into the bag to make sure my money and passport were still there. Then zipped it up and checked the zip again.

'Do you want to go?' she asked.

She looked at me, searchingly, from my eyes to my bag. I wanted to tell her about my own experiences. Share my shame with her so that it would have company. To tell her that the incident between my grandfather and her daughter had had as much of an impact on me and my family as it had on hers: that the argument that resulted in the car crash killing my mum and brothers had happened as a direct consequence of my parents receiving a letter from Cyprus telling us everything that she was telling me now. If ever there was a time to really talk about this, it was now. But I couldn't stir up that hornets' nest any more. I had dealt with it. That was before. I was moving forward.

'Your dad and his brother are very different,' she said, as if reading my thoughts. 'Your father is like the old man, yes?'

Bloody hell. She was razor sharp. I was getting very uncomfortable. The Fat Murderer might not have been as obvious as his own father, but in many ways his restraint was more depraved and had manifested in other ways that were just as damaging. He wore his depravity. I could see it. Irini could see it too.

'Your father sends the old bastard spending money every month, while your uncle has to pay for the retirement home. Did you know that?'

'No.' But I bet my mum knew.

'How can he be like this, knowing what the old man has done? Xenia was young, she's forgotten it now, but if I hadn't come in at that moment, who knows what he would have done.'

Well, I could have told her. And I could have told her that Xenia wouldn't forget. Not entirely. It was there. Somewhere in her memory, pecking away at the carcass of her self-worth like a vulture.

A sick chill went through me as I stared at the corner where it had happened. I thought about the times I had fallen prey to my grandfather's perversions, his opportunistic grabs as I passed him on the stairs at home, the soft knocks on my closed bedroom door, that simpering, begging, pathetically lewd look on his face, mixed with the threat of who knew what if the secret came out. I wanted to be sick.

The words were almost there in my mouth. I could not let them out. But I didn't need to. Irini knew. She knew I knew she knew. It was a whole circle of knowing. And it was too much.

I should have stayed. But I didn't want to hear any more. I didn't want to talk. I needed to get away. From this house. From Cyprus. And I certainly didn't want to go to visit my disgusting old grandfather with The Fat Murderer. I wanted to be with my mum. Or David and Marc. Or Vas. But they were all gone. He'd seen to that.

'I'm sorry, Irini,' I said, and walked through the yard and out to the old town. I really wanted to see Hambis.

Siesta was over, but The Greek Philosophers weren't at the café. I checked inside. I bought a small coffee and drank a glass of water and waited. Half an hour passed by but there was no sign of any of them. I crossed the road to Kyriacou's house, but he wasn't there.

I would go to Hambis's orchard. He'd be there and, if he wasn't, I could stay and see his apricots and greengages, his lemons and oranges. I would watch the barn swallows swooping in and out of their nests under the eaves of his old house.

I walked along the road that led out of the old town towards the swathe of golden countryside. Just a small way along the dusty track was Hambis's house. The door was ajar.

It creaked as I pushed it open and stepped in to find Kyriacou and Panayiotis slumped over whiskies at the kitchen table. Immediately I knew something awful, something that couldn't be undone, had happened. 'Hambis?' I asked. They nodded. He had died in the night. Alone. I left and never saw The Greek Philosophers again.

39

It was approaching our final weekend in Cyprus. It was September, though no one had informed the weather, which was still in the throes of a stifling heatwave, building pressure, making any movement heavy and tiring. Everyone had agreed that the best way to escape the heat would be to decamp to the Troodos mountains.

We had been there once before during this summer, at the start of our visit. We had stopped at Pano Platres, a small mountain village cut off by snow in the winter months. Just above the village, you could camp where it was mercifully cool and green and the streams ran like liquid ice over rocky beds. It had been a hair-raising ride but worth it. The road up was barely scraped out of the side of the mountains, which made the going slow and rough. We had had to lie down in the flat bed for fear of being bounced right out of it and over the edge. The jeopardy had made it thrilling. The track had crumbled and broken away as the heavy tyres ground against it, my uncle's truck fishtailing as it kept its tenuous grip on the loose powdery earth, mini rockfalls sprinkled stones and grit into our hair. But we had been in good hands. My uncle and his friends had driven these roads all their lives. They knew every turn, they had negotiated every hairpin bend, they knew where the road was soft, where it was treacherous, they could spot a rockfall before it happened. Nevertheless, they never relied on their knowledge because they were wise enough to know that the road was always changing.

I'd never understood why people got so excited about camping holidays in England. I couldn't see the point of having to pretend you were enjoying a miserable, soggy holiday where you were less comfortable and more hungry than usual. Greek mountain camping was something else entirely. This was an adventure, and because it was a Greek Cypriot adventure, no one would endure any level of discomfort and no one would go hungry!

That first time, we had parked by a crystal mountain stream where we had anchored crates of soft drinks and beers into its icy flow. We had piled up enough food to last several lifetimes: cured hams, cheeses, breads, ripe tomatoes and cool crispy cucumbers, slabs of pork and lamb, pastries and cakes. We chopped and sliced and skewered and barbequed and consumed until we were full and sleepy. When night fell we had lain down *bablomas* – pink quilts handmade by the *yiayias*. We slept in a long row under the vast starlit sky, until the sun returned and warmed us awake.

Of course, being Greek Cypriots, and having absolutely no regard for personal safety, we had parked ourselves on the edge of a dramatic precipice. It was a wonder that a few people didn't just roll off and disappear. The Fat Murderer took the side closest to the mountain edge. I had considered the possibility of slowly rolling over to make him move in his sleep until he fell off. But that would have meant sleeping next to him and actually touching him, and I didn't have the stomach for it.

That first mountain morning, desperate for a pee, I had awakened while everyone else was still sleeping. I had opened my eyes and looked to the horizon, where the dawn was breaking. In my confused state of semi-somnambulance, I thought the mountains must have caught fire. I gasped as I stumbled out of the line of sleeping bodies and fell into a fiery dreamscape so lurid, red and orange that it scorched my eyes. It had taken me a few blurry waking moments to realise that it was the sunrise, working itself into full radiance, a magnificent lava flow spectacle spreading across a purple sky, burning up the valley towards us. It was consuming and powerful. It was proof of a universe. An infinite universe filled with infinite possibilities. For one small second, I almost heard The Calling. Mesmerised, I reached out to take its hand and I almost had it and then ... then it slipped away, as it always did these days. I adjusted my money belt containing my Getaway Fund and passport and went for a wee in a bush. When I returned, the flames had almost extinguished and clouds had moved in under us and it became another lost dream.

On this next trip, our last, we were going all the way to the top. To Mount Olympus. Further for The Fat Murderer to fall, I thought to myself, weakly. Thoughts of killing him had taken a real back seat since I had been in Cyprus. It would be a fitting end to the trip – not my dad falling off the mountain, although that too, but to be away from Dhali and the sadness of Hambis's death.

My dad and I had packed our suitcases, except for the few things we would need to take with us to Troodos, after which we would be returning to Dhali for one last night and then flying home the following day, Tuesday. Flying home Tuesday and flying the coop Wednesday, I thought with terrified glee. Once I was back in England, I would craft an existence for myself and become the person I could be. And there was fuck all anyone could do to stop me. I'd just started saying 'fuck all' and it had fast become my favourite phrase, especially when The Fat Murderer was around, who I was now annoying even more by insisting on calling him by his name. It was priceless and not without some serious intention behind it. My dad was getting very stressed the closer it got to our return to the UK. One of The Philosophers had told me that ongoing stress or a sudden burst of anger or other strong emotion could cause a brain aneurysm. I was doing everything I could to assist. It would be a bonus.

By Thursday evening we were pretty much ready to go. My cut-in-half uncle came home from work, showered the sawdust off his gnarly body, and we sat down to a peasant meal of macaroni and chicken doused with lemon, olive oil and grated haloumi. Outside, a hen squawked. I guiltily stuffed a piece of chicken breast into my mouth and made a mental note to think about becoming a vegetarian at some point down the line. My moral musings were interrupted by a huge slurping noise. The Fat Murderer was sucking macaroni into his oily mouth and dabbing at the grease with bread before shoving that in as well. I could have thrown up right there and then. 'Christakis,' I said, with my mouth full – we all talked with our mouths full, there was no sound reason not to; Greeks love talking and eating and they love talking and eating at the same time even more – 'when we go to Troodos tomorrow, can I be in the truck?'

There were two reasons for the question:

1. I didn't want to have to sit in Stavros's dad's Mercedes-Benz all the way, with Stavros breathing down my neck and watching my chest. Since he had topped up

the contents of his testicles by racing me to the island at Fig Tree Bay, he had been almost predacious.
2. I wanted to be in the flatbed truck for one last thrill ride.

No answer.

'Can I go in the truck?' I asked again, forking a few pieces of macaroni. 'Uncle? Irini?'

Irini glanced up at my dad. Some exchange passed that I couldn't quite fathom, but it was an exchange nevertheless.

'What? What's going on?' I said, my free hand drifting down to rest on my money belt.

My aunt doubled down on her eating, staring maniacally at her plate. My uncle left the table.

'What?' I said. 'What?' I put down my fork and folded my arms, looking at my dad, ceaselessly shovelling food in. 'What have you done, George?' I asked him, levelly.

'DonbeblattyrudeandstopcallingmeblattyGeorge,' he snapped, speaking English now, rat mouth full of partially masticated macaroni and chicken. Not a pleasant sight. 'We going to see you grandfather tomorrow.' Shovel, shovel.

I was momentarily pleased that Irini had mentioned my dad's intention to drag me to see his useless old father. So I was ready for the fight.

'I'm not seeing that arsehole.'

'He wants to see you.' Shovel, shovel, shovel.

'I bet he does.'

'He doesn't got long to live.'

'Good. I hope he dies today so I don't have to see him tomorrow. I want to go to Troodos.'

'You come with me to see your *bapou*.' He carried on

loading macaroni into his horrible fat oleaginous rodent face. He picked up another piece of bread and used it to dab grease crassly from the corners of his mouth then chucked it in. 'Then we go to Troodos later.'

'I don't want to see that old bastard,' I said vehemently. 'I hate him.'

'You seeing those blatty old bastards in the old town though, innit? Stavros says you've been going there all the time.'

Ah, it fell into place now. Stavros. The monobrowed turncoat. He had snitched to my dad about my Greek Philosophers probably because I hadn't let him feel me up at the beach. The spying duplicitous groping moron.

'What of it?' Guilt pricked at me – not for hiding my activities but because I had abandoned those dear, dear men for reasons I now couldn't justify. I felt terrible about the way I had handled Hambis's death. I missed him. I hated The Fat Murderer even referring to them. They were mine. Not his.

'You don't think I see it, but I know you go to the old town sitting with the old men, drinking and smoking, and that's going to stop.'

'Well, Stavros was there too, so is he being told to stop?' I asked, knowing full well what the next comment would be.

'Stavros is the man. Is different.'

Christ give me strength. I couldn't wait to get out of this small town with its small-town ideas and its small-town gene pool.

I looked at my aunt. She was seething. But not nearly as much as I was. It was the old control trick, wasn't it? Here, in Cyprus, I had wandered freely only because The Fat Murderer thought I was under his direction. I was never really free, was I? Now he was reeling me in so that I was back under his thumb once we were home. Well, he had a surprise coming. Because I was off as soon as we landed. I wasn't even going to wait until we got back home. I would disappear at Heathrow and he'd never see me again.

'She doesn't have to see him,' said Irini. 'You can see she's distressed.'

'Yeah. I am. I'm not coming. You go and see him. I'll see you in Troodos.'

'You coming with me. The end of the conversation.' Dab, dab, scoff, scoff. Urgh, urgh.

I looked at my aunt. 'You have anything you want to say, Constantina?' she asked, almost pleaded, and threw a threatening look at my dad, who kept his eyes on his plate.

I thought about it. 'No. Nothing.'

She nodded at me. 'Go. We will see you in Troodos. I promise.'

I couldn't finish my food. I went to my room and tried playing my guitar, but all I could think of was what it would be like to see my grandfather again. He had been the very genesis of The Well of Shame and, if I dug deep enough, I could still feel the shadow of fear he had cast over me as a small child. Maybe it was time to dispel that fear. After all, he was just an exiled old man, destitute and dispossessed, had it not been for my dad's money. I was also morbidly curious to see The Fat Murderer and his pervert father side by side. Maybe I'd see a link, fathom a chain of connectivity between their sins. Whatever the reason, like an idiot, I agreed to go to see the old bastard with The Fat Murderer.

40

Friday afternoon was oddly bleak. The weather had changed. The wall-to-wall sunshine was now patterned with patches of passing cloud. During the shadowy moments, and without the kind blessing of sunlight, Dhali was exposed as its real self: dull and downbeat. It was depressing.

I sat on my aunt's veranda waiting for my dad to come back with a car he was borrowing from Stavros's granddad, which would take us to Nicosia to see The Pervert and then on to Mount Olympus. I played some guitar, but I kept making mistakes on easy pieces. So I put it in its hard case and propped it up beside me. I tightened my money belt. I was surprised to note that my waistline had shrunk, most likely due to the lack of Curly Wurlys out here.

I watched a colony of ants busy at work with a dead cockroach. They would make a gargantuan effort to shift the roach slightly and then the roach would hit a bump in the ground and slip backwards again, and they'd be back where they started. I watched the trail and saw where the ants wanted to take the dead insect. I could have picked it up and placed it there for them in a second. But I wondered if they would consider my intrusion an assistance or whether it might just highlight their collective weakness and make them feel bad. Perhaps it was better to let them struggle. In the end, we all have to make our own way, don't we? I did some long dribbling for old time's sake.

The Fat Murderer pulled up in an enormous old banger that looked as if it had been in a field somewhere since the end of the Second World War. It backfired twice after he'd shut off the engine. We could have hired a car, or taken a taxi, but no, we were going to drive to Nicosia to see my pervert grandfather in an exploding death trap.

My dad put his hand out of the driver's-side window and opened the car door from the outside. He stepped out of the car and came towards me, treading on several ants and the dead cockroach. I was feeling reckless and angry. Mostly at myself for agreeing to do this.

'Come on, Conniecon! Let's go,' he said, pointing to the rust bucket.

'I'm not getting in that pile of shit, George,' I said, wanting to wind him up – there was still time for that aneurysm.

'Is a blatty good car, this one. Stavros's grandfather drive this for years. Starting every time,' he said, looking as proud as if he had made the thing with his own hands.

'It's fucking ancient, George,' I said.

'Conniecon, stop calling me George.'

'George, stop calling me Conniecon.'

'Get in the fackin' car.'

I read the insignia at the rear of the car. 'What the hell is a Humber?' I said.

'Get in, Conniecon.'

I wanted to run right at that moment, but somewhere deep down I knew it was important for us both to see my grandfather together. I needed to see evidence; to step out of the partially illusionary state I'd been drifting in and out of for much of my life; to see it there, in front of me, so that I could *know* it was real and not something half imagined nor the half re-written memory of a bereaved child. That I had not misinterpreted things that were not always tangible. Once I left this behind, I had everything to look forward to.

For The Fat Murderer it was the exact opposite. He needed me to be there as his audience, to witness the evidence of his innocence; to prove to himself that the shame that he knew deep down to be real was a mere illusion. That he wasn't just like his own father. If he acknowledged one particle of the shared blackness that both he and his father possessed, then all the light he so zealously shone on himself would be snuffed out. We were, each in our way, seeking to escape the evil that was our only bond.

The Fat Murderer and I didn't speak all the way to Nicosia. I had placed my guitar case between us so that our arms wouldn't accidentally touch. It kept getting in the way of the gear stick but he dared not say a word. I was on board for the ride but I was gelignite.

We parked, with just one backfire, in a suburban street outside a large, grey building that looked a lot like every other downtrodden municipal building in Cyprus: spare and temporary. There was a shabby sign outside, which read '*Katoikia Yia Ilikiomenous*', which I assumed translated as 'Home for Elderly Perverts and Arseholes'. A few old men sat on cheap chairs placed randomly on a raised concrete veranda. Some of them were lying on sprung bedsteads covered with thin mattresses. I think we were both shocked at how terrible it was.

My dad forgot that the car door on his side wouldn't open from the inside. The handle flapped uselessly. He started to wind down the window and the winder came off in his hand, leaving him with no way out. I looked at him over my guitar case. 'Typical,' I said. He ignored me.

He put the winder back on its fixture, carefully wound down his window and opened his door from the outside.

'Just needs some tapple you tee forty,' he mumbled. As if he was going to find WD-40 in this godforsaken hellhole.

As I got out of the car, I felt a release of blood in my underwear. I had started my period. Great. Today just got better and better.

'George, I have to go to the pharmacy,' I told my dad.

'What for?' he asked, sensing some plot to get out of going inside The Bleak Home For People No One Cared About.

'Because, George, I have started my period.'

'No, you haven't.'

'I have.'

'Why now? The second we get here?'

I was barely in control of reason. Plus, I was bleeding quite heavily now. I could feel it.

'Well, any minute now blood is going to be coming through my shorts so I really need to get some tampons. Give me some money.'

Still looking sceptical, my dad handed over a few lira.

'That's not nearly enough,' I said. It was more than enough.

He handed me a few more grubby notes.

'More than that,' I said.

He handed me a bunch of notes.

'Bring me the change,' he said.

'Sure thing, George,' I replied, intending to add the entire lot to my Getaway Fund – minus a few shillings for tampons. I went off in search of a pharmacy.

'Leave your blatty guitar in the car,' he called as I left.

'No chance, George,' I said, mostly to myself. I was taking it with me. It was a small reminder of who I was. I checked and double-checked my money belt – it was like a tic these days. 'No bloody chance.'

I dragged out tampon leave for as long as I could, taking backstreets and skirting through the shady parts. It was well past midday now and the weather was hot and heavy. My guitar case kept bashing against my legs with an irritating thwap sound. Sweat was running down my neck and chest and my inner thighs were beginning to chafe. I was feeling inconsolably ratty.

I found a pharmacy on Ledra Street, just before the Stoa Tarsi, the last cross road before the Greek–Turkish border. I hadn't expected to fetch up so close to this symbol of separation, to see homes cut in half by a line that people were afraid to cross; to see the physical evidence of all those long conversations with The Philosophers that I hadn't understood nor really cared about. Now I got it. And it stopped me in my tracks. Control. It was insidious and cruel and it was a game of power and fear. Whether you were nations or individuals, whoever had the power wielded the fear. Cyprus had been whole and now it was bifurcated. One side brutally excised from the other. Like my family.

I felt rather than heard the footsteps behind me. It was the pharmacist. 'Terrible, isn't it?' he said, looking at the barrier. 'Yes, it is,' I replied, though I doubted we were thinking about the same thing. I went inside the shop and he followed. He locked up for siesta as I left.

'One Cyprus' had been spray-painted on a broken wall. I wanted to cry.

Tampons in hand, I found a café that was closed but had

an outside toilet that wasn't locked. It was a terrible toilet. The old Greek drainage system in Cyprus was too fragile and narrow for modern toilet paper. When you wiped, you had to place the paper in a wastepaper bin by the loo. This bin hadn't been emptied for some time. The stench was overpowering. There were flies buzzing around the soiled tissues spilling onto the floor and there were mosquitos on the walls. The toilet had no seat and was a study in yellow sticky patches and pubic hair. The microbes must have been having a banquet. I tried not to inhale or touch anything. I hovered to wee, used my pants to wipe and threw them in the bin, disturbing a cluster of flies, which rose irritably in a buzzy black cloud before settling back down to their task of consuming faeces. Fully tamponed up, I couldn't think of anything else to do other than to go to the old people's home.

 When I arrived, the old bastard was lying prostrate on one of the flimsy mattresses, his eyes covered with one gnarly hand, pretending to cry, bemoaning his lot. He was wearing a white vest and grey baggy trousers. The fly was only half zipped up. Of course. His belly flopped over the waistband. He had dusty bare feet with hard yellow toenails. He reeked of stale perspiration and cunning. He hadn't changed much. He looked a lot like my dad. I looked a lot like my dad. What a frightful triptych we made. I wondered how much it would cost to have a new face done with plastic surgery. It would be worth it, whatever the cost.

 When he saw me, the duplicitous old bastard revved up the tears and held his hand out to touch me, imploring. I shrank away and dared my dad to say something. The old perv boo-hooed loudly, staring at me morosely and asking my dad why

I wouldn't come close. Fucking cheek. Had he conveniently forgotten what he done? Or, like my dad, did he condone it. He repulsed me. They both did.

I sat on the edge of one of the filthy chairs as far away as possible with my hand on my money belt and my guitar case in front of me like armour. I said nothing while The Fat Murderer and The Pervert spoke. A light rain began to fall from a mostly blue sky. It was strange.

I watched them both, hoping for some revelation or education or explanation as to how it had all come to this: a grandfather outlawed from his own village, his son having murdered his wife and children, and, in turn, his daughter who'd spent the last eighteen months thinking of ways to kill her father. Bloody hell.

The Fat Murderer tried to encourage me to embrace his father when we left, but I was having none of that. The old bastard stunk worse than the bloody tampon toilet and, if I was ever going to touch him, it would be to wring his baggy old neck. He laid on the crocodile tears again.

A light but steady rain was falling now. I walked to the car and waited while my dad exchanged last words with his dad. He took a bundle of notes out of his trouser pocket and counted out a whole wad and gave it to the old geezer, who didn't even look at it but threw it on the table by his side as if it was of no importance to him. The sly old fuck. It was important all right; I saw the greedy glint in his eyes. My dad undid the driver's-side door, got in the car, and attempted to wind down his window. The winder came off in his hand. He fixed it back on and managed to work the window down an inch until it refused to budge any further. He didn't look at me as the car coughed and lurched into action.

The rain got steadily heavier as we approached the foothills of the Troodos mountains. A band of black, dense cloud clung to the middle section of the peaks, but we could see, from this distance, that the top was bestowed with a mellow late summer sunshine. If I was going to be here at all, I wanted to be at the top, to be with other people and to be free from the pall of this hideous day.

My dad was driving angry. I was an angry passenger. We were both angry with me. He was angry because I had added ignominy to his habitual wrath; I had failed to deliver whatever it was he had wanted to get from this disgusting charade. I was fuming. I had learned nothing from the exercise. I hadn't observed a single revelation. I hadn't confronted anyone about anything. I had achieved nothing. Again. It had got to the point where I couldn't blame anyone else for my shitstorm of a life. I was the architect of my own downfall. Time and time again, it occurred to me now, I had engaged in one foolhardy thing after another without ever really thinking it through to a satisfying outcome. I hadn't managed to kill my father and I probably never would. I was really, truly deeply disappointed with myself. I was in such desperate need of comfort. And it was now, if at any time at all, that I could do with remembering my mum's name, but I just could not bring it to my mind no matter how hard I tried.

As we climbed, the rain quickened. The closer we drove to the band of cloud, the harder it came. Then we were in it: rain hammering the car. The shaky old wipers were useless and just smeared rain and dust across the windscreen, so it was difficult to see anything.

'Just turn them off, George,' I said to my dad. 'They're making it worse.'

He ignored me and made them go faster, which just smeared the windscreen more efficiently.

I peered into the grey murk that was now enveloping us. I couldn't see beyond the nose of the car. Water was cascading into the vehicle through the inch of open window on the driver's side. My dad's shirt was wet down one arm and part of his chest. I saw him reach for the winder to close the window and it came off in his hand again. He pressed it back onto its fixing, where it wobbled and threatened to fall on the floor.

I was no expert driver, but it was obvious to me that the car wasn't up to the journey. On the steeper switchbacks, my dad had to stop, put the handbrake on, go into first gear, and ease the car into a precarious hill start. Each time he slid into second gear the car would just judder and stall and we'd have to start all over again.

'We have to go back down,' I said. 'We won't get to the top. This shit car is going to conk.'

My dad stared ahead dementedly.

'Sunshine is come soon,' he said, through gritted teeth, as the car lurched into second gear again, stalled and rolled backwards. He pulled up the handbrake and the car did a little skid.

I snapped.

'Jesuschristalfuckingmightygeorge, just find somewhere to turn around and let's get this coffin back down the mountain.' It would be some kind of weird poetry if he managed to kill me in a car accident too, wouldn't it? But the numbskull kept going.

Where the track was rocky, there was at least some traction, but the Humber's balding tyres slipped on softer, wetter ground. My uncle could have done this journey with his eyes closed, but even he wouldn't have attempted it in this weather – nor, come to that, in this heap of a car. My dad hadn't driven these roads since he was my age. I could see he was losing it, starting to panic. I thought he was as close to an aneurysm as I could hope for, but I really didn't want him dropping dead at the wheel while I was his passenger.

'Calm the fuck down, George. You getting your knickers in a twist isn't going to help anyone,' I said. He swore in Greek.

The rain was relentless now. Crashing down on the windscreen, falling in sheets, obscuring everything. The car slipped sideways, stalled again and backfired. He tried to start it. And start it. And start it. It just coughed, a little weaker each time.

'Stop starting it,' I shouted over the rain pounding on the windscreen. 'You're flooding the engine.'

He took his foot, mercifully, off the accelerator.

'You are going to stay here,' he said.

It was hard to hear him, so loud was the smashing of the water on the car.

'What? What did you say?'

'I says, you are going to stay here.' He was almost shouting.

'Why? Where are you going? There's nowhere to go, George. We're stuck.'

'You going to stay here in Cyprus. To live.'

It took me a moment.

'What do you mean I am going to stay here in Cyprus? To live? We're going home on Tuesday.'

'No.'

'What do you mean, *no?*' My guitar was sitting between us; I moved it to the side slightly so I could see him properly. 'I've had enough of it here. I have to get back to school. We have to go back. There's no discussion.'

The rain redoubled its efforts. It washed down the windows like a monsoon. Condensation was building up inside the car and, despite the cool rain, the car was pounding hot and stuffy. I tried cranking my window but water came in, beating down on my arm. I wound it back up.

'I'm going back,' I said, flatly.

'I am going back,' he said slowly. 'You going to stay here, in Cyprus.'

'No, I'm not. I'm going back.' I was afraid now. This wasn't all there was coming to me; I could feel it. 'What the fuck am I gonna do in Cyprus?'

'You going to get married.'

'I'm not.'

'You going to start a new life here, a good life with good people.'

'My life is in England...'

'Conniecon, since you mum and brothers died, you been crazy. You talking to yourself in you room all night, you stealing money, you putting dirty socks in my pockets, you smoking and drinking the whisky, you treading on the marrow plants, you going out and fucking the boys. Time to stop. Here is good for you. You like Stavros.'

I laughed. A sort of hollow ha ha ha. So that's why he hadn't minded my hanging around with that dirty snitching dimwit. God. Would I ever stop being an idiot?

I turned and looked at him squarely.

'I'm not marrying Stavros.'

'You getting engaged this weekend. We have a party in Troodos. I come back next year and we have the wedding. We have big wedding. You'll be very happy.'

'You can have a wedding, but I'm not gonna be there. You can't make me. Stavros? *Fucking Stavros?*'

'Stop with this fackin' all the time, Connie.'

'Fucking Stavros. Are you mad? Has the last sane cell finally left your brain? *Stavros?*'

'Yes, blatty Stavros. Okay?'

'He's got the personality of a cockroach. A cockroach with brain damage. His bloody eyebrows meet in the middle. I don't even fancy Stavros.'

'You don't have to fancying him. Is not about the sex. Is about partnership. He is come from a good family.'

'You can't make me. You can't. You can't.'

I was speechless. I had finally run out of words. This was insanity. Could he make me marry Stavros? *Could he?* What was the age of consent here? Was I Cypriot? No, my passport was British and it was right here in my money belt, with my stash. I thought of Auntie Roulla. If I could get to a phone when we were back in town, I could call her. She would know what to do. But, then, some bingo ball in my brain, one that had been rattling around in a sticky corner of my mind, suddenly fell into place. Bingo. I thought of how Auntie Roulla had been before we left England. How she had tried to tell me in Vas's bedroom before her husband had silenced her.

'Auntie Roulla knew about this, didn't she?' I said quietly.

'Is got nothing to do with Roulla.'

'You made her not tell. She was my only one.'

Please remember I tried for you ... whispered in my ear the last time I saw her.

'You fucking bastard. You fucking bastard.'

'Shaddap,' he spat.

'Does Irini know? Does she?'

'No, she can't be trusted, that one. She's liar and a big mouth.' He snarled spitefully.

'What, because she was right about your shitty father? And she had your number right from the start, didn't she? Who else knows? *Who else?!*'

'No one. Just Stavros family and the priest who is going to marry you.'

Oh, bingo again. The priest ... of course, Panayiotis's brother. And The Philosophers ... all those conversations about women's choices. They knew. It was right there in front of me and I couldn't see it. Well, I was crystal-clear now: I wasn't going to marry Stavros. And I wasn't going to stay in Cyprus. I started making mad lightning-fast plans in my head. I'd steal away tonight and make a run for it while they were all sleeping on the *bablomas*. I had money; I had my passport. Or I'd kill him in the night, stab him in the chest with the kebab knife and blame it on a mysterious stranger who had come in the night and stolen away again. I'd stab myself a bit to make it look authentic. Well, there was nothing to lose now ...

I pulled back my fist and smashed it into The Fat Murderer's face. It was a lame punch because it glanced off his greasy fat chop, but I pulled back again and landed a better one. I opened the car door before he could hit me back. Sod it. I was going now.

'Where you going, stay in the car,' he said, grabbing my sleeve.

'I'm not staying here. I'm not marrying anyone. I have plans. You know nothing.' I shook him off, grabbed my guitar and threw it out of the door. I stepped out of the car into the drenching rain and the car lurched forward. I jerked backwards, letting go of the door and it swung open, forcefully.

'Whoah! Connie, what's happening?' The Fat Murderer said, alarmed now.

I walked around to the back of the car and saw that, when we had slid to a halt, we had skidded sideways and the car was now sitting across the narrow track. The offside front wheel was suspended in mid-air, no ground beneath it, floating above nothing. The nearside wheel was barely holding on. Now that my weight had been removed from the passenger side, the car rocked, threatening to tip.

'The front wheel is hanging off the road,' I shouted through the driving torrent. Water was building up fast, flooding now, running down the track towards us, under my feet and under the car. It was hard to stand.

I ran back around to the open passenger door, slipping and going down in the mud twice in quick succession, afraid to steady myself on the car in case I upset the delicate balance and sent it over the edge. The Fat Murderer was trying to open his window so that he could stick his arm out and open his door. The winder came off in his hand and he dropped it somewhere in the footwell. He bent down to get it, sending the car rocking wildly again.

'Stop moving! On your side. Your wheel. It's hanging off,' I shouted through the open passenger door, pointing. 'What do I do?' I was breathing fast and heavy; everything was going blurred and then coming back into focus.

'Connie, get back in the car, sit in the back seat and don't move,' he shouted back. 'Then I climb across and get out of the car on your side and then I sit on the back of the car and you can get out slow then I jump off. Okay? Trust me.'

This was more logic than I had heard from him in a lifetime. And it may have worked. The car groaned and pitched again. I couldn't see through the mist and the rain, but I was pretty sure, beyond the precipice, there was nothing but a deep drop. I stopped and thought. And listened.

Somewhere up above the clouds I could hear two buzzards calling to each other. A plaintive cry: keeew keeew, echoing around the mountains, soaring and swooping, keeew keeew, keeew keeew . . . And then it came. The Calling, after all this time, it was here, somewhere above the clouds and somewhere deep within me, a perfect union. I could hear it now and its message was clear. Visions came jumbled up, slowly at first then faster and so furiously:

My mother's face as he drove away on that night in 1974 . . .

A surge of water came down the hill, lifting the car. I watched in awe as its back end wavered and its front end lurched. It just needed a small nudge. I nudged.

Marc and David torn to shreds . . .

I leant against the car a little harder. It wouldn't budge, it continued to seesaw back and forth, back and forth. The movement caused the passenger door to swing and click shut.

The Great School Disco Disaster of 1975, the look on those troubled faces as I was dragged from the school hall . . . The Well of Shame overflowing at the cinema . . .

'Connie!! Blatty wake up, you fackin' stupid cow!!' The Fat Murderer was banging on the passenger-side window.

Telling me that no one would ever want me, denying my mum the yellow kitchen she had wanted for five years, for five bloody years, the stench of his sickness in the bathroom, the bruises and the lies . . .

He was panicking now. I could see through the torrent of water running down the glass that The Fat Murderer was scrambling around in the footwell looking for his window winder. He banged on the window, bloodshot eyes rolling around in terror. Who was wielding the fear now, eh?

How do you like that? Huh? How does it feel to be on the receiving end for once?

'Connie, open the blatty door!!! I'm going to fackin' kill you!'

I leant against the back end of the car with all my weight; it rocked dangerously, making an agonised creaking sound.

Tearing apart my beautiful love with Vas, giving carte blanche to perverts like his own father and Peter Pervy Roy to handle me like the damaged goods that he'd made me into, and me being so polite like such a good girl because that's what he told me to be ...

The car was bouncing now, gaining momentum with each push I gave it.

... and inside screaming and squirming and blotting it out so that I could get through another day and now you think you can just get rid of me and marry me off to a total stranger. Well, that's the wrong way round. I was supposed to get rid of you, all those attempts at trying to kill you and you justwouldn'tfuckingdiesohowdoesitfeelnow, you Fat Fucking Murdering Bastard!

I filled my lungs with air and threw my head back. I emptied my soul with a guttural cry, answering The Calling at long last and, with all the strength I had, pushed the car over the edge. It disappeared into the mist as it crunched and scraped, until I could hear nothing but the rain.

Then, I picked up my guitar and I walked away.

The date was September 16th, 1977. The day Marc Bolan died.

2007

41

The Guitar Bar stands on the edge of a small village, on the south coast of Cyprus, about 2km from the beach. It's my bar. You'll know you've come to the right place because, although we don't have a sign outside, we do have a huge neon electric guitar on the wall inside. Corny, isn't it? I admit it, I am a bit corny these days. And, at forty-six, well, so what?

Most people still bypass the village, drawn instead to the bigger attractions of Limassol or Paphos nearby. I'm happy with that. The longer the tourists stay away from here, the better. The Guitar Bar has avoided the inescapable onslaught of tourism so far. You have to know it's there to know it's there, because we are set back from the road in a small citrus grove, totally obscured from passers-by. If you do come looking, find the ancient twin olive trees on the road as it leaves the village. Walk between them and you'll discover a narrow dirt path, edged with small white rocks, which winds its way through the grove and opens out to a small clearing. At the far side of the clearing are three broad steps leading up to a white veranda, upon which sits The Guitar Bar. It's a small building, just one storey with a flat roof terrace, painted in brilliant chalky white with azure shutters and doors, and swathed in jasmine and bougainvillaea. There are tables and chairs on the veranda, which spill out into private little corners of the orchard where you can sit amongst the trees, unseen and in perfect peace. Here, you step into an old world, a world that doesn't care what you wear or who you are, a world where how much you own or where you've been have no currency. A world where dreams can come and go as they please and who is to say what is real and what is not? And people do find us. The right people. Most people are familiar faces. They come back year after year to eat and drink or sometimes just to sit and drink and think. But always to hear the music. They come to be nourished, not merely fed.

I have my gang: they're not famous pop stars or Greek philosophers; in fact, they're mostly animals and lunatics, but we get along well. There are the cats, of course there are cats. They were here first and considered our moving into their grove not so much an encroachment as the arrival of staff. Before we arrived, they ate geckos. Now they eat souvlaki. The cats are full and the geckos are relaxed.

Last year I took on a chef: Mohammed is all contradictions. He says he is 'religiously fluid' and has been known to accept the tenets of Buddhism, Zoroastrianism and Hinduism. He is actually half Egyptian, half Greek by birth, and he worships in both the mosque and the Orthodox church. He extolls the virtues of both nationalities and is certain that he has inherited them all, in particular a worship of cats, 'Like my direct ancestors, the pharaohs.' He makes The Guitar Bar cats three square meals a day and gives them far more attention than they require. His favourite is a superior-looking overly pampered tabby he has named Queen Fattyma. Mohammed insists he doesn't overfeed her: 'She has a thyroid problem.'

To be fair to Queen Fattyma, all the cats are overweight, but they are fat and happy. They love the music and they love the people. They are perceptive little creatures. Where food and drink fall short of succour, they give people the warmth and solace they need. And to their credit, they never shit near the bar.

And then there's Charalambous, the aged and sprightly waiter who tends my tables. Charalambous is a tiresome bag of armchair psychology and homespun philosophy. He insists he is a 'people person' and that he 'can spot a spirit twin' immediately. More accurately, he's part waiter, part nosy parker. He loves to uncover the secrets that people bring to the grove. He calls the more interesting guests The Onions, and seeks to peel back their layers to find who they really are at their core. I think it is somehow due to him having to deny his own real identity for such a large part of his life.

When Charalambous first wandered into my grove looking for freedom and somewhere to belong, he told me we had met before in another lifetime (we hadn't). He said one day I would remember it too (I won't). I nodded pleasantly just to appease him. I changed the subject and complimented him on what he was wearing: a tie-dyed sarong and a David Bowie *Diamond Dogs* T-shirt.

We both spoke our 'truths', as he liked to call them. Charalambous was frank about his past. He came from money and was married by arrangement when he was nineteen and, after a good deal of electric-shock therapy treatment to try to cure him of his perversions, he had conformed to being a good husband and father. When his wife died and his two children had grown up and left Cyprus, he left the tiny mountain village where he had lived under heterosexual camouflage his entire life, and blossomed. He wore the Bowie T-shirt because, he said, the song 'Rebel Rebel', from the *Diamond Dogs* (AKA Dog's Dinner) album, had come along just when he was at his lowest ebb. The song's words had spoken Charalambous's truth to him before Charalambous had even known it was his truth, 'really, totally, bang on, exactly', and had given him hope.

I refrained from telling Charalambous that it was a shame he had chosen such a turd of a song as his anthem. Instead, I told him that I had killed my father. Charalambous's father was not dissimilar to mine and he said it was a good job I had finished him off. I said it was a good job that he, Charalambous, had finally come out of the closet and that he could stay for as long as he wanted. He said he didn't need a job, but I said he might as well make himself useful. I've been bossing him around and paying him nothing ever since.

I live in a modest but gorgeous old house on the plot. It's set way back in the trees, steeped in honeysuckle and birdsong. I walk to and from there to work every day. Mohammed lives in the village. I don't know where Charalambous actually lives. When he's not staying in my spare room, he's what he calls 'staying over with new friends'. I think he'd love to be more explicit. 'Come on, let's swap sexy stories!!' he says, but swapping tales of sexual exploits isn't professional, I tell him. Though it's mainly because I've got none to tell.

I bought the grove five years ago when land was still cheap. I think it must be worth something these days. I get a lot of sweaty developers snooping around, asking if it's for sale. When I move on, and I probably will, I won't sell. I'll just leave everything here, as it is, and let it remain a refuge of the old world, pure and nostalgic. It's not a solely philanthropic idea. I'll get a lot of joy out of fucking with the developers. They're a bunch of cunts.

The irony of my settling in Cyprus after a lifetime of moaning about Greeks isn't lost on me. I changed my mind and I don't care if I'm a big hypocrite. To be honest, I had no intention of ever settling in one place. I loved travelling across the world with my guitar and had always avoided any job that might take me back to the scene of my crime. Yet, wherever I went, no matter how hard the sun shone or where the jasmine bloomed, I noticed I could never find the *feeling* I'd had when I spent the summer of '77 in Cyprus. Some places touched me in a similar way but left me unsated. Later, I began to hanker after it, The Cyprus Feeling. The otherworldliness of the place. I missed this nation of hard-working, hard-loving eccentrics. I was shocked and pleased to note that what I really wanted – *needed* – was to be immersed in the utter, fabulous nonsense of the Greeks. Their pride and warmth, which I had once scorned as suffocation, was now something I valued and, actually, craved. I missed them. And I'd never say this out loud, but I *was* them! I got The Calling to come home. And here I am.

Which was all great and ooh la la, etc, until the thing that happened last week. The week that will be forever known as The Week of the Great Mind Fuck of 2007.

42

I hadn't thought about those initial years after The Murdering of the Fat Murderer for a long while. I couldn't wait to put them behind me. I had made it out of Cyprus in 1977. I spent a few days in a cheap pension on the coast at Larnaca, swimming, thinking, worrying and overeating, then flew to England on the return flight we had booked. I didn't go back to our London house or the Greek Freaks for three badly-thought-out and therefore not very good reasons:

1. There was nothing there any more. (Wrong: there could have been money, comfort, support and the Rive Gauche-scented bosom of Auntie Roulla. But I wasn't thinking straight on account of having just done a murder by pushing my dad off a mountain.)
2. I never felt bad about killing my dad, not for a second. I was as pleased as pie to be shot of the bastard. But I harboured an illogical fear that the police would be there, waiting to arrest me for murder, and I'd finally end up in Holloway Prison trying to find the biggest lesbian to befriend for my own safety. (Wrong: it was an accident. Just like my dad's other so-called accident. I simply expedited it. And, anyway, lesbians never fancy me, which I've always found quite hurtful.)

3. I had this notion that I could start over again. That I had finally answered The Calling and was moving inexorably towards a new wipe-clean me. (Wrong again: there are no new beginnings, we can never truly wash off our stains.)
Oh, and
4. Vas. Once upon a time, I had considered us equals. The chasm between us was so vast now that I couldn't bear to look in his direction, let alone move in his circles. He was at Oxford; he had a relationship with someone normal. He *was* clean. He had a life. I was grubby and homeless. I barely had an existence.

Bearing in mind my psychological glitching, it's a wonder that I survived those few first years. Because they were truly difficult. I stayed in some pretty skanky places and probably spent more of my stash of cash on disinfectant than food. I was isolated and confused. Eventually, just when the cash was running low, I saw an ad in a restaurant window for a musician. They were desperate and asked if I could play that evening and it became a regular gig. I got a lot of recommendations and a lot of free meals.

I contacted Ms Liz Liddle. I told her I couldn't afford to come to Guildhall, as I needed to earn money. She had a friend who was a musical agent and introduced us, and my career as a session musician began. I travelled all over the world playing for bands who weren't talented enough to play for themselves. And some who were talented but needed an extra guitar on stage. Those were my favourite gigs. When I wasn't touring, I was in a recording studio. I was most comfortable in the recording studio, away from the world, just me and my guitar.

I still couldn't remember my mum's name. I had a stint with a chain-smoking therapist called Arthur Spooner. In between clearing mucus from his permanently congested bronchi, he told me I was suffering from PTSD and that one day I might be triggered and the memory would come back. He agreed it was best if I remembered it myself. If someone else gave me the name, it may not register as real. Anyway, I had no one left to ask, so it was a pointless point. He wasn't much help psychologically, but I did give up smoking.

When I tell people my story, and I rarely do, they look distraught, pitying. But that's not the way I'm telling it. It's what they've been conditioned to think and feel. The bad stuff is only a part of me. Not all of me. People think that when something bad happens to you, it *is* you. It is not. It's just one part. I wasn't broken by what had happened. I was changed. I was fortified.

And that worked very well for me until The Quiet Man arrived.

43

He came the second week of September, when the shadows were just beginning to lengthen. Outside, the pavements were still being baked through long days of uncompromising heat. But here, in the grove, the sun had made peace with the shade and had turned mellow and compassionate. He would come to The Guitar Bar. He would always sit at one of the tables amongst the trees, partially but not entirely hidden.

When The Quiet Man first arrived, Charalambous was in the bar singing his favourite tune in a strong Greek accent – 'If you the boy or the girl . . . Rrrrebel Rrrrebel . . .' He is always trying to get me to play it on guitar for him, but I refuse to be drawn into a karaoke singalong. He was busily singing and spraying his 'Corner of Culture', as he likes to call it, with Dettol. He has instigated a book exchange system, which is basically a virus exchange system as far as I'm concerned. I said Charalambous could have his free book club but that he had to keep the books germ-free. To give him his credit, he has done so.

I interrupted Charalambous's spraying and wiping and singing and told him to serve our new customer. He came back to the kitchen, after taking the order, looking a little perplexed. He checked his badly applied makeup in the mirror. He nodded, satisfied with his reflection. I looked in the mirror with him, wondering what on earth he was seeing that I wasn't.

'Charalambous, your makeup looks terrible,' I said.

'You don't know. You don't wear makeup,' he replied.

'You are the most ridiculous homosexual I have ever met,' I said.

'And you are the most in-the-cupboard lesbian I have ever met,' he replied.

'I'd rather be a lesbian than an old poof.'

'I'd rather be an old poof than a cupboard lesbian spinster.'

'It's a closet not a cupboard.'

'Cupboard, closet, men or women, Constance, you ain't getting none of anything, sister! So the point is a moot.'

The routine never gets old. He jerked his head back at the man sitting at the table.

'He speaks very quietly, that Onion. He doesn't say anything.'

'Well, what did he order?'

'I asked him and he said "anything".'

'Just give him the usual, then.'

'What if he is a vegetarian?'

'Did he say he was?'

'No.'

We decided he probably wasn't a vegetarian, then. Had he been, that would have been his first sentence. 'Hello, I'm a vegetarian.' So, we gave him the day's special: souvlaki and salad with a glass of wine and some water. He finished it all and spent a quiet hour reading a hefty-looking tome that he had hauled out of his satchel. I spent a quiet hour behind the bar, elbows on the surface, watching him through the open door. I was using my powers of subliminal suggestiveness to urge him to turn around so that I could see his face. He never looked up.

'What are you staring at The Quiet Man for?' said Charalambous, staring himself. He lit a cigarette and shook out the match with a series of dramatic flourishes.

'Put that fag out, no one wants to be waited on by an ashtray. Give him a complimentary coffee, and find out what he's reading.'

'*Panayia mou* ...' said Charalambous, tapping out his cigarette.

He came back looking pleased with himself.

'Poetry. He's reading poetry.'

'What poetry?'

'Poems.'

'God give me strength. Give him a complimentary ouzo and find out which poetry.'

'*Gamimeni Kolasi* ...'

'Fucking hell, yourself. Go.'

He came scuttling back.

'George Herbert. He's reading about somebody called the George Herbert.'

'How old is he?'

'I don't know. Forty, fifty, thirty. I don't know ... he won't let me peel. I ask him and he gives me nothing.'

Charalambous picked up his duster and his bottle of Dettol and continued wiping down the books.

He came four days in a row, in the mid-afternoon when the bar was at its quietest. I always spotted him when he was already seated, his back to the bar, head buried in a book. Once or twice, he left his book on the table and his satchel bag on the floor and wandered through the gardens. I was itching to have a look in his bag, but didn't have the nerve in case he came back and caught me. I tried to get Charalambous to do it but he refused.

The Quiet Man stirred me up. There was nothing I could put my finger on. He had no distinguishing features that I could see. He was tall but not very tall. He was average build and from the back looked like any other person. He wore jeans and a black T-shirt and sometimes made notes in a small leather-bound book. I liked his arms. I liked the way he turned his pages. In a very short time I had become obsessed. It was discomforting. I felt nervous, star-struck. I drove Charalambous round the bend because I kept sending him over to spy and come back with information.

'Ask him what he's here for.'

A funeral.

'Ask him if he's married.'

Yes.

'Ask him if he's got kids.'

Two.

His patience would always run out, but I got the sense that he was as intrigued as I was.

The Quiet Man made me feel nostalgic for things I hadn't thought of for many years. As if I were sleepwalking backwards, drifting in time. I thought I saw shadow people from a past I had deliberately forgotten.

And then they emerged from the shadows into a glaringly bright spotlight.

It was that perfect time, the no man's land between day and night. I sat outside a café in town, drinking coffee, watching the old Greeks taking their *peripatos*, their evening walk. It was only the old ones who had time for walking now. Everyone else was in a rush. At once, I got a waft of a perfume, a familiar, long-ago smell I couldn't place. Rive Gauche? Why did I think Rive Gauche? Then, almost immediately after, I saw a familiar helmet-shaped hairdo on the other side of the narrow road, followed closely by two other helmet-shaped hairdos. I stood up to see better. It took a moment for time to catch up with me, but it was definitely them: the aunties. Doulla, Goulla and my beloved Roulla. I sat down and sank low in my chair.

I should have followed them. I should have made certain. Back at The Guitar Bar, where things were tangible, I wasn't so sure. I sat at one of my tables, pressing my hands against the wooden surface for reassurance that I was still real.

Charalambous minced over. Mince was the word he insisted I use to describe his walk. He would make me watch him walk and ask, 'How is my mince?' He had been waiting for most of his life to have the freedom to mince, and he was mincing for mankind. He had been experimenting with lipstick and was waiting for me to notice. It looked bad.

'You look like a clown,' I said.

'Well, you teach me how to do it, then.'

'I can't be arsed, Charalambous. Just find another colour.'

'You're in a funny mood,' he said.

'I am.'

'Is it The Quiet Man?' said Charalambous. 'He came back again today after you left.'

'What? What do you mean he came back?'

'He came back.'

'What did he want?'

'He wanted to see if you were here. I think he fancies you.' He poked me in each breast playfully, saying 'Boing boing' to augment each poke. I ignored it.

'What did he say?' I asked.

'He says he would like to speak to the woman.'

'Has he mentioned me by name?'

'No. He just says the woman. I never told him your name, he never asked.'

'Thank you, Charalambous. You've been absolutely useless as usual.'

And then, on day six of The Week of the Great Mind Fuck of 2007, the slowly crumbling rock face of my sanity fell, full force. I saw Peter Pervy Roy. Peter. Pervy. Roy.

I had gone for a swim. I was drying off on a lounger when I felt a shadow cast across my early autumn sunshine. I looked up, shielding my eyes from the light spilling around the silhouette in front of me. He had his hands on his hips and his legs spread wide in a revolting power stance.

'Well, bloody hell, Connie Costa, you haven't changed a bit.'

I couldn't see the face through the glare but I knew the voice; slimy and cocky.

I thought three things:

1. Is he real?
2. He is real.
3. I wish I was wearing more clothes.
    Oh, and
4. I wish he wasn't real.

I reached into my beach bag and pulled out my wrap. I stood up and tied it around myself. I shifted position so that Peter Pervy Roy had the sun in his eyes. Feeling less vulnerable and with the advantage of a clear view, I felt better. He must have been knocking seventy, but I was pleased to see that he had not worn well at all. His face was puffy. His paunch sat over the waistband of his shorts. His legs were skinny and knobbly with varicose veins. I hoped they were painful.

I'd played this scene in my mind over and again through the early years. The adult me, confident and strong, meets an old assailant. Him. What joy it would bring. How ready I would be; how cutting and punishing. Now, I had nothing.

'So, this is where you've been hiding yourself, is it?' he said. Christ, he was still trotting out the same old lines.

I was about to say 'I'm not hiding', when I caught myself. *You are a grown-up, Constance.*

'What are you doing here?' I said, consciously relieving my face of the painful smile. *Remember who you are, Constance.*

'Well, that's a nice greeting for your old Uncle Pete,' he slimed.

After an uncomfortable pause, he shifted his stance and folded his arms in front of him.

'Shame about the way your dad went,' he said, suddenly.

Fuck. What did he know?

'Why are you here?' I said, as coldly as I could.

'Same reason you are. Your dad's funeral,' he said, assuming I was up to date with whatever he was blethering on about. 'It was so sudden, wasn't it? Poor George. One minute he was fine, then, last week, poof, he just went, like that.' He snapped his fingers. 'Terrible. Terrible. Terrible . . . He was a good man, your dad.'

I still said nothing. I was focused on trying to keep both feet planted on shifting ground.

'I was surprised we didn't see you yesterday at the get-together.'

I gave no response.

'Yeah, George's wife got us all together for drinks. It was lovely meeting some of your dad's old mates. Funny, innit?

We all knew your dad but never knew each other. But that's funerals for you. I s'pose you know 'em all, Mikis, Marios and them?'

I could have spontaneously combusted right there and then. How dare he speak to me as if we were old friends, this rundown, flabby bag of reek. And also, what the holy mother of all fucks???? I picked up my bag and slipped on my sandals. I had to get away and think. I left him mid-sentence and didn't look back.

Holy mother of all fucks. All the way back to The Guitar Bar, that's pretty much all I said to myself. Holy mother of all the fucking fucks.

Charalambous had washed the veranda and was setting candles in jars on the tables. When he saw me, he came running so fast that he slipped on the wet steps and windmilled his arms to try to regain balance. He landed on his backside and with a bounce he had no right to in his advanced years, he sprang back up and grabbed me by the shoulders.

'The Quiet Man came again,' he said, out of breath with either exertion, excitement or both.

I nodded. 'Okay.'

'He says he can't come back tomorrow, but he will be here the day after to see you and to please be here at three o'clock.'

'Charalambous, I may not have killed my father ...'

Charalambous's face dropped. 'Wait, you sit. I'll get some coffee.'

He shouted to Mohammed. '*Parte kafe. Grigora.*'

'And a Metaxa too, please.'

'*Kai Metaxa. Megalo. Grigora. Einai epinigon.*'

It *was* an emergency.

We sat at The Quiet Man's table.

'Tell me your truth now, Constantina *mou*. We have time,' said Charalambous, handing me the brandy.

God, him and his truth . . . He sat back; hands folded in his lap. 'Drink up, my fatty *dídymo pnéuma*.'

'I'm not your sprit twin.'

'Yes, you are. Start from the beginning.'

I took a deep breath.

Charalambous listened without interruption. Then said, 'I'm sorry you didn't kill your father, Constance. It's a terrible shame.'

44

I was air-drying my hair in the afternoon sunshine when he arrived. Charalambous had tucked a napkin into the neck of my T-shirt in case I spilled my coffee on my white clothes. White wasn't a sensible colour for me, but all those years on tour I just wore be-in-the-background black. Now, I wore white as an antidote.

I had spent a fraught five minutes looking at myself in the mirror. I had grown old. The skin under my chin was looser than the last time I had checked and I detected the beginnings of some horrendous jowl manifestation. My nose was bright red and shiny from my day at the beach. Charalambous had suggested I put on some makeup.

'No, Charalambous. Bugger it. Bugger it all. I don't have to impress this person. Who does he think he is?'

The Quiet Man arrived. He took his usual seat, facing away from the café. He took a book from his satchel and placed it on the table. Charalambous went over to take his order. I watched him nod and make small talk, then make his way to the kitchen. The man opened his book and began to read.

I scooped my hair up into a scrunchie. I stepped off the veranda and moved through the sun-dappled grove, everything in slow motion, gravity losing its grip. The lemons were just starting to turn from hard green to pale yellow. They would be ripe soon.

I tapped his shoulder. He turned to look at me. I nodded.
'It is you, isn't it?' I said.
He nodded.
'It is you, isn't it?' he said.

45

I sat cross-legged on the chair opposite Vas, tucking my feet in tightly. Charalambous brought a rattling tray with two glasses and a bottle of our finest local wine. He unloaded the tray and minced away, buttocks clenched tightly, feet at ten to two. He turned and, lips pursed, blew me a small kiss.

'Fucking hell, eh?' said Vasos.

'Fucking hell, indeed,' I said.

'We need cigarettes,' he said.

'I don't smoke any more,' I said.

'Me neither,' he said.

Charalambous flitted over and placed his own packet of cigarettes and matches on the table.

'You are welcome,' he said.

'Stop eavesdropping,' I said.

He gave me his archest squinty eyes and disappeared into the bar.

Vas took a cigarette from the pack, lit it, and passed it to me. I took it begrudgingly. Vas smirked as he lit his own cigarette.

'That was almost gracious of you,' he said, still grinning.

'That was almost sexist of you,' I said, grinning a little myself now.

'Nice bib,' he said, nodding at my napkin.

Charalambous appeared and whipped the napkin off my

T-shirt. 'Sorry, this was my fault. She's a spiller and she wanted to look nice today. For you.'

'Charalambous, will you please go away and stop listening to our conversation.'

Charalambous rolled his eyes at Vas and they shared a moment.

'Also, don't mention the big red clown nose, she's sensitive about it,' said Charalambous, tapping his own substantial trunk. 'I told her, foundation, but she doesn't listen.'

'Is there enough foundation in the world to cover that nose, though?' said Vas.

Already, Charalambous had been Vassed: I had to smile at my old friend's unfailing ability to ease any situation.

'Charalambous, kindly piss off.'

He smiled and wiggled his backside as he walked away.

'Oh, and put some music on so you can't earwig everything we say.'

'Okay, I'll put on Wham!'

'Don't put on Wham!'

He immediately went to the CD player and slotted in *Music from the Edge Of Heaven*. By Wham!

'So why the whole International Man of Mystery act, then?' I asked Vas, once Charalambous had gone back into the bar. 'Why didn't you just say something?'

'I wasn't sure.' Vas shrugged, same old shrug. Age suited him. 'I found this place and then I saw you, Conno.' Of *course* he had found this place. This place was made for people like him. People with magic in their veins. People with poetry in their hearts.

'At first, I thought it was you, but then I wasn't sure. So, I had to come back. Then I thought maybe it wasn't you because, if it was you, you'd have recognised me. Then I thought it might be you but that you might not have recognised me. Then I thought that maybe you had recognised me but hadn't wanted to speak to me, or I thought that maybe you did want to speak to me but didn't know how to. Then I thought maybe I should just go for it and ask you to meet me.'

'Bloody hell, Vas, that's a lot of thinking for one person.'

'Why the spooky disappearance for thirty years?' said Vas.

'Of course ... you don't know, do you?' I had, until this moment, never considered there to be a different version of my life story out there. 'Christ, where do I start?' I said.

'All I know is you got married. Without telling me.' Vas tapped his cigarette in the ashtray.

'I didn't get married.'

'Yeah, you did. To some wealthy nightclub owner called Stavros. Your dad told us.'

'Seriously? That's what he told you? God, I hope he's rotting in hell with his arse on fire.'

'So, you didn't marry?'

'No. I didn't. My father lied. He always lied.'

'Wow. I know he was a bastard, but that's a huge lie to tell. Why would he do that?'

'Because he's the Olympic Lying Gold Medallist.'

'I don't understand. If you didn't get married, why didn't you come back? *Thirty years, Conno.* You knew where we were. You were still in touch with your dad.'

'I wasn't. Is that what he said?'

'Well, yeah.'

'It's a complete fabrication, Vas. I don't know how that man lived with himself. I really don't.'

'So, what did happen?' said Vas, looking highly confused.

'It's complicated ...' Was it, though? It was kind of simple in a way.

'How?' prompted Vas.

'I thought I'd killed my dad, so I did a runner.'

Vas smiled. It was his old smile, a smile of affection and private amusement.

'Brilliant, Conno. Just classic Constance Costa. Okay, let me just absorb that,' said Vas, speaking very slowly. 'You thought you had killed your dad, so you did a runner?'

'Yep.'

'For thirty years?'

'Yep.'

'Right. Well, he was very much alive until last week.'

'So I gather. This has been a shocker of a week for me, frankly.' I took a huge gulp of wine and a big puff on my cigarette.

'I bet.' He looked unconvinced now. 'But ... he always said you were okay. That you had married, had kids and worked part-time in a clothes shop.'

'And you swallowed that hook, line and sinker, did you?' I drained my glass.

We sat for a while, saying nothing. I poured wine in both our glasses.

'You never got in touch,' I said, breaking the silence, some of the old hurt creeping back.

'I did! I did, Conno.' Vas looked at me now, earnestly. 'I bunked off school and came to your house a few weeks after Christmas, must have been ... January 1977 ... you weren't there. I waited for hours and then your dad came home and bollocked me big time. He told me I was never to bother you again. Then he told my parents and they bollocked me. I was getting bollocked left, right and centre. I was totally heartbroken. And in desperate need of one of our tremendous shags.'

'Oh, well, you soon found that elsewhere,' I said. 'Dina told me about your supermodel super-intelligent girlfriend in Dulwich.'

'How do you remember that after all these years?' said Vas, surprised and touched.

'I just do,' I said, in place of: 'Because you never forget a pain that profound.'

'It wasn't the same as it was with you, Conno,' said Vas, in place of: 'I'm sorry you still feel that pain.'

'How do you remember that after all these years?' I said.

'I just do,' he said, with a slight smile.

'You didn't wait long to sort yourself out, though, did you? I mean, our bed was barely cold before you were hopping into someone else's,' I said, feeling chagrined up to the eyeballs.

'We didn't have a bed,' Vas said, smiling. 'We shagged behind trees . . . not funny? Too soon?'

'A bit, yeah.'

'I'm sorry. I did wait a few months, but I honestly believed we were doomed and I just wanted to move on. It wasn't a serious relationship. Just a fumble, you know.'

We both took a sip of wine.

'When did they tell you I was getting married?' I asked Vas now.

'When you didn't come back from Cyprus. I thought we might see each other before I went to uni, but you were gone.'

Vas looked at his hands. 'I had no choice but to believe it. At the time I felt guilty, Conno. I thought maybe my going to boarding school had sent you over the edge.'

'It did, a bit,' I said. 'But also get over yourself.'

'I'll try to. I have always felt bad about that last conversation we had; you know, when I called you to say I was going away ... I was a bit ...'

'Dramatic?'

'Yeah.'

'Cruel?'

'Well ...'

'Selfish?'

'No ...'

'A self-interested immature feckless male with no sense of loyalty?'

'Yeah, that was it.' We both laughed a small laugh. 'Then boarding school – did you know your dad paid half the fees?' I shook my head, more in wonder than anything else. I had known at the time that The Fat Murderer was at the bottom of the whole boarding school fiasco. Vas continued. 'And the pressure of fast-tracking for uni and my mum and dad on my back and Roulla moping around all the time, telling me she had a terrible secret. It was just all too much.'

'Auntie Roulla knew. She tried to tell me, but Uncle Mikis stopped her. I was disappointed, really. Why would she just let me go like that.'

Vas looked up from his hands now.

'Well, you know what it was like in those days. The men had a societal mandate to bully their women and the women had to put up with it. Roulla had no choice with Mikis and your dad closing ranks.'

'Still,' I said. 'It was my Roulla, she was my only one.'

'She's only human, Conno. Roulla was cut to pieces. She was furious with your dad. Hated him. Things really changed after you left. It all sort of fell apart.'

Oh good, I thought.

'Oh dear,' I said. 'What happened?'

'Marios and Adonia moved to Tottenham. Your dad wasn't welcome at the Papachristodoullous', Roulla made sure of that. And something went down with my dad and your dad, which I never got to the bottom of. So there were no Greek Nights. Which was a mercy at the time.'

Vas rubbed his forehead. 'I was so fucked up, Conno. I mean, me and you. We were, you know, Vas and Conno. And we'd only just been brave enough to tell each other ... remember that night after Marios's wedding? Remember when we said, you know ...?'

How could I not remember that night, when I danced on air to the love song of blackbirds. It was the brightest light in my sky full of stars, and none had shone brighter or warmer since. We both thought our own thoughts for a moment.

'Did you like it, boarding school?' I asked.

Vas took a long drag on his cigarette.

'No, I hated it. It was full of posh wankers who kept calling me Bubble – you know, Bubble and Squeak, Greek?'

'Wankers,' I agreed.

'Fucking wankers,' he added.

We had both thawed a little.

I drank some wine. We needed another bottle. I looked around for Charalambous, but he was nowhere to be seen. Why was he never there when I needed him?

'I am sorry your dad lied. I'm sorry I believed it. I'm sorry you went through, well, all of it ...' Vas put his hand on my hand. I pulled away. Too soon. Too soon for intimacy. And I wasn't interested in pity. To accept pity equated to accepting my status as a freak and I'd got rid of that idea a long time ago.

'Well?' said Vas tentatively. 'If you didn't get married ... what the hell happened?'

'He tried to make me marry a bloke with a monobrow, so I killed him.'

'Would you care to elucidate?' said Vas, crossing his hands in his lap.

I didn't really want to tell my wretched little tale to Vas, who, I already knew from Charalambous's onion peeling, had gone on to marry and have children and be normal. And now here he was, back in my life, stirring up silt just when the waters were finally running clear. That old feeling of always being at the centre of my own shame had started to creep over me.

I got up and turned my chair around, I sat down, legs either side, and rested my arms on the chair back, hands clasped for ballast, and, for the second time that week, told my story.

'I don't see how The Fat Murdering Bastard could have survived,' I finished. 'It was a long drop. I saw the car go over. He was indestructible, that man.'

Vas drew his eyebrows together, thoughtful, perplexed, working something out.

'He did talk about a car crash. Obviously, he survived. In the context of what I now know, I'm sorry about that. But he never mentioned you were part of it. When he came back to London, he said that you had agreed to marry and that you were happy to stay in Cyprus. He was pretty convincing.'

'I told you, he's a good liar.'

'Fuck.'

'Yes, fuck, but also, not fuck,' I said. 'I was lucky. I had a vivid imagination I could escape to. It saved me from going under with all the other victims of the psychos and the perverts.

Some of them never resurface. And if they can just manage to tread water, it's always there, in the background, like Jaws, waiting till they bleed, homing in on the scent of blood and dragging them back under. They have nothing. But I had that. And I had you.'

I drew a deep breath.

'And I always had music. Sometimes it was a beating heart for me when I was so tired that I thought my own heart might stop. I feel sorry for people who don't have music in their lives. That's why I built The Guitar Bar.'

I shrugged.

'It's for the broken and the wounded. And I think it calls to those people. Does that make sense, Vas?'

'Yes. It does.' He nodded with simple acquiescence.

I liked his answer. It was without sympathy and without solicitousness. I picked up my wine and, on the way to my mouth, spilled it on my T-shirt.

I sighed, rubbing at the stain in agitation. Vas pulled my hand away from my T-shirt. 'Leave it. It doesn't matter, Conno.'

'You're going to have to stop touching me, Vas. I'm not in the mood for being touched.'

He held his hands up in supplication, just as he used to when we were younger, and sat on them.

Now I realised that I had a new misery to ponder: not only that I had failed to kill my father, but that *he had left me*. The big irony of my life was that I hadn't walked away from him, *he had walked away from me.* By trying to get out from under the shadow he had cast over my young life, I had cast another shadow of my own making, a shadow that had lasted thirty years, a shadow that was real only to me.

But then, had I killed The Fat Murderer, he'd have had

it coming to him anyway. As I hadn't killed him, well, I was innocent and unencumbered. And, either way, I had survived. I had loved my weird, expansive, ad hoc life full of music and laughter and travel.

'... he picked up another family pretty quickly too.' Vas was still talking, but I hadn't heard what he had been saying until now. 'Got married and had kids. He retired to Limassol about five years ago.'

I had to laugh. We had both retired to the same part of the world at the same time.

'I don't care,' I said to Vas, but more to myself. 'I don't want to hear about him. It's got nothing to do with my life. I'm glad he's dead.'

I felt rather than heard Vas exhaling with relief.

'I never liked him, especially after you left. And I think it's fair to say he didn't like me much either.'

I felt much calmer now.

'If you didn't like him, Vas, why are you here?'

'My parents are too old to travel alone. Marios and Adonia didn't want to come either. But I couldn't cope with all the parents and aunties on my own. I don't see them much, but Marios always brings you up in conversation. He liked you. He liked the thought of us, actually. And I know Roulla missed you terribly.'

'I've seen them. Around town. Why aren't you all in Limassol?'

'We're staying out here because it's cheaper. You know how the Greeks like to save money.'

'Do they know?'

'Know what?'

'That I'm here?'

'No.'

'I don't want to meet them, Vas,' I said. 'Roulla and your parents and everyone. It's another lifetime. It doesn't mean anything to me any more.'

I couldn't do it. How do you reassemble the pieces of something so shattered?

'Okay,' Vas said. 'But they'll be here for a few weeks visiting all the rellies – what's left of them, they're dropping off like flies – so if you did change your mind . . .'

'I won't.'

He nodded. 'I get it. I do.'

I wanted him to hold my hand now, but he was still sitting on both of his.

The sun had been slowly setting and sky fires lit up through the branches of the orange trees. The firmament was turning from powder blue to deep feathery pink. I hadn't noticed the guests arriving. Nearly all the tables were full.

Vas and I had finished our wine. I was suddenly very hungry. I called out for Charalambous. He came scurrying out of the bar carrying a tray of food. He was wearing a white frilly apron and a sailor's hat. He looked pretty good, as it happens. He offloaded the tray at a table en route with a weird tense curtsey, and bustled over. He was flustered and had a line of sweat on his top lip. His lipstick had bled into the corners of his mouth.

'Excuse me, Your Royal Highness, are you going to help tonight?' he asked, resting one hand on the table and leaning in too close. 'Because we are very busy.' He didn't seem quite so enchanted with my and Vas's reunion now. He turned his back, pointedly, on Vas.

'No,' I said. 'Can you bring us some souvlaki and more wine, please? And some olives. And bread.'

Charalambous looked at Vas.

'And anything for you, Your Lordship?' he said, reaching for and achieving some admirably high-end derision.

I stood.

'Vas, I'm going to have to help him. He's rudderless without me, aren't you, Charalambous?'

Vas laughed.

'But don't go yet,' I said to Vas. 'We have an amazing guitarist coming this evening, he plays like Paco de Lucía and the night is only just beginning. Can you stay?'

'Oh, this one is going nowhere,' said Charalambous, wiping his forehead with his apron. 'He's helping too.'

Vas and I both shrugged.

And, just like that, we were back.

46

The last guests were leaving, meandering through the trees and out into the real world.

It had been a wonderful evening serving dish after dish of Mohammed's sizzling souvlaki, and mountains of fresh salad glistening with pungent olive oil and shiny scarab olives. We worked well together, Vas and I, under the direction of a dictatorial Charalambous. And while the guests ate honeysweet baklava and became drunk on ruby red wine and the intoxicating air, the guitarist, Demitrakis, played. And oh, how he played. He was almost as good as David Gilmour out of Pink Floyd . . . He cast enchantments and conjured entities. He wound his way through the loops and spaces of human emotion until we were all bound within his spell.

His music still lingered, though he had packed up his guitar and left an hour ago.

Vas and I wandered back to our table. The scents of citrus and jasmine filled the night.

Charalambous had left us a few plates of food and some water. He came back now with a pot of coffee. I told him that I would clear the tables and cash up later, that he should go home, wherever that was tonight. He handed me a sweater. 'It's getting chilly, even for a fatty bum-bum like you.' He gave my arm a meaty slap and then trailed through the grove, quietly singing his favourite song. He was all right, Charalambous. I don't believe in an afterlife, or ghosts, other than the ones we carry around with us, but were she still a consciousness, my mum would be silently thanking Charalambous for his timely arrival in my life. And for his limitless kindness.

Vas and I took stock of each other for few moments as we sat together, saying nothing. I wondered what he thought of me. He hadn't changed much at all. He was older and sturdier and his black curls were laced with grey. His beautiful Grecian nose was, perhaps, a little less defined these days, but he still had the same dark eyes and long lashes that threw spidery shadows onto his cheekbones. I watched him eat. I used to love watching him eat, watching his lips part, his jaw work. I liked it now. I could have remained this way for a long time. This night was rare. But time was precious. We had lost so much of it and I didn't know how much was left.

'Your turn,' I told Vas, carefully keeping my voice low so as not to upset the stillness of the night.

'Not much to tell, really,' he said, slowly and quietly. I watched him chewing bread for a bit.

'You got married and had kids.' I had a thought that made my stomach sink. 'You didn't marry Dina, did you? Please don't tell me you married Dina.'

'God, no! They tried, though. I had a narrow escape there.'

I felt a little shy now.

'So, who did you marry, Vas?'

He took a deep breath, spoke in a measured tone as if he, too, sensed the danger of tearing the delicate fabric of the night-time.

'I married a very wonderful woman called Andrea. We met

at Oxford, where she was on secondment from Harvard. I was teaching English Literature. We had two kids, Andrew and Nicholas.'

Great; brilliant, educated, childbearing and American. I bet she could pop ping-pong balls out of her vagina as well.

Now my stomach jolted from the minimal threat of Dopey Dina to the real threat of the Awesome Andrea. I could feel myself drifting away from the shield of the night. It was no accident that I had never insisted Charalambous ask The Quiet Man for his name. Though we both knew it. I didn't want to know that The Quiet Man was Vas because I simply didn't want to face the inevitable facts that I now learned: that Vasos was happy, that he had found someone more worthy of his inimitable qualities, that he hadn't been saddled with a fuck-up like me. That he wasn't free. I knew it was ridiculous, but in the addled section of my brain that had stopped at 1977, Vas and I had always been on pause. I'd never expected to see him again and yet I had expected to find him precisely as I had left him.

'Is she here with you?' I asked, going for casual and sounding as if I was being garrotted.

'No. We don't live together. She's a bit older than me. Once the kids went to uni, she really wanted to go back to the US to retire. She's from Montana originally.'

They didn't live together. The ligature around my neck loosened. I felt mean for being happy. Still . . . I felt into the night. It was still safe. I moved forward carefully.

'So . . . you're divorced, then?'

'No, no point. I mean, we might do one day, but right now neither of us are interested in getting married again. We've been very mature. You'd like her, Conno.'

I doubted that very much.

'How about you, did you ever settle down with anyone?' he asked.

'There were a few. Not for a while. I'm happy as I am.'

'No kids?'

'No. Too selfish. I'd have made a terrible mother.'

'True. The worst.'

'I'd have been Emma Bovary,' I sniggered.

'Queen Gertrude.'

'Rose West,' I said.

'Margaret White,' said Vas, and gave me a sideways look and a grin.

'Hah! Carrie's mother! You *have* read Stephen King!'

'Yeah, I can do trash, occasionally,' he smirked.

We sat in more silence now. The darkness folded around us, cool and damp, and I shivered. I reached for my sweater and put it round my shoulders. Vas watched.

'I'm sorry that stuff happened to you, Conno. Despite all that, I hope you had a good life.'

'I have had an *amazing* life,' I said, with real passion. 'I really have. I'll tell you about it one day. You'll be really jealous. Much better than being an institutionalised professor in a dusty old university, with a failed marriage and two estranged children.'

'Well, I wouldn't put it quite like that, but coming from a bitter old spinster such as yourself, I suppose it's to be expected.'

'So,' I said, dreading the answer, 'when do you go back to the UK?'

'I'm not in a rush. I'm taking a year's sabbatical. I'm supposed to be writing a paper on George Herbert.'

'God, you poor thing. Still the metaphysical poets, eh? Not progressed much, have you?'

'What are you reading? Stephen King, Peter Benchley, James Herbert, all the greats?'

'I'm reading James Joyce at the moment. In Greek. Actually.'

'Nah, you're not.' He looked at me. 'Did you ever think of me?'

I stared back. 'Never. Did you ever think of me?'

'Not once.'

Vas lit a cigarette, took a drag, and passed it to me. We passed it back and forth.

'Don't suppose you've got any weed, have you?' he asked.

'What are you? Fourteen? Of course I haven't got any *weed*.'

We sat, both staring ahead, passing the cigarette back and forth, letting our fingers brush lightly. After a long time, Vas took in a deep breath and sighed it out. As if acknowledging something to himself.

'This feels right, doesn't it?' said Vas, shaking his head as if to clear his mind.

'Yes, it does,' I replied, and a little bit of magic trickled between my shoulders and down my spine.

'Do you think there's any chance that, at some point, you might want to see my willy?'

'Is it bigger than before, because, as I recall, it was minuscule,' I said.

'Oh yes, it's a showpiece now. It's won awards.'

'In that case, I probably do.'

We talked deep into the night and made love as the waves ebbed and flowed, ebbed and flowed, and crashed on the shore, and then crashed again – several times, in fact – after which we fell into each other's arms, exhausted from our ardour, knowing we would never again be apart.

We didn't really. Things never turn out like that. Not in my life anyway.

Vas went back to his hotel, because, as much as he was willing to show me his prize-winning winkle, he was tired and he's got this hip thing where he needs to lie down for a bit with a pillow between his knees. I cashed up the night's takings and spent a frantic hour rifling through Charalambous's germy bookshelves trying to find a copy of *Ulysses* that I recalled someone had left on a table once.

As I turned the lights off and made my way through the citrus trees, I remembered an ancient phrase I had attributed to a pop star from another life, Marc Bolan: 'To see the stars, you must first look into the darkness.' When I was a teenager and everything seemed bleak, it was my way of telling myself things would be okay.

It was September 16th, which, until now, had always been a bleak anniversary for me. It was the day one car accident had taken Marc Bolan and another had killed my father. Or so I'd thought. Thirty years on, it was finally a good date. It would always be the day that Vas and Conno made up.

I looked up. The stars were in glorious abundance.

47

Vas and I are strolling through the orchard towards the bar, drunk on the scent of almost ripe oranges, tangy and sweet. The stars are hanging low and there's a slight chill in the air. We had an earth-shatteringly magnificent making-up-for-lost-time shagfest earlier and we are holding hands. His hands are so lovely. I have sausage fingers, but his fingers have actual bones in them. I keep un-entwining and re-entwining our fingers until he says, 'Fuck's sake, Conno, stop fidgeting.'

We got back on the horse, sex-wise, pretty sharpish, Vas and I. We've both picked up moves along the way. Vas is a little less athletic than he was in his teenage years, on account of his dodgy hip, and I really do have a touch of asthma these days – it's all the cats – so I make sure I take my inhaler beforehand, just in case I get the wheezies. But when we are alone, when the night is deep and silent but for the chirping of cicadas and the distant wash of the sea, we fit together perfectly. Every time.

Vas has been here for almost two weeks now. He's unpacked his suitcase, but his stuff is all over the bedroom floor. Andreas, the carpenter, is coming round tomorrow to make him a wardrobe. I like Vas being here. I like his things. I touch his toiletries. I secretly smell his clothes too. He caught me doing it once, but he just looked at me for a moment then said, 'It's a good job I like you so much, Conno.'

He hasn't written anything about George Herbert yet and

spends most of his days swinging in a hammock he has rigged up between two lemon trees. It's where he does his thinking. I tried to get in it with him the other day and he said, 'You can't get in here, Conno, you'll pull the trees down.' Which I thought was an outright cheek, but he and Charalambous had a good old chuckle at my expense. When I told Charalambous he was a turncoat, he said, 'Bros before the hos, fatty bum bum.' They've also started calling me Conkstantina, in reference to my nose. Which is a double bloody cheek, as neither of them have been short-changed in the beak department.

Vas and I have not yet actually said that we love each other. It's too soon. And the last time we declared our love, everything went tits up straight afterwards. I believe in love, but it's a thing that should be felt. It doesn't have to be said. To trifle with such a fragile and beautiful thing is wanton. I am still aghast at how easily people will squander the love they find. But I do love him, and it's really pissing me off that he doesn't say it first.

Considering the wonderfully coordinated culmination of our afternoon delights (intentionally plural, not just a Greek S), I'm surprised Vas isn't a little more relaxed this evening. He's jumpy and keeps looking around as if he's anticipating something. I'm so chilled I'm almost horizontal. I lean my head on his shoulder.

'I'm not doing any work tonight,' I tell him. 'Ask me why?'
'Why?'
'Because I am shagged out!' I laugh. 'I have spent the afternoon with the Shagmaster General. Shagginton Shaggy. Mayor Shagman of Shagsville Arizona, Shag—'
'This isn't the time, Conno,' Vas snaps.
'Ooohooh, touchy ...'

He suddenly spots what he's been looking for and breaks away from me. He grabs my hand and squeezes it a bit too tightly and says, 'Please, Conno, don't be angry with me', then turns and walks briskly along the path between the trees.

He returns with two enormous floating hairdos, under each of which sits an older woman wearing support tights and white mall-walker sneakers, both carrying an assortment of tubs and bags. You could knock me down with the smallest of feathers. Doulla and Goulla. As I live and breathe. It's Doulla and bloody Goulla. And then she's there. Auntie Roulla, holding on to Marios's arm. God, he looks like a film star, and he's still got all his hair, which is a miracle, because Uncle Mikis was as bald as a coot by the time he was thirty. Though why I'm thinking about this now is beyond me. His handsome face lights up when he sees me: 'Constance!' I am undecided. Should I stay or should I go? I'm not angry, though. 'I'm not angry,' I say to Vas, over Marios's shoulder, as he pins my arms to my sides in a fierce embrace. He smells expensive.

Auntie Roulla is an orchestra of emotions: fury, relief, love, sorrow and disbelief playing across her face in concert. 'Constantina *mou*, my lovely girl, we find you after all these years. Oh, I'm sorry. I am sorry,' she says. She's revving up for a boohoo, I can tell.

'There's nothing to be sorry for, Auntie . . .' I say, trailing off. This is a lot to take in. It's been thirty years . . . She's shrunk a little with age, or maybe I just remember her bigger, but her hair adds a good eight inches to her height, and she's wearing hazardously high heels. She clasps the loose skin under my chin and jiggles it ferociously. She shakes her head sadly. 'Darling *mou*, you grow into a lovely chunky lady, so sad to be without your family for so long . . . we are here now and everything is going to be okay. We do your hair tomorrow, make it bigger so your nose look smaller, then you will be perfect.' She breaks down and sobs into a hanky.

Vas moves to my side. 'Is this okay?' he asks quietly, and only to me.

I'm not feeling quite as shagtastic as I was two minutes ago, but I am strangely okay. 'Yes. It's okay, Vas.'

Vas steers us to a table. He and Marios seat the aunties, taking the tubs and bags off them, setting them down on the ground.

'I did explain that you have a restaurant, Con,' says Marios, with a twinkle, 'but they insisted on bringing food.'

'I am pleased someone has brought food.' It's Charalambous. He is looking particularly uptight and sweaty in Dr Scholl's sandals, a kilt and his old *Diamond Dogs* T-shirt.

'People are asking who is playing tonight,' he says, manic eyes swivelling from me to Roulla, me to Vas, Vas to Marios and the aunties, and then back to me again. 'Demitrakis is sick. He can't play.'

'Never mind,' I say, justifiably distracted.

He leans in closer, almost nose to nose now. I feel his spit hit me on the mouth as he explodes very quietly.

'Never mind? Neverbloodymind? Someone has to play (spit), Constantina (spit). It's called The Guitar Bar (spit). We have slow service and no music.'

'Why is the service slow?'

'Because Mohammed doesn't want touch the pork, because he's Muslim today, so I have to cook it and serve it and pour the drinks and write the bills and take the money and make nice with the people. *Who come to hear guitar music.* You must play.'

'Why aren't we serving lamb?'

'Because Mohammed gave the lamb to the cats.'

'Tell Mohammed to serve drinks.'

'HE. IS. MUSLIM. He won't touch booze. And anyway, he has taken Queen Fattyma to the doctor because she ate too much lamb and can't do a poop. You need to play. Please.' He presses his palms together.

'I can't play, Charalambous, I have people ... this is my Auntie Roulla, Auntie Roulla this is—'

Charalambous pushes in front of me, like a sort of auntie cock block, and almost screams, 'Aaaaauntiiiie Rrrrrroulaaaaa, *the* Auntie Roulla? Constantina's only one Auntie Roulla? No. Can't be. How, why, oh my God! Vasoulaki, you are a wonderful Onion.' He looks like he's going to spontaneously combust. 'Welcome, welcome – oh, and who is this handsome devil?' he gasps, looking at Marios. 'Hello, I am Charalambous, Constantina's spirit twin.'

'He's not,' I manage, before Charalambous continues.

'I am. We will share our truths later, young man. But now, please, Auntie Roulla, she must play. Tell her. She listens to you.' As if thirty years hadn't just happened.

'Play!' says Vasos, patting Charalambous on the shoulder. 'I've never heard you play, Conno. I'll help with the drinks, Charry.'

'Don't let us stop you. Play, *please*,' says Marios. 'We'll be here afterwards, for the truth sharing, won't we, Mum? We've got nowhere else to be.'

'Play, *agabi mou*. We sort the food,' says Roulla, waving me off with a man hand, already unpacking the tubs.

I've played in front of thousands of people and yet I have avoided picking up my guitar around Vas. It's like the two worlds shouldn't cross. But now all the worlds are coming together whether I like it or not.

I have a Hummingbird guitar these days. But, tonight, I choose my old favourite: the Kay. The man in Denmark Street all those years ago was right. It *is* special. Although I haven't played it for some time. I sit on a stool on the veranda, and tune up. I perch my guitar on my left inner thigh, old style. At first my fingers are strangers, as if this is the first moment they have ever made these moves.

It occurs to me that my playing has always been linked to my father. I played, at first, as the person who wanted to escape what he had done to me; then, as the person who wanted to escape the repercussions of what I had done to him. I have, in one way or another, always played as a fugitive. Ms Liz Liddle's advice comes back to me now. 'You need to take a stance when you play. You'll only be able to do that when you know who you are. Less con, more stance.'

I play some easy pieces by Carulli, some trickier pieces – *Asturias* by Isaac Albéniz. My fingers move of their own volition and I accept a simple truth that is both scary and elating: I don't have to build a future or run from a past. I just have to be here. In this moment. With these people. Because whatever I have been searching for may have finally arrived.

With service coming to an end, Vas moves towards the veranda and sits on the steps. He watches me play. Charalambous stands behind him, stroking Vas's hair, his lipstick freshly applied and wildly crooked; a small, black trickle of mascara running down each cheek. I think the whole evening has been too much for him. He is an emotional wreck.

My hands begin to play one of the most beautiful pieces of music ever written: the adagio from Rodrigo's *Concierto de Aranjuez*, the piece I played for Ms Liz Liddle, on my last day at school, in place of words and sentiments I was too young to utter. The piece my mum had loved when she was dancing and alive and full of the promises my father was yet to take from her. And I am awash with memories. Memories spinning webs so thick and fast that I must brush each one aside to see the next. Memories of the aunties in the Petrideses' kitchen dishing out plates of unconditional love; of Vas and I under the tall trees in Essex, trying to make our bodies fit together; our dance at the wedding; Marios looking at my bruises and saying 'I hate to think what the other fella looks like' – all of it so tender and honest. It all comes back. And then, then I remember.

I suddenly feel frivolous. I stop playing the adagio and, instead, play an all-too-familiar glam rock riff. I wink at Charalambous. He can't allow himself to believe what's coming. He stops stroking Vas and clasps his hands to his heart and joins in with a surprisingly rich baritone, 'You don't know if you are a boy and a girl ...' Jesus H. Christ, you'd think he'd know the correct words by now.

Everyone knows the chorus, of course they do. It's 'Rebel Rebel' by David Bowie. And I have to admit, Charalambous's anthem is a fine one. And as we sing the last drawn-out phrase, we are all bound together by the music: the stars, the people, the cats, the night, all as one, and floating amongst us are the spirits of those we still love. I remember her face. Her smell. I remember it all now.

I think I might cry, but then Charalambous leaps onto the podium and, with great magnanimity, announces that all drinks are on the house for the rest of the evening. If I paid him, I'd take that out of his wages.

I sit down on the steps next to Vas. We hold hands, loosely.

'You can *really* play, Conno,' he says.

'You took a risk, didn't you, Vas, getting them here?' I say.

'I did. But the thing is, Conno, if I had pretended that I didn't know where you were, I'd have been as bad as your dad, wouldn't I? I know they're bonkers and you wouldn't want to take them out in public, but they *fucking love* you, Con. And they're family.'

He is right, of course. He is always bloody right.

'It's hard to let people in, in case I lose them again,' I say.

'Well, if you don't let people in, they're already lost to you anyway. Aren't they?'

'There's so much to unpack, you know?'

'There's nothing to unpack. It's unpacked already. We're Greeks and whether we like it or not, everybody knows everything about everyone.'

'When I last saw them, I felt I was a nobody. It took me years to be a somebody again. And I did it without them. I don't need them.'

Vas nods. 'I know, I know that, Conno. But they need *you*. I didn't have to persuade them to come here, they insisted. They deserve a chance. And you deserve them.'

'I do deserve them,' I say to Vas, but mostly to myself.

'We *both* do. This, what we are, what we have after all this time, it's *fucking amazing*, Conno, and it's selfish to keep it to ourselves. It's bigger than just us two. If you can't let them in for yourself, then do it for us.'

Us. Not me. Or you. *Us.* He said it and it's making my heart go *so* bananas that, right now, I can't keep it from fluttering up into my throat. I haven't really had much 'us' in my life. Not that you need to be an 'us' to be fulfilled. I've had friends and lovers, but now I think about it, they were never *us*. It was me and them. I must admit, some 'us' would be nice. And I do love them. All of them, the aunties, Marios, Charalambous. I just have to let them love me back.

'Christ, just look at them!' says Vas, laughing. 'If nothing else, they're priceless entertainment.'

Doulla and Goulla are clearing tables and bossing Mohammed, who has returned with a retinue of felines. Auntie Roulla is standing at the foot of the path giving guests complimentary leftovers in tinfoil packages as they leave the grove, 'In case you get hungry later.' My spirit twin, Charalambous, is peeling poor old Marios's onion, two inches from his face. What a lovely mess they all are. That Cyprus feeling, the one I couldn't shake, that led me here; it wasn't just about the way of life or the place. It was about them. All of them. The Calling had always called me away, but now it was calling me back. And back is where I wanted to be.

I lay my head on Vas's shoulder and breathe him in.

'You smelling my neck again?' he says. I nod. 'It's a good job I like you so much, Conno.'

'That line is never going to wear thin, Vas,' I say, as I turn his head towards me and trace his mouth with my finger. His lips part slightly and he inclines his head and kisses the palm of my hand.

'You know she's gonna make you go to the hairdressers tomorrow and you're gonna come back with massive hair?'

'I don't mind. It's time I had a 'do.' I shrug.

'I'll enjoy messing it up when you get back. After all, I am The King of Shagland.'

Vas brings his hand to the back of my head and pulls me in, close, how he always did. He kisses me lightly, once, twice, three times, and does that weird, proprietorial lip bite thing.

He says, 'You know, right?'

The Greeks are waiting patiently now. Sitting at their table, lost and found in their reveries, as are we all, old souls bound together at long last and with so much still unsaid.

'Shall we do this, then?' says Vas.

'Yes,' I say, 'I'm ready.'

And, I really am.

48

My mum's name was Rose.

Acknowledgements

That's the trouble with letting clever and nice people into your life, isn't it? You're obliged to acknowledge their contribution to it. Still, here they are.

THE BOOK-TYPE PUBLISHING/AGENT GANG

What a gang! They are great because ...

1. Given the choice between working with them or eating miles of chewy toffee covered in creamy Cadbury's milk chocolate, I'd forgo the Curly Wurly every time.
2. Not only do they have good hair, but they are also exceptional at their jobs.
3. Every single one of them has been a complete pleasure and a laugh and made these the most enjoyable few years.

They are as follows:

a. Literary agent and fellow pigeon fancier Sarah Harvey, at CAA UK, who is a total and utter groover of the highest order. If there was an Olympic category for grooving, they'd have to invent a medal that was better than gold just for her. Thank you, Sarah, for perceptive, game-changing suggestions and for getting Connie so quickly. It took approximately one nanosecond to know that I wanted to work with you. And thank you to the team at CAA UK. Special mentions to: Daisy Meyrick for getting the ball rolling in such an intuitive

ACKNOWLEDGEMENTS

way; Devon Lee for expertly spinning international plates like a Greek waiter at a shotgun wedding; John Ash and Felicia Hu for stepping in and stepping up.

b. Literary agent and Glamour Queen Alexandra Machinist, NY agent extraordinaire. You rock! You rock as much as Dave Gilmour. You live at the very top of Rock Mountain, Rocksville, Arizona. Your enthusiasm and steadfastness mean everything. Every time I think of you, I cheer up and thank my lucky stars. Major recognition to the team at CAA NY, especially Xanthe Coffman.

c. Executive editor, and Taker of No Prisoners, Sara Birmingham at Random House NY, for signing the novel at lightning speed ('sentence one', I love you for that and your rare but effective use of the F-word) and for coming up with the title. I didn't need to speak to anyone else, you had me at, 'Hel—'

d. Senior commissioning editor and future fantasy wife of Vas Petrides, Amy Batley at Hutchinson Heinemann. You were so quick to get this book and to understand my characters better than I (I love you for that and your subtle powers of persuasion). And I was quick to get you. There was no other choice.

Amy and Sara, you are magnificent women. You edited the book in tandem in a weirdly workable transatlantic way which no normal human can fathom, and you each deserve equally overblown accolades. I am stretched to find superlatives grand enough to express how very grateful I am for your perceptiveness, your expertise, your support, and for just being really, exceptionally talented, and lovely people. With great hair.

e. The brilliant team at Hutchinson Heinemann: Anna Hervé, thank you for spotting the things we all missed and for allowing me to noun a verb. Joanna Taylor for turning my

ACKNOWLEDGEMENTS

novel into an actual book and for being excellent at ramping up the excitement factor. Gemma Wain for admirable – and face-saving – expert pedantry. The UK sales team: Kirsten Greenwood, Emily Harvey, Alice Gomer. The international sales team: Anna Curvis, Barbora Sabolova. Marketing: Instagram Policeman and cocktail appreciator Lucas Lockyer, marketing designer Beth Maher, and Hannah Park. Publicity: Marie-Louise Patton (irritatingly good hair), the indomitable Laura Brooke, and fellow Suzi Quatro wannabe Charlotte Bush. Design: Zahraa Neseer (the fox ... you genius), thank you. Production: Nicky Nevin. And last but deffo not least, HRHs publisher Helen Conford and the actual MD of Hutchinson Heinemann ... Venetia Butterfield.

f. The equally brilliant team at Random House New York, especially the utterly delightful Azraf Khan and Caitlin McKenna, editorial director, who wrote an epic email that I probably wasn't supposed to see but which rendered me speechless with joy. And not forgetting production editor Robert Siek, managing editor Rebecca Berlant, production manager Sandra Sujursen. The A Team: publicist Rachel Parker, marketer Madison Dettlinger, deputy publisher Alison Rich = Wow x3 – what a pleasure it has been working with you, thank you for your knowledge and dedication. Thank you also, Maria Braeckel, Milena Brown, exec VP Andy Ward and editor in chief Ben Greenberg for your kind support and vision.

g. Jennifer Mannion. Thank you, dear Klacker.

THE NON-BOOK-TYPE GANG

If I ever get rich, I may replace you all with more glamorous friends. You're safe for now but don't get too comfortable.

ACKNOWLEDGEMENTS

1. Dorothy Atkinson – thank you for loving Connie and for your absolute belief in the story. You and Martin Savage made me feel proper and always do. It's deep.
2. The Crazee Gang – thank you for believing I could do it and for treating me like a non-freak even though I don't like football or going to the pub.
3. Kirsten Soar who said, 'Why are you editing someone else's book and not writing your own?' And me thinking, 'That's a good point . . .'
4. Chris Smith for being my book buddy and utter . . . it begins with a C.
5. Sarah Vaughan – thank you for being the first person to read the book and for your never-ending generosity of spirit and encouragement.
6. My spirit twin, Anya Jones. Thank you for missing Connie when she wasn't there. Let's swim and rock out forever.
7. George Barnett. You are all over these pages; your humour, your musicality, your discernment. Thank you for listening to me laughing at my own jokes and for giving me the voices of David Bowie and Marc Bolan. You still have no idea how funny and brilliant you are, which is probably best as you'd be insufferable.
8. My family. Love, always.

I thought the entire book was solely down to me. Now I realise it seems to have been a bit of a collaboration. Who knew?!

With love and sincere gratitude,

Alex x x x